Praise for the novels of

"*The Paris Housekeeper* is the beautifully writte[n] women caught up in the Nazi occupation of [ ] characters of Rachel, Camille and Vivian ju[mp from] every page. Highly recommend!"

—Karen Robards, *New York Times* bestselling author
of *The Black Swan of Paris*

"In this *Upstairs, Downstairs* look at the Ritz during World War II, three lives entwine: a wealthy American widow and two maids at the Ritz, one of whom is in deep peril by virtue of being Jewish. What will they risk? Perfect for fans of Pam Jenoff and Kristin Hannah looking for more stories of heroism in World War II France!"

—Lauren Willig, *New York Times* bestselling author
of *Two Wars and a Wedding*, on *The Paris Housekeeper*

"*The Secret Society of Salzburg* is a heart-wrenching yet uplifting tale about the importance of art and beauty in the darkest of times. Renee Ryan weaves a masterful story of the life-or-death struggle Jewish refugees faced anchored by the unbreakable friendship of two extraordinary women. A must-read."

—Julia Kelly, internationally bestselling author
of *The Last Dance of the Debutante*

"*The Secret Society of Salzburg* is a gripping, emotional story of courage and strength, filled with extraordinary characters and tender relationships. Renee Ryan reminds us that the universal languages of art, music and friendship bring light and hope amid even the most challenging of times. I loved every word."

—RaeAnne Thayne, *New York Times* bestselling author
of *The Beach Reads Bookshop*

"*The Secret Society of Salzburg* is a powerful journey of bravery, secrets, and subterfuge. In a world where beauty and art are set amid the ugliness of hate and oppression, two friends emerge to save those most at risk despite being under constant threat of danger. Renee Ryan is a brilliant storyteller and this book is definitely one you don't want to miss!"

—Madeline Martin, *New York Times* bestselling author of *The Librarian Spy*

"*The Widows of Champagne* is a heady concoction of everything I love about historical fiction—history, drama, and passion as effervescent as the resilient LeBlanc women and the champagne that bears their name. I highly recommend!"

—Karen White, *New York Times* bestselling author
of *The Last Night in London*

Also by Renee Ryan

The Widows of Champagne
The Secret Society of Salzburg

The PARIS HOUSEKEEPER

RENEE RYAN

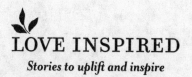

LOVE INSPIRED

Stories to uplift and inspire

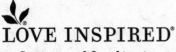

LOVE INSPIRED®

Stories to uplift and inspire

Recycling programs for this product may not exist in your area.

ISBN-13: 978-1-335-44858-3

The Paris Housekeeper

For questions and comments about the quality of this book, please contact us at CustomerService@Harlequin.com.

R is a trademark of Harlequin Enterprises ULC.

Love Inspired
22 Adelaide St. West, 41st Floor
Toronto, Ontario M5H 4E3, Canada
www.LoveInspired.com

Printed in U.S.A.

To Hillary, my daughter, my heart, my inspiration.
You make being a wife, a mother, a nurse and a friend look easy.
To say I'm proud wouldn't be enough. I'm truly humbled.

The Invasion

Chapter One

Rachel

14 June 1940.
Paris, France.

Paris was out of time.

The French government knew it. The people knew it.

Now, nineteen-year-old Rachel Berman knew it, too. And as she sat with her family in her parents' living room, listening to the minute-by-minute updates on the wireless, she understood something else. Something truly horrifying.

Victory belonged to the enemy.

The German war machine stood poised just outside Paris, neither invading nor retreating. The troops—all three hundred thousand of them—had arrived yesterday. They'd had twenty-four hours to make their move, and still, even with dawn breaking over the horizon, and not a hint of inclement weather, they didn't invade the French capital.

The cause for this perplexing hesitation was unknown. There'd been speculation, of course, but nothing concrete that would explain it. Was this a military tactic to frighten Parisians? If so, it was working. One thing was certain, at least to Rachel, and anyone paying attention. Paris would fall into German hands by nightfall, possibly sooner, maybe even within the hour.

What then? What would it mean to be a Jew living in German-occupied France?

Would the Nazis bring their anti-Semitic racial policies with them? Would they mark off whole sections of Paris, as they'd done in the Polish city of Lodz, and then force all Jews to live within the small, designated area?

They could do it. Probably would do it.

Trapped behind barbed wire, held there by ignorance and hate. The thought made Rachel feel hot, sweaty, and mildly nauseated. She had to close her eyes to let the sensation pass.

A feeble sound filled the room. Her mother weeping into a handkerchief.

Rachel whipped open her eyes and sent her gaze around the apartment, taking in her family with a single swoop. Her mother, all soft curves, always ready with a smile or kind word. Her older sister, Basia, so pretty, beautiful, actually, with her coal-black hair and startling green eyes. No one would guess the twenty-four-year-old was a seamstress working in a fashion designer's atelier rather than one of the models hired to show off the exquisite clothing.

Would Basia have a job after today? Would any of them? So much uncertainty. Even after completing two accounting courses, and being very good with numbers, Rachel couldn't find the proper formula to explain the rapid defeat of what had been deemed the world's mightiest army. Strong only on paper.

On the other side of the room, Rachel's father sat upright and still, remarkably stoic in his silence, his eyes barely blinking beneath the bushy flop of salt-and-pepper hair. Rachel adored Ezra Berman. She respected him even more. He was the quintessential hardworking Polish immigrant, a tailor by trade, who'd opened his own shop in their middle-class neighborhood ten years ago, after much toil and sacrifice in his adopted city.

At fifty-five, he was too old to be conscripted into the army.

At barely seventeen, Rachel's brother, Srulka, was too young.

"Our soldiers have fought valiantly. French casualties are high. Their deaths, I fear, have been in vain." The disembodied voice crackled from the wireless, proud and strong, but also angry. Rachel understood the anger, felt it herself.

Her mother still wept, softly now, a sort of whimpering, and her father remained calmly resigned. There was no wailing or gnashing of teeth on his part, and suddenly Rachel could stand his silence no longer.

"Papa," she blurted, rushing to kneel before him, her hands reaching for his, holding fast when his fingers closed over hers. "It's not too late to flee the city."

It would have to be soon. They had hours, possibly less.

"We would need to leave immediately," she urged. "If we are to beat the Germans."

A flinch crossed his face, gone as quickly as it came. It was the first real emotion her father had shown all morning and gave Rachel the courage to press on. "The Germans—*the Nazis*—will march into Paris at any moment. There will be no escaping the city then. We must go now. Right. Now."

A deep, staggering silence met her impassioned plea. Not even her siblings joined in the argument, though she knew they shared her concerns. "Surely you agree." She squeezed her father's hands. "Surely you understand the danger we're in."

Someone cleared his throat. Her brother. Rachel ignored him. "Papa, please. Let us leave Paris."

With slow, careful movements, he released her hands and spoke in his deep, gravelly voice heavily accented with his native Yiddish. "We stay."

Rachel blinked, stunned. She opened her mouth to argue.

He stopped her with a fast shake of his head. "We have discussed this, Rachel. We will not abandon this apartment, our home. I will not forsake my business and give my customers cause to find another tailor."

"What customers do you have left? Most have enlisted in the army or fled the city."

"They will return, and when they do, I will clothe them as before."

"Papa," Rachel whispered. "The battle is over. Paris will fall. This is not something that *might* happen. It *will* happen. Then we will be at the mercy of Nazis."

"I have lived through worse." He was referring to his previous life in Poland after the Great War, the days of desperate want and need, the poverty that had led him to immigrate with his wife and daughter to a new city, in a foreign country. Paris had been good to their family.

That Paris no longer existed.

"This war will not be the same as the last," Rachel said. What was happing in Poland was proof of that. "This enemy, these new Germans, they are harder, angrier, and more ruthless. Hate lives in their heart. Hate for people like us."

Her father's chin went hard. "We are French citizens."

"No, Papa. We are Jews." The words came from somewhere deep inside, from a well of something she hadn't acknowledged, not fully. Fear, anger, outrage that her father clung to his false sense of security. That somehow German occupation in France would be different than what the people of Poland suffered.

"*Nebbish!* Rachel, *hertzeleh*, you worry too much. Our neighbors, they are good people. They will protect us from the Nazis. We are safe in Paris. Now. Enough of this arguing." He rose abruptly, sending Rachel scrambling to her feet as well. "The Germans have not entered the city, and so we will go on as we always have. Me, to my shop. Srulka to school. You and your sister to your jobs."

Basia left the apartment first, a soft sigh and brief wave her only farewell. Her father and brother were the next to go, leaving Rachel alone with her mother. The older woman took her in her arms, and Rachel had to fight not to cling. "Do not fret, *schatzeleh*. Your father is never wrong about these things."

For several moments, Rachel couldn't respond. Her eyes were hot, and she wanted to cry, but the tears were stuck in her throat, hot and painful. "I hope you're right, Mama."

"We must trust your father. Now." She patted Rachel's cheek and gave her the same goodbye she'd given the others. *"Sei gesund."* Be well.

She nodded. There were no more arguments to make, no more words to say, and yet Rachel didn't want to leave the safety of her mother's arms, or the familiar aroma of oil and goose fat that permeated the air in their small apartment. They were the soothing scents of her childhood, so comforting and normal, a reminder of her Polish heritage.

Despite what her father wanted to believe, the Bermans were not French, not even Rachel and her younger brother, who were both born in Paris. No, they were still foreigners. Still Jews. Irreligious, and fully assimilated, but of a different race. Separate and apart, foreigners.

No, Rachel thought, she didn't want to leave the safety of her home, but she did.

Out in the hallway, she could hear a dog barking from somewhere in the building, and—she thought maybe—a baby crying. Another thought came then, a foreboding that the poor sobbing child would not see his next birthday. It was a dark, ugly thought, and one Rachel couldn't suppress now that it had come into her mind. She blamed her black mood on her disagreement with her father.

Pressing her lips together, she exited the building. The hot, humid air greeted her with suffocating precision. It was as if she could feel evil drifting on the light breeze. As she made her way down the wide boulevards and long avenues, the city felt too large, empty. Void of nearly two million Parisians who'd already escaped, the streets were a concrete desert, every sound magnified exponentially, as if coming from inside a cave. A dungeon of echoes.

Rachel hurried her steps.

A burst of wind whipped a slip of her black hair free from her blue chenille beret. The loose curl slapped against her cheek. Rachel tucked the wayward strand beneath the cap and picked up her pace. She took the final corner onto Rue Cambon, a sigh of relief on her lips. She'd made the entire journey without crossing paths with a single German soldier.

Paris was still a French city.

For how long?

She looked to her left, to her right. Even here, there was little activity. Rachel took another moment to study the Hôtel Ritz, where she worked as a chambermaid. The exterior looked like a palace from another century. The interior was just as grand. The hotel was actually a combination of two buildings with two separate entryways, four stories each and a row of dormer windows on the top floor. Most guests preferred the main entrance on the Place Vendôme, but employees were required to enter via the service entrance on Rue Cambon.

Rachel made her way to the women's locker room and began unpacking her uniform from her satchel, then worked on steaming out the creases. Employees were never allowed to wear their uniforms outside the hotel. Madame Ritz was adamant on this point. She wanted to create an image that her staff existed only inside the walls of the Ritz. Like a fairy tale, they were to appear fully formed, conjured as if from dreams, always available to provide the hotel's signature luxury service.

Once she donned her uniform and pinned on her lace cap, Rachel left the locker room. A wave of desperation rolled through her, and she had to pause a moment. There was that sense of helplessness again, creeping down the back of her neck. She leaned against the wall and tried to breathe through the anxiety fluttering in her chest. She heard voices coming from the laundry room, but only as if from a great distance. Tears threatened. She fought them back. To cry, here and now, was an indulgence she could ill afford.

She must be strong.

Rachel squeezed her eyes shut, and quietly admitted she

feared what the Germans would do once they entered Paris. To her, her family, the other Jews who'd remained in the city.

We are French citizens.

Her father had spoken with great calm and authority. Clearly, on the surface at least, he wasn't worried about the German invasion. Her mother seemed to agree. Rachel would try to do the same. Jaw set, she forced herself to shrug off her own fears and take on the mantle of her father's confidence in their French neighbors. She opened her eyes, pushed from the wall, and entered the laundry room. Her supervisor, Madame Bergeron, spotted her at once and pointed a bony finger in her direction.

"You, there. The Jewish girl. Come with me."

The Jewish girl.

Already, it started. The labeling, the setting apart, the being treated as different and thus somehow less. These were the thoughts that plagued Rachel as she followed her supervisor out into the corridor and down the two flights of stairs that ended in the dimly lit hotel basements.

Never talkative, the lead housekeeper was resolutely solemn this morning. Rachel was glad for her silence. Something felt wrong about this errand.

You, there. The Jewish girl.

She desperately wanted to turn and run. Where would she go? Home. Her mother would only send her back. With her father losing clients daily, the family needed her extra wages to survive. She sighed, focused on putting one foot in front of the other. Stony and pinched-faced, Madame Bergeron carried the scent of stale cigarettes on her clothing. Rachel wondered if she were the smoker, or if she'd been in one of the guest rooms.

At last, they reached the bottom of the stairs, turned to the right, and continued, with Madame Bergeron taking the lead. The lack of light was a physical presence, as if the dark were closing in on Rachel. Suffocating her, shadows melting into one another to form a forest of cold emptiness.

Eventually, the head housekeeper stopped in front of a closed door, and Rachel was able to take a decent pull of air. Of course, she thought. *Of course.* They stood before the closet where the hotel kept a back stock of bed linens and towels.

Madame Bergeron retrieved the metal ring of keys at her waist and clattered one into the lock. She reached to the single light bulb hanging from a fine, frail wire, now swaying from the fresh wave of air from the open door. It was too dark inside. There were no windows, the only light supplied by the forty-watt bulb. The walls were lined with shelves from floor to ceiling, each overflowing with bedsheets, pillowcases, and linens of every shape and size.

"Grab as many towels as you can carry," Madame Bergeron told her. "I will get the rest."

Rachel reached out, then paused when a series of shouts rang out from somewhere overhead. Voices twisted into a garbled cacophony of rapid-fire words and sentences. One black, ugly word leaped out of the chaos. "Nazis."

Shock jumped into the other woman's eyes, followed by an unmistakable thread of fear. "The Germans. They've entered the city."

In unison, they said, "We must get back."

Without looking to see if Rachel followed, Madame Bergeron took off in the direction of the stairs. Rachel allowed herself one crumbling moment of weakness to let dread wash over her, to grieve. Then she raced after her supervisor.

They took the stairs two at a time, the shouts and wails their guide. Back among her fellow employees, the noise was the first thing Rachel noticed, an earsplitting roar of too many people speaking over each other. She stood frozen near the doorway, hovering half in the room, half out, her muscles straining, her heart beating too fast. Already, she'd lost sight of Madame Bergeron. The older woman had disappeared in the pandemonium.

Snatches of conversations drifted over Rachel...*utter collapse of leadership...the government let go of Paris without a fight...not one shot fired in the city's defense.*

But what came as the greatest shock was the announcement

that the German invasion was both orderly and peaceful. No violence on their part. Not a bullet loosed to make a point. Rachel hurried outside with the rest of the staff and found a spot on the crowded sidewalk. And then...

"There!" someone shouted. "There they are. The Germans."

Rachel saw them. An uninterrupted flood of foot soldiers and tanks, armored cars and cannons, and rows upon rows of trucks approaching from the south. She went silent under the horrible sight of all that military precision, more terrifying than anything portrayed in the newsreels. The scene was the stuff of nightmares, the sound worse.

Horror drained the heat from her face. Her fingers and toes turned to ice. She opened her mouth to cry out, but no sound came forth. The soldiers, they were so young, most of them close to her own age. But their gazes were hard and intense, and proud. The air was filled with the sound of their jackboots, like hammers to nails.

The Germans continued parading past. The thunder of their footfalls seemed to be getting louder. Someone on Rachel's left moaned. The man on her right openly wept. But others—too many of them—cheered and waved at the endless line of cold-eyed soldiers. They seemed happy to welcome the enemy like some sort of foreign dignitary come to make their lives better.

The open acceptance of the German marauders, the gleeful welcome, this was a far grimmer sight than the troops themselves goose-stepping brazenly through the Parisian streets. Of course they would make their presence known in the center of the city first, at the very heart of French commerce and wealth.

Rachel had seen enough.

Turning on her heel, she went back inside the hotel and made a promise to herself. She would confront German occupation with courage. She would not break, nor would she be alone. She had her family. Together, they would face what came next. They would carry on.

They would survive.

Chapter Two

Camille

14 June 1940.
Paris, France.

Camille Lacroix moved through the darkened apartment, her steps heavy, her progress slow, and if she didn't hurry, she would be late for her shift at the hotel. She must not be late. The job was too important for her, for her family.

Assuming, of course, she still had a job. *You still have a job.*

The Hôtel Ritz needed every member of the skeleton staff to operate at its usual efficiency. Many—too many—of Camille's fellow chambermaids had fled Paris in the mass exodus, making it possible, even necessary, for her to pick up extra shifts like she did today. She needed the hours. The additional wages. The chance to provide for her family after failing them so completely with one terrible, selfish choice.

She moved quicker now, taking rapid, purposeful steps, and stopped abruptly. A movement caught her eye at the spot where the floor met the wall. There it was again. That small flurry of motion. Camille held steady, her gaze carefully picking over the shadowy contents of the room. That's when she heard it, the dreaded scratching of tiny little rat claws.

Her stomach dropped. This was not the first time she'd encountered her unwanted roommate. The rodent seemed to think he belonged in the crumbling old building as much as she. He'd probably been here longer, and she was wasting precious time.

She took a tentative step, listened a moment, and heard nothing. Not from the corner of the apartment or from the deserted Parisian streets outside. That lack of sound from the once bustling Rue Androuet was barely two weeks old and as jolting as a gunshot.

The noise came again. Scratch, scratch...*non*. Not a scratch, louder. A knock. Banging, actually. Coming from the front door.

"Mademoiselle Camille. I know you are in there. I beg you. Answer the door. You must answer the door." The thick Polish accent belonged to her elderly neighbor from the apartment one floor below. But that couldn't be. Madame Kauffman was supposed to have left Paris last week. Something had gone wrong.

"Mademoiselle?" The voice held the barest hint of defeat, as if the older woman was on the verge of giving up on Camille, as so many others had done in her life.

"I am here," she called out.

"Oh, bless you, my girl. Open the door. Please, hurry."

Camille did as her neighbor requested. She hurried through the still air, made somehow heavier due to the blackout paper on the windows. The lack of light was not unwelcome. She preferred the gray, murky veil that shrouded the cramped space she rented in the Montmartre neighborhood.

The apartment was affordable, but also shabby and threadbare, and impossibly small. So small that Camille was out of the bedroom in a handful of strides, through the sitting room with just a few more. A quick twist of her wrist to release the lock and the door swung open.

She blinked, hard and fast, forcing her vision to adjust to the dimly lit corridor, another result of the blackout rules. A few ribbons of light slipped through the darkness, falling over her neighbor. The woman was thin, white-haired, and breathing hard. But what caught Camille's attention was the dented piece of luggage resting at her visitor's feet, held shut by two pieces of frayed rope.

"Madame Kauffman," she said in way of greeting, inspecting the woman a bit closer, not liking what she saw. The skin under her eyes was a purplish shade of gray. No trick of the light, Camille knew, and she wondered when was the last time her neighbor had slept through the night? Probably not since the Germans had bombed Paris eleven days ago, destroying buildings, and killing nearly a hundred innocent civilians. "You are still in the city."

It was an inane comment, seeing as her neighbor stood on her threshold, her eyes rounded with equal parts despair and confusion. Oh, yes, something indeed had gone wrong.

Camille sensed she would be late for work, after all.

Perhaps she could dispatch the woman with a few kind words. "Madame Kauffman?" she prompted, trying to keep the impatience out of her voice. "Is there something you need?"

The woman opened her mouth, shut it, opened it again. Her bottom lip trembled, and her voice, when she finally managed to speak, was little more than a whisper. "My son," she rasped. "He does not answer my calls. I fear he has left the city with… without me."

Camille had no response, only a gasp. She reached out, let her hand drop just as quickly. She and Madame Kauffman weren't close, barely passing acquaintances. "There must be an explanation for his delay."

There had to be. Surely, a son would not leave his mother to fend for herself in the deserted city. Surely, a family member would not abandon another. *You did it.*

It wasn't the same. She'd had no choice. That's what Camille told herself, what she almost believed. But there was a part of her that secretly savored the distance from family and why she avoided going home. Why she sent money in her letters with very few words.

What was Monsieur Kauffman's excuse? Was he like her, or more like so many other Parisians ruled by their fear and panic? Ever since the bombings a week and a half ago, most of the city had gone slightly mad. Ruled by desperation, two-thirds of them had packed up their belongings and joined what was being called the mass exodus. In their frenzy to escape death, some left elderly parents behind, family pets, even children, and not always by accident.

An unpleasant reality of war.

"My son and his wife, their daughters, they are all gone. Everyone I know is gone. Everyone, but you. Camille." She lifted her face, her anguish clear in the limited light. "You will take me out of Paris with you when you go, yes? *Oui?*"

Camille's heart wrenched. What this woman asked of her, it wasn't possible. She couldn't leave Paris, not today. "I think it best you wait for Monsieur Kauffman."

"He is not coming," she said, her voice soft, tortured. "You are all I have left."

Something in the tilt of her head, her lingering focus on a spot just over Camille's shoulder, spoke of pain, the pain of betrayal, and Camille felt it again. The shock, the outrage, her own guilt over her selfish choices. The need to help was too strong to ignore, and Camille was no longer torn. Her soul was not so black as to deny a person in need. Not again. Never again. And yet. What could she do?

Most Parisians had left the city weeks ago. Most, but not all. Some had waited until the last minute to flee. Perhaps one of them had space in their car or pushcart. "I will help you."

"Oh, bless you. Bless you, my child."

Camille drew in a tight breath and opened the door a bit wider. "Come inside," she said, reaching down for the battered suitcase with one hand, using the other to draw her neighbor into the apartment. "Let me finish gathering my things, and we will be on our way."

"You are a good girl."

She wasn't. Her sole act of selfishness had brought tragedy to her family. A loved one dead, forbidden a proper resting place among the faithful for his terrible deed. Another one changed forever, left behind for others to care for, with little hope of... *Non*, now was not the time to think of such things. Now was the time to act on this woman's behalf.

Perhaps in saving her neighbor, Camille would come one step closer to achieving redemption for her own mistakes. "Wait here." She guided the older woman to a chair in the sitting room. "I'll be quick."

Madame Kauffman nodded, then gave a slight turn of her head toward the lone window in the apartment. Camille followed the direction of the woman's gaze, sighed at the slats of gloomy light that slipped past the crooked seams of the black out paper she'd taped to the glass. Fabric had been unavailable, as had the suggested glue. Those thin threads of light proved just how badly she'd failed to follow the guidelines given to the French people.

No one had shown Camille how to do the job properly, another casualty of the government's passive attempt to defend Paris. No more effective than the instruction to wear the gas masks only a select few owned. As useless as the air raid sirens going off without trained officials to direct the people to safety.

Was it any wonder so many Parisians had abandoned their homes and businesses?

What did it matter now? Camille shoved aside every doubt and focused on what must be done now, this morning. She would convince some kind soul to escort Madame Kauffman... somewhere.

How hard could it be? she wondered, as she reached for her chambermaid's uniform—the black dress tailored to fit her lithe frame, the starched white pinafore and matching lace cap, the sensible shoes made for comfort rather than fashion—and tucked it into her bag.

Her movements were painstakingly slow, weary even, as if she'd lived double her twenty-one years on this earth. Every muscle ached from the hours she spent scrubbing floors, changing bedsheets, sanitizing bathrooms, and generally seeing to the guests' every need, no matter how frivolous or absurd. One resident in particular came to mind. The wealthy American widow who'd taken a liking to the way Camille styled her hair, often calling her away from her other duties on what seemed a last-minute whim. The generous tips she paid were always sent home. More restitution, but never enough.

Slinging her bag over her shoulder, she left the bathroom and moved into the main portion of the tiny apartment. At the sight of Madame Kauffman sitting so still and resigned, Camille was once again overwhelmed with the urge to pull the older woman close, to assure her everything would turn out well.

She was not that much of a liar.

Taking the battered suitcase in one hand, she reached for her neighbor with the other, and quickly, carefully, drew the woman to her feet.

Outside, the heat hit like a fist, while an eerie silence wrapped around them. Under that shocking lack of sound, Camille could no longer feel the heavy June air. Instead, a chill prickled her skin. Today the mood was different, more solemn. The empty street felt wider, somehow, as if built to accommodate the enemy's tanks. Panzers, they called them, short for *panzerkraftwagen*, massive landships made to destroy anything in their path. And they loomed just outside an unprotected Paris.

Hurry.

"Yes, well," she said, trying not to push her companion too hard, but knowing the clock worked against them. "Come along, Madame Kauffman."

Putting the dazzling white domes and bell towers of the

Sacré-Coeur Basilica behind them, Camille took Madame Kauffman's thin hand, wrinkled flesh over brittle bones, and headed for Rue des Trois Frères. She adopted what she hoped was an acceptable pace, even as one word kept moving through her mind. *Hurry.*

They'd barely taken a smattering of steps when the older woman tugged free of Camille's hold, pivoted, then set her gaze on the building they'd just exited. "Thirty years I have called Paris home. I will miss this grand city, as much as I once missed Warsaw, and—" she turned to smile at Camille, the stain of old age and a fondness for coffee on her teeth "—I will miss you, too. Very much."

Camille tamped down her impatience and forced herself to smile. "And I, you."

Sighing, the older woman shook her head. "This world, it is not right anymore."

"*Non*, it is not."

"Monsters walk among us now."

"They do."

A bird flew overhead, squawking a sort of warning, startling them both.

"Come." One arm locked with Madame Kauffman's, the other carrying the battered suitcase, Camille guided her neighbor through a world turned upside down toward a destination not yet known. As they rushed along Rue des Trois Frères, then turned left onto Rue Tardieu, they had the advantage of caring little where the woman ended up, only that she escape Paris.

Another few blocks and there, at the bottom of the hill, on Boulevard Marguerite de Rochechouart, was the expansive line of automobiles, bicycles, and pushcarts overflowing with household goods. Camille tugged Madame Kauffman along at a steady pace. Entirely too slow. It could not be helped. Her elderly neighbor was already showing signs of fatigue in her hitched breathing and limping gait.

They went from one vehicle to the next, stopping at each, no matter how large or small, and Camille asked the same question, over and over: "Do you have space for a small lady with a single piece of luggage?"

The answer rarely varied. "We have no room."

Camille refused to be discouraged. Trying not to run, she all but dragged her neighbor from car to car, doing most of the talking, her request either ignored or denied.

Was no one willing to help an old woman? Did no one care?

A drip of sweat rolled down the side of her face. Her heart pounded against her ribs. Again, Camille stopped at a car in the queue and motioned to the driver to lower his window.

The man mouthed his refusal. *Non.*

"Please, monsieur. I—"

He turned his head and focused on the line of cars in front of him, his message clear.

"It's hopeless." Camille heard the dejection in Madame Kauffman's voice, felt it herself. Still, she made herself take a long, deep breath and offered what encouragement she could muster, which was to say not very much.

"I am not giving up."

Even with her neighbor's arduous, awkward pace, they moved faster on foot than anything with wheels, though it required great attention to avoid being pushed to the ground or rolled over. Then, up ahead, Camille noticed another car. A space in the back seat clearly visible.

She didn't waste time explaining the situation. She simply pulled the older woman along with her. *Come along*, she wanted to yell at her neighbor. *Move.* She didn't need to say the words. Madame Kauffman propelled herself forward on her own. One step, then two. Another. Finally, they were striding alongside the car, and Camille asked the driver the same question as all the ones before. "Do you have space for a small lady with a single piece of luggage?"

His response came without hesitation. *"Oui."*

It took a moment for her to process the word. When she did,

relief nearly buckled her knees, and she offered her gratitude with a voice barely above a whisper. *"Merci."*

Her hand shook so hard, it took her three tries to open the car door. Once she had the older woman settled in the back seat, Camille leaned in through the open window and kissed the papery skin on the weathered cheek. "Take care, *mon amie*," she said, wondering if she would ever see her neighbor again, thinking probably not. *"Au revoir."*

"Au revoir, Camille."

Eyes stinging, she stepped back, then suddenly realized she had no idea of the car's destination. What if Madame Kauffman's son came for her, after all? He would want to know what had happened to his mother. "Where?" she asked the driver, a rotund man with a bushy mustache and balding head. "Where are you going?"

"Rennes," came his response. "My brother has a house near the train depot."

Camille breathed in deeply, let it out in a whoosh of air. Of all the possible destinations, her neighbor would journey to Brittany, to a city barely thirty miles from Camille's home village of Dinan.

Again, the thought whispered in her head: *I want to go home.*

She could leave now, right now. Better yet, she could return to her apartment and pack her things, everything that meant anything to her, in twenty minutes. She could retrieve her bicycle and join the line of cars. So easy, so simple. Home in a matter of days. Back to living in the picturesque medieval village with her mother, who even now was working in their family's floundering bakery. Two of Camille's sisters joined in that never-ending battle, while the other only watched with those wide, empty eyes.

Her heart gave a flutter at this thought of escape. Ah, but her mind was not so quickly led into the fantasy. *How will you feed your family, yourself, if you leave Paris?*

How, indeed?

It was an argument she had with herself daily, sometimes more than once, always with the same outcome. There were no jobs to be found in Dinan, or Rennes for that matter, certainly nothing that paid as well as her position at the Hôtel Ritz. It was settled, then. There would be—could be—no escape for Camille. Only duty. Obligation. And perhaps, in time, restitution, for the past, for herself, and for the lives she'd ruined with a single thoughtless act. And if a part of her was relieved she wouldn't have to face what she'd done, well, that was between herself and her own conscience.

She offered a final farewell wave to her neighbor and hurried toward the center of Paris, her course set on the dark road that lay ahead—a road growing darker by the day.

Chapter Three

Vivian

14 June 1940.
Hôtel Ritz. Paris, France.

By mid-afternoon, on what was proving, ironically, to be a beautiful balmy spring day, Vivian Miller stood on the balcony of her hotel suite and tried to make sense of the day's events.

It could not be done.

There was no logic to be found in war. Foolish to think otherwise.

As an American, Vivian had thought herself immune to European politics. More foolishness on her part. She lived in the heart of Paris, in a luxury hotel where clandestine meetings had been occurring for months. Just last week, Winston Churchill had taken a room in the Ritz and met with other world leaders. He'd been very visible, eating in the hotel restaurant, or sitting in the bar, whiskey glass in hand, head bent in furious discussion. Usually—always—him trying to convince his contemporaries of the evil lurking in their midst. None of them listening.

None of them believing.

Europe—Paris—*the world*—would suffer for their refusal to heed Churchill's warnings.

For her part, Vivian had known what was coming. Of course she'd known. Even if she hadn't been paying attention to the dignitaries and their comings and goings, she'd lived through another war. The signs were all there. The grasping for power. The claiming of territory that belonged to others. Threats masquerading as diplomacy.

Hitler had not been subtle.

Now German troops marched on Paris. Vivian could hear their boots thumping the pavement, each strike a death knell to peace. She knew she had precious little time to choose whether to remain in the city or escape with the rest of the two million frightened souls. For weeks, she'd put off making the decision. Something always held her back. Something that could not be fully explained, except for one important fact.

People relied on her.

It always came down to that.

Oh, sure, there were others who could take her place. But did they have her money, her contacts? Vivian could think of only a very few. With caveats. So. Maybe. Not even one.

Was that enough reason to stay?

Be smart, Vivi. The words came to her in her late husband's flat Midwestern accent. *You're an American. This is not your fight.*

That was the kind of head-in-the-sand rationale that had allowed Hitler to rise to power. The kind of thinking that belonged to appeasers. Did Vivian want to join their ranks?

Surely, she was braver than that.

She gripped the wrought-iron railing in front of her and cast her gaze over the hotel gardens. She'd chosen this room for the view, preferring to wake every morning to birdsong and manicured lawns rather than to the frenetic bustle of the Place Vendôme.

Three years, that's how long she'd lived at the Hôtel Ritz,

every one of them without her beloved Rupert. Alone. So alone. She breathed in, breathed out, fought for control.

It helped to concentrate on the view.

The sun shone through the green of the trees, casting the army of flowers in bold relief, each bloom more perfect than the one beside it. Beauty found a way to thrive. Light existed within the dark. Good eventually prevailed, even after evil triumphed.

And always—always—God was in control.

Where was He now? Why had He taken his hand off France?

Only time would tell, Vivian thought, returning to her suite. At the same moment she stepped off the balcony, a knock sounded from the entryway. It came again. Faster, louder. Such persistence warned Vivian she would not like what she found on the other side of the door.

It could not be avoided.

Blinking away the harsh sunlight dotting across her eyes, she hurried through the suite, the clack of her heels silenced by the thick carpet. At the entryway, she undid the latch and opened the door. Her heart gave a quick stutter behind her rib cage.

Hans Elminger, the Swiss nephew of the hotel's most important investor, stood on the threshold, expression grim. His presence on her doorstep meant nothing good. Behind him, a blur of moving bodies rushed by. Another bad sign.

With an apologetic tilt of his head, Elminger relayed the devastating news Vivian already knew. "The Germans have entered the city."

"Yes." She could think of nothing more to say.

"The Métro has closed," he continued. "And most exits out of Paris have been blocked by German troops, though not all. It is not too late to escape the city."

Not too late to escape.

Vivian looked again at the river of panicked humanity streaming down the hallway, all of them believing that safety could be found outside the city. Were they right?

A sudden, awful, terrible thought occurred to her. Hans El-minger was at her door for a reason, and it wasn't to give her hours-old news. "Are you shutting down the hotel?"

He shook his head. "At the moment, no. But that could change. Madame Ritz is in conversation with the Board, and she has advised me to inform our guests that while we will do our best to accommodate you for as long as we remain open, we cannot guarantee your protection from the German invaders."

Vivian had not believed otherwise. "Understood."

With a lift of his chin, he gave a pointed look over his shoulder. "Many of our guests are leaving now."

And all of them, Vivian noticed with a pang, were carrying nothing but a single suitcase.

A viselike grip tightened in her chest as she considered her priceless antiques in her suite, collected from around the world. Her Renaissance tapestries. The furs and fine jewelry that had been gifts from her husband, each piece representing a moment of their life together.

Possessions could be replaced. The sentiment behind them could not.

"If I choose to leave with the others," Vivian began, sweat breaking out on her brow, the only outward sign of her uncertainty, "will this room be mine when I return?"

Because, surely, she would come back. The Hôtel Ritz was her home now.

"If we stay open, yes. The suite is yours. Assuming the Nazis do not requisition the building or…" He left the rest unsaid. He didn't need to expand. They both knew German soldiers would be swamping the hotel lobby at any moment. They would dine in the restaurant and drink in the bars. And possibly—probably—take ownership of valuable items that didn't belong to them.

"I'll let you know my decision within the hour."

"Very good, madame." He gave her a curt nod and departed, disappearing into the crowd at a cool, steady pace, his head bobbing above the fray, as if he were a buoy riding the waves in a stormy sea of uncertainty.

Vivian shut the door and turned back to her suite. For a paralyzing moment, she stood clenching and unclenching her fists. Stay or go?

Stay and risk her life for others? The moral choice. Go and put her own safety first? The selfish decision. But also, the practical one. Vivian didn't need to live in Paris to continue her work. It was wiser to leave. More efficient, expedient, to remain.

If only Rupert were still alive. He would tell her what to do.

Smoothing a hand over her hair, she looked around her suite, barely taking note of the subtle blend of high-end French design mixed with Old English charm.

Her head pounded miserably, and she had to blink away the excesses of the previous night. All part of keeping up the appearance of a wealthy, empty-headed widow with more money than sense. Having deep pockets mattered a great deal in Paris, yet even with all her millions, Vivian was still an outsider, even among her fellow American expats.

It had always been that way. From the beginning of her marriage to the much older, much sought-after Midwestern industrialist, she'd been scorned by the social elite. First in Cleveland. Then New York. London had been a little better, but not by much.

What had Vivian done that was so wrong? She'd found herself a man with a vast fortune who'd adored her, that's what. For a self-indulgent moment, she let her mind drift back in time to her frenetic yearning to belong to someone, anyone. No, not just anyone. A man who didn't use his fists to make his point. She hadn't expected to find love. The immediate attraction she'd felt for Rupert Miller had come as a surprise. Their whirlwind romance equally so.

Those first awkward parties as an engaged couple had been a taste of what was to come. The disappointments and compromises. The snubs by her "betters." Vivian had endured the humiliation, for Rupert's sake. She'd smiled, and pretended she was fine—just fine—until he took her home and it was just the two of them.

They'd been happy for ten remarkable years. Blissfully happy, and her sweet husband was still with her, always, alive in her memories, his dark brown eyes warm with affection. His thick gray hair tousled as he leaned over to whisper in her ear, *Remember, Vivi, I love you.*

He'd been the only one. Her passive, indifferent mother hadn't shared the sentiment. Her father had shown her the true meaning of violence. A loud bang jolted her back into the present and she spun to face the entryway again, heard the commotion beyond the door.

What did the past matter now? Rupert was dead, Vivian was alone, and German soldiers marched on Paris. The French had been given nine months to prepare for this day, and yet they'd continued living as before, without any meaningful variation in their routines.

Parisians had thought it impossible. The fall of their country, their precious city. They'd put their faith in their government, and their army touted themselves the strongest in Europe, foolishly believing the Maginot Line, that flimsy wire and concrete barricade from Luxembourg to Switzerland, would hold back the monsters.

Make your decision.

If Marie-Louise Ritz—Mimi—closed the hotel, Vivian would have to find another place to live. And that would be that. But first, she needed more information. Slipping out of her suite, she stepped into the middle of the frantic crowd rushing to presumed safety. Her years as a combat nurse for the American Red Cross should have prepared her for the hysteria.

In some ways, she supposed, it had. In others, not at all. Vivian felt their panic as if it were her own. A tangible, living thing she could nearly touch. As she headed to the stairwell, she was tossed about, teetering at times, forced to reach for the wall now and again to stay upright.

The disconsolate voices, the scent of fear, it was strong, leaden, and Vivian remembered the days when ambulances came roaring up to the Italian hospital with their wounded cargo. Today there was no blood, and there were no missing limbs. Oh, but the wails of anguish. Those were very much the same.

As Vivian descended the first flight of stairs, she saw Coco Chanel five steps below, travel case in hand. A stunned-looking chambermaid chased after the famous fashion designer, her arms overflowing with more bags. Coco never traveled light. Vivian called out to her friend, but she either didn't hear her or chose to ignore her.

Just as well. Their destinations were not the same. Coco was a Frenchwoman with friends and family all over the country.

Vivian had no one.

In the lobby, she approached the doorman, Jacques, a man she'd enlisted in her clandestine work on more than one occasion. "Have you seen Madame Ritz?"

He answered without looking at her, "She's in the hotel bar with the others."

"The others?" she asked, but he was already turning away to help an elderly couple into a car with a dubious-looking driver behind the steering wheel.

Sending up a prayer for the pair, Vivian hurried down the narrow passageway leading to the hotel's Rue Cambon entrance. At the end of the corridor, she briefly looked over her shoulder, then entered the famous bar where, on most nights, a collection of artists, singers, and expatriates told tall tales, smoked cigarettes, and swilled too many drinks.

Although the mahogany counter gleamed, as always, and the brass was polished to a near-blinding shine, everything else about the bar was different from what Vivian had grown accustomed to. For starters, too many bodies were crammed into the small, confined space. Staff and guests alike had gathered side by side around a wireless in the far corner of the room.

There were no divisions or social barriers, no separations of rich and poor. Chambermaids linked arms with women draped in furs. Kitchen boys and front desk clerks stood beside men in tailored suits.

Vivian had zero desire to join them. She was here only for enough information to make her decision. Another, more thorough glance around the bar and, finally, she spotted Madame Ritz, small, elegant, dressed in her black dress in the familiar Edwardian style. She sat at a table, deep in conversation with Georges Mandel. Like Vivian, the celebrated journalist and former French Minister of the Interior was a permanent resident of the hotel. The poor man looked as exhausted and as rumpled as his overcoat. There were lines of worry around his watery, red-rimmed eyes. Vivian knew the feeling.

Not wanting to interrupt what looked to be an important interchange between the two old friends, she discreetly seated herself at the table next to theirs. It wasn't a stratagem, per se. If they wished to include her in their discussion, all they had to do was give her a small nod. They never once looked her way.

"I cannot stomach the idea of leaving France," Mandel told the widowed hotel owner. "It would be akin to running away."

It was Mimi's turn to wear a worried expression. "Georges, my friend, I beg you to reconsider. You are, after all—" she leaned forward and whispered "—Jewish."

"It is because I am a Jew that I won't go. It would look as though I were afraid."

"Perhaps you should be afraid. Perhaps you should accept Churchill's invitation to join him in London."

"I won't play the coward. *Non*, I won't do it. We will speak of this no further." He took the older woman's hand in his. "You did not seek me out to discuss my future, but yours. You have a tricky dilemma that must be settled at once."

Mimi nodded, sighed, nodded again. "My Board has given

me their advice. Now I wish to hear yours. Tell me, Georges, do I keep the hotel open, and suffer the indignity of those foul Nazis milling about my property, or do I close my doors for the duration of the war?"

"The way I see it, you have but one option. No, Mimi." Mandel held up his hand. "Do not interrupt. Let me finish. If you shut down operations, the Germans will requisition this hotel. Then, I fear, you will never get it back, not a single room or furnishing within."

The argument made sense, but the hotel owner did not appear persuaded. "I will, perhaps, lose my hotel for a while. But surely, I will regain ownership once the Nazis are good and soundly defeated."

"Why take such risk? You, my good friend, are Swiss. Your homeland is neutral. Therefore, it stands to reason that you are also neutral."

She seemed to think this over. "The Board came to a similar conclusion, but with more direct words."

"Then let me also be frank. Your hotel will be occupied by Germans. It's a given, but if you remain neutral, and do not take sides in this war, you will have a better chance of maintaining ownership of your hotel."

A small, satisfied smile crept across her face. "I thank you for your candor. That's exactly what I needed to hear."

She rose and called for quiet, lifting hands bejeweled with diamonds and other precious gems. A hush fell over the room. Someone clicked off the droning, staticky newscast that brought only bad news.

"Everyone in this room should know who I am. For those who don't, I am Marie-Louise Ritz, the owner of this hotel and the President of the Board of Directors. I am also Swiss, and like my country, I am neutral in this war. Therefore—" she paused for dramatic effect "—the Hôtel Ritz will remain open. My decision is final."

That was it. The hard-nosed, pragmatic hotel owner had

spoken. Vivian still had a home. Unfortunately, in a matter of days, she would likely be living among *those foul Nazis*.

A chill ran through her, a sort of primitive warning that forced her to accept the truth at last. She'd known this day would come. She'd known the Germans would take Paris and steal all hope from the innocent.

She'd also known what she would do when the inevitable happened.

There'd been no uncertainty in her heart, not really, no waffling. In truth, Vivian had made her decision months ago. The moment she'd supplied the first set of falsified papers to a family of Jews wishing to escape Europe.

Chapter Four

Rachel

14 June 1940.
Paris, France.

Rachel leaned against the wall, twisting her hands together at her waist until her fingers went numb. She'd lost track of time and thought it might be close to the end of her shift, but she wasn't sure. She wasn't sure of anything anymore. Every muscle in her body screamed for her to sit, to rest, to let her growing fatigue win. She remained standing, her right shoulder aligned with one of the guests, her other pressed to another chambermaid.

What was her name? Camille. Yes, that was it. Camille Lacroix. A pretty French name for a pretty French girl. Tallish, on the thin side, she was only a few years older than Rachel, with light blond hair, delicate features, and pale blue eyes. The enviable combination earned the girl second looks. And smiles. Many, many smiles.

Rachel didn't receive smiles. She did, however, attract second looks. But the attention thrown her way came with speculation and whispers. *Is she Jewish? Of course she's Jewish. Look at her hair, the swarthy color of her skin, the shape of her nose, the black eyes.*

Labeled, set apart, considered different for physical traits she had once been so proud of, because they came from her sweet, kind, beautiful mother. The need to rail against such obvious racism burned hot in her belly.

"The Hôtel Ritz will remain open," Madame Ritz declared in a solemn tone better suited for a funeral. "My decision is final."

Rachel felt the floor shift beneath her feet. *Remain open.* She turned the words over in her head, wondering: What did that mean? She knew, though it made her stomach twist in a kind of roiling sickness. German soldiers would eat in the hotel's restaurant. They would drink in the bars, and Rachel was glad— so very, very glad—that she worked in a department where she was expected to remain invisible.

If she kept her head down, and avoided notice, then she would be…what? Safe? Free of the whispers? Was such a thing possible in a city occupied by Nazis?

The hotel manager approached Madame Ritz. As the two engaged in a private, hushed conversation, Rachel was thankful someone had thought to turn off the broadcast announcing the fall of Paris. In the ensuing silence, she could close her eyes and pretend that evil lived outside French borders. Far away from Paris, the hotel, her parents' apartment.

Oh, Papa, why did we not leave the city when we had the chance?

Madame Ritz addressed the room again. "German occupation need not be terribly inconvenient for our guests." She nodded to several of the long-term residents—the famous novelist who'd fought in the previous war, the French film star tucked inside her fur coat despite the heat, the American widow sitting at a table, her brow knitted together in quiet contemplation. "You may return to your rooms with confidence that we will provide the same white-glove service as always."

Rachel sucked in a breath. How could she make that promise? The depleted staff was already run ragged. They could not hope to continue the brutal pace indefinitely. Was she the only employee who thought this? She shifted her gaze to Camille. The other chambermaid seemed to visibly sag under the weight of the hotel owner's declaration. Rachel reached for her hand and squeezed. Camille squeezed back.

Neither let go, both seeming to need the comfort of the brief human contact. Rachel wished she knew more about the girl. They didn't speak about their lives outside the hotel. And yet they'd formed a tentative bond in the past few weeks, each continuing to show up for work as others abandoned their posts, often without notice.

Camille drew her hand away, and Rachel noticed something she'd missed under the chaos of the day. "You aren't wearing your uniform."

"No, I…" She looked down, grimaced. "I'd only just arrived for work when the Germans entered this part of the city. There was no time to change."

But that would mean… "You were late?" Rachel heard the shock in her voice. There was nothing for it. Camille was never late. "That's not like you."

"Yes, well." The girl looked away. "I was unavoidably detained."

Behind Camille's eyes, Rachel could see the agitation, the worry. "You were stopped by German soldiers?"

"*Non.*" She went silent a moment, lost in thought, and then something else appeared in her expression. The sort of steadfastness that spoke of resolve. "A neighbor needed my help escaping the city. Securing transportation proved difficult."

Rachel thought of her father's confidence in the French people. For the first time since leaving her apartment, she felt a little less desperate. She nearly smiled at Camille, nearly reached for her hand again, but a surge in the crowd pushed them apart. The moment was gone.

Madame Ritz continued making promises, assuring the guests they were important to the hotel. "Until we can assess the situation, we will be closing the dining rooms. That's not to say we won't provide food for our guests, but from a limited menu. We will bring trays to your rooms and—"

She was cut off by the sound of male voices. German voices. Shouting. Rachel's mouth went instantly dry. The Nazis were here already, inside the Hôtel Ritz.

"How many of them?" someone whispered, her voice wavering. "Have they come for food?" another asked, while someone else posed the question, "Do you think they want our rooms? Are we to be tossed out onto the streets in the middle of the night?"

Questions upon questions. It wasn't until Jacques, the head doorman, rushed into the bar that answers came, if not the ones the assembled guests and staff sought.

"The German army has taken over the hotel." Panic coated his voice. "Soldiers have pushed their way through the Place Vendôme entrance. Their muddy boots sully the carpets. They do not take off their hats. They do not hide their guns. They only make demands, insisting we provide them with food and lodgings."

The whispers became a roar.

"Calm down. Everyone, please. Calm down." Madame Ritz shoved through the crowd, ordering people to move aside, pushing them when necessary, until she stood before the wild-eyed doorman. "How many Germans are in my hotel, Jacques? Give me a number."

"No fewer than two dozen, madame. Possibly as many as fifty."

The older woman went silent, as if calculating the number in her head and then applying the result to the vacant rooms in the hotel. "We will do what we can to accommodate them."

Another explosion of shocked whispers rent the air, louder than before, but not by much. Then came the outrage, the heated arguments to reconsider her decision, but nothing could sway Marie-Louise Ritz. This was her hotel. Her word stood.

This was it, Rachel realized, her heart pounding. The beginning of the end. And there was that sense of helplessness again, creeping down the back of her neck, sliding to the base of her spine. She began to shake. But then, something happened inside her, a sort of rebellion that she hadn't known herself capable of, turning her fear into something equally fierce. A will to survive. Her anger fed the sensation.

Organized chaos filled the next minutes, as guests retreated to their rooms and employees went back to work. The housekeeping staff was tasked with preparing the empty rooms for their unexpected guests. Guests? Rachel nearly sneered. German soldiers were not guests. They were marauders. Here to do harm, to take—to steal—what did not belong to them.

She wanted to howl in frustration.

She went to work instead, hoping the menial tasks of changing bed linens and scrubbing floors would occupy her mind. For a time, they did. Then, they didn't, and she had to remind herself she needed this job. Her father's business had lost too many customers, and Rachel's next accounting class was due to begin in a couple months. Tuition must be paid.

The chambermaids were dismissed at 7:30 p.m., and only because the Germans had initiated a curfew that required all French citizens to be inside their homes by eight o'clock.

Camille caught up with Rachel in the locker room. They shared a look, somehow realizing this was a big moment. They'd worked side by side turning over the rooms, and what had been a tentative bond only this morning had found a stronger footing. They were friends now, solidarity through adversity.

Camille broke the silence first. "Where do you live? Close enough to walk?"

Rachel shook her head. "I usually take the Métro, but with it being shut down…" She didn't finish the sentence. "Anyway, I live on Rue Rochechouart."

"We're headed in the same direction," Camille said. "I'm only a few blocks up the hill from you, in Montmartre. You shouldn't be out there alone."

"Nor should you."

They agreed to brave the streets together, out of necessity, but also out of a new kinship. By the time they'd changed into their own clothes and exited the hotel, the sky had turned a dingy charcoal gray that reminded Rachel of worn bed linens washed too many times. A light breeze kicked up, but did nothing to suppress the heat, or still the strange combination of scents. Motor oil mixed with diesel fuel, horse sweat, and, weirdly, jasmine.

There were others on the street, hurrying, like them, to get home before curfew began. A head poked out from a slit in the door of a darkened restaurant. A shadow appeared on the sidewalk, and then went quickly on the move, the dark silhouette shifting and bending with the curves of the street. In a swift shuffle of feet, Camille moved in front of Rachel, as if to protect her, and Rachel wasn't sure whether to be grateful or offended. She was Jewish, not helpless.

They followed a similar path as the shadow, their footsteps picking up speed as if catching his urgency. Neither spoke. They passed a building where a group of German soldiers stood huddled together on the rooftop. The men worked as a team, moving as a single unit. Their efficiency was smooth and frightening. They let down a Nazi banner that bore a black swastika inside a white circle against a bloodred field. An evil tapestry signifying the death knell to Paris.

Camille's hand reached for Rachel's. "We should hurry."

"We really should."

They completed the final blocks with their palms pressed together. Outside her apartment building, Rachel tugged free of Camille's hold and pointed to the third floor. "I live there."

"It's nice." Camille studied the building a moment longer, her eyes sweeping over the stone facade and gabled rooftop. "Will I see you tomorrow?"

Rachel wanted to say, *No.* Never again would she turn over a room in preparation for a Nazi soldier. But that would be her pride speaking, so she gave a short, reluctant nod.

"We will stick together," Camille announced, "and look out for each other, *oui*?"

It was a lovely idea. "I'd like that."

Camille turned, took a few steps, then stopped, and hurried back. She clearly had something more to say, but words seemed to fail her. Rachel wanted to sigh. She knew what was on the girl's mind. It was there in her uneasy expression. This wasn't the first time someone tiptoed around the subject of her ethnicity. "You want to know if I'm Jewish."

"No, I… Well. I already knew that. What I want to know, is…" She looked away, back again, giving into the sigh Rachel herself had repressed. "Do you, or rather, are you—"

"Protected?" Rachel supplied. "Safe?"

"Prepared."

One word, the insight behind it, and all Rachel's worries roared to life. Regardless of her father's faith in their neighbors, no one really knew what the future held for French Jews. If German occupation in Poland was the prevailing model, then there was much to fear. But at this point, it was all conjecture. "As prepared as any of us can be."

It wasn't really an answer, but it seemed to satisfy Camille. Though not completely, for she pressed the issue. "You will let me know if matters grow difficult?"

What could this young Frenchwoman do if the Nazis built ghettos in Paris? Not much, surely. Nevertheless, Rachel said, "Of course."

"*Très bien.*"

This time when she turned to leave, Camille didn't stop or look back. Rachel rolled her shoulders and entered her apartment building. The interior was unnaturally silent. Eerie, even. A sure sign more people had left the city. Rachel had not been honest with Camille. Her family wasn't prepared for German occupation, not with her father's willful reliance on their neighbors.

Would they protect them? Hard to know. Although the bulk

were French, most of them were Catholic. Only a few were Jewish. The *Israelite bourgeois*, as they called themselves. Living in this building was proof of Ezra Berman's social climb out of poverty.

Admirable, except on their ascent into the middle class, Rachel's parents had forgotten any sort of religious practice. They'd fully assimilated and had insisted their children do the same. The Bermans didn't attend the local synagogue. They didn't recognize the High Holy Days. There was no menorah in their home. No lighting of candles to signify the beginning of Shabbat or the recitation of the traditional prayers.

There were times when Rachel resented her parents for pulling away from their faith, just to fit in better with their neighbors. The rituals and prayers, the hymns, they would have been a comfort now. To be fair, Ezra and Ilka Berman hadn't given up being Jewish. They'd just stepped away from the religion. Her mother still cooked traditional kugel, one of her father's favorites, no matter that the symbolic references had been lost years ago.

Rachel sighed, wishing for something missing in her life she couldn't form into concrete images. Thoughts in turmoil, she entered her family's apartment, noting that the scene was much the same as this morning. No, she thought again, they weren't prepared for German occupation. Her mother and sister sat together, hands clasped, their faces twisted in grief. Her father and brother were farther away, their faces equally grim.

Shutting the door, Rachel crossed the room and sat at her mother's feet, saying nothing, forcing down her panic, her fear, and forced herself to listen to the announcer explaining what was expected of French citizens living in occupied Paris. He touched on the new curfew, explained the rules of rationing, and how to acquire coupons for staples such as bread, sugar, and milk. The German-accented French was jarring, the guttural language hard on Rachel's ears.

Sighing again, she placed her head in her mother's lap. Tears slipped from her eyes. She let them come. From above the top of the hill, in Montmartre where her friend Camille lived, the bells of the basilica tolled eight hollow notes, marking the moment of Paris's first night of the new curfew set by the Germans occupiers.

And so it begins, Rachel thought, the dark, frightening existence under a dictator who hated Jews. Without a plan, without hope. Would any of them survive?

Chapter Five

Camille

14 June 1940.
Eighteenth Arrondissement. Montmartre. Paris, France.

Camille paused halfway up the hill and looked over her shoulder just as Rachel disappeared into her building. Although curfew loomed, she lingered a moment, thinking about the Jewish girl. There was an innocence about her that reminded Camille of her little sister. It was that similarity that made her want to protect Rachel, as she tried to do for Jacqueline.

Neither could help the world they'd been born into, a world where judgment was commonplace and acceptance scarce. A bone-rattling fatigue suddenly hit Camille, digging deep, like a hook snared in her flesh. She could feel the beginning of a headache, a dull persistent throb behind her eyes. Paris had fallen so quickly. French propaganda had alleged that the German army was weak and undernourished, poorly armed, and not fully committed to the Nazi ideology. This afternoon's spectacle had contradicted that narrative.

Now her mind was on her father. If he were alive, he would have stood among the other veterans of the Great War, his medals pinned to his suit coat. Like them, he would have openly wept. He'd once been so proud of his German ancestry, passed down through his mother. But that had been before he'd gone to war for France. Before his capture that had resulted in interrogation and torture. He'd relived the ordeal in his nightmares, thrashing about and muttering in his mother's language. At her own mother's insistence, Camille had learned German to better understand his rantings. Only to wish she hadn't been so successful.

She passed three young Frenchmen—teenagers. Boys. Loitering. Their thin faces were full of rebellion, and they held cigarettes between their fingers. A small defiance, the smoking, as was their presence on the street so close to curfew.

Did this make them brave or reckless? Both, she decided, and hurried past them. Rue Androuet was strange in the dull darkness of night. The route she knew so well in daylight retreated into shadows. The cafés were empty. The sidewalks bare. No noisy children playing ball. No vendors hawking their wares from pushcarts. Vacant and still, yet she felt eyes on her and practically vaulted inside her apartment building.

She paused, took a deep breath, and was instantly sorry for the hesitation. The slap of heels on stone signaled the approach of the building's concierge. Camille let out a sigh just as Louise Thibodeaux appeared. The woman was an intimidating presence. Tall, thick in the waist, large-boned, she carried a perpetual frown on her face. Her wiry hair tended toward gray. But her eyes. Camille had long ago worked out why they seemed strange. It was their color. So dark it was impossible to tell where the irises ended and the pupils began. That lack of contrast gave her a blank, soulless stare.

"A letter arrived for you, Mademoiselle Lacroix." Her tone bore a hint of hostility. The concierge didn't like Camille, though she couldn't think why. She paid her rent on time and generally stayed out of the woman's way.

"A letter came today?" She wasn't sure how that could be

possible. The Germans had shut down all routes for commu-nication this morning.

Still frowning, Madame Thibodeaux dug around in the pocket of her apron, pulling the material wide, as if needing to inspect the contents with her eyes as well as her large hand. At last, she retrieved a crumpled envelope but held it aloft in-stead of passing it over to Camille, which didn't keep her from recognizing her mother's handwriting. *May it be good news*. Though she feared it was not. She noted the postmark. Sent three days ago.

Why was the concierge only delivering the letter tonight?

When she asked the question, the woman gave a very French shrug. "It has been a busy time for me. I lose tenants daily, one only just this morning."

She was speaking about Madame Kauffman. Too weary to explain the situation, Camille stuck out her hand. "May I have the letter?"

Sighing heavily, the concierge handed over the rumpled en-velope, reluctance evident in her dreadfully slow movements. Camille made to go. But the woman wasn't done with her. She gave Camille a suspicious glare, her frown digging deeper. "What do you know of Madame Kauffman's disappearance?"

And there it was, the purpose of this uncomfortable inter-change all along. The woman could have just as easily slipped the letter under her door, as was her usual practice. Instead, here they were. "I believe she planned to flee the city with her son and his family."

"I see." The concierge sniffed in annoyance. "Yes, well, if you hear anything from Madame Kauffman, you will let me know. If she has indeed left the city, I will need to rent out her apartment. And it won't be to someone like *that* woman."

"That woman?"

"A Jew."

Camille blinked, feeling sick and, if she were honest with herself, slightly afraid. Madame Thibodeaux's face had changed, her frown turning into something darker, sinister even, similar to the glint in the eyes of the German soldiers.

Was this how the concierge had always felt about her Jewish residents? Was she emboldened to speak her mind now that Paris was in the hands of like-minded racists?

An image of Rachel came to Camille. The sweet girl who never complained, no matter the menial tasks she was given, and worked twice as hard as the other chambermaids. What could be done for her? Suddenly, Camille felt appalled all over again and didn't even try keeping the disgust out of her voice. "If there's nothing else…"

It was an obvious dismissal, and the concierge knew it. Her face went hard and pinched, but as if sensing she'd gotten what she could out of Camille, relented. "That's all for now."

Camille headed up the stairs. On the second landing, she paused, her eyes seeking the door to Madame Kauffman's apartment. Who would rent the space now? A horrible thought occurred to her. With so many German soldiers in the city, there would be a need for politicians and administrators. Office workers, too, secretaries, typists, file clerks. Camille could imagine one of them taking the apartment still fully furnished with Madame Kauffman's belongings.

Her stomach pitched again. *Nothing you can do.*

She patted the letter, now in the pocket of her skirt, and trudged up the final flight of stairs. Her apartment felt like a crypt, the air silent and stale and thick from the day's lingering heat. She ached from the weight of the silence. The loneliness. The emptiness of her life. And always, the guilt.

Her mother's letter would not carry good news, but it must be read. Camille went to the lamp, her hand hovering over the switch. Now that the Germans had taken the city, was a blackout still necessary? She doubted there would be bombings tonight. Unless… Was France now an enemy to her previous allies? Was a bomb deposited by a friend any different than one dropped by the enemy?

Best to keep the apartment dark.

She sat on the window ledge. The moon had yet to rise. She would not be able to read the letter yet. Compromising, she lit a candle.

Hand shaking, she retrieved the letter and quickly discarded the envelope. Through the page's single fold, her eyes hooked on her sister's name. Another sigh slipped past her lips.

Jacqueline, the source of so much love and guilt. But also, shame. The thought of harm coming to her sister while Camille was here in Paris stole her breath, the pain much like a punch to the gut. Lips pressed into a flat line, she shimmied her finger beneath the fold and flipped open the paper. Her mother didn't open with a greeting or empty salutation.

Camille,
I have done what you asked. I have been patient with your sister.

Your sister. Not "my daughter," not "my beloved child," but *your sister.* Sighing, she looked up at the ceiling. A sort of blank, terrifying anger filled her, but she didn't know who it was directed at—her mother, or herself? She continued reading…

There was an incident at the school, and she cannot return. Nor can she go unsupervised. As you well know, I cannot spare your other sisters from the bakery. I have found a local woman to help out during the day. And thus, I come to the reason for this letter. The matter of the caretaker's wages is not yet settled. I turn to you for resolution and expectantly await your response.

Camille shut her eyes. Although her mother had been careful with her words, she knew what Solange Lacroix wanted. But how? How was she to find the money to pay for Jacqueline's caretaker? She already worked extra shifts and earned substantial tips when she styled the American widow's hair. There had to be a way to make more, and Camille would find it. It was her duty. Her sister's declining mental state was, after all, her fault.

Your fault.

She opened her eyes and reread the letter, seeing only Jacqueline's tortured face when Camille had found her in the basement, leaning over their father, begging him to wake up. Camille tried to quash the memories. They came anyway, an unwelcome tether that bound her to the mistake she could never undo and a terrible choice she could never remedy.

She'd left her sister alone with their father, knowing the risk. All because of a boy. Camille didn't even remember his name. Oh, but how she'd wanted to be with him, so very badly, and had agreed to meet him at the river's edge. She'd been selfish, single-minded. She'd known her father suffered bouts of depression and battled waking nightmares, and still, she'd left her seven-year-old sister in his care.

Claude Lacroix had chosen that afternoon to take his own life, a gunshot to the head. Had Camille been home, maybe she could have prevented the senseless tragedy. Or at least, she could have kept Jacqueline from being in the basement when he pulled the trigger. Five years later, her sister suffered her own bouts of depression and waking nightmares.

Your fault.

It was up to Camille to provide for Jacqueline's care. So far, the family had been able to keep the girl's condition secret from their neighbors. It would be harder now that she'd been expelled. Matters could not be more dire. Hitler's desire for a perfect race was well-documented. Camille knew what the Nazis did to mental patients. She'd found proof in the many German newspapers and journals she'd read at the Paris Public Library. Ever grateful her mother had insisted she learn the language of her father's family, she'd read how German doctors openly conducted experiments on mental patients and often euthanized them as a final solution when no cure was readily found. If they brought those policies to France…

Your fault.

Camille pressed a hand to her mouth. She'd forgotten to breathe. She needed to breathe. She took a pull of air. Pushed it out. Calmer, she read the letter again, her eyes latching on to two words, *local woman*. No name, no identity. She could be anyone. Her sister was about to be put in the care of a stranger. Camille needed to go home and meet this woman.

It would require missing a day of work, and spending money on a train ticket. It had to be done. She couldn't hide out in Paris any longer, rationalizing her absence. Jacqueline was her sister. It was Camille's duty to protect her. Her stomach growled, reminding her she hadn't eaten since this morning, a piece of stale bread and a slice of hard cheese.

Her roommate showed himself, his pointy little rodent claws scraping across the scarred wood floor mere feet away from her perch on the windowsill. Fitting, Camille thought, living among rats, inside her apartment, and out.

The latter was far scarier than this little guy. They carried guns.

The bold creature scurried closer, close enough for her to see his pink nose twitching. Mildly annoyed, but only just, Camille gave in to the silent plea and went into her tiny kitchen to find a morsel or two for them both.

The Occupation

Chapter Six

Vivian

23 June 1940.
Paris, France.

Almost two weeks after Paris fell, at precisely six o'clock in the morning, Vivian pressed her ear to the polished door of her suite and listened, heard nothing. Time to go. Dressed in an elegant black suit, matching black pumps, and a turban-style hat with a polka-dot ribbon and jaunty bow, she was proving to herself—*to them*—that she was unafraid of their presence in the hotel.

But of course she was afraid. She harbored illegal papers in her room, some void of photos and official stamps, others ready to hand over to their new owners. American passports for some, French identification cards for others, all skillfully rendered by an expert. The same expert she was scheduled to meet this morning. That made twice this week. There would be more rendezvous in the coming days. Friends, and friends of friends, required her help. So many of them in desperate need to leave the city or, barring that, to hide in plain sight.

She made her move. Slipping into the hallway, she shut the

door carefully behind her, quietly, without a single snick of noise.

So far, so good.

At the top of the grand stairway, carpeted in the Ritz's signature blue, Vivian took in the ornate gathering area one floor below. Not a lobby, per se, but there was a reception area that met the needs of guests and visitors alike. Despite the occupiers making themselves at home, the gorgeous tapestries still hung on the walls. The crystal chandelier sparkled as always. And, as Mimi had promised, the Hôtel Ritz continued operating at the highest level of service. The depleted staff still fetched and polished. They straightened and dusted, and, when a guest approached, slipped smoothly into one of the nooks or cupboards, out of sight. Out of mind.

Vivian adjusted her tote bag, took hold of the banister, and made her descent.

A sentry in the ugly gray-green uniform of the German *Wehrmacht* met her at the foot of the stairs, hand outstretched. She knew what he wanted. Her identity papers, her *Ausweis*. Like so many of his kind, this soldier could not be more than twenty years old. He had the requisite stiff neck, the rosy complexion of youth, and the golden hair venerated by the Nazi regime.

He also knew her, this arrogant boy.

They'd been through this process multiple times. Still, he kept his hand outstretched, palm up, German belligerence radiating off him. Sighing, she dug out her American passport. Smelling of sweat, and emboldened with German pride, the soldier took his time inspecting her credentials, as if trying to prove his superiority. Vivian nearly sneered. The pistol resting in the holster at his belt was all the authority he needed.

Another few seconds passed and, at last, she was back in possession of her passport and free to go. Frustration propelled her out into the stale morning air that still held the stench of petrol, German haughtiness, and French despair. Tote slung over her shoulder, Vivian put the Ritz behind her and set out toward her destination. The sun had yet to rise, and the streets took on a sinister aura. Paris was a different city at this hour, without light, without activity and sound, everything it had once been erased.

How had the French people—the politicians—the world—let this happen?

They'd underestimated the enemy, clinging to their policy of Appeasement. They'd refused, almost willfully, to acknowledge the true nature of Nazi aggression and the depths of Hitler's savage ambition. When they'd been proven wrong, they'd crumbled like a cheap suit, signing a treaty that cut France into two zones, one free, the other handed over to the enemy. The government officials hadn't remained to face the consequences of their actions. They'd fled to the south, to the resort town of Vichy, in the Free Zone, and had left everyone in the Occupied Zone to fend for themselves. Cowards, all of them.

Vivian's country was no better. The land of the free and home of the brave had looked the other way, still looked away. Vivian would do her part to help as many people as she could.

Mind firm, purpose set, she continued her gradual drift north. The stagnant scent of the Seine was faint on the air, covered by the fainter smell of blooming flowers from gardens still damp from last night's rainstorm. The sun began its approach, spilling pink fire on the stagnant pools of water at her feet. This was usually Vivian's favorite hour of the day, when she most loved to stroll through Paris, when the city was at its most beautiful.

Not this morning. This morning, Paris was sullen and ghostlike. Telephone and postal service had been restored, but not much else. Vivian hurried, her destination a nook hidden in an alleyway near the famous French opera house, the Palais Garnier. When she arrived at the majestic building ten minutes ahead of schedule, she let her gaze skim the columns and brush over the bronze busts of Mozart and Beethoven and on to her favorite sculptural group at the apex of the south gable. *Apollo, Poetry, and Music* never failed to take her breath away.

The air changed, suddenly, charged with some new, looming threat. She heard it, the sound of roaring engines approaching from the distance. Seconds later, she saw it. A convoy of armored tanks, automobiles, and motorcycles roaring through the mist. At the center of the eerie vision was a convertible Mercedes-Benz. A man dressed in full military gear stood, very straight, very proud, one hand holding on to the rib of the windshield. The little black mustache beneath the bill of his cap gave away his identity.

Vivian's mouth opened and closed, and she felt her eyes widen like a gaping fish.

Hitler had come to tour the conquered city.

She slipped behind a column just as the vehicles zigzagged around concrete barriers at an impossible rate of speed. Only once the last motorcycle roared around the corner did Vivian step into the light. Heart pounding, mind reeling, she attempted to continue, but her legs were shaking too hard. It was one thing to see German soldiers milling about the Ritz, quite another to witness the *Führer* himself on the streets of Paris. All the more reason to meet her forger and offer a future to three desperate souls.

She set out, moving quickly. Hitler's arrival had put her behind schedule. Here, too, Paris was an abandoned city. No people, no activity, hardly any sound. Quite eerie, really. Made even more sinister by the darkened windows looking out over the streets like empty, hollow eyes.

Shivering, she entered the alley and slid into the alcove, her back against the building.

A few seconds later, a shadow shifted, and she was staring at the best forger in France. He was a small man, slight of build, and near to her in age, somewhere in his forties. He was not a handsome man. But his skills were unsurpassed and, as Vivian had discovered the first time she'd engaged his services, expensive. Luckily she had the money and was willing to pay his outrageous asking price.

The man moved into the alcove, standing too close, and completely by design. Should someone stumble upon them, they would see two lovers. Vivian suddenly wanted to hurry along this meeting. There was a sense of danger in the air, made more immediate because Hitler was touring the city.

Thankfully, the forger got straight to the point. "You have the money, madame?"

"I do, monsieur." They never used names. Safer that way. "You have the package?"

He hesitated only a second, then pulled out a small canvas bag from his jacket.

Vivian took the package, spread the drawstring opening, and counted three *Carte d'Identités de Francais* inside. She quickly reviewed each one, checking for the bearer's photograph—provided by her—nationality, profession. The date and place of birth, current and previous addresses, and, last, physical characteristics such as hair and eye color.

Satisfied, Vivian returned the cards to the canvas bag, then dug deeper, all the way to the bottom. From beneath the first layer of lining, she retrieved the agreed upon fee, five hundred American dollars. Using a quick sleight of hand that would put any three-card monte con artist to shame, he pocketed the money.

With movements just as quick, just as skilled, Vivian tucked the identity cards beneath the false bottom of her tote. The entire transaction took less than three minutes.

They spent the next five discussing Vivian's upcoming needs— American passports for a desperate couple newly arrived from Poland. The cost for acquiring these documents was steep, but acceptable. They settled on the day and time they would meet again, and their business was done. They separated without speaking, heading in opposite directions. No backward glances.

Vivian returned via a different route. When she arrived back at the hotel, she heard the church bells calling the faithful to mass. Ah, but the streets remained bare. Too much fear even to attend service. Conversely, she was met with a buzz of activity that communicated the arrival of more dignitaries. Had Hitler's motorcade stopped at the Hôtel Ritz? Was the *Führer* himself to take a room? She didn't think so. There were none of the vehicles she'd seen earlier idling at the curb. Still, German uniforms swarmed the grand hall. Vivian strained to catch sight of a familiar face. She didn't have long to wait. Hans Elminger appeared and took her elbow, propelling her to the reception area.

"What's happened?" she asked. "Why the commotion?" And on a Sunday. Apparently, the Nazis didn't honor the Sabbath any more than the French.

Neither did the Hôtel Ritz. One more casualty of Occupation. "The *Luftwaffe* has requisitioned the hotel for its headquarters. *Reichsmarschall* Göring has reserved the Imperial Suite and will take possession once we refurbish the room to meet his specifications."

Vivian felt the shock move through her limbs. This was it, then. The Hôtel Ritz confiscated, the best suite in the house seized by Hitler's second-in-command. Vivian's would surely be next.

She opened her mouth to ask which of Hitler's favorites had taken her room, and how long would it be before he took possession, but Elminger anticipated her. "You need not worry about your lodgings, Madame Miller. You are welcome to remain at the Hôtel Ritz."

Something like relief shot through her. "I am not to be kicked out of my suite, then?"

Elminger grimaced, apology written on his face. "I didn't say that."

Impatient now, Vivian gave him a haughty look. "What are you saying, Hans?"

"You are, as I said, welcome to stay in the hotel. However,

orders from Berlin assert that the suites on the Place Vendôme will accommodate German officers only. For these rooms—" he leaned in close "—they have taken a ninety percent discount."

Appalled, Vivian did the math in her head. Ninety percent. The Nazis would be paying a mere twenty-five francs a day for the most luxurious lodgings in Paris. It was shameful, criminal. "If I choose to move to another room—"

"—on the Rue Cambon side."

"If I choose to take a room on the Rue Cambon side..." she repeated, thinking how ironic that the Hôtel Ritz was to be divided into two zones, much like France herself. "Will I receive the same discount as the Germans?"

"I am sorry, madame, but no. You will be required to pay the same as before, plus an additional twenty percent."

"Orders from Berlin?" She glared, not caring that she sounded waspish.

"That is correct."

The hot burn of outrage heated her cheeks. She didn't care about that, either. "Should I agree to these terms, how long do I have to move my personal belongings?"

Eyes not quite meeting hers, Elminger consulted a spot over Vivian's right shoulder. "You have until tomorrow afternoon."

"One day? That's all?"

"I'm afraid your suite has been reserved for one of the officers still en route to Paris."

"His name?"

"I am not at liberty to say."

Of course not. Elminger was nothing if not professional. And now Vivian faced another difficult choice. She could find a different hotel or leave Paris. Neither option fit her needs. Nearly half a dozen Jews awaited new passports, and nearly twice that required travel visas. Perhaps, in time, there would be another solution. For now, the Hôtel Ritz would have to do. "I'll take the other room."

"As you wish." He handed her a room key.

Vivian didn't bother looking at the room number. What did it matter if she was on the second, third, or even fourth floor? She was being kicked out of her home. She turned to go, then immediately pivoted. "I will need assistance packing. Please send the chambermaid who does my hair on occasion up to my room in exactly one hour, not a moment sooner. Her name is Camille."

"Very good. I will see to this myself."

"Thank you." Before returning to her suite, Vivian made a brief detour to the other side of the hotel. She wanted to see her new accommodations for herself and make an assessment as to what furniture could move with her and what would have to be stored. She bypassed the sentries at the foot of the grand stairwell, avoided eye contact with the German soldiers milling about, and absolutely—positively—without question ignored the Nazi flags on display in urns that once held potted plants.

Once inside her new room, on the third floor, as it turned out, she felt the beginnings of genuine despair. Elminger had given her one of the smallest rooms in the hotel. Her furnishings would never fit inside these walls, much less her substantial wardrobe and jewelry. At least there was a tiled bathroom en suite, and a working telephone—she checked—a vanity, writing desk, dresser, and one armoire. The room would suffice. Vivian would make it so.

Mind working, she went to the cupboard Mimi built into every room and glanced inside. She then moved to stand before the dresser, the armoire, calculating sizes, weights, and finally formulating a plan to keep her valuables out of Nazi hands. Satisfied her scheme would work with a little help, she returned to the other side of the hotel, up to the second floor this time, and breathed a sigh of relief. Nothing had been moved, nothing touched. Her furs still hung in the built-in closet. Her jewelry rested safely in drawers and velvet cases. Most important of all, the illegal papers were in their hidden compartment, tucked under layers of folded lingerie.

Vivian gave a short nod, then just as quickly frowned as she realized how much needed to be done in twenty-four hours, with the help of a single chambermaid. By her own design, but still. The sheer magnitude made her want to weep. Ernest Hemingway, while on one of his notorious benders, once told her nothing bad happened to guests in the Hôtel Ritz. Vivian hadn't believed him then. She certainly didn't believe him now.

That didn't mean she would go down without a fight. She was Vivian Miller, a survivor, Rupert Miller's widow, and one of the wealthiest women in the world. She moved in all the right circles, and a few of the wrong ones, which added up to a strong network already in place to do good work, righteous work. What could possibly go wrong?

Everything, a voice in her head whispered, as she began emptying drawers and tossing their contents on any available space. A knock heralded the arrival of the chambermaid. Time to put her plan in motion. She straightened, threw back her shoulders, and went to greet her newest recruit in her network of trusted partners. Though the girl didn't know it yet.

"Hello, Camille." She greeted the girl with one of her winningest smiles. "Do come in. Hurry now. We have a lot of work ahead of us if we are to finish before the end of the day."

Chapter Seven

Camille

23 June 1940.
Paris, France.

Camille blinked in surprise. She couldn't decide what was more alarming—Madame Miller's disheveled state or the excessively warm welcome. They weren't close. They certainly weren't friends. This woman was her superior in every way. And while the wealthy American was always kind, and tipped well, she was never this enthusiastic with her greetings. Nor was she ever in possession of such a bright, happy smile. Camille didn't trust that smile.

The woman wanted something from her, and it wasn't a new hairstyle copied out of the latest fashion magazine. She suddenly wanted to flee from whatever scheme the American had in mind. There were some things she would not do. Illegal things, unethical or immoral things. But then, she thought about the letter she'd sent home a week ago, asking for more information about her sister's new caretaker, and her mother's lack of a response.

Camille needed to go home, which meant missing an entire

day of work and the purchase of an overpriced train ticket. A generous tip would solve both problems.

There was also the reality of her position. It was her job to cater to a guest's whims.

Returning the American's smile, Camille stepped into the suite and found herself battling to hide her shock once again. For a moment, she thought she'd entered the wrong room. The entire suite was in disarray, as though the widow's closet had exploded, sending her clothes atop every available piece of furniture. She couldn't find the words to speak. Vivian Miller was usually so careful with her things. She didn't fling her blouses on chairs or toss her shoes on top of tables or drop pieces of jewelry onto the floor.

"Madame, have you been robbed?"

Distracted, she responded in a thicker American accent than usual. "In a manner of speaking."

"Have you alerted the authorities?"

"They are the ones who rob me."

Seemingly unaware of Camille's shock, the widow moved to the opposite side of the suite and frowned at the disarray. Alarming, to be sure. But what really surprised Camille was that the woman looked little better than her room. She'd discarded her suit jacket, revealing a large coffee stain on her untucked blouse. Her long red hair had come undone from its usual chignon and now fell well past her shoulders in chunky tangles. Even her eyes looked different. No longer full of fierce resolve, but a sort of uncertainty.

Rolling her shoulders as if shrugging off something uncomfortable, she eyed Camille. "I know what you're thinking. You are thinking I have lost my mind." She laughed, a short, gruff sound that held no humor. "And maybe I have."

A dozen thoughts fluttered at the speed of hummingbird wings. Camille could only look and stare. Sometime before she'd arrived, the widow had thrown open the doors, and now a stiff breeze blew in, tousling her hair, making her seem, as she herself had said, as if she'd lost her mind.

But she hadn't. Camille had seen the real thing in her father, her sister. Suddenly, she knew exactly what to say. "You've had troubling news."

"And then some." She reached for one the fur coats she'd draped over the edge of a chair and ran her fingertip along the silky collar. "I've been informed I must vacate my suite immediately."

Camille gasped. "Can they do that?"

The widow closed her eyes and gave a slight shuddering sigh. "Apparently, they can do many unjust things."

She meant the German invaders, but also the hotel's leadership who abided by their captors' rules. The chaos in the sitting room made sense now, as did the woman's untidy state. "What are you going to do?"

"What I must."

It was a bold statement. In the abstract, it was the equivalent of a warrior's cry. Reality was another thing altogether. German soldiers were everywhere in the hotel. They made themselves at home in the restaurants, the bars, and now, apparently, Vivian Miller's personal suite. "Will you be leaving the hotel?"

"They can't run me off that easily. No, no." The widow dusted off her hands and set them on her hips. "I have been given twenty-four hours to relocate to another, smaller room on the Rue Cambon side."

Camille could feel an undertow of swirling emotions rolling off the other woman.

"I need to move all of this, or as much as I can, but I can't do it alone." She put a hand to her forehead, shoved at her hair, shifted. "Will you help me, Camille?"

Across the expanse of clothing and furniture and differing social standings, time seemed to shift and bend, and Camille sensed—somehow, knew—that this woman, this American, was asking for more than her help moving to another suite.

Camille nearly said no. She could not put her job in jeopardy, not even for a guest who tipped generously. *No.* The word was there in her mind, finding purchase in her throat. *Just say it, Camille.* Why couldn't she say the word? Because the American had never required anything untoward from her before, and so, she nodded. "Of course I'll assist you."

"I knew I could count on you." Triumph threaded through the words. "Let us get to work, shall we?"

And work they did, quickly, efficiently. The stakes were high. The time short.

The widow gave Camille orders in her soft, easy voice. Her French was not perfect, but it was very good. She pointed Camille to the bedroom. "Gather up my furs and bring them to me."

The task proved daunting. There were at least fifteen, most of them full-length coats, a few stoles, each one worth more than Camille made in a year. The widow took charge of her jewelry herself, shutting up the finer pieces in locked cases.

They were barely an hour into the project when the door banged open, and they both startled. A German soldier appeared in the doorway. Vivian made a gasping noise, a cross between, "Oh!" and a sharp intake of air. Then came the outrage, every bit of her anger spilling into her voice. "What is the meaning of this?" she demanded, approaching the soldier with eyes as hard as his.

He hadn't bothered to announce himself, and didn't even bother to meet her eyes. "I have come to inform you that your furniture stays."

"But that's impossible." Her hands fluttered, then gripped together at her waist. "I assumed all of my possessions would come with me."

"You may move whatever you can fit onto two hotel carts, nothing else."

"Nothing else? But…" She spun in a circle, her gaze landing on the antiques, the tapestries. "This, all of it, belongs to me."

The soldier said nothing, and his gaze remained hooked on the wall directly behind her left shoulder. It was the ultimate in rudeness, and it was Camille's turn to make a gasping noise between "Oh!" and a sharp intake of air.

Vivian was not so reactionary. She was, however, clearly taken aback. "You are telling me that I am to surrender what is mine to whatever German has reserved this suite?"

Once again, she was given no response. The soldier simply spun on his heel and left the room, his boots hitting the marble in the entryway, then going silent as they struck carpet in the hallway. He did not close the door. Vivian did that herself, with a loud, rattling bang.

Flinching, Camille set the fur coat she'd been carrying onto the chaise longue. The scent of Vivian's perfume clung to the garment, her signature blend of roses, jasmine, and vanilla at odds with the tension in the room. "This is the last one."

Eyes glassy, the widow came to stand beside Camille. She ran her hand over the coat, her fingertips barely connecting. She looked stricken. It was strange seeing Vivian Miller without her usual air of confidence. The woman was always so cool, so in control. Not now.

"Okay, then. They want to play dirty, then so will I." She began filling suitcases with fast, furious flicks, one right after another. She tossed in dresses at random. Shoes, hats, but oddly none of her furs found their way into any of the luggage.

She snapped a lid shut, then another, and another, until only one was left. Instead of reaching for a fur coat, the widow straightened. Her eyes landed on Camille. She had to lock her knees in order to maintain her composure under the woman's thorough inspection.

After an endless moment, she lost her nerve and shifted slightly, swallowed heavily. And still, Vivian Miller stared at her. "I wonder," she mused. "How far can I trust you, Camille?"

She thought of her sister's condition, the circumstances that led to it, and answered truthfully. "I know how to keep a secret."

"Your own, perhaps. But can you keep someone else's secrets?"

The question hung in the air, ominous. Important. Camille wasn't made from goodness and light, far from it. She had never felt in control, even before the day her father had taken his life, before she'd abandoned her youngest sister to witness the horror alone. How scared she'd been when she'd come home and found her father, her sister. How scared they'd both been. Something sad and hollow opened inside her. The sensation bloomed large, making her crave to be more than she'd ever been before. A woman of honor. "I don't gossip."

"No, you don't." She glanced toward the door. Camille followed the direction of her gaze. The two of them were alone.

"It's no secret the invaders have no conscience," the widow began, the words revealing her fury, but something more. "They take their plunder without remorse, without conscience. They're crooks, every one of them."

Camille couldn't disagree. She'd just witnessed their thievery firsthand.

"They take my furniture, my art, but they will not get all my possessions." She stroked the fur again, gave a sad ironic smile. "However, if I am to succeed, I will need your loyalty. And because I ask this of you, I want to say that I have already given you mine."

"I... That is, Madame Miller—"

"Call me Vivian."

She shook her head, appalled. "I couldn't. I can't. It's against the rules."

The widow waved away the argument. "You can, Camille, and you will. Because I am a valued guest. But also, what I need you to do will require complete and total trust on both our parts. The kind of trust that transcends social status."

Camille felt a surge of unease, and the skin on the back of her neck prickled. "What is it you want me to do, madame?" She paused. "I mean, Vivian?"

"I need you to help me hide my most treasured possessions."
Camille looked to the furs.

"Yes," Vivian confirmed. "Those, but other items, too."

It was a huge thing to ask of her, what amounted to treason against the Third Reich. She wanted to run out of the room. But she didn't. Partly due to her shock, but also because Vivian had already involved Camille. She wanted to be angry, and maybe she was, but she was also flattered that this woman trusted her. Something no one had done in a very long time. Not since her father's suicide.

"I will pay you for your silence. No, don't shake your head at me. To deny me this gesture would be to insult me."

Camille felt a moment of shame, and also a need to prove herself worthy of this woman's trust. The money didn't matter. But of course, it did. "I would not wish to insult you."

"Good. Very good." Vivian pressed money into her hand.

Without looking at the quantity, Camille stuffed the bills into the pocket of her dress. "Tell me what you need from me."

Vivian directed her to the cupboard cut into the wall, now empty of the woman's clothes and other personal items. Camille knew what to do. She reached for the first fur and, folding it gently, found a place on the top shelf. Vivian followed with the next one. They worked in silence, moving from the furs to cases of jewelry. Small pieces of crystal went in as well.

The antique tapestries were the final occupants of the space, which Vivian rolled herself. She shut the cupboard door, and Camille immediately spoke what was on her mind. "I would think the German taking over this suite will look in there."

"Ah, but you assume he will know the cupboard exists." She moved to the armoire positioned farther down the wall and put her hand on the smooth wood.

Understanding, Camille took her place on the opposite side. They pushed and shoved, then shoved and pushed, until the wardrobe sat directly in front of the cupboard. Stepping back, Camille studied the placement. "It looks like it belongs there."

Vivian joined her, linking their arms in the way of old friends. "It really does."

There was still work left to do.

While Camille continued gathering the rest of the widow's clothing, Vivian sat at her antique writing desk. She touched the smooth wood with her fingertips, her gaze distant and sad. Camille sensed she was lost in memories from another time, another life. The expression deepened as the widow began opening drawers and pulling out photographs, postcards, a stack of papers yellowed with age.

"Don't just stand there, Camille. Come here. I'll want all these to come with me."

"As you wish." She put the first stack in a box, added the next, and the next, but when she reached for what looked like a leather portfolio, Vivian placed her hand on top of the case.

"This one, I carry myself."

The move took hours and required a lot of heavy lifting. So much so, that when Camille's shift came to an end and she was back in the locker room, she could hardly move her arms above her head. Wincing, she closed her locker and waited for Rachel to do the same. "Ready to head home?"

"More than." The girl blew out a sigh of exhaustion.

Camille's sentiments exactly.

Outside, she pulled in a tight breath at the sight of the swastika banners, more today than yesterday. Hanging from rooftops, on buildings, and in some places, it seemed as if they grew right out of the stone. It had been a long day, full of subterfuge and secrets and what amounted to treason in the eyes of the occupiers. Vivian had promised Camille her loyalty. She had to believe the woman was sincere.

Out of the corner of her eye, she noticed she wasn't the only one who'd had a long day. Rachel's steps were sluggish. They took the usual route home. It would have been faster to take the Métro, now that it was reopened, but the money. It was always about the money. Camille remembered the cash Vivian had given her. She would be able to travel home on Friday, which she'd negotiated with a promise to work two extra shifts a day on both Saturday and Sunday.

The sound of heavy footsteps cut off the rest of her thoughts. Camille reacted instinctively, her hand shooting out, reaching for Rachel's arm. She tugged the girl close. A single look shared and they were increasing their pace together.

A high-pitched scream filled the night air, followed by shouts in guttural German mixed with angry French. Then came the sound of glass shattering on the concrete. Rachel's feet ground to a halt. Camille stopped, too, frozen in the wake of that terrible noise. She gaped, unable to react, too stunned, too terrified to comprehend fully what she saw, the truth of what Occupation meant for Paris. What German brutality looked like. And the ugliness contained in the hearts of weak men.

Camille blinked into the madness. A mob had gathered, fueled by emotion, and growing larger by the minute. They held bricks and rocks in their hands, spewed foul words from their mouths.

Suddenly, a child stumbled out of a building. The sight of her hysteria was more terrifying than the breaking glass. The girl appeared uninjured and was so small the congregation of angry men didn't seem to notice her. She ran hard, and when she saw Camille and Rachel, she ran harder still. Whatever she'd endured inside that building had left her with wild, tangled hair, panicked eyes, and an inability to speak. Her mouth worked, but the most she could manage was wordless, primitive sounds. Her breathing was fast, too fast, and there was something animalistic in that, too.

Reminded of her own little sister caught in one of her fits, Camille swallowed against the pain in her throat, the pain that was always there. The sensation paralyzed her, freezing her into immobility. Rachel didn't have the same problem. She took off in the child's direction, scooped her up in her arms, and ran away from the mob, across the street and down to the other end of the block.

By the time Camille caught up with them, Rachel had set the little girl on the ground and was crouching down in front of her. They seemed lost in their tiny world of two, one Camille could never inhabit or fully understand. Because no matter how hard her life was under German occupation, it was much, much worse for Jews.

Chapter Eight

Rachel

23 June 1940.
The Berman Apartment. Paris, France.

Rachel's fear had a taste, a thickness in the back of the throat, and a feeling, too, formed as a knot of sickening dread tight in her stomach. The urge to grab the child and run was strong. The need to understand what was happening, *why* it was happening, was stronger.

She locked eyes with the little girl and felt a twist of grief. Whatever she'd witnessed had changed her forever. Rachel opened her mouth to say something. The words stuck in her throat, and something cold moved up her spine. Defeat, the sense of powerlessness. The world, *her* world, which she'd thought was so solid and safe, was made of straw.

The absence of calm created a sinister milieu that was nearly tangible. And the heat. So hot. The scents. The tinny smell of blood. The sounds. The shrieks. There were two of them. One, a collection of racial slurs tangling together. The other climbing up Rachel's throat.

And then, there was this tiny, small, terrified little girl. Rachel knew her. Naomi Wozniak. A sweet child of seven. She lived with her parents above their bakery. The one being targeted by the mob a half block away. More foul words. More bricks and rocks hurled into the air. More shattering glass. The destruction of a single business seemed to be the goal. The life's work of an honorable family destroyed out of hate.

Rachel knew why.

The Wozniaks were fellow Jewish immigrants who'd lifted themselves up to this bourgeois neighborhood. Unlike her family, they were religious. They owned a kosher bakery, the only one for three blocks in any direction. The one that was now being vandalized by German thugs. She glanced toward the madness and noted a familiar face among the looters. A French boy from the neighborhood and beside him, two more. That they were a part of this made the situation even more insane.

Rachel leaned in toward the child, careful to keep her voice soft, her touch light. "Where are your parents, Naomi?"

The girl shook her head, seemingly unable to respond. It didn't matter. The truth rode on the feral wind. It sounded in the angry shouts, the shattering of glass, the throwing of bricks and rocks. Rachel shuddered. There was something animalistic in the mob's behavior. "They are in the bakery?"

"Yes." The word was hardly audible.

"Rachel." She glanced up and straight into Camille's face. She'd forgotten about her friend. "The child shouldn't be on the streets. We need to get her away from here, before—"

"—curfew. I know." Rachel refocused on Naomi. She recognized something in the depth of that gaze, something from her own inner thoughts. The vast, horrible knowledge that the world was a hard, mean place for them. That their neighbors, people they'd once trusted, wanted to do them harm.

"Naomi, are your parents...are they...injured?" Rachel asked the question carefully, not knowing how to put her greatest fear into words.

"They...they're...in...the shop," she said, shaking her head.

"I ran. I wasn't supposed to leave our hiding place. I was supposed to stay. But I ran. They shouted at me to come back. I ran anyway." She dipped her head, her voice barely above a whisper. She was shaking with fear and shame, but Rachel could feel only relief. Naomi's parents were still alive.

"I would have run, too." Aware of a bubbling anger stoking her courage, she stood and took the child's hand. Camille moved in beside her, clearly prepared to enter the fray with them.

"You don't have to do this," Rachel told her. "This isn't your fight."

"It isn't yours, either."

There she was wrong. This *was* Rachel's fight. An injustice against one Jew was an injustice against all of them. Or perhaps, Rachel thought, Camille did understand. She was standing firm with Rachel. The very embodiment of her father's words. *Our neighbors…they will protect us from the Nazis.* Rachel's mind went quiet, her thoughts no longer scattered. They needed to get the child off the streets. She and Camille, together.

She looked to her friend, and there in her eyes was a loyalty Rachel knew was real. Words weren't necessary. A nod, that was all it took for them to become a single unit.

"We'll take her to my parents' apartment," Rachel said.

Camille spoke to the child in a low, calming tone. "It's going to be all right, Naomi."

There was something safe and decent about Camille Lacroix, in the way she leaned toward the little girl, her gaze soft but steady. They managed to propel the child forward, but her fear worked against them, and their progress was slow. She stumbled, nearly taking Rachel and Camille down with her.

Camille recovered first, dragging Naomi to her feet with a gentleness that was at odds with the violence surrounding them. They crossed the street, quickly, silently, and entered the apartment building with Rachel leading the way. Camille shut the door behind them, and all sound suddenly stopped, the silence as jarring as the shouting had been.

"Which way?" Camille asked.

"Up." When Naomi blanched, Rachel stooped down. "It's all right. I'll carry you." She picked up the child and led the way to the third floor, climbing the stairs as quickly as possible with Naomi's additional weight in her arms.

At the landing, Rachel set the girl back on her feet. At the same moment, the door to her parents' apartment swung open and out rushed her mother, clearly anticipating their arrival. Still, Rachel lifted her eyebrows. "How did you know we were coming?"

"We saw you cross the street." Before Rachel could respond, Ilka Berman dropped to her knees. "Oh, my dear sweet child. You must be so frightened. Come to me." She opened her arms in invitation.

The little girl accepted with no hesitation. Once in the shelter of the motherly embrace, the child broke into loud, agonizing sobs. Helpless in the face of all that sorrow, Rachel found herself frozen in indecision.

Not so her mother.

"That's it," she soothed in Yiddish. "There, now. Let it out, *bubelah*. That's right. Let it all out."

Rachel watched, feeling disconnected, distant, as if she was looking through a wall of frozen water. Her mother, like Camille, seemed to know what she was doing. Her words and kindness made it easier for the traumatized child to give into her fear and grief.

With Naomi's sobs slowing, her mother looked up and smiled at Camille. "You must be Rachel's friend."

Rachel made the introductions, but it was her mother who invited Camille into their home in her accented, broken French.

"I can't. Curfew approaches." She didn't need to say more. The consequences for being on the streets after 8:00 p.m. were steep—arrest and possibly worse. "I'll come back another time."

"Are you certain you don't want to wait a few more minutes?"

"Very." Her eyes swept to Rachel then, held steady, a host of meaning in her gaze. "We should walk to work together in the morning."

"I'll be fine." Was that true? Was tonight an isolated event, or was this frenzied vandalism only the beginning of what Jews living in Paris could expect?

"Rachel." Camille's voice flowed over her like a soft breeze. "It's not safe to be out on the streets alone."

Something in the way she said the words, or rather the ones she didn't say, had Rachel speaking harsher than she'd meant. "And yet you are about to head out into the fray right now."

"Yes, well, I'm not a...a..."

"A Jew."

Camille winced. "Please, Rachel. I'm not trying to insult you. It's just..." She reached out, briefly touched her sleeve, let her hand drop. "There is solidarity in numbers."

She was right. "Yes, we will walk to work together." Then, as Camille made to go, she added, "Be careful getting home."

"Always." They didn't hug. They weren't that kind of friends, but Rachel watched until Camille was gone before following her mother and Naomi into the apartment.

The rest of her family stood at the row of windows overlooking Rue Rochechouart, their necks craned identically to the left, presumably to watch the activity down the block.

Rachel took up position next to Basia. From this vantage point, she could see only silhouettes. There was Camille's, melding into the shadows, unnoticed by the mob. Rachel could feel their frenzy, their hate. Eventually, blessedly, the crowd seemed to lose interest in their evil, twisted game. The shouts became murmurs. Stones were set down. And people began slithering away like snakes into their holes.

The vandalism was over. The horror, Rachel sensed, was only just beginning. Was this to be their fate as Jews in German-occupied Paris? The police had never shown up. Their neighbors had stayed inside their homes. Where were the good people of France? And where were Naomi's parents?

As if hearing her question, the couple emerged from the bakery. They ignored the destruction in favor of twisting to the left, the right, frantically searching. It dawned on her why. They were looking for Naomi. Her hand flew to her mouth. "We need to let them know we have her. They will want to know she's safe."

She moved to the door. Her father stopped her with a hand to her arm. "No, *hertzeleh*. I'll go."

Rachel saw the emotion in him. Tears were in his eyes. Unshed, but there. Rachel had never seen her father cry. He wasn't crying now, but she could tell it cost him to maintain his composure. In the next minute, he was gone, reappearing outside the building, arms flailing as he tried to gain the Wozniaks' attention. Rachel saw the exact moment when the couple understood their daughter was safe. Relief slumped their shoulders. And then, her mother was outside on the sidewalk, too, Naomi's hand in hers. The child's parents saw her at the same moment, their heads lifting in tandem.

Their smiles widened.

Again, Naomi was running. This time, toward her parents.

Even as she watched the happy reunion, Rachel couldn't prevent images from earlier in the night. They flashed in her mind. So much violence. The hatred in the men's eyes had been on a new level, one she would have not thought possible before this evening. If any of them had looked in her direction, and seen her and Camille with the child, would they have directed their anger toward them? Would bricks have been thrown at their heads?

Bile suddenly rose in her throat, tasting like acid on her tongue. She tried to swallow it down, tried to remind herself that they hadn't seen her and Camille. Her stomach rebelled anyway. Hand over her mouth, she ran to the bathroom, slammed the door behind her, and sank to her knees. Alone, she let the sickness come, let it empty the meager contents of her stomach.

When she was done, she noticed that her cheeks were wet. What was that sound? Sobbing. Her own. She tried to stand, couldn't, so she just sat, right there on the tile floor. Hands shaking, she squeezed her eyes shut and willed her breath to slow. She still felt sick. Tears slipped down her cheeks. She wiped at them, over and over.

"Rachel," her mother called through the door. "Are you all right, *ketsl*?"

Somehow, she managed to find her voice. "I—I'm fine. I just need a minute."

It took longer than a minute for the nausea to subside, closer to five. Finally, she rubbed at the sting of emotion still burning behind her lids and, gaining her feet, left the bathroom. Her mother was waiting in the hallway when she emerged, and as she'd done with Naomi, she opened her arms in silent invitation. Rachel rushed into the offered embrace. Too exhausted to cry, she clung, enjoying the feel of their shared heartbeats.

After a moment, her mother stepped back and cupped her cheeks between her warm palms. "You will want your dinner now."

Rachel wasn't sure she could eat, but her mother looked so hopeful, as if the simple chore of feeding her child brought her some semblance of peace. "Yes." She swallowed. "I… Yes."

Later, when she was alone in her room, Rachel pulled out her journal and flipped to a blank page. She took accounting classes because everyone told her she had a head for numbers. And perhaps she did. She certainly liked it when columns added up, and her father was so proud of her. Lately, though, in ways she couldn't fully explain, things had begun to change in her heart, and she craved a different future than the one her parents wanted for her.

The world—her world—had teetered off its axis, throwing

all she knew into confusion. Nothing was certain anymore. A bright future was no longer guaranteed for Jews living in a German-occupied city.

Rachel woke at night, sometimes from haunted dreams, and always with an inexplicable tug at her soul. She desired a different fate. A world without fear. Trying to capture that feeling, she'd begun putting her thoughts in a journal. She could spend an entire evening trying to put her feelings on the page. Some nights she would agonize over a single sentence for hours.

Other nights, the words flowed. Words upon words poured from mind to pen to page. She wrote it all down, every bit of thought swirling in her head, no matter how ugly or raw or terrifyingly wistful. And when she finally shut the book, it was with a sense of relief, always, to know that she'd found a small piece of solace in the act of writing.

Cathartic, but nothing could erase what Rachel now knew to be true. The sense of safety she'd known all her life was dissolving, slipping from her grasp like water through splayed fingers. And the worst of it was that there was nothing she could do. Nothing but watch everything she held dear wash away into the gray mist of Nazi hate and French indifference.

Chapter Nine

Camille

28 June 1940.
Dinan, Brittany, France.

Friday arrived. Camille hadn't slept much. She'd lain awake, thinking of that little girl on the street even though Rachel had assured her no one had been hurt, and that, while the bakery had suffered damage, the family had been reunited. A blessing, but then, there was nothing to distract Camille from worrying about her sister. Never again would she leave the girl in the company of someone who could do her harm.

With still no new letter from her mother, Camille rose before dawn. The journey from Paris to Dinan would take approximately four hours by train each way. That would give her very little time with Jacqueline, to see for herself she was in good hands.

She dozed on the train, falling in and out of a troubled sleep. The nightmare that haunted her at night toyed with her now. She managed to resist the worst of the images. The guilt? That, too, she pushed away. She was going home, wasn't she? She hadn't abandoned Jacqueline completely. A lurch startled her awake, and she looked outside.

The sun was a perfect round orb hanging prominent in the sky. The countryside showed the green of summer, and Camille immediately recognized the craggy terrain of her home region. They were close now, and the quicker the train sped through Brittany, the stronger she felt the melancholy of homesickness. She pressed her forehead to the window, hungry for her first glimpse of Dinan since moving to Paris. Up ahead stood the ancient walls of the medieval village and its fifteen towers dating back to the eleventh century. Beyond that stood the imposing castle, the Château de la Duchesse Anne.

The train pulled into the depot with a series of metallic creaks and groans. The earsplitting sound of the whistle announced their arrival. The trip had been blessedly uneventful. There'd been no checkpoints. No demands to show her identity card. She knew that wouldn't last. For now, she was home. Then she remembered why she'd come, and every reason for staying away came rushing back. The guilt came next because, deep down, she hadn't missed witnessing the consequences of what she'd done every time she looked at her sister.

Jacqueline is not a consequence. She is your sister.

And Camille loved her fiercely. The depth of the emotion, that was what caused her so much pain. Sighing, she slipped her hand in her pocket and closed her fingers over the original letter from her mother. She'd reread the words a hundred times, a thousand.

"All those for Dinan," called the porter. "Dinan. All those for Dinan, please disembark."

Home. The word whispered in her brain. *I am home.*

The pull was still strong.

She disembarked into a village that was not her home, not anymore. The Nazis had put up their hideous swastika flags everywhere. Soldiers in their gray-green uniforms carried guns slung over their shoulders. The arrogant stare of the victor shone in their eyes. Some even had vicious-looking guard dogs with them, straining at their leashes.

What would these men do if they discovered Jacqueline's condition? Would they arrest her, send her away?

The Nazis' sense of entitlement manifested itself in unconscionable persecution of people they deemed unworthy. It had taken some digging to uncover their policy for mental illness. *The Destruction of Life Unworthy of Life*. Hitler himself had issued the memorandum stating that a person with mental illness required either permanent institutionalization or, in some cases, premature termination by medical measures. German professors of psychiatry and directors of asylums had agreed such a program was warranted.

Would they bring this policy to France? They'd brought others just as foul.

A sense of urgency reared, and Camille hurried along the platform. Sleek gray clouds moved overhead like smoke smearing the sky. Gray uniforms, gray clouds. The mood on the cobbled streets was equally gloomy.

Her family's bakery was in the heart of town, on the Place des Merciers. The business had been in her mother's family for five generations, handed down from mother to oldest daughter. They were known for their signature *pain des amis*, a pastry Camille knew was as good as any found in a Parisian patisserie.

She felt it again. The homesickness. The loss of her dreams. She'd never planned to live in Paris. She'd hoped only to take over the family business when it was her turn. She missed the feel of dough between her fingers, the scent of butter and flour as she kneaded it into submission. She was stalling, but she needed one more minute. Just one more.

The bakery was on the first floor, the family home on the top two. The building had lost most of its charm in recent years. But the pointed gables, wood shutters, and antique doorway hadn't changed. What *had* changed was the long line of customers snaking out the bakery and down four blocks. Most would leave empty-handed. Not because her family didn't want to sell them bread and pastries, but because businesses were subjected to rationing just like individuals.

Proving Camille's point, the display window was bare but for a handwritten sign alerting shoppers that supplies were limited. She tried to push to the front of the line, only to be elbowed and yelled at for her effort. Giving up, she went around to the back and stepped into the pleasing scents of yeast, butter, and flour. She navigated her way through the kitchen, toward the shop where her family sold the best baked goods in the village.

There was no sign of her mother. Two of her sisters worked the counter at a frantic pace. Lily, barely fifteen and reed-thin, took the orders, slowly and deliberately, never making a mistake. She looked like Camille had at that age, but without the carefree manner that had been her trademark as a child. Knowing the war wasn't the only reason, a sudden pang sparked in Camille's chest, and she looked to their other sister. Seventeen-year-old Angeline favored their mother, as did Jacqueline, and with that thought came another spasm of pain.

Camille bit her lip. Her heart filled with a complicated mix of love and regret, rolled up in the scents of flour and sugar. "Good morning, mademoiselles."

"Camille," shouted Lily, the happy child of old in her expression. "You're home."

"Only for the day," she said, hugging her fiercely and doing the same with Angeline, who stepped back and swallowed, and Camille knew matters were not good here. Worse than not good. "Where's *Maman?*"

She swallowed again, and Camille could count the emotions passing across her face like shadows flitting across a valley. "Upstairs…" She trailed off, took a breath, started again. "With Jacqueline."

"Thank you." She hugged each sister again, then wove back through the kitchen, past the ovens and industrial mixers, the giant sink, and mounted the back stairs. She didn't glance toward the door that led to the basement. Not once.

Halfway up, Camille paused in the darkened stairwell. Caught in the quiet nothingness between the two worlds of her childhood, the bakery below, her home above, she needed to stop. Stop and embrace the momentary freedom of no one needing her.

She took the moment, relished it. Then her innate sense of duty won out, and she finished the climb. A cloud of cigarette smoke encircled her, and Camille's stomach twisted in distress. Her mother was smoking again, though she'd promised Camille she'd quit. Cigarettes cost money they simply didn't have.

Irritated, she blinked past the throat-clogging fog. Her eyes landed on her sister, and her mouth filled with the nasty taste of regret. Jacqueline sat on the floor, her legs tucked in close, her arms crossed over her knees. She rocked back and forth, humming a tune their father had sung when he was most himself.

Although Jacqueline's voice trilled over the melody in perfect pitch, her hair was wild, her dress rumpled, and purple fatigue shadowed the skin beneath her eyes. It hurt to look at her. Beautiful, tortured Jacqueline, her body that of a young girl on the verge of womanhood, her mind that of the seven-year-old child who'd witnessed the horror of death.

It wasn't fair. Her sister should not be paying the price for Camille's selfishness. But where was her mother, or the woman she'd hired? There was no sign of either, save the stale scent of cigarette smoke. A bad sign. "Jacqueline."

The girl looked up. Her gaze, as wild as her unkempt hair, chased around the room, finally landing on Camille. She released a small, frightened squeak and backed away. There was no recognition, only fear. Camille felt tears well. "Don't be afraid," she said softly. "It's me. Camille."

A cry of dismay tore from the cracked lips, and the rocking resumed in earnest. "No. Not Camille. Camille left. Just like Papa."

Camille's breath stalled in her throat. The situation was worse than she thought. Her move to Paris had been one more abandonment for the girl. One more desertion. And deep in her heart, Camille had been secretly relieved to go. She wasn't relieved now. In the time it took her heart to take a single beat, she crossed the floor and went down on her knees. "Oh, my dear, sweet girl." She reached out but didn't touch her sister. Not yet. "I'm here. Right here."

"No, no, no." She dipped her face into her hands and started to cry.

Camille was reminded of the child from the other night, and she thought her heart might break. "I'm here, *mon doux enfant*. I'm home."

Jacqueline went still. Slowly, she lifted her head. There was an indistinct glitter in her eyes, something not quite of this world. Then, her expression cleared. "Camille?"

"*Oui. C'est moi.*"

In the next instant, Jacqueline was in her arms, both of them crying. Seconds turned into minutes, and Camille was no longer sure who clung harder. Had she been wrong to move to Paris?

What else could she have done? The family needed her wages, even more now that rationing had been set in place, all but crippling the bakery from making a profit.

Her mother's voice interrupted her thoughts. "There's no need to baby the girl."

Camille sat back on her heels. But she kept her hands on her sister's shoulders as she glanced up at the face of the woman who'd birthed her. Her expression was bleak, her shoulders stooped. She'd aged in the six months since Camille had left for Paris, as if she'd taken on more than her fair share of the work. "I thought you hired a local woman to help with Jacqueline."

"I sent her on an errand."

"What errand?"

"Doesn't matter."

Somehow, Camille knew that it did. "She went to buy cigarettes."

"Yes."

The way she said the word, sorrowful and defeated, so utterly defeated, Camille knew her mother was broken, and something inside her broke, too, knowing she was partially to blame. "I'm sorry, *Maman*."

"I know you are."

Jacqueline went back to singing to herself. When the rocking started, her mother collapsed in a chair and touched the side of her face. Only then did Camille notice her hand trembled. "The tantrums," she whispered, "the constant fear of discovery, I can't take it anymore. It's too much. She is my child, and I love her. But I can't seem to reach her, not like you. And now she is in decline. Her outbursts grow more violent."

Camille didn't want to hear this, not any of it. She didn't want to feel the guilt, either, knowing her absence had all but fractured her family. "It was your idea to send me to Paris."

Her mother sighed. "We need your extra wages. You know this, Camille."

She did. Nevertheless, her eyes filled with tears again, and everything in the room took on a misty tint.

"It's time we send Jacqueline to Rennes."

Camille had known this was coming. A part of her understood, and still, she opened her mouth to argue. "What about the local woman? Is she not working out?"

Her mother shrugged. "She has family in the Free Zone and wants to join them as soon as she is able to renew her identity card."

This was not good news. "How long will that take?"

"I don't know."

"Perhaps someone else could take her place."

"There is no one else."

"But—"

"Enough, Camille. Jacqueline is not my only concern. I have two other daughters, each of them working hard downstairs."

What about her fourth daughter? The one working hard in Paris?

"I've tried it your way," her mother said. "Now we will do it mine."

Her mother would not be swayed. But if they sent Jacqueline to a public hospital specializing in psychiatry, weren't they handing her over to the Nazis? Then again, if the girl was getting worse, she was no safer in Dinan.

The situation was ugly and complicated, and Camille started to cry. *My fault. My fault.*

She hadn't known she'd spoken the words aloud. But suddenly, her mother was on the floor with her, rocking her back and forth, finally saying the words Camille had spent five years waiting to hear. "It's not your fault, Camille. My sweet, clever girl, none of this is your fault."

Chapter Ten

Vivian

1 September 1940.
Paris, France.

Vivian woke late, as was becoming her habit, especially now that she'd been downgraded to a room she hated, on a floor with people she didn't especially like. She had to drag herself out of bed for a meeting with a member of the American government working in the ambassador's office. Before the declaration of war, she'd gone weeks between meetings.

Now the immigration rules were more stringent for Jews seeking asylum in the United States. Falsified identity papers and fake passports were difficult to obtain. But American visas were nearly impossible, even with Vivian's deep pockets.

She'd like to think her efforts were for purely altruistic reasons, but she knew better. Her motivation stemmed from a secret desire to keep Rupert's legacy alive. He'd been a committed philanthropist, giving vast amounts of financial support to worthy causes. To continue in his name kept him alive in her mind.

It was raining when she left the hotel. She hurried along the narrow streets, holding her umbrella at a jaunty angle to better highlight her matching raincoat. She passed a little park with blooming flowers, their color in stark contrast to the gray sky. Everywhere she looked, Paris had become a carbon copy of Berlin. German soldiers played the tourist, snapping photos of themselves and their friends. They even grabbed locals, mostly women, and forced them to pose with them. Some did so willingly. Most did not.

Parisians were returning home, but they found a very different city. The street signs were in German now, with the original French names in smaller print underneath. Most telling of all, Vivian passed café after café, business after business, with words written on blackboards perched near the doorways: *Les Juifs ne sont pas admis ici.*

Jews are not allowed here.

She couldn't comprehend why the French people ignored this bigotry, as if by failing to acknowledge what was happening, then it wasn't, well, happening. Frowning, she entered Café Voisin, placed her order at the counter, and chose a table by the window. She wanted to witness her contact's approach. The rain came down harder, turning the scene slate-colored and smudgy.

People rushed past the café. Their expressions were set, their pace fast. Some carried umbrellas. Most did not. All looked grim. Watching them, as they *endured*, Vivian was overcome with a sense of bone-deep weariness. Paris was lost. The city was no longer a celebration of art, beauty, and light, but a dismal world of people with their heads down, navigating the real-life horror of Occupation.

Her thoughts were as gloomy as the rain.

She reached for one of the pastries. It was nearly too pretty to eat. The scent of strong coffee flavored the air. No rationing in Café Voisin. It was, after all, a favorite lunch spot for German officers billeting at the Hôtel Ritz. So many of them. It was only a matter of time before they implemented even more Aryan policies of hate and destruction toward Jews and other people they deemed inferior. Soon, Vivian feared, discrimination would turn to persecution or worse. At least she was able to prevent disaster for a few.

A few was better than none, but not nearly enough. How long before her efforts were swallowed up by the Nazis' need to erase entire groups of people? People who breathed the same air as they did, who walked the same streets, who had families and friends and dreams worth pursuing? Oh, yes, her thoughts were indeed gloomy.

She took a delicate bite of her tart and tried not to fume. He was late. She made use of the time by sliding her hand in her purse. She pulled out the bank draft that would hurry along the visa process for a Jewish couple and set it beneath the cloth napkin beside her plate.

That done, she placed a serene look on her face, and settled into the role of a wealthy, pampered American who cared nothing of politics. It was far from the truth, but people saw what they wanted to see. Lies. Subterfuge, donning a persona contrary to her true self. This was what her life had become. Would Rupert approve of what she did for the war effort? Would he be proud of the way she used his money? She'd like to think so.

The door swung open and in walked three German soldiers in their closed-collar service uniforms. Not *Wehrmacht.* *Schutzstaffel.* SS. She'd learned to discern the difference. The German army officers were much more understated. The SS, not so. They wore silver braided shoulder boards, an eagle on the peaked cap, runes on the right collar, rank tabs on the left. And of course, the iron cross was always pinned at the neck.

Even if they were in civilian clothes, she would know them for Nazis. It was in their attitude. Their arrogance. They appeared to have not a care in the world, laughing over something one of the three said. Good, she thought. Let them laugh and order their food and ignore this lone woman sitting by the window. She heard one of them mention the Ritz. Another remarked that his accommodations were acceptable.

Acceptable? *Acceptable?* How absolutely, utterly German of him.

Feeling sick, Vivian slowly turned away from the trio. No sudden movements. That, too, she'd learned in the months since the hotel had been overrun by vipers and their sycophant friends. She'd nearly avoided their notice when one of the three, the one who'd spoken in moderate terms about his *acceptable* accommodations, snapped his gaze in her direction.

Vivian froze, and she knew, in that instant, he was a very dangerous man. He was also unbelievably attractive, a near perfect male specimen. Female gazes turned in his direction, but he seemed to have eyes only for Vivian. She'd attracted interest from his kind before. None had been so bold in their inspection. Nor had her response been so full of immediate, blood-pumping animosity. Something about him. Something cold and reptilian in the way he stared at her.

He'd removed his hat and had tucked it under his arm, leaving his fair hair uncovered. He wasn't young. But he wasn't old, either. He had dark blond hair, chiseled features, and an aristocratic bearing that reeked of entitlement. He was almost beautiful, but in a terrible sort of way. It was his eyes, she decided. Pale blue, icy, soulless. And he was looking straight at her.

She couldn't look away. She didn't dare. To do so would be to lose some precious piece of herself. It was an odd thought, but one Vivian felt to the very marrow of her bones. An aura of danger emanated from him, and one word came to mind. *Trapped.* She was good and truly trapped in the man's gaze. And then he smiled, a miniscule lift of perfectly formed lips. So confident in his charm, his looks, his power over others.

An instant surge of emotion swept through Vivian, something unnatural for a woman who'd known the love of a decent man. Hate. Vivian hated this Nazi.

The visceral reaction was stronger than anything she'd felt before. Such intensity, and personal to this man alone. She became aware of other people moving around her, the buzz of voices. He started toward her, then stopped after only a step and turned back to his companions.

Now that she was free, the tail end of a breath hissed from her lungs.

Ten seconds, that's all it had been, and Vivian knew, without a shred of doubt, that the man was not someone she ever wished to know. But he'd taken a room in the Ritz, and that meant their paths would cross. The thought made her hands tremble. She couldn't grasp her cup. She gave up after two attempts and simply stared out the window. The rain had stopped.

He soon left the café, but not before he sent another look in her direction. She had a bad feeling about that man. This fear in her, it made no sense. She'd done nothing wrong, as far as the Nazi knew, and though she'd like to leave, she still had important business to conduct.

She would give the attaché from the American embassy another five minutes, then return to the hotel, albeit reluctantly. For weeks the building had been under construction. Sawdust and workmen were everywhere, mostly on the Place Vendôme side.

Mimi Ritz wasn't saying why she'd approved the renovations and, more specifically, why now, which left Vivian wondering how the woman defined *remaining neutral*. Most of the hotel guests were German officers. All of them made impossible demands and treated the Ritz as if it were their personal retreat for private indulgences. They ran the staff ragged, sending them on ridiculously frivolous errands.

Vivian made sure to keep an eye on Camille. They were united now, because of Vivian, and that meant that she was responsible for the young woman. She also kept an eye on the other one, the girl Camille had befriended. Oh, yes, Vivian knew all about Camille's friend. The Jewish girl, that's what the head housekeeper had called her when Vivian had asked her name, which was rather baffling. There were other Jewish employees in the hotel. Why label that girl and not the others?

The café's door swung open, and Vivian connected her gaze with the tall man who'd entered the building. He wore a precisely tailored suit and gray silk tie two shades darker. His severe face held the signs of aging. If she had to guess, she would say he'd spent a minimum of seven decades on this earth.

She adopted a pose of nonchalance and waited for him to make his move. He passed her by, did an impressive double take, then made a grand show of spreading pleased recognition across his features. "Vivian Miller, how remarkable to run into you here. Why, you haven't changed a bit since I last saw you." He gave her a good once-over that bordered on insulting, before adding, "This ensemble you wear, the hair, the makeup, *très chic.*"

It was a convincing performance. She almost believed they'd come across one another by accident. "Archie, old boy, what a pleasant surprise."

"Indeed." He greeted her with two air kisses, one for each cheek. "It's been too long, *ma chere amie.* I have missed your beautiful face and witty conversation."

She offered him an ironic twist of her lips, as if to say: *Laying it on a bit thick.* "Please." She made a sweeping motion with her hand. "Won't you join me?"

His hesitation took her by surprise, as this was their usual pattern. But then he smiled and claimed the seat opposite hers.

Returning the smile, she offered him a tartlet as they discussed their mutual friends, none of whom existed. "I ran into Marge Morton last evening at the opera," she said. "She was with Richard Unger and his wife, Gladys."

"Ah." Archie held perfectly still, his eyes never leaving her face. "They are well?"

"Very well, but like so many Americans, they've tired of France. They miss New York." There. It was done. He now had the names for the travel visas and the city of their hoped-for destination.

All that was left was Archie's agreement, and Vivian would pass over the payment.

"New York is lovely this time of year," he said.

Not true. The city would be blazing hot and full of soupy humidity that taxed the lungs and frizzed the hair. "Is there any wonder they miss the city?"

He held her gaze. "Indeed."

The response she'd been waiting for. Finally, he'd agreed to provide the visas. Vivian felt the tension drain out of her. This process hadn't needed to be so difficult, but that was Archie. He enjoyed a bit of drama. "I believe our mutual friends hope to leave for America within the next two weeks," she said.

"I would think the end of the month quite soon enough."

A longer wait than the family had hoped, but these things took time. "Perhaps I had the details of their departure wrong. I am not always the best of listeners." She gave a delighted laugh, then leaned in close and said in a low whisper, "A month is acceptable."

"Very good."

And that was that. All done. The money exchange proved a bit trickier. Vivian tapped on the napkin covering the bank draft, then lifted the edge for Archie to take a quick glance. When her companion spilled his coffee—a quick study, this one—she slid both napkin and check in his direction. A fast grab on his part and the draft went in his pocket while the napkin mopped away the liquid puddling beneath his overturned cup.

They talked a moment longer, about nothing in particular, nothing beyond the weather and the upcoming opera season. Then Vivian made to rise. "I must go."

"Before you do…"

She sat back down, eyebrows lifted.

"You were a combat nurse in the previous war, yes?"

Not sure how he'd come by this information—she'd been

Catherine Vivian Pierce at the time—she nodded. "That's correct."

"You were stationed in France?"

Vivian frowned. What sort of game was Archie playing? If he knew she'd been a nurse in the Great War, he also knew where she'd served. "Italy."

"Ah." He toyed with the pastry beneath his hand, breaking off pieces of the flaky crust, then popping them into his mouth. "I wonder. Are you still interested in caring for wounded soldiers?"

It was not a question she'd expected. But now that the idea was in her head, she could see returning to the woman who'd known what it meant to give of herself. Even if it was only to sit at a bedside and read a story. Or write a letter for a soldier who'd lost his hand—or any number of duties. She could do it. She could work for the American Red Cross again. "It's been years since I trained as a nurse. I'm no longer qualified, but I—"

"You misunderstand." He stared at her in dismay. "I am not asking for your services as a nurse. I am asking for your support of a new hospital solely dedicated to wounded soldiers."

Humiliation stiffened her spine, making her feel exposed. Archie didn't want her. He wanted her money. What had she expected? She had a role to play in this war, and it wasn't to make a personal sacrifice. It was to open her checkbook. Always, it came back to the money Rupert had left her. Even the forged papers and visas were about how much Vivian was willing to pay. She tried not to let her disappointment show, but she was no actress. Her skills went only so far. "How much *support* are we talking about?"

He had the grace to break eye contact, but not before he said, "As much as you are willing to give."

She'd known he'd say that. She'd *known*. Forcing a smile to hide the ache in her heart, she threw out a number so impossibly large that her companion choked on his coffee. He recovered quickly enough. They set another date to meet, at another café in Montmartre, where he would give her the visas and she would hand over the money for the hospital. It was all so polite, and still, Vivian felt dirty. She wanted a bath, and she wanted it now. "If that is all, I have another appointment."

Giving him no time to respond, she left the café. Her umbrella was sufficient protection from the pouring rain that had started up again, but not the lingering looks tossed her way. She didn't care. What did it matter that a handful of German soldiers watched her cross the street? They didn't frighten her. Even before her meeting this morning, she'd known her role in this war.

She still knew her role. It wasn't a comfort. It wasn't terrible. It wasn't anything. It just…was.

The German

Chapter Eleven

Vivian

1 September 1940.
Hôtel Ritz. Paris, France.

Occupied with thoughts of wounded soldiers and Jewish refugees, Vivian kept her head down, her feet moving. Even after the skies cleared, she continued her random wandering. She had no idea how long she'd been walking or which direction she'd taken after she left Café Voisin. Her disappointment was sharp.

How she used her money mattered. She was not so naive as to think otherwise. She also understood that lives were saved with every falsified identity card she had forged and every travel visa she wheedled out of the American government. But she'd wanted to do more, be more, than her money. At least soldiers injured on the battlefield would have a fighting chance at survival. Many would be healed and return to their loved ones.

Still, Vivian felt empty, as unnecessary as her umbrella now that the rain had stopped. No one needed *her*, not on a personal level. She had no children, no extended family. Her life had become a round of parties, attending the opera, the ballet, and sometimes the occasional film, with nothing to break up the monotony other than the coordination of falsified documents for people desperate to leave Europe.

A crow swooped overhead, practically clipping her on the shoulder before landing on a low-hanging branch. The feathers on his big black body gleamed in the rain, as if they'd been coated with layers of motor oil. He readjusted his feet, swished his tail a few times, then stared at her with those fathomless black eyes.

Vivian shuddered. Crows were depicted in literature as bad omens. Sometimes they were mediators between this world and the next. In real life, they were shameless scavengers, feeding on the dead. She quickened her pace. Practically running now, she entered a world made of concrete and marble, the Vendôme tower at the center.

The iconic white awnings of the Hôtel Ritz beckoned.

She slipped around the sandbags stacked on either side of the Place Vendôme entrance and hurried past the archways, stopping only long enough to hand her umbrella to a bellman. Once she was inside the hallowed walls of Paris's grande dame, she took a moment to breathe. The hotel gleamed. All polished wood, marble, and gilded furnishings. The sounds of construction were louder today, more frenzied, as if the SS soldiers milling about presented a need to hurry. Vivian knew Hermann Göring was due to arrive any day now, which probably explained the hectic mood.

Her eyebrows lifted when several soldiers carrying a massive, oversize bathtub labored up the grand staircase. It didn't take deductive reasoning to understand that the corpulent *Luftwaffe* commander enjoyed a long soak. Probably while sipping champagne.

The idea that he'd confiscated the Imperial Suite for himself, all but evicting another wealthy American, made Vivian feel slightly ill. What could Laura Mae Corrigan do? She was just another American widow with deep pockets and few skills outside throwing exclusive dinner parties. *No different than you.*

They were very much the same, and Vivian wondered why it had taken the hotel so long to "relocate" her fellow heiress. Even Coco Chanel had been kicked over to the Rue Cambon side upon her return to Paris. Vivian's eyebrows went higher as a row of soldiers carted cases of Bollinger champagne up the stairwell in the bathtub's wake. She started to shake her head, then stilled. Something had shifted on the air, and she felt eyes on her.

"Mademoiselle, or should I address you as madame?" The flawless French fell over her like a silk scarf, the rich baritone almost musical, and she knew the owner had to be the Nazi from the café. The sensation of being trapped was too strong for him to be anyone else.

Slowly, very slowly, she glanced over her shoulder and locked gazes with the same pale blue eyes she'd met this morning. He stood too close, and Vivian felt the urge to run. But that would require turning her back on him. She knew better. Oh, yes, she knew not to take her eyes off this man. She pivoted until they stood face-to-face.

He continued staring, his gaze boring into hers as if he meant to look straight into her soul. She tried to brazen it out, but she faltered and dropped her eyes to a spot on his chin. "It's madame."

"Ah." His eyes took in her face with something akin to reverence. "Has anyone remarked how much you favor Rita Hayworth?"

Many, many people. "A few."

"She is a favorite of mine. You, I think, are even more beautiful." There it was again, that near-worshipful tone. And yet there was also a sense of entitlement in his manner, as if she should consider herself fortunate to have gained his attention.

"Thank you. I consider that a great compliment."

"It was meant as one."

He spoke with typical German arrogance, and that was enough to have her taking a longer look at his face, just in time to catch him taking her measure, from head to toe, in a slow, insolent inspection full of an intimacy that had no place in a public building. In that moment, Vivian saw a man who took what he wanted, and right now, he wanted her.

"I assume your husband is with you in the hotel?"

He could obtain this information in many ways, some that would include gossip. She did not want this man hearing anything about her marriage or her beloved Rupert that didn't come from her own lips. "My husband passed away five years ago."

"I'm sorry for your loss."

He didn't sound sorry. He sounded delighted. This man, this Nazi, he was not so hard to read. Already his mind calculated and planned. A predator selecting his prey. The back of her neck prickled in alarm. This man, he frightened her. It wasn't only his interest. It was the underlying intensity of his fascination. Men had been obsessed with her in the past. It had never ended well.

"You are a guest in this hotel?" he asked.

"Yes," she said, her eyelids lowering ever so slightly. "On the Rue Cambon side."

"Yet you loiter in the reception area on the side of the hotel reserved for German officers. I have to wonder why?"

Her heartbeats seemed to be bumping into each other. Not good. Not good. She must remain calm. "There is buzz among the guests about an important man moving into the hotel. I wanted to see what all the fuss was about."

"Have you satisfied your curiosity?"

There it was again, that sensation of terror she hadn't felt since her childhood. She thought she'd known what sort of man she was up against. She'd been only half-right. He was a predator, yes, but was also handsome and charming, with an edge of cruelty some women would mistake for mysterious. Vivian knew many men like this one. Her father, with his abusive hand and evil intent, had taught her well. "I have seen all I came to see."

He took a step toward her, and then another, until the distance between them was mere inches, six at the most. Vivian could smell his scent, a combination of sandalwood, coffee, and French tobacco. It was not an altogether unpleasant scent. A man cloaked in the vile uniform of the enemy should smell worse.

The hotel manager approached, taking in their interchange without comment. "Your suite is ready, *Herr Sturmbannführer* von Bauer. I apologize for the inconvenience you suffered due to the inadequacy of your previous accommodations. We will, of course, reimburse any fees you were charged." Elminger thrust out his hand. "Your key."

Vivian lowered her eyes, immediately wishing she hadn't caught the room number. A growl of outrage tried to work its way past her lips. This vile, unpleasant Nazi was to live in her former suite, among *her* precious furnishings she'd been forced to leave behind.

It wasn't right. It wasn't fair. Then again, nothing about German occupation was right or fair. And the Nazi marauder smiled at her with a self-satisfied glint. Somehow, he seemed to know that he'd taken her suite.

"You will dine with me tonight in the hotel restaurant." The crooked smile he gave her was not unpleasant—charming, actually. Vivian knew what kind of man lived behind that smile.

She should decline. Politely, of course. "I'm afraid I already have plans."

His eyes went hard. Not so charming now. "Break them."

She stiffened, sensing something about this man. She knew his type. Violence was a drug for men like him. *Tread carefully, Vivian.* "If you mean to suggest that I would disappoint—"

"It was not a suggestion."

She gaped at him.

"We will meet in the dining room at eight o'clock sharp. Dress for an elegant evening."

He turned from her then, just turned away, dismissing her without a second glance, and as she watched him mount the hotel's *grand escalier*, she had a moment of clarity. She'd been here before, at the mercy of a man who held all the control. Her father had been the worse sort of brute. He'd hurt her, physically, mentally. She still had the scars. She did not want more.

Vivian wondered what the Nazi would do if she didn't show. It would be dangerous to find out, too dangerous. They lived in the same hotel, he on the side of the victors, she on the side of the defeated. She would dine with him, but she would do so fully armed.

Her greatest weapon was not her beauty, as many men had failed to learn. It was her brains. She would use them now. The first step was to gather information. From the one man in the hotel who knew every person, every liaison, every coming and going.

Frank Meier, the inscrutable hotel bartender, had no family, and, like Vivian, seemingly no life beyond the Ritz. He was one of her partners in her forgery scheme, often setting up contacts when hers ran dry. He also had his own gambling ring from his spot behind the mahogany bar, and many already wondered where his loyalties were in this war.

Vivian knew the answer. Frank was half-Jewish and American. He was no Nazi.

The corridor between the two hotels was dark as a tomb. Shadows shifted across the wide, empty space, slithering along the floor, disintegrating into the walls like secrets blown away with the wind. Vivian wondered, would anyone miss her if she disappeared into the walls like just another shadow?

It was not a thought she wished to consider too deeply.

A pinprick of light guided her forward, straight into the Little Bar where Frank had served as the head bartender since 1921. The air was thin and filled with the scent of stale liquor that no amount of cleaning could fully eradicate. Odd, how she never noticed the odor when the room was full, only when it was empty but for the man behind the bar. Dressed in a black shirt beneath his plain white jacket, he'd parted his hair in the center and slicked it back with what appeared to be half a jar of pomade. He held a bar towel in his hand and was wiping away a smudge on a martini glass only visible to his discerning eye.

"Frank."

"Ah, Vivian," he said, barely looking up from his task. "I don't usually see you in my bar at this hour."

She heard the censure. Understandable. Their clandestine work was better conducted beneath the din of a crowded room. Interacting in the light of day was dangerous—if she was here to conduct their usual business. She ordered a club soda and waited for him to set the bubbling water in front of her before saying, "I met the hotel's newest resident."

"Hermann Göring has arrived?"

"I meant another." She didn't state his name. She didn't know it, not fully, and if she did—well, she wouldn't want the nasty taste of it on her lips.

Frank didn't have the same aversion. "You must mean Hans-Dieter von Bauer."

"That's the one." She glanced around, ensuring they were alone, then: "What do you know about him?"

Still polishing the same martini glass, Frank shrugged. "Not much. He's in charge of a construction project in Drancy, top priority. At the moment, that's all we know."

That's all we know.

She stared at Frank for a long moment, waiting for him to say more, praying he would. When he didn't, she sighed. "He suggested I dine with him this evening. I will, of course, bring him here for drinks afterward."

There was nothing more to say. It was understood that Vivian would find out what she could about the Drancy construction project. Wishing there was another way, *any* other way, she accepted her fate and drained the rest of her glass.

Pushing back from the bar, she made it only a few steps when Camille entered the bar. She was dressed in her chambermaid's uniform, looking efficient and professional, but her expression gave Vivian pause. Something terrible had put that pain in the young woman's eyes.

It's none of your business.

And yet, somehow, she thought maybe it was. Hadn't she only moments ago wished to be more than a checkbook in the eyes of her government? She'd just agreed, sort of, to suss out information about an important Nazi project with her unique talents and skills.

Now this young woman was in need of something only Vivian could provide. A listening ear that could be trusted. Camille knew one of her secrets. Vivian could offer to return the favor and carry one of hers. She opened her mouth, then glanced around. Not here, no. This was not the place for confidences. Later, in her room.

She would send for the maid, under the guise of needing her hair styled for tonight's dinner engagement. Not a complete ruse. Facing off with a man like von Bauer would require a high level of feminine armor.

She passed Camille, gave a single nod. The maid returned the gesture.

Out in the hallway, Vivian paused. Camille had approached Frank with an unusual request, desperation in her voice. Frank denied her request, but Camille refused to give up. There was additional back-and-forth, and Vivian had heard enough. She retraced her steps, prepared to do battle for a young woman in need.

It felt good to have a purpose. It felt right.

Chapter Twelve

Camille

1 September 1940.
Hôtel Ritz. Paris, France.

Her mind on Jacqueline, Camille held Frank Meier's stare. Her mother's voice played in her head. *It's not your fault. None of this is your fault.*

There had been such sincerity in those words, given to her for the first time since her father's death. She knew her mother meant them. But her terrible choices could not be undone by a few heartfelt words whispered in her ear. Redemption was not so easily won.

And so she continued trying to convince the hotel's famous bartender to hire her. An entire lifetime came and went in the seconds it took him to cross to the other end of the bar and slip behind the long expanse of wood. In those precious moments, the memory of Jacqueline's tortured face, all twisted and confused one minute, beautifully empty the next, mocked Camille's pitiful efforts to find additional work in the hotel. Frank Meier was her last resort. She'd already approached the pastry chef, and the head of laundry, even the hotel manager.

Their responses had been succinct and always the same. No, no, and no. "Please, Monsieur Meier, I will do any task, no matter how menial. I will empty ashtrays, wash glasses."

"You ask the impossible."

He didn't even look at her when he spoke, just kept prowling back and forth behind the long strip of polished mahogany. Frank Meier was the most famous employee in the hotel, a force unto himself. He'd published his book on cocktails back in 1936. Camille should have read *The Artistry of Mixing Drinks* before approaching him. Too late now. "Monsieur, you are woefully understaffed. I can help you with that."

"I only hire men to serve in my bar."

"I would wear the same uniform." A crisp white shirt, a white jacket, and snappy black bow tie. "I will slick my hair tight against my head." She would lose all signs of her femininity, go to any lengths, whatever it took for him to hire her. He did not say no.

He did not say yes, either.

"Please," she intoned. "Please," she said again. There was nothing else worth saying.

"I only hire male bartenders."

So he'd said. Several times. "I could deliver drinks. I would move quickly. Quietly. No one would notice. Please," she added a fourth time, the desperation evident even to her own ears.

He opened his mouth, but a stern female voice spoke over him. "Hire her, Frank."

They both swung to stare at Vivian Miller standing in the bar's entrance. She was dressed in a stylish black suit gathered at her waist with a matching pencil skirt beneath a raincoat the color of a Paris sunset.

The bartender seemed not to notice her smart attire. He was too busy scolding her. "Madame Miller, this is a hotel matter between the staff."

"Look at her. The blond hair, the blue eyes. The Germans will not take offense."

"I only hire male bartenders," he repeated like a mantra.

"We are at war, my friend, and men are scarce. Think on it. What the girl proposes could prove valuable to your business endeavors." There was a touch of sly triumph in Vivian's voice, as though she said one thing, but meant something else entirely.

For a moment, the bartender appeared not to know what to say, and hope rose in Camille's throat. She didn't understand why the American widow was championing her. To do so had put the man in an awkward position. It was one thing to deny a chambermaid's request, quite another to refuse a guest's wishes.

"Think it through, Frank. The women will mostly ignore her. The soldiers will see only a pretty French girl whose life's work is to serve them."

He said nothing for so long, Camille thought he wouldn't respond at all. But then he shot her an irritated look. "What you ask is impossible. And before you interrupt, I should not have to remind you there is a new curfew in place. The girl cannot be out past nine."

"Then you will send her home before nine. Or I can arrange a cot in my room if the hour grows too late." Vivian switched to English, and the rest of the conversation was lost to Camille. She picked up a few words that sounded familiar—*secret, paper, clandestine*—but she wasn't certain the words were the same or just seemed the same.

Eventually, Frank returned his attention to Camille and, switching back to French, addressed her directly. "Do you understand what you are asking, mademoiselle? Working in my bar will mean interacting directly with the Germans. If you have any reservations, now would be the time to voice them."

Camille didn't want to interact directly with Germans. A kind of sickening dread replaced the earlier spark of hope, but it must be done. She must take this gift that had been handed to her. "I have no reservations."

"You are certain?"

She nodded queasily. Something in her silent agreement

seemed to strike the right chord, because he said, "All right. We will try this, but I make no guarantees. You begin tomorrow night. Then we will see what we will see."

Now the questions popped into her head, and the sickening dread nearly buckled her knees. Somehow, though, she managed a sort of muffled, "Thank you."

"Go away now." He flapped a hand in her direction. "I have mixers to prepare."

She did as he requested, moving quickly.

"Camille, a moment, please." Vivian took her arm before she could protest. "Come with me. Up to my room."

She blinked in surprise. "Now?"

"I wish for you to style my hair. I have dinner tonight with, well—" she made a face "—it doesn't matter with whom."

Torn between curiosity and duty, Camille admitted, "My break is nearly over."

"I'll alert your supervisor you're with me."

When they arrived at Vivian's room, the American pulled a key from her coat pocket, opened the door, and stepped aside to let Camille enter first.

She was struck all over again by the differences in the two rooms. The entryway wasn't nearly as grand as the woman's former suite. No marble, but also no harsh chill in the air. The room itself was empty except for a few pieces of furniture that had seen better days two decades ago. Still up to the Ritz's high standards, but with a lived-in elegance that spoke of old-world charm.

"Wait here while I hang up my coat and call downstairs to let your supervisor know where you are. I'll only be a minute."

That minute turned into five, and when Vivian returned, her hair was out of its pins and hanging unadorned at her shoulders. She'd changed into a light blue robe belted tightly at her waist, and she sat at the vanity table. Familiar with the routine, Camille took her place behind the American and caught her gaze in their shared reflection. "Thank you for speaking on my behalf with Monsieur Meier." She needed to get that out of the way. "I'm in your debt."

"I assume you need money." She brought out the words without so much as a nod to delicacy. "That's why you asked for the extra work."

"I approached other departments first."

"I see."

What did she see, Camille wondered, this woman with more money than she could spend in ten lifetimes? Something of her thoughts must have shown on her face, because Vivian spun around and faced Camille directly, watching her closely, cool and confident, but also with something inexplicable in her eyes. A sort of unspoken compassion that had been absent in their previous interactions. No one looked at her that way anymore. Her mother had, once upon a time, before the burden of raising four daughters on her own had broken her.

Suddenly, Camille felt undone, a pale, shallow version of herself. And she couldn't stop herself. She wept a little, soft, hopeless tears she could not hold back.

"Oh, my dear, dear girl. What is this? Tears? No, no, this will not do. Come now." She stood and took Camille in her arms. "I did not mean to upset you."

"I—I— It's—" She couldn't seem to speak past her shame. She pulled away from the comforting embrace and crossed her arms at her waist. She tried to make herself smaller, invisible even, anything to stop the tears and the humiliation that came with them.

"It's the Germans," Vivian guessed. "The idea of serving them. It scares you."

"Well, yes," Camille admitted, and more tears fell. A river of them, streaming down, down her cheeks, making her feel weak and needy and desperate to unburden herself. "But also, no. I am not afraid of them for myself." But for her sister? Rachel? Others like them.

"I don't understand. So, you will explain it to me." Vivian

guided her to a chair and, applying soft pressure on her shoulders, urged Camille to sit. Kneeling before her, she took her hands. "You know the secret I have hidden behind the armoire in my former suite, and you have carried this burden well. Now you will let me carry one of yours."

Camille nearly snorted. Hiding a few furs and pretty baubles from greedy Germans was not the same as hiding Jacqueline's condition from men seeking to build a master race. And yet what this woman offered, this momentary relief from carrying her burdens alone, tugged at her. Made her crave to share her suffering. A new sense of desperation made her reckless. "It's my sister. She's ill."

The words were out before she could stop them, and now it was only shame she felt, the shame of betrayal. What did she know of this woman? Nothing, really.

"I'm so very sorry."

Camille heard the sincerity, but she also knew words were easy to say, hard to mean.

"What have the doctors told you?"

There'd been no doctors. Her mother had been adamant. No one was to know about Jacqueline's condition. They'd lost enough customers due to her father's erratic behavior. They couldn't lose more. Considering the Nazis' policies on mental health, the stakes were now higher.

No, Camille realized, no one was to know about Jacqueline. Not even this woman. This stranger. She'd already said too much, but Vivian was waiting for an answer to her question. "Her condition, it's not treatable."

Instead of probing for details, Vivian simply asked, "Was she born this way?"

"It started with my father. After he came home from the Great War." She struggled to keep her tone neutral. "He wasn't the same. He'd...changed."

Vivian nodded, and in her eyes was a sort of knowing, no

judgment, no condemnation. "We called it shell shock. I saw it often." Her gaze turned distant, sad. "Too often."

"You... How?" Had her own father suffered, or possibly her husband?

"I was a combat nurse with the American Red Cross in the last war. The condition manifested itself in various ways. There were similarities between patients. Also, differences."

Nothing about Vivian Miller would have led Camille to believe she'd once treated men like Camille's father. The rest of the story was tumbling out of her mouth before she could stop herself. Her father's bouts of melancholy, his fits of anger, the confusion and nightmares, the disappearing for days, returning no better, sometimes worse. The attempts at ending his own life.

"He eventually succeeded," she said, very calmly, very slowly, keeping her own role in the tragedy out of the narrative.

Vivian looked at Camille with genuine pain in her gaze, a sort of tragic understanding, and she had the disquieting impression that the woman saw through her deception, all the way to the truth of her negligence. That she'd abandoned her baby sister in the care of a madman. "Oh, Camille." Vivian squeezed her hands. "Tell me you weren't there. Tell me you didn't witness your father's death."

"Not me, my sister." She blurted out the rest of the story, including her own culpability.

"You could not have known your father would choose that day to take his own life."

"I should have known. How did I not know?"

Vivian stood, placed her hands on her hips. "This is your burden. You blame yourself for your father's death, and your sister's condition, all because you couldn't prevent this tragedy."

She nodded, stunned this woman, this stranger, had summed up her pain so succinctly. "Because of my selfishness, my sister suffers the same as my father. If the Nazis decide to target people like Jacqueline here in France, as they do in Germany, they will take her away. They will hurt her. They will…" The rest of what she meant to say dissolved into soft, quiet sobs.

"Who knows of her condition?"

"Only my family. Her previous caretaker, who has left the country, and now you."

"So she is safe."

Camille nodded. "For now."

"Promise me, Camille. Promise me you will let me know if the situation changes."

"I…I promise."

She was still trying to sort through why this woman cared, when she found herself tucked into Vivian's embrace. "You are not to blame."

She barely heard the soft proclamation. Her guilt had become a part of her, ingrained into every piece of her body and soul. There was room for little else.

"Camille, listen to me." Vivian set her at arm's length and stared into her eyes. "What happened to your father and sister were tragic accidents. You are not to blame."

Her mother had said something similar. Two women, different in every possible way, but one. They'd taken Camille into their arms and said the words she'd wanted—needed—to hear for five long years. *It's not your fault. You are not to blame.*

If only she believed them.

Chapter Thirteen

Vivian

1 September 1940.
Hôtel Ritz. Paris, France.

Vivian wasn't especially hungry when she entered the restaurant. Her mind was too full of Camille's pain and the memories she herself carried from the front lines. War was an ugly business that left men wounded in ways that didn't show until after the weapons were laid down. They suffered terribly. Their families suffered. All because men like von Bauer and his covetous *Führer* wanted more land, more power, more everything.

This current war was not like the last. The battlefield was vastly different, as was her role. She wasn't to provide healing. She was to fight in a new and different way. Tonight was only the beginning. She'd arrived early, one step ahead of her opponent. A defensive move. The man was no vapid socialite looking to trip her up. Von Bauer could do far worse than skewer her name among the social elite.

The maître d'hôtel met her with his usual smile beneath his thin mustache. Very French, but also very affected. "Will madame be dining alone?"

"There will be one more." She scanned the room. "I'm early."

"Very good." He reached for two menus and tucked them against his chest with military precision that was no doubt meant to impress his German diners. "You will follow me."

At a table for two, he pulled out her chair and set the gilt-edged menu before her. The final piece of theatrics involved a flick of his wrist as he unfolded the crisp napkin with its mono-grammed *R* and handed it to her to place in her lap.

A black-clad waiter appeared next and began filling the empty water glasses from a crystal pitcher. With a brief nod and a promise to return shortly, he was gone.

Alone, Vivian allowed the music of cutlery and the soft lilt of a distant violin to flow over her. She circled her gaze around the restaurant, her eyes landing on familiar faces. So. She would not be the only woman dining with the enemy. Most of the men had left their uniforms behind, favoring black tuxedos and white ties.

Vivian also noted a few French dignitaries preening beside them, and one oily US ambassador. William Bullitt should not be here in the Ritz. He should not be in Paris at all. He should be in Vichy supporting, or rather monitoring, the new French government. He remained in Paris instead, hobnob-bing with Nazis.

Like you. Vivian could hear her husband's voice in her head, urging her to pack up what was left of her belongings and re-turn to America. To what end? No one would welcome her. If they did, they would not do so graciously. In Paris, at least she had a chance to do some good. *And get yourself killed.* Rupert's voice again, reminding her just how much she missed him.

She closed her eyes, feeling his presence practically fold-ing around her, as real as if she were wrapped tightly in his arms. Not dissimilar to how she'd felt pulling Camille into her arms and letting the girl cry out her pain. The girl's tragic story reminded Vivian of her days as a nurse when much of her duties entailed giving soldiers a chance to vent their fears of never healing.

Vivian would like to think she'd given Camille comfort. It was hard to know. The girl had swallowed her sorrow quickly. She'd then dried her eyes and had styled Vivian's hair in silence. Neither had spoken about the tragedy of her father's death, not then, nor when Vivian sent the girl away with a sizable tip. The money, she knew, was appreciated. But she hoped she'd given Camille something more. A moment of peace.

She felt eyes on her again. It was a curious sensation, a prickle of warning in the back of her throat. She knew who was watching her. Yes, well. Let him stare. Let him marvel over the glorious waterfall of red curls Camille had created so expertly.

The enemy had his weapons, and so did Vivian.

Slowly, she opened her eyes and found herself staring into a pair of piercing ice-blue eyes, so light they were nearly colorless. Much like his hair, also pale, also colorless. The quintessential Aryan. Up close, she could see his age, somewhere near her own, perhaps a few years younger. He was undoubtedly attractive; she'd noticed that in the café, and in the hotel later—and like both of those times, female eyes watched him as hungrily as he watched Vivian.

"Good evening, *Herr Sturmbannführer*."

"Such formality."

"I don't know your full name." The sudden animosity she felt for this man, it stole her breath. "I know only your rank."

He stepped forward, leaned down, and said, "SS *Sturmbannführer* Hans-Dieter Gunther von Bauer." In perfect French, he added, "My friends call me Diti or *der Rab*."

She lifted her eyebrows. *"Der Rab?"*

He bent further, still quite tall, with the height of an athlete and, oh, how she disliked him. "It means *raven*, and you never told me your name."

"I think you know who I am."

"Vivian Miller, the American widow my colleagues call *Snedronningen*."

Unfamiliar with the German term, she waited for him to explain.

"The Snow Queen. That glorious villain from Hans Christian Andersen's fairy tale."

"I'm familiar with the story."

Still, Vivian went pale. The Germans had given her a nickname that linked her with a morally ambiguous witch who possessed the ability to manipulate ice and snow. They thought her a woman with a frozen heart living alone in her palace, separate from the world, untouchable, in a battle between good and evil.

The Snow Queen versus the Raven. The witch pitted against the harbinger of death. Vivian's cold to von Bauer's hot. Her iron will to his sinister agenda. Good versus evil, only one of them surviving the battle.

He sat and reached for the water glass with his left hand. She saw it then, the silver ring encircling the third finger on his left hand. The swine was married.

Why had she expected anything different?

She turned her gaze to her plate, either that or let him see her disgust. In a rush, Vivian saw her future flash before her, the loss of her soul, banishment, ultimately death, all because of this wicked man who'd set his mind on having her. She was not so naive as to think he desired a platonic relationship. "What else do your friends say about me?"

"They say…" He lifted the water to his lips, drank slowly. "You are a woman who knows how to get what she wants. In that, we are the same."

Of course he would think she was an opportunist. Like most men with power, he saw in her what he knew to be in himself.

The waiter appeared as if out of mist, and von Bauer ordered a bottle of champagne—from one of the grandest French winemakers. Vivian suspected he received an outrageous discount for the wine, as he did for the suite he'd stolen from her. She felt dirty, sitting here with such a man. When the waiter returned and poured the golden liquid, von Bauer rattled off their orders, a piece of rare meat for each of them, smothered in crisp *pommes frites*—the French version of steak and potatoes. Rupert's favorite. Vivian felt even dirtier, the kind of sullied sensation that could never be fully washed away with water and soap.

"May I ask why you chose to remain in Paris when so many Americans left?" He leaned forward. "You share this with me, and I will tell you something about me very few know."

Oh, he was a clever one, she thought, curling her hand into a fist, and nonchalantly setting her chin on top. Already interrogating her. She sorted through possible responses quickly, choosing, discarding, landing on the simple truth. "This is my home."

"You mean, Paris is your home, or the Ritz?"

She told herself to remain calm, stick with the truth. "Both."

She did not expand. He did not press. But again, she felt the weight of his stare. "Tell me, *der Rab*—" she would never call him Diti, too intimate "—what brings you to Paris?"

"I go where my *Führer* sends me."

She could see the pride dancing in his eyes, thick and bold. A man of ambition, who moved in circles with the most important men in the Third Reich. "Adolf Hitler personally sent you to Paris?"

"I have been assigned an important project in Drancy."

This, here, now, was her opening. The chance to uncover useful information about the Nazi agenda in France. She should take it. She must. She would. She did. "I don't know much about that section of Paris. What about Drancy has attracted *Herr* Hitler's interest?"

He didn't answer right away, choosing instead to take a slow, measured sip from his champagne coupe. The look in his eyes was not so nice, and Vivian found herself hastily adding, "Never mind. I'm sure it's none of my business." She put an indiffer-

ent note to her voice. "We have each shared something of ourselves. What next?"

The change of subject had him lowering his glass. No longer
looking suspicious, he gave a slight hitch of his chin. "You see
that man over there, three tables over? The large one."

Her gaze settled on a fleshy, sweaty man holding court as
if he were a Roman emperor and the rest of the diners at his
table were his lowly subjects. He guzzled champagne between
impossibly large bites of food. He was rather grotesque in his
decadence.

A young effeminate man stood attentively behind him.

"That is *Herr Reichsmarschall* Göring, the *Führer's* second-in-
command, and general of the *Luftwaffe* air squadron."

Adolf Hitler's foremost lackey had finally arrived to take
over the Imperial Suite. The man was not what she would call
a model of military fastidiousness. Word was he had a notorious
addiction to morphine, among other things. "I have heard," she
ventured, "the *Reichsmarschall* has a penchant for pretty things."

"This is true."

If that was true, were the other rumors as well? Did Göring
enjoy wearing women's evening gowns, impossibly high heels,
and dancing with *his boys*?

The waiter chose that moment to deliver their steaks. She
tucked into her meal with far less enthusiasm than either Hitler's right-hand man or the Nazi at her table. When the plates
were cleared, she sat back and retrieved a cigarette from its silver case. She'd barely brought it to her lips, and von Bauer was
already reaching to her, lighter extended.

"Tell me about your husband."

She didn't want to speak about Rupert and couldn't think
why he would want to do so, either. She kept her answer simple. "He died of a heart attack."

"And you never remarried?"

"No."

The light in his eyes changed, turning lascivious and knowing, a man ready to play. "Perhaps," he began with a sly twinkle, "we should take this conversation upstairs to my suite."

Not tonight. *Not ever.* "I think a drink in the bar first."

"Of course." He stood, strolled to her side of the table, and helped her stand.

She let him guide her out of the restaurant in his nonchalant manner that made the moment seem less significant than it was. It did nothing to erase her nerves, nothing to erase the unsettling feel of his hot hand resting at the small of her back. She resisted making eye contact with the other diners, already knowing what she would see. Curiosity, judgment, and, in some cases, vindication that they weren't the only ones cozying up to a German.

There was jealousy in several pairs of female eyes, misplaced envy that Vivian had captured the attention of such a beautiful male specimen.

How little they knew her.

She had no desire to land the role of von Bauer's mistress. She planned only to use this relationship to gather information for the war effort. She didn't let herself think about what she would have to do to get this information. A friendship, that was all, a little flirting perhaps. Nothing nefarious. Nothing that would dishonor her husband's memory.

Already she'd become proficient at lying. Even to herself.

They crossed through the reception area, where officers mingled with female guests and Frenchwomen who, Vivian knew, did not rent rooms in the hotel.

The scene was the same in the bar. More officers with their female companions mingling, smoking, most of them drinking Frank's famous Bee's Knees cocktail. It physically hurt to watch the jeweled hands lightly grazing uniformed arms. To catch the demure glances given through heavily kohled eyelids.

Again, she avoided eye contact, somehow especially gutted at the sight of the French actress Arletty draped on a chaise longue, gazing up at a young SS officer at least fifteen years her junior. The woman looked absolutely transfixed. In love, even. Appalling. So many had turned into collaborators. And now, Vivian's name would be thrown in among their ranks.

She couldn't do this.

You have no choice. Except that she did have a choice. She could leave Paris. She could choose self-respect over protecting innocent lives. Her own morality as opposed to turning a blind eye to persecution. When she thought of the people with so much to lose, she knew she would not walk away. It was inexcusable, the way these invaders took what didn't belong to them. For the moment, men like von Bauer held the power, but maybe not for long.

He pressed his lips to her ear. "We're going to have some fun, you and I." He slid his fingertip along her bare shoulder. "One roaring good time."

Not tonight, she vowed, flicking a glance in his direction, seeing the reality of what was to come in that bold, unwavering gaze. He was more than a little hungry for her. He was smitten. One step shy of obsession. Her creative attempts at putting him off had only served to make him want her more. A gross miscalculation on her part. Now, she would have to pay for her mistake.

She forced herself to breathe, and with as much dignity as she could muster, smiled at the man who'd targeted her for his mistress. Deep inside those cold blue eyes she saw the brutal end of her life, and something inside her said, *So be it.*

Chapter Fourteen

Rachel

3 October 1940.
Paris, France.

Rachel wasn't allowed to attend her accounting class. The instructor claimed she missed the deadline for registration. That wasn't the reason, she knew. She'd been denied because she was Jewish. Her once-imagined future was gone. Eradicated the day German soldiers marched on Paris, now swarming every part of the city, always with their guns holstered at their belts or their rifles slung over their shoulders. Swastikas taunted from doorways and rooftops and from treasured French monuments. Signs banning Jews from restaurants and cafés were everywhere. German films played in the cinemas. Strauss and Wagner blared from Radio Paris.

And Rachel, though her job was still secure, knew only quiet despair. She was not alone. Ever since the vandals targeted the Wozniaks' bakery, the mood in the Berman home had dissolved into hushed silences and frowns. The first toss of a rock and their world had gone gray. And yet Rachel's father still relied on the goodness of the French people. He believed the anti-Semitic policies were temporary and didn't apply to them.

They weren't religious, he argued. They were not affiliated with their local synagogue, or any synagogue, and thus they were safe from the decrees coming down from the Vichy government in their attempt to appease their captors.

Rachel wondered, where were the French people? Hiding in their homes, afraid and panicked they would be targeted next, or simply, conveniently, looking the other way?

Not *all* of them. There was Camille Lacroix, who stood by Rachel at work. If there was one, there were others. Hope. Rachel wondered whether that wonderful, slippery, bittersweet emotion ever truly died in a heart. Her optimism dropped the minute she sat at the breakfast table and saw the lone hunk of bread. She looked at her mother, the very heart of their family, sitting across from her. Something about the way she held her shoulders, stiff and set at an odd angle, didn't feel right. A sort of waiting hovered in the air. "Where is the rest of the family?"

"Basia wanted to get a head start on her sewing. Srulka is at school, and your father—" she paused, looked away, sighed "—he wanted to speak with Chaskiel Perelman."

"Why would Papa need to consult with the other tailor?"

"Another decree was passed by the French government."

Rachel's gaze dropped to the slip of paper resting on the scarred table between them. It looked official. She craned her neck, trying to read the words, and gasped at what she saw written in dark lettering across the top. *Statut des Juifs.* Law on the status of Jews. "What does it mean?"

There was such sorrow on her mother's face as she pulled the folds of her threadbare wrap tighter around her shoulders, and Rachel knew whatever was written beneath the caption was not good. "The Vichy government has defined what makes a person a Jew."

No! Rachel reached for the paper and, pulling it closer, skimmed the ordinance.

Her mother did nothing, absolutely nothing, as Rachel read the definition aloud. "'A person belonging to the Jewish religion or having more than two Jewish grandparents is considered a full-blooded Jew.'"

The ordinance also instructed that all people meeting this description living in the Occupied Zone must report to their local police station and register as Jews no later than the twentieth day of October. All Jewish-owned businesses were required to affix a sign in both German and French by the end of the month that identified them as such. The German term JÜDISCHES GESCHÄFT at the top, and the French version EXTREPRISE JUIVE beneath. The worst, the very worst, was that the decree came not from the German but the French government. The oily bureaucrats lived in the Free Zone and yet made rules—laws—for Jews in the Occupied Zone.

Panic constricted Rachel's breathing. Everything she knew that was good and right in the world was slipping away each day Germany held power, and a collaborating puppet government followed their lead. She slapped the paper back on the table. The heat of her humiliation, her fury, shot her to her feet. "Surely, we won't submit to this."

"What choice do we have but to follow the laws set before us?"

There was something very, very wrong about her mother's quiet acceptance, and something hotter than shame in Rachel's heart. Fueled by her fury. Rebellion. "We resist, Mama. That's what we do. We don't obey. We don't register. We...we... *resist*," she said again.

Her mother sighed. "Our neighbors know us by name. They know who we are by the language we speak, by the clothes we wear and the food we cook. They know we are Jewish. One of them will report us to the authorities if we don't do it ourselves."

Bitterness was a flood washing through Rachel's veins. Everything that they were, every family member that had come before them, their ancestors, their *people*, all of it was cast in a dark light, a bruised shade of hate. "Then we will escape Paris. We will leave under the cover of night and make our way to the Free Zone and—"

"How will we do this? By train, on foot? There are checkpoints everywhere, where we would be required to show our identification papers."

Rachel moved to stand next to her mother, facing her, her fists clenched. "We can't just accept this," she hissed, her voice a screaming whisper.

"Your father will tell us what to do."

Rachel's heart went hard as stone, and she had to swallow several times to keep from saying words she could not take back. She was so angry. At the situation. At the French government. And, yes, also at her father for his blind trust in their silent neighbors.

What next? Would her family be forced out of their home? Already they were banned from most businesses. "It's not fair."

"No. It is not."

Rachel lowered her head. Her eyes fell on the uneaten piece of toast, and she thought about the restrictions on food and fuel and even clothing. Necessities that required coupons and then waiting their turn to purchase even the simplest of items they'd once taken for granted.

"Your father is head of our *mishpokhe*, our family. He wishes for us to register together and so we will."

"When?"

"He will tell us what day."

Rachel nodded, immediately feeling a sense of doom. Her eyes shut of their own accord, and the air tightened in her lungs. But she sat back down and, saying not a word, attacked her meager breakfast with single-minded intent. From beneath her lowered lashes, she studied her mother. She looked so defeated. "What can I do to ease your burdens?"

"You are doing it," her mother said simply. "You are working at the hotel. The money you bring home is important to our family."

Her wages came at a cost. Rachel thought about the treatment she received from the other chambermaids. They made snide remarks loud enough for her to hear. The slurs had been general at first. They'd become more personal ever since Madame Bergeron stopped calling her Rachel and referred to her only as The Jewish Girl.

The Jewish Girl. The name had stuck, and now the rest of her coworkers looked at her with sidelong glances, never directly. Never as if she were a person. Rachel lived with the insults. She just swallowed her anger and humiliation and lived with it.

To be fair, not everyone judged her. Some simply ignored her. And then there was Camille. Her friend. Her one and only friend.

Resolve, she felt it move through her, all the way to the hotel, where she did what she was told without argument. She cleaned the nasty toilets, scrubbed the dirty floors, changed bedsheets that carried stains better not questioned. None of it mattered. Nothing mattered but the wages she took home to her family.

At the end of her shift, arms aching, eyes blurry, she entered the locker room and sat on the wooden bench. She needed a minute. Just a minute, before heading home. The door opened, and in walked her supervisor. She came straight to Rachel, saying not a word, giving not a smile, and towered over her with a frustrated glare. Her large frame was hunched with exhaustion. Finally, she said Rachel's name. A first in months, but there was something mirthless in the tone. Maybe even a little bitterness.

Rachel quickly gained her feet.

"I need you to deliver this telegram to a room on the Rue Cambon side of the hotel. It's important you put the envelope in Madame Miller's hand directly. Do you understand?"

No, she didn't. This was not a task typically assigned to a chambermaid. But her supervisor was looking at her expectantly. "I'll deliver it right away."

"See that you do." This time there was no mistaking the coldness in the woman's voice, a frigid sort of displeasure she didn't try very hard to hold back.

Rachel accepted the yellow envelope and rushed out of the room. Madame Bergeron said something low and indiscernible, but her tone sounded biting and full of disgust. It didn't matter, she told herself. She had a job to do.

Vivian Miller opened the door with a dramatic flourish, clearly expecting someone else. She was wearing a dress made of green silk with gold thread woven through the fabric. Her hair tumbled past her shoulders in a gorgeous cascade of red curls, kind of wavy and full of dimension. Rachel didn't know what to think of the woman. Camille had only good things to say, and she trusted her friend's judgment. But the American dined with Germans and took tea with women who did the same.

She was certainly stunning, almost too beautiful. A light so bright she nearly burned, and Rachel realized she was staring. She cleared her throat. "A telegram has arrived for you." She thrust the envelope into the space between them. "I was told to place it directly into your hand. So, um—" she wiggled the paper "—here you go."

Confusion knit the American's eyebrows, pulling them into an inverted triangle that did nothing to detract from her beauty. "Doesn't a bellman normally deliver telegrams?"

Although Rachel was equally baffled, it wasn't her place to question decisions made by management. "Not this time."

The woman took the envelope, said a sort of *hmm*, then pressed a tip into Rachel's hand. Her expression turned soft, and kind, and Rachel sensed there was at least one person in the hotel besides Camille who saw her as a person. Not *The Jewish Girl*. Not a nameless chambermaid, but a living, breathing person, separate from her position.

There was only one way to respond. "Thank you."

On her return journey to the locker room, Rachel tried not to look left or right. She hated this darkened route down the back stairwell. The quiet of it, the emptiness, the way the walls seemed to press in on her. The air took on a heavy feel, cold and slightly ominous, and seemed to creep through her uniform. She shivered and, unable to stop herself, cast a glance over her shoulder.

Had the shadows grown longer? Picking up speed, she continued. She thought she heard a squeak of the floorboards, but another glance told her she was quite alone. Nevertheless, her heart gave a quick stutter behind her rib cage. To distract herself, she reviewed her brief encounter with the wealthy American. Was Vivian Miller trustworthy, as Camille seemed to believe? Was she someone Rachel could trust?

The answer was obvious. Rachel trusted no one in the hotel save Camille. This, she realized, was what it meant to be a Jew living in occupied France.

Chapter Fifteen

Vivian

3 October 1940.
Paris, France.

Vivian had tipped the chambermaid generously and sent her away with what she hoped was an unspoken assurance that she meant her no harm. She'd provided enough passports and visas to Jews to understand the sort of discrimination the girl suffered. Every day new ordinances were passed by both the Germans and the French. No longer an appeaser, Philippe Pétain, the leader of the Vichy government, was a collaborator. A sobering reminder of how far France's leadership had fallen into moral decay.

Vivian's fingers curled over the telegram, reminding her why the young chambermaid had come to her room in the first place. She stared at the familiar yellow envelope with the Western Union logo. No one from America sent her telegrams anymore, not since Rupert's estate had been settled years ago.

Frowning, she slipped her fingernail beneath the envelope's seal and pushed the flap aside. The words *Western Union Telegram* were splashed across the top of the paper, the bold text all but obscuring the company's logo beneath. The time stamp read:

1940 OCT 3 AM 10 33

Below that, also in bold type, was:

MRS VIVIAN MILLER STOP
THE HOTEL RITZ STOP
PARIS FRANCE STOP

Vivian scanned the rest of the message and gasped. "What? No! This can't be right."

She blinked several times, the words blurring, her stomach burning with an emotion she barely understood. The empty, terrible ache had no beginning, no end. Everything she'd built was gone. Wiped out with a single piece of paper sent by a Washington bureaucrat. Worse, so much worse, were the innocent lives that would be lost. Individuals, entire families, without a means of escape. Without hope.

Perhaps she'd misread. Yes, yes, that was it. She'd misread. She took her time on the second pass, digesting each word carefully.

YOUR FRIENDSHIP WITH HIGH-RANKING GERMAN SOLDIERS HAS COME TO THE ATTENTION OF YOUR GOVERNMENT STOP

YOUR BANK ACCOUNTS HAVE BEEN FROZEN INDEFI- NITELY AS WE LOOK INTO THE MATTER OF YOUR LOY- ALTY STOP

WE REQUEST YOU DISCONTINUE ALL PERSONAL RE- LATIONSHIPS WITH GERMAN SOLDIERS UNTIL FURTHER NOTICE STOP

UNTIL THAT TIME YOU WILL BE GIVEN AN ALLOW-
ANCE OF FIVE HUNDRED US DOLLARS A MONTH STOP

WILLIAM C WILSON
ASSISTANT TO THE SECRETARY OF WAR

Vivian's knees gave out, and she crumpled to the carpet, her legs twisting at an awkward angle. She hardly noticed. Her own government had turned her into a pauper, and for what? Because someone had seen her eating in the hotel with the despicable *der Rab* and had assumed she'd thrown her lot in with the Germans?

The injustice of the accusation burned her throat. The empty, terrible ache throbbed into a dark, bottomless hole inside her soul, swallowing light and time, narrowing down to one question.

Who had informed on her?

She read the telegram again, seeking a clue to his identity. Or hers. This time her mind roiled in a tangle of fury and disbelief. The lack of punctuation was the final gut punch. The American government had seized millions of her dollars, and they'd used the word *Stop* instead of periods and commas, all to save money. Punctuation, after all, cost extra.

Her legs began to throb, and she adjusted her position on the carpet.

The anger inside her ran deep, something that maybe had always been there, lying neglected and silent until now. Her father's fists hadn't pulled the rage to life. The snubs and dismissals from Rupert's friends and family hadn't touched it. But this insult? This betrayal? It was too much to bear. A low wail escaped her throat, rocketing through her. Her fingers closed into hard fists. The telegram crumpled under the added pressure.

She'd played by the rules. She'd taken her father's abuse, her mother's neglect, and had swallowed the pain of rejection from the social elite. Vivian was done. Just done. She would not let this stand. The US government would not steal what was hers.

Someone would hear what she had to say. Someone at the American embassy. Not Archie. He was a mere attaché. She would go to the top. Straight to the ambassador himself. With that thought came clarity, and suddenly she knew who'd betrayed her.

Mouth set, she found her coat, shoved on her gloves, pinned a hat on her head. Her outrage fueled her out the door and down the hall.

She kept her gaze focused straight ahead as she made the journey from her room to the first floor to the sidewalk outside. It was an easy ten-minute walk to the embassy. It took her only eight. She paused at the corner where Place de la Concorde met Avenue Gabriel and took a deep breath. It was still business hours. He would be in the four-story chancery building. She'd been here a few times and knew the way.

In no mood to play politics, she breezed past the guards stationed at the gate with a quick flash of her American passport. She stopped briefly at the reception desk to state her business—a personal matter—and her destination—the ambassador's office. The man with the clipboard would alert Bullitt of her arrival.

The click of her heels on the tile matched the staccato of sound in her ears, hammers to nails. Her rapid pace earned her sidelong glances, but again, she sailed past the guard stationed outside the ambassador's office with a smile and a nod of acknowledgment. He didn't try to stop her. So, yes, the man at the front desk had alerted the ambassador of her arrival.

It wasn't until she was pushing into Bullitt's inner sanctum that she found real resistance. His secretary scurried around her and barred the way with his skeleton-thin body. "Mrs. Miller, you cannot—"

"Oh, but I can." And she did.

William Christian Bullitt Jr., the United States Ambassador to France, sat behind his massive wooden desk. He did not stand to greet her. He did not even glance up from his paper-work. He was a hard, severe-looking man with a large forehead, dark unemotional eyes, and thick, bushy brows that seemed always scrunched in a perpetual frown. In his youth, he'd been a freethinker and somewhat of a radical. He was a conservative now and had the aura of a prison warden. He'd held this position since 1936 and, like Vivian, was firmly established in Parisian society. Their paths had crossed often, though they weren't friends.

He was once a close friend with President Roosevelt. However, they'd had a falling-out when Bullitt insisted on remaining in Paris after the German invasion instead of following the French government to Bordeaux to look after US interests there. That had been a mistake on his part. His career was on the skids, and Vivian suspected he'd played a role in her current impoverished state, seeking a way to get back into Roosevelt's good graces.

It made the most sense.

Bullitt ate in the Ritz's restaurant. He swilled drinks in the Little Bar. He'd been there that first night she'd dined with von Bauer, and many times before and after. It was the before that she remembered now. Bullitt had made a clumsy pass at her. Her skin crawled with the memory of his hot breath on her cheek, the sticky hands on her back. She'd scorned him, and now he'd taken his revenge.

Without being asked, she took a seat in the chair facing his desk and cleared her throat.

Finally, he looked up.

"Mrs. Miller." He spoke in English, using his upper-crust accent that pegged him as a man from Philadelphia. "I have an enormous amount of work to do before I leave for the day. Important work, you understand. This is a delicate time for our country."

He was trying to give her the brush-off. With a flicker of irritation, she sat back, physically settling in. "I'll be brief."

He, too, sat back, as if admitting defeat. "You have five minutes to state your business."

"I only require two." She retrieved the telegram and slapped it on the desk.

Bullitt didn't even look down, but a change had come over his face. It was that cagey look of triumph that confirmed her suspicions. The rat had informed on her.

Now she wanted to hear it from his own lips. Those thin, twitching lips he kept firmly pressed together. Vivian marshaled her resentment and pressed on. "I received an interesting telegram today." With the tip of her red-lacquered fingernail, she scooted the nasty piece of business across the polished wood of his desk. "Any thoughts you wish to share?"

He pulled the telegram toward him, bringing it closer to the lamp.

Vivian waited while he read.

When he finally looked up, she saw the unrestrained glee before he masked it behind a bland expression. Oh, yes, this was her guy. And Bullitt was enjoying this moment, thinking he held all the power. Maybe he did. Maybe this was a wasted trip.

Even so, Vivian wasn't leaving until he explained himself. "You have nothing to say? No explanation to give as to why the American government questions my loyalty?"

"Perhaps if you dined less often with Nazis, and kept to your side of the Hôtel Ritz, the American government would trust you more."

Vivian gritted her teeth, feeling a mix of frustration and annoyance. "So says the man who also dines with Nazis in the same restaurant, nearly every night of the week. Tell me, Bill, were *your* assets frozen? Were *you* also turned into a pauper overnight?"

His mouth opened and closed like that of a gaping fish. Clearly, she'd shocked him with her directness. He recovered quickly and made a scoffing sound deep in his throat. "You are not a pauper, Vivian. Your money sits there, untouched, merely frozen, and lest you forget…you have been given a sizable allowance."

"Five hundred dollars a month is not a sizable allowance. It's an insult."

"Many in Paris live on less."

He had a point. But so, however, did she. "My money was good enough to fund a hospital for soldiers wounded in battle."

"The hospital is for French soldiers. America is not in this war."

We should be. "How am I to continue my various—" she paused "—let's call them philanthropic efforts without access to my money? *My* money, Bill, not to put too fine a point on this."

He sighed, shook his head. "Vivian, Vivian, you must know how your friendship with von Bauer looks to the rest of the world."

"Do tell." She could not keep the sarcasm out of her voice. "How does my friendship look to the rest of the world?"

"The US government cannot risk your money falling into the hands of a known Nazi. Whether by accident, intentional, or something in between, you will not be allowed to aid the fascist war effort."

Her own government thought her weak-willed at best, capable of treason at worst. The realization struck like a blow. She wanted to storm out, but she couldn't. Her feet were made of lead. And her voice, when she spoke, came out hoarse and slightly tortured. "You know that would never happen."

"Do I? You have been seen cavorting with the enemy all over Paris. You have not hidden this relationship. You flaunt it in public."

"I am not his mistress."

"Yet."

She gasped at his audacity. Had she been sitting closer, she would have slapped him for the offense. "You go too far."

"I understand you're upset."

He had no idea. "Do you know how distasteful it is to live

among Nazis? Do you know how humiliating it is to sit with those vipers in their own nests and pretend it is exactly where I want to be? I do this to gather information that I pass on to people who fight in secret."

"Who are these people?"

Oh, no. No, no. "You did this, Bill. You turned me into a villain to forward your career. You have told tales about me, adding an ugly spin no doubt, and have now tied my hands."

He sighed, finally, pushing the piece of paper across the desk in her direction. "What's done is done."

That was all he had to say? She decided to be more direct. "How am I to continue helping people escape persecution?" Faces flashed through her mind. The ones she'd saved. The ones waiting on passports and visas and identification papers. "How?"

He shrugged, pushing the paper a smidgen closer. "It is in your own power to remedy the situation. The instructions are right there in the telegram."

"I am to discontinue my friendship with high-ranking German soldiers. Even though I've explained why I seek them out?"

"Excellent. You know what must be done. Now, if you will excuse me…"

Dismissed so casually, Vivian left the embassy with her head spinning, her heart heavy, her resolve growing. There had to be another way to continue her work with the refugees. She would find it, without her extensive bank account or her government's help.

When she arrived back in her room, a rush of tears wanted release. She refused to give in to them. Her anger was another matter. That she relished. Let it sharpen her thinking.

She had no real money to live on, a mere five hundred dollars a month. Barely enough to cover her hotel fees. She looked around the room, noting the creases in the pink wallpaper, the scuffs on the furniture, the missing threads in the carpet. The Nazis had stolen her home. They'd stolen her property.

The Americans had stolen her money. But it wasn't over. It was never over when a strong woman was pushed to her limit.

So she didn't have access to her money? She still had assets, a veritable fortune in this room but also hidden in another. And that, she realized, was her answer. A private liquidation sale to the very men she'd been accused of befriending. Poetic justice or revenge, what did it matter? Vivian would have the money she needed to continue her secret work.

It was not the way she wished to honor her husband's legacy. It was, however, a way to battle the darkness creeping into her heart.

Chapter Sixteen

Camille

October 1940.
Eighteenth Arrondissement. Montmartre. Paris, France.

Not your fault. Not to blame. The words sounded in time with her footsteps as Camille half jogged, half sprinted up the stairs to her apartment. It was bleak and cold inside the building, and her back was on fire from working two shifts at the hotel and another half shift in the bar.

Not your fault.

Almost two months had come and gone since Vivian repeated her mother's words. She'd spoken with an understanding that came from experience rather than empty platitudes, and still, Camille regretted confiding in the American. It wasn't that Vivian treated her any differently. Yet Camille's throat constricted every time they interacted, her guilt always with her. No amount of kindness could erase the tragedy of her father's death. That was Camille's reality, her truth.

She moved deeper into the apartment, her legs hardly steadier than her nerves, and tried not to let the memories come. But they were there, circling around in her head, tethering her to the past. Mouth pressed in a grim line, she moved to the couch, sank down, and leaned her head against the worn fabric.

The familiar sound of rat claws told her she wasn't alone. She could hardly muster the energy to care. Every muscle ached with fatigue, and her skull felt stuffed with thick wool. She shut her eyes. An insistent knocking startled her upright, immediately transporting her to that morning when Madame Kauffman came seeking her help. Camille hadn't thought of her neighbor since. Her brow furrowed, wondering if the woman had been reunited with her son.

Camille would never know. That, she realized, was why she'd let herself forget. She simply couldn't bear more bad news. The knock came again.

Sighing, she stood, relieved herself of her shoes, and shuffled across the scarred floorboards without making a sound.

"Mademoiselle Lacroix? Are you in there?"

The familiar voice of the concierge sounded strange and oddly urgent coming through the slab of wood between them. "I am here."

"Another letter from Dinan has come for you."

Her first thought was of Jacqueline, and Camille flung open the door. She had no time to greet Madame Thibodeaux before the woman was pushing into the apartment. Her gaze chased over the clutter Camille was always too tired to put into order. She saw the judgment in her landlady's stiffened shoulders. Her audacity was nearly too much, but then Camille noticed the envelope in her hand, and she had a fleeting image of Nazis seizing her sister, of loading her onto a train bound for Berlin, or worse, a containment camp in an undisclosed part of Germany.

The worry grew fangs, and all Camille could do was wait out Madame Thibodeaux. From experience, she knew she would get nothing out of the woman until she'd taken her inventory. Vaguely, she noticed how the concierge moved through the apartment, confidently avoiding the hazards—the floorboard that stuck out, the carpet's rolled edges. Clearly, she'd been here before, probably more than once, conducting a similar search.

Camille could look for another building and—she sighed—confront the same issue. Already, stories were running rampant about the corruption of concierges. They collaborated with the Nazis and were paid well for informing on their tenants. Sometimes they charged their tenants for their silence. Often they played both angles. A nasty business all around.

Finished with her inspection, the older woman faced Camille directly, hands parked firmly on her hips, the envelope crushed between her fingers. "You keep an untidy home, mademoiselle. For a professional housekeeper, I would expect better."

The insult barely registered. Camille was too focused on the envelope bearing her mother's handwriting. "You mentioned a letter from Dinan? Is that it?"

The woman looked down at the balled-up envelope in her hand, gave a little shrug, said, "Oh," and made the transfer with a shove in Camille's general direction.

Camille fumbled with the letter, nearly dropping it, and waited for the other woman to take her leave. Her feet remained firmly in place, and so, with her own little shrug, Camille directed her attention to the letter, noting the envelope had been opened with only mild finesse. She wasn't sure if her landlady had read the letter, or the Germans.

Please, Maman, *may you have not written anything to alert the censors.*

She read quickly, relieved to find her mother had been careful, wisely choosing to be vague, almost too vague. Camille wasn't sure what she meant to say. A thin tendril of frustration wound through her mind, into muscle, and even into bone. *Oh,* Maman.

"Trouble at home?"

Camille flinched at the question. She wasn't sure how to answer. The only thing she was sure of was that her sister needed her. The desire to see Jacqueline again was strong and complicated, a layered feeling that painted every thought with self-reproach.

She needed to speak with her mother. Now. That meant swallowing her pride and asking this woman for a favor. "Madame Thibodeaux. May I use your telephone?"

It seemed the concierge might refuse, but she shocked Camille, agreeing easily, then adding the reminder, "They will be listening."

Camille nodded, thinking war made the strangest of allies. "Come with me."

Inside her sitting room, the woman pointed Camille to a black telephone sitting on a waist-high bookcase decorated with fancy trinkets. A few she recognized as once belonging to Madame Kauffman. She wanted to sigh. War might create unexpected allies, at unexpected moments, but it also created thieves. In this instance, both were true at the same time. The concierge was neither completely decent nor wholly immoral.

Camille picked up the telephone receiver. Angeline answered on the third ring. When Camille identified herself, she said, "You're calling about Jacqueline."

"Yes."

"Let me get *Maman*."

A muffled sound followed, and then her mother's voice sounded in her ear. There was no greeting. Just: "Do not come home, Camille. She is already gone."

The news came like a punch to the throat. All the air whooshed out of her lungs, nearly choking her. *Too late. I am too late.* She snatched in a breath. Another. Several more. "Gone where?"

"Rennes."

Closer than the facility in Lyon, to a well-known public psychiatric hospital run, for now, by French doctors. How long would that be the case? Anger bled into Camille's heart, joining another emotion already flickering there. Guilt. Always, she lived with the guilt. How many times would she fail Jacqueline? Her eyes darted to Madame Thibodeaux, who made no pretense of giving Camille privacy.

Nevertheless, she had to ask. Had to know. "When?"

"A week ago, Camille," her mother said patiently. "It's an exceptional facility and close to home. The fees are reasonable, and the doctor is a good man. I made sure of this. She will be safe there."

No one was safe in occupied France. "Who is her doctor?"

"Pierre Garnier."

A French name meant Jacqueline was in the care of a French doctor. He could be old. He could be young. Competent, or not. He could have an agenda, be aligned with the Nazis, as so many were in Paris. People disappeared all the time and never came back. Many feared they were next. With Jacqueline, the fear was very, very real.

Camille had left her sister with a man unworthy of that trust. She would not do so again. This Pierre Garnier could be many things. There was only one way to know for certain.

Rennes, Brittany, France.

After a long week and a half of anxious thoughts, Camille made the journey to Rennes. It had taken some creative negotiating with her two bosses for time off. Now, as she stood on shaky legs before an iron gate twice her height, she wondered if coming had been a mistake. What if she found Jacqueline worse? How would she live with that guilt on top of all the rest?

She peered beyond the meticulously tended courtyard, where the Guillaume-Régnier Hospital loomed large and impressive against the blue sky. A normal-looking building behind the wrought-iron fence. No concrete walls, no barbed wire, just a lovely-looking structure that boasted wide bay windows on the ground floor. No turrets or gargoyles anywhere to be found, just a pretty ivory facade and a rooftop that mimicked the buildings in Paris.

There were no Nazi guards, either, not here at the gate, or at the entrance of the hospital. No Nazi flags flew over the building. The morning air was still and calm, and she gave her name to the man at the gate. He checked his clipboard, nodded once, and, smiling, directed her to a narrow door cut right into the fence. She stepped through, then followed the gravel walkway to the visitor's entrance.

A woman sat behind glass in the sterile-looking reception area. The walls were white. The sitting chairs were white. The marble floor was white. The woman, however, was dressed in all black but for her crisp *white* shirt. The ensemble made her look as though she'd been plucked from an office building. "My name is Camille Lacroix. I have an appointment with Dr. Garnier."

The receptionist referred to a ledger of some kind, her fingertip trailing down the page. "Ah, yes, Camille Lacroix, here you are." She lifted a telephone, spoke something unintelligible in the receiver, then set it down again. "He'll be with you shortly."

"Thank you."

Camille avoided the chairs and wandered around. When one minute turned to five, then seven, she sat, stood, walked around again. Then she saw him, a man in a white coat over a charcoal-gray suit. He was not what she expected, and her breath came in a quick, sharp rasp. He was so young, past twenty but not yet thirty. The lines of his broad shoulders suggested he'd been an athlete once, and his face had the features of a grown man who'd been a rather charming boy. The cut of his jaw was severe, but not unattractive, and though there were lines of fatigue around his amber-colored eyes, there was also kindness in them, too.

That frustrated Camille on some deep level, a knotted emotion she couldn't quite parse into consumable pieces. There was something otherworldly about the sensation, something that hinted at a deeper emotion she knew not to explore.

"Mademoiselle Lacroix?"

"*Oui*, I am Camille Lacroix."

The lines around his eyes deepened with his smile. "I'm Pierre Garnier."

Again, she found herself captivated. She hadn't expected his voice to be so deep and soothing, like a balmy breeze. The thought came from nowhere, and another, equally confounding one, followed. There was something upright about this man that brought her comfort.

Camille wanted to breathe in his clean, pleasant scent. She'd been surrounded by women for so long, she'd forgotten how pleasant it could be simply to be near a man who saw only her, spoke only to her. He reached out his hand, jolting her out of the dreamlike unreality of her thoughts. His fingers were long and elegant, more suited to an artist than a man dedicated to ministering to the mentally ill, and Camille found herself wishing she'd met him under different circumstances, outside of war and the fear of Nazi bigotry.

"It's a pleasure to meet you, Dr. Garnier." She took the offered hand, surprised at the warmth curling through her as their palms met. Again, she experienced a sense of safety. It was too much. She pulled away quickly.

The abrupt move didn't faze him. "You will want to see your sister, but before I take you to her, I'd like to discuss her condition."

This was why she was here. So why did his request, asked in that soothing tone, make her think of Nazis, and bright lights, and interrogations? *Because you work among monsters who hide their evil behind smiles and veiled leers.* It made sense she harbored suspicions, when Jacqueline's future, her very life, depended on this man's goodness. "Of course."

"Follow me." He led her through a door she hadn't noticed in her wanderings. They ventured down a long corridor—more doors—another hallway—*more doors*—until, at last, he directed her into an office that made her think of a gentleman's study. Warm wood, plush chairs, a desktop full of papers and journals, writing utensils and pads, and books. They were everywhere. On shelves, on the desk, even the floor.

"How long have you been a doctor?" The question was out before she could contain it.

"Seven years."

"That long?" She'd expected half that and found herself reassessing his age. Thirty.

"Have a seat." He indicated that she take one of the two chairs facing his desk.

Outside in the hallway, Camille thought she heard voices, but this room was quiet, and again she found herself relaxing as she waited for him to walk around to the other side of the desk. He took the chair next to hers instead. "I know your time is short, so let's get right to it. Tell me about your sister."

There were so many ways to begin, so she started with the most important point she hoped to make today. "Jacqueline doesn't belong in a mental hospital."

"Where does she belong?"

Home. With me. But did she? Camille's days at the hotel were long and exhausting, and the city was overwhelmed with Nazi soldiers. "I don't know." She hated that she sounded defensive and panicked. *You are defensive and panicked.* "My sister isn't crazy."

"No, she's not."

Who was this man, this doctor, who was agreeing with everything she thought she would have to argue against? It was all so easy, a relief even, like a stolen hour with a friend. For a moment, Camille wanted to forget about the ugliness outside this comfortable office, where the world was scary and complicated and where she carried a stifling guilt that snaked into her dreams most nights. "What's wrong with my sister, Dr. Garnier?"

His gaze was suddenly an abyss. Dark, unreadable, yet oddly hypnotic. "Let me reiterate, Mademoiselle Lacroix, your sister is not mentally insane. She is, however, suffering from a malady we are only just beginning to understand. We don't have an official medical term for the condition, but I can tell you that her symptoms are not dissimilar to what we've seen manifested in some soldiers after returning from combat."

"Like my father."

"Yes. Exactly."

He knew. He knew what she'd done, and what she hadn't done. Clearly, her mother had been subjected to a similar conversation and had shared their family's secret. Deep, deep inside her soul, the place where Camille kept everything ugly and shameful, familiar guilt roared to life. "You know how my father died."

"Yes."

"And do you know that Jacqueline was there with him when he pulled the trigger?"

"I know that as well."

His matter-of-fact tone filled Camille with an otherworldly calm. The sensation wasn't based on anything she'd ever experienced before, a need to confess all, every bit of her culpability. "Are you aware, Dr. Garnier, that *I* left Jacqueline in my father's care that day?"

"I am." His eyes never left her face, and in his soft expression, Camille saw the woman she wanted to be. She also saw acceptance, and bone-deep understanding, and sorrow. Not for Jacqueline, but for her. Warmth spread in her heart, and she thought she might cry.

For years, she'd longed for someone to see past her mistake, to the woman underneath.

"Mademoiselle Lacroix, I know you are worried about your sister. Considering the world in which we live, your concern is warranted. But the burden of her illness is not yours to bear."

"I left her alone with him."

"No, you left your sister in the care of her father. Listen to me, mademoiselle. Please." This time, she didn't pull back when he reached for her hand. "You could not have known he would choose that afternoon to take his own life."

"I *should* have known. He seemed well before I left. He seemed happy playing jacks with her, but he wasn't okay. Why didn't I know he wasn't well?"

Something came and went in his eyes. Genuine pain, quickly blinked away, but Camille had seen it. Then he was placing his other hand on top of hers, one now below, the other above, and she'd never felt more cherished than in that moment with her hand nested inside his. "You couldn't have known, Camille."

She broke eye contact and turned her head away, certain he could see her desperate need to believe him. "Had I been home, maybe I could have prevented my father's death."

"You can't know that."

She lowered her head, studied their joined hands. She watched him out of the corner of her eye, noting how his midnight hair fell across his brow, how his eyes still showed pain and sorrow. There was a strange intimacy in that look, one that soothed the toxic brew of her worry and guilt. "I failed my sister."

"I believe the tragedy of your father's death left its mark on your sister. But I believe it left one on you as well."

"I…" She couldn't say more. No one had ever spoken of how her father's death affected Camille. Not even Camille herself. Suddenly, she couldn't pull air into her lungs.

"Let's take a break." He released her hands. "We'll visit your sister, and then, once you've seen her, we will finish our discussion."

Unfolding himself from his chair, he stood, slowly reaching his full height, which was considerable. She hadn't noticed that before. She let him draw her to her feet. There was a small scar on his left cheekbone. The imperfection on the otherwise handsome face made him seem normal, approachable.

He led her out of the office and down a long hallway with tiled floors and concrete walls. She walked slightly behind him, saying not a word, trying not to trip over her own feet as she took inventory of the hospital. She didn't really know what occurred within these walls.

Were chains hooked to the walls in some of the rooms? Were there hoses spewing icy cold water? Massive amounts of sedatives swallowed or pumped straight into collapsing veins?

As if he could read her mind, Garnier slowed his steps. As she drew alongside him, he said, "We are very progressive in our treatments."

Was there truth in his words? Or did he tell lies made of smoke that reflected off mirrors?

"We provide activities to soothe the troubled minds of our patients. There are games to play and puzzles to solve. The patients participate in crafts, and there is a garden meant for tending. Your sister prefers spending time outdoors. Come, I will show you."

They passed an elderly woman dozing in an armchair, her snores low and even. Another worked a puzzle. There was an air of normalcy about her, certainly nothing lunatic, but for her quiet humming. Outside, Garnier pointed Camille to a garden of colorful late-blooming flowers. And there, beneath a pretty pergola, was her sister.

Remembering their previous interaction, she approached the girl slowly, and sank to her knees. She hardly noticed the sharp bite of a twig beneath her left shin, or the wind that sent her hair in a wild tangle around her face. Her sister was calm, serene even. "Jacqueline."

The girl looked up, and Camille saw a sister she hardly recognized. Clear eyes, cheeks painted a healthy pink, lips smiling. "Camille? Is it really you?"

"It's me." Her voice sounded watery in her own ears, and then they were hugging.

Camille had seen the fence surrounding the hospital as a tool to trap her sister. Now she saw a different purpose for the metal and iron hinges. She saw a way to keep the Nazis out.

They spoke about the section of garden Jacqueline tended. They discussed the girl's sessions with Dr. Garnier. Each coherent sentence brought a new revelation. After a while, Camille said her goodbyes and followed the doctor back to his office.

"Thank you, Dr. Garnier. Thank you for giving me back my sister."

He didn't respond right away. "Today was a good day, but there is still much work to be done before she can go home."

"How long will it take to cure her?"

"It's hard to know, and *cure* isn't precisely the right term. There are new treatments, many of which have been tried with great success on soldiers suffering from battle fatigue."

Camille's mind went to torture tactics, and the sigh she pushed out shook a little. "You are referring to drugs, surgeries, and other barbaric practices."

His shoulders stiffened. "We practice the most humane treatments, mademoiselle. Drugs, sometimes, but only as a last resort. The rest, no. Not here."

Camille heaved another sigh, then took a hard swallow, as if working her throat might free the maelstrom of emotions swimming in her head. "What if the Nazis take this facility?"

Something like resolve came into his voice. "Your sister is safe under my care."

With those doctor eyes trained on her, their depths full of meaning, she sensed—*she knew*—he was saying far more with silence than with his words. But she needed to know. "The Germans, they oversee this hospital?"

"Not yet."

Not yet. But they could. Any day they could seize this hospital and take away the patients. The scene ran in Camille's mind, her sister being carted away, disappearing into the black void of Nazi policy toward the mentally ill. Distantly she felt her spine straighten, her chin lift, even as images drowned her in a panic so deep it felt as if she were breathing water.

Strong hands closed over her shoulders, pulling her back to

the now. "Your sister is safe with me, Mademoiselle Lacroix. I won't let them take her."

She closed her eyes, wishing she could believe him.

"I vow it to you now." He took her hands and pulled them to his heart. "I will protect your sister from the Nazis. This is my promise to you."

Camille opened her eyes, and when her gaze landed on his young, handsome face, she saw his truth. "I...I believe you."

They spoke awhile longer, mostly of the specifics concerning Jacqueline's care. Garnier promised to send weekly progress reports with an agreed-upon code that involved the use of gardening terms. Some of the procedures he suggested came with a fee, and it was Camille's turn to make a vow. "You will have everything you need to treat my sister properly."

Chapter Seventeen

Rachel

20 October 1940.
Paris, France.

On the last day for Jews to register at their local police station, at precisely seven o'clock in the morning, Rachel joined the rest of her family in the entryway of their apartment. They'd shared a silent, pitiful breakfast of stale bread and watered-down tea. An unfortunate start to the day, but what she would remember most was the contrasts. The bright autumn sun streaming through the window and the solemn mood of their gathering.

No one spoke. They'd held off registering until the last possible opportunity. Not because they'd needed to coordinate their various schedules, although that had played a factor, but because her father had been adamant they wait. As if putting off the loathsome task would somehow make the law disappear. It did not.

There was no escaping what they must do.

No escape, no escape, no escape. That was where Rachel's mind went on this bright, chilly morning, where it always went when she thought about the decrees and edicts the Vichy government issued, sometimes daily. Each one aimed at erasing yet another liberty from the Jewish people. Persecution was their way of life now. Citizenship had been rescinded for immigrants like her parents, no matter that they'd fully assimilated. It was criminal what the French authorities were doing to the Jews.

And still, Rachel's father believed if they obeyed every new law sent up from Vichy, they would be left alone. He actually, truly, believed that if they gave up their weapons and radios, and followed their rules, and renewed their identification cards to show their ethnicity, if they rode in the last car on the Métro, then they would be safe.

Clinging to a lie and calling it hope. That was what her father had done, was still doing, and what he'd taught the rest of his family to do. Except Rachel. She experienced oppression at her job and could not accept that doing so was right. No longer was she able to serve in the public places within the hotel. Soon, she would have no job at all.

What then?

Her mother bustled between each of her children in the same way she'd done when they were small, asking unnecessary questions: "Do you have your gloves? Your scarves? What about your identity cards?"

A half-hearted laugh slipped out of Rachel, brittle and dry. Of course they had their identity cards. By law, every Parisian sixteen and older was required to carry them, always.

As if reverting to the child he'd once been, Srulka spoke in the small, whiny voice he'd adopted back when he was a toddler. "I don't see why we have to register as Jews, Papa. We aren't even religious."

"This is not about religion," Rachel said before her father could respond. "It's our ethnicity that has, according to the Germans, turned us into contemptable creatures."

"It's not fair."

"No," their mother agreed, placing her hand on his cheek. If she'd meant to calm her son, she failed. He slapped her hand away with the petulance of the toddler he'd once been. "It's stupid."

"Do not speak to your mother in that tone."

Her father had stood silent and brooding prior to Srulka's outburst. Now he wore the mantle of the family patriarch, as austere as the black suit he wore as a sort of uniform. "It is for my customers," he would say in his defense when Rachel questioned the somber color. "It is not my place to outshine them, but to make them look their very best."

He was clear on this.

He'd also been clear about his unhappiness over leaving his shop unattended this morning. So single-minded, Rachel thought, wondering why he only considered the immediate present, never looking to the future. They were here, in this awful moment, still in Paris, undergoing yet another suppression of their basic human rights because he lived moment to moment. Always so sure everything would go back to normal once the Germans were defeated.

Rachel wanted to feel her father's confidence. She wanted his faith in their neighbors. But she understood, as her father did not, that to be a Jew in Paris was to be dirty and that she was somehow less than human. She felt it at work, when the other chambermaids turned away at the very sight of her, like she was a stain on their humanity.

Basia linked arms with her. "We will do this detestable thing today, and then it will be over, and we can go on with our lives."

Rachel sighed. Her sister seemed the least upset, and why not? Basia's boyfriend lived with his family in a gorgeous home on the elegant Avenue Victor-Hugo. His father was close friends with several high-ranking staff members in the German embassy. "I hope you're right."

"Of course I'm right. I'm the older, wiser sister who is never, ever wrong."

Rachel tried to laugh. The sound came out like a choked sob.

Ezra Berman placed his hat on his head, reached for the doorknob. "We go."

They left the apartment single file, her father at the front, her mother at the back, the rest of them in the middle, organized by order of birth. *Le commissariat de police* was seven blocks to the west and three blocks to the south of the family's apartment.

Already, the streets were crowded with Jews, all heading in the same direction. The throng so thick it looked like a shapeless mass. Apparently, the Bermans were not the only family who'd put off this detestable errand until the last minute. A foreboding swirled in the air, and quiet despair resonated from the crowd. So many unknowns.

The weather turned a half hour into their painfully slow journey. Rain oozed from the sky, a fine, cold mist that descended over the streets in a watery gray trickle. The line of Jews pressed on, moving silently in the gloom, their collective breaths huffing, their expressions grim.

A truck carrying German soldiers whizzed past, and a spray of water hit Rachel's cheek. Through the gaps in the crowd, she glimpsed the police station in the distance, where they would present their identification cards and be put on a list. What the authorities would do with that list, well, that was where Rachel's mind stopped.

She glanced at her father's black-clad back as he navigated around pools of dark muddy water. By the time they drew close enough to see the building's entrance, Rachel was wet and cold, and she could feel the water dripping past her collar, down the hollow of her spine. She shivered when she saw the men in charge. Not German soldiers, but French policemen. She had not imagined it would be local authorities herding them along. Insult upon insult.

With each hour that passed, the crowd grew larger, vying for a spot in the queue and pressing in from every angle. *Almost there*, she whispered to herself when they were but a block away, and yet so far. The rain continued to fall, as if the sky was weeping for the people who were being herded along like cattle.

Would this endless, humiliating torture never end?

The crowd condensed, moving as one solid pack at a pace more suitable for a funeral procession. The foul-smelling web of wet wool and sweating bodies shoved, pushed, and jockeyed for position, as if their miniscule efforts could hurry along the humiliating process. A hard jostle from behind sent Rachel's feet tangling over one another. For a half second, she lost her balance, and her grip slipped from Basia's arm. With a small gasp, her sister reached for her, caught her just before she dropped to the ground. A pause, a merging of gazes, where neither spoke of the despair in their hearts.

Rachel's gratitude shuddered past dry cracked lips in two simple words. "Thank you."

For a fleeting moment, Rachel allowed herself to close her eyes. Not to pray—she didn't have those words in her head—but to gather her inner fortitude. Basia's voice fell over her. "Don't worry, sister. We'll get through this together."

Together. As a single unit, the entire family rounded the final corner, *together*.

Once again, there were no German soldiers on the street, only French policemen in their blue tunics and stiff kepi hats, keeping order among the crowd with pokes from their batons.

The sound of labored breathing had Rachel looking to her mother. Ilka Berman's lips were raw from biting them, and when she tried to smile, her skin pulled apart the cracks, releasing small droplets of blood. Rachel was suddenly too tired to feel anything but love for this small, frail woman on the verge of breaking. Everything in her softened, and she looped her arm over her mother's shoulders.

She stole a discreet glance at the policeman closest to them. As if sensing her eyes on him, the tall, gawky man leaned forward, shoulders bunched, and looked straight at her. Panic seized her. The sensation felt as though a noose had been cinched around her neck and pulled too tight. She shifted in front of her mother, shielding her from the official's direct line of vision. The move proved a mistake. Her grip slipped. And then, her mother was gone. Just…gone.

She spun in a circle, searching, searching. Where was her father? Her brother?

Basia?

Helplessness washed over Rachel. There were too many of them to keep track of in this crowd. They should have prepared for this eventuality. Should have planned better. She reached out frantically, shouting her mother's name first, her father's, the others. She lifted onto her toes and there, up ahead, were her father and brother.

Where were the others?

Her name. She heard someone calling her. It was Basia, half a block behind her. Her mother was there, too, waving a hand over her head, calling her back. But her father, her brother.

What to do?

Hurry ahead, or push her way backward through the crowd? Back, definitely back, to her mother. With each step she took, she was shoved two more in the wrong direction. People shouted at her in an angry tangle of languages, French being only one of the many. Nevertheless, Rachel persevered.

She pushed and pushed, until she could go no more. The crowd had grown too thick, as immovable as a brick wall. Rachel had no other choice but to wait for her mother and sister to catch up, knowing that her father and brother were moving farther ahead. She breathed a sigh of relief when Basia's hand touched her shoulder and her mother's smile fell onto her face.

The rain stopped suddenly, and the sun came out in a hazy halo of splintered light through the trees. Heat and humidity circled up from the sidewalk, wrapping them in a damp oppressive blanket. The three Berman women were reunited with the rest of their family mere feet from the police station's entrance.

There were no hugs exchanged, no warm greetings, but the

relief was there, almost palpable in the small tentative smiles that spread among them. Inside the building, they approached a long wooden table where a man wearing wire-rimmed glasses sat perched on a ladder-back chair. A variety of official-looking papers lay in neat, organized piles, and there was an expression of hatred on his face so fierce that Rachel felt his animosity deep in her bones.

The collection of *fichiers*—files—on his desk was extensive, no doubt gathered throughout the day. That stack, coupled with the man's scowl, established, without a doubt, that the French police were nothing but a collection of Nazi sympathizers here to do their occupiers' bidding. Already they proved themselves deadly efficient as they hustled whole families through the registration process.

The man directed her father to present his identification card first. Her brother was next. Her mother. Basia. Then it was Rachel's turn. As he'd done with each of her family members, he compared her face to the picture on her identity card, then said in a flat, hard tone, "State your name."

"Rachel Berman."

He shuffled around a stack of papers, clearly for show, then plucked one free from the top and set it directly in front of him. "Age?"

"Nineteen."

She gave her address next.

"You live alone?"

"*Non*, with my parents, Ezra and Ilka Berman."

More shuffling of papers, presumably to compare the address she'd given him to the one her father had also given. The distrust was astonishing. As if being born Jewish made them liars.

"Are you currently employed, Mademoiselle Berman?"

"I work at the Hôtel Ritz."

His head snapped up, and his gaze thinned with obvious suspicion. "You are allowed to interact with guests?"

Rachel thought of Vivian Miller and their brief interaction

a few weeks ago that culminated in a substantial tip. "I do not speak directly with the guests." The lie slid easily off her lips, mostly because it was based in truth. "I am allowed to clean the rooms on the Rue Cambon side of the hotel and only when they are empty."

"What is involved with cleaning these rooms?"

She kept to the basics. "I enter when the room it is empty. I proceed to scrub the floors and toilets. I either replace or refresh the towels in the lavatory, depending on their condition. I change the bed linens, dust every surface, and vacuum every floor."

"And when there are no rooms to clean?"

"I work in the laundry room."

For a long, tense moment, he said nothing. A beat passed, and then another. At last, he glanced back at the form he'd been filling out, made several notations. "One final question."

Rachel swallowed, trying unsuccessfully to untie the knot in her throat, and waited.

"Where were you born?"

The answer was in front of him, written on her identity card. "Paris."

He nodded, then reached for a file folder, a red one, the color of blood. Rachel felt the sting of fear as she watched him place the form with her information inside the folder, then write her name on the tab. Her brother's information had gone into a gray folder. Her father's into a black one. The forms belonging to her mother and sister were set inside yellow files.

Rachel realized there was a system in place, a sort of cipher, with a simple encryption based on the color of the folder. Rachel's mathematical mind easily cracked the code. French citizenship obtained by legal means didn't matter to these men. Nor did they seem concerned with address, Occupation, or social standing. That had been for recordkeeping mostly and perhaps an intimidation tactic. The point of these interviews was to classify every Jew by gender and origin of birth.

Men born in France went into one category. Immigrants into another. Women were classified in a similar way. But why? What reason was there for these distinctions?

What, Rachel wondered, did they plan to do with this information?

It was a question she hoped never came with an answer.

Chapter Eighteen

Camille

15 December 1940.
Hôtel Ritz. Paris, France.

Over the next two months, Camille remained preoccupied with worry over Jacqueline. Dr. Garnier kept his word and sent weekly reports, though he disguised them in chatty letters about his life in Rennes, more friend to friend than doctor to patient's concerned sister. In those letters, Camille discovered a clever wordsmith. The descriptions of Rennes made her wish to visit the city and see its beauty with her own eyes. His letters were full of wit and charm, and he was vigilant with his reporting on Jacqueline's health, usually one of three vague phrases. Camille preferred the happiest, *we continue to see progress*, over the less than positive, *matters are no worse*, or the most dreaded, *challenges remain, but do not fret, Camille, this is common.*

He never requested money, not even when he mentioned a new treatment he'd discovered, often couched inside a phrase about tending his *little garden*, a direct reference to Jacqueline. Camille sent what money she could anyway. Yesterday's report had included the happiest of the three missives, and so, feeling less anxious than most nights, she stood in the hotel bar, half-hidden in shadow. Blinking through the gauzy haze of cigarette smoke, she watched the crowd with detached aversion.

How did Vivian stand the noise, the foul smells, the high-pitched laughter? Some of her disgust must have shown on her face because Frank approached her with a censorious scowl. "Try to keep your thoughts off your face, Camille. You are supposed to blend in, not draw attention to yourself."

She shut her eyes, pushed down images of Jacqueline, and replaced them with the doctor who'd given her hope, and adopted the approximation of a serene smile. "Better?"

"Marginally."

She readjusted her stance and glanced over the room again, past the smoke. Her eyes landed on Vivian and that detestable German. Why him? Why allow a known Nazi to woo her when she could have any man in France?

"Don't judge her too harshly."

Camille startled at Frank's admonishment. "I wasn't judging her."

Obvious skepticism lifted his eyebrows. "No?"

"Well, yes, maybe I was. She deserves more than what a man like him can give her."

Frank didn't argue the point. "She has her reasons."

Camille couldn't think what would motivate such an unholy alliance. Too many women had chosen a similar route, disappearing into a comfortable life vastly different from the early days of Occupation. At first they'd stumbled about, eyes blinking in disbelief at the strange new world thrust upon them, but then, life at the Ritz had returned to a semblance of normalcy.

Parisian women dined with hard-eyed Nazis. They met each other for lunch and gossiped about the ones missing and ignored the fact that outside these hallowed walls, Paris was not back to normal. Anything but. Laws were passed that forced Jews to register, and prohibited them from certain professions like law, medicine, teaching.

Even Rachel was relegated to serving solely in the laundry. She was no longer allowed to venture into guest rooms, not even to change soiled towels and straighten rumpled bedcovers. If only Camille could shield her friend from the prejudice and ill treatment she received from their coworkers. She stood up for her when she could, but it wasn't enough. "It's not right."

Frank misunderstood her meaning. "What would you have her do? Would you have her stay in her room, and what? Read the night away?"

Yes, she thought, Vivian should not be among these vipers, but she said, "No," and covered her mouth to hide a yawn. "It just seems like an empty way to fill time."

"Again, I will caution you, mademoiselle, from jumping to conclusions. At least she is not alone."

"But she is alone." How did he not see this? "Look at her, Monsieur Meier. At all of them. Their laughter and gaiety, it's not real. It's forced."

To watch them now, with their hands wrapped around German arms and the desperate glee in their eyes, was to witness a charade of the worst kind. They pretended the men courting them were not the enemy. Most were Frenchwomen. A few Americans, like Vivian, but there were also sleek blonde German secretaries assigned to administrative work in Paris.

The Nazis in their SS uniforms, they understood it was a new day, a new world, where they were in charge. The victors playing a joke on the rest of them. Their eyes were watchful, while their mouths curved with a hint of amusement. Some of the women were their equals, dangerous and capable of conforming their ideals with the men they took to their beds. Camille hoped Vivian knew which were which and whom to avoid.

"Stop gaping," Frank told her, his voice curt. "Here. Take these used napkins to the laundry, then deliver this package to Madame Miller's room." With a flick of his wrist, he revealed a nondescript envelope concealed inside the bundle of soiled linens. "Place the packet in the top right-hand drawer of her writing desk."

Camille nodded.

"Touch nothing."

She nodded again, knowing what was expected of her. In the past few weeks, she'd performed similar errands for the bartender. Always to Vivian's room on the Rue Cambon side. Always an envelope that held what she suspected were identity cards. Possibly forged. Maybe not. She never looked. What she didn't know now, she couldn't be forced to tell later. But then an idea struck her. If Vivian was supplying false papers, could she not do so for Rachel and her family?

"Once you're through with this chore," Frank continued, "you may go home. And, Camille, drawing conclusions on insufficient information is never wise. Things aren't always as they seem. Remember that the next time you glance over the guests and think you know who they are or why they behave the way they do."

"*Oui*, monsieur." Sufficiently reprimanded, Camille collected the bundled linens and left the bar without a backward glance.

Once inside Vivian's room, Camille was, as always, struck with the lack of luxury compared to her former suite. Was that the reason she allowed the Nazi to seduce her? So that she would have access to the room that hid her valuables behind a heavy armoire? It was a terrible thought to have about a woman who'd shown Camille favor.

Quickly now, she moved to the writing desk and put the package away as Frank instructed. Behind her, the door opened, and Camille heard the click, click of high heels. She glanced over her shoulder and met Vivian's gaze. The woman looked brooding, angry even—until she saw that it was Camille in her room, and her expression relaxed.

Spinning fully around, Camille stood under the unwavering gaze, her hands clasped at her waist. For several moments, the American divided her attention between Camille and the desk. Camille. The desk. Something in her eyes, a wariness, told her not to ask about identity cards and favors for a friend. She would ask later. That much Camille promised herself.

Still watching her, Vivian took a quick draw on the cigarette in her hand. The overhead light was bright and quite unkind, in that it showed Vivian's true age. The gold streaks in her red hair tended toward ash, and the forty-plus years that had come and gone had left their mark in the small permanent creases at the corners of her eyes and mouth. Camille then realized she had yet to explain why she was in the room. "Frank sent me to deliver a package."

Vivian nodded, her gaze locked on Camille, and then she went on the move. Camille followed her path across the room with her eyes, expecting the other woman to retrieve the package. Though she'd never done so before during one of these exchanges. Vivian did indeed sit at the small writing desk. But she opened a different drawer and pulled out a different envelope than the one Camille had deposited only moments before.

"Read this," she said, keeping her voice neutral and a little distant.

It was the distance that made Camille's heart palpitate. With shaking fingers, she teased open the envelope and retrieved the piece of paper inside. The words were in a foreign language, and completely unintelligible to a woman who spoke only her native tongue. As far as anybody knew. "I can't." Her face heated with embarrassment. "I only know how to read French."

She didn't mention her proficiency in the German language. Some secrets were best kept to herself.

"Right. *Pardonne-moi.* I wasn't thinking." Vivian took the paper. "This—" she waved the yellow slip in the air "—is from the American government and explains why I make nice with the detestable Nazi who has captured my suite for himself."

Camille remembered Frank's warning. *Things aren't always as they seem.*

"The US government believes I am a willing collaborator

with the Nazis." She said this as if the very idea tasted vile in her mouth, and Camille felt a moment of raw shame. Had she not believed the same? Was that not the reason Frank had rebuked her?

"My own government has frozen my bank accounts because they believe, and I paraphrase, that my money will somehow fall into enemy hands." She snorted. "As if I am some idiot woman incapable of protecting what is mine."

Camille couldn't blame Vivian for the bitter tone. "I... Oh."

"Oh, indeed." Frowning, she jumped to her feet and paced the length of the room, her breath coming in fast, angry snatches. "I will be manipulated by these evil men. This is what they say to me. What they think of me." She paused, took another pass across the floorboards. "So now, I am to be given a pitiful allowance." Vivian continued moving, her arms pumping, her face pale and furious. "I will not see a dime over five hundred dollars a month of my money—*my money*—until I prove my loyalty."

Camille watched Vivian pace, her own lungs burning with outrage on the woman's behalf. "What will you do?"

"What I must."

Camille said nothing. She didn't understand why Vivian was telling her this. Except, maybe she did. The woman had been put on an allowance that couldn't possibly be enough to maintain her current lifestyle. Much would have to change. Economies would have to be put into place. There would be no more extra work for Camille, no more generous tips. No more special treatment of any kind. And certainly, no favors for a friend in need.

"Will you have to move to another hotel?" *Or return to America?*

"I cannot, not yet. Too many people rely on me." She didn't explain further. Camille didn't need to hear the details. She knew about Frank's gambling business, everyone knew. His forgery operation was not so well-known. And now Camille understood, without a doubt, that Vivian was involved in the latter.

"How will you manage?"

"There are ways. I have many items of value still in my possession and, as you know, more in my former suite."

Camille remembered helping Vivian stow away her valuables in her former suite, hidden from the man living there now. The man she allowed to court her.

"My value is more than money. I know how to make *friends* with powerful men." She gave Camille a meaningful look. "In this instance, I must become close to the Nazis. Not all of them, not even two of them, just..." She stopped, looked down at her feet, shook her head. "One. I shall make him my very special friend."

Camille was not so naive as to mistake her meaning. Vivian intended to become von Bauer's paramour. To use him as he would surely use her. It would be dangerous, and a terrible, awful way to serve the people who relied on her. Her mind searched for a proper response. "You are going to allow that Nazi to make you his...his..." She couldn't say the word.

She didn't have to. "Yes."

"You will be hated by many."

Vivian took another turn around the room, a short journey that ended almost as quickly as it began. "I have thought this through. I can no longer put off the inevitable." She moved to stand before the mirror. The thoughtful expression did nothing to minimize her beauty. "I have been given tools with which to fight this war. It's time I utilize them."

"I don't like it."

"There is no more holding him off. He grows impatient. It is now or never."

"I don't understand." But she feared she knew exactly Vivian meant to do.

"My relationship cannot only appear real. It must *be* real."

Her look of absolute dread did not match the statement. "This is where you come in. I need your help, Camille."

She repeated her earlier words. "I don't understand."

"I want you to start a chain of gossip among the staff. You will give details of my liaison with von Bauer, only a few, most of them vague. Your coworkers will come to the right conclusion."

Camille was appalled. "I don't gossip. You know this. It's why you brought me into your confidence all those months ago."

Taking her hands, Vivian held her gaze. "Your integrity is one of your most endearing qualities, as is your loyalty. I ask for both now. You will spread this rumor for me. Everyone must believe I am von Bauer's willing paramour, including your friend, Rachel. She more than anyone must believe I am, for all intents and purposes, what some call a horizontal collaborator."

"Why must I spread these lies?"

"They won't be lies."

It was exactly what Camille had not wanted to hear, and everything she'd feared.

"If the staff is gossiping about me, the guests will eventually hear the rumors. The power of a good scandal has no social boundaries. Word will get out about my relationship and eventually circle around to von Bauer, who will see this as confirmation of my affections."

This plan of hers made a strange, awful, horrible sort of sense, except for one small portion. "But Rachel," Camille said. "Surely, she doesn't need to believe these lies."

"There you are wrong. A woman willing to become a Nazi's mistress cannot befriend a Jew, not even by way of a friend of a friend. It's too dangerous."

"For you."

"For us both. It would not be wise to shed unnecessary attention on the girl."

She was right, of course. Still, Camille pulled her hands free, her teeth grinding together in frustrated agony. "You've truly thought this through?"

"I have."

"You are certain there is no other way?"

"You will help me?"

She nodded. But in truth, she wasn't sure her participation was needed. The staff already gossiped about Vivian, and many of the others who slept with Germans. When she said as much, Vivian took both her hands again, this time in a grip so gentle that mist had more substance. "If I am to do this terrible thing, I need to know that someone sees me, the real me, not the Nazi's mistress, or a vapid woman seeking her own comfort and luxury at the expense of her morals."

The wording made Camille wince. "You are sure there is no other way?" Perhaps if she asked the question enough times, Vivian would eventually give a different answer.

"My course is set. So, Camille, you will be my ally in this ugly business?"

Camille made her mind go blank. It was all she could do. It lasted only a moment, then: "What about Frank? Will he know?"

"Only you." She squeezed Camille's hands. "I trust only you."

Another burden laid upon her shoulders. "I hate that people will think badly of you, and I won't be able to correct them."

Vivian released her. "Having you on my side will take some of the sting away."

Would it be enough for the widow, living a lie with only one true ally? Camille didn't think so. If the Germans lost this war, and they would—they must—what would become of her? Would collaboration be labeled as treason? Would she be tried and hanged? Perhaps her clandestine work would outweigh sleeping with the enemy.

Vivian would do this, Camille knew, with or without her

help. She could not, in good conscience, let her walk into a viper's nest alone. "All right, I'll do it. Tell me what I am to say."

It took fewer than three days for the rumor to spread through the staff, a journey full of expected and unexpected twists. Each lie grew in depth and size, gathering momentum. At regular intervals, Camille, coached by Vivian herself, added a few half-truths. Others added their own, attaching salacious details that shocked Camille when the stories wound their way back to her. Apparently, Vivian Miller spent the night in her former suite with its current occupant every night—not true. She wore diamonds stolen from wealthy Jews—possibly true, though Camille prayed it wasn't. And there was more. Always more.

On the third day, when she and Rachel were walking home, her friend asked, "Is it true? Has Vivian Miller become the mistress of a Nazi?"

"Yes." The worst part was that Camille knew it was no longer a lie.

"I thought you said we could trust her."

Camille took a long deep breath, the sound rattling in her lungs. "I was wrong."

It hurt to say the words, but say them she did. She would not, could not, take them back, no matter how disgusted Rachel looked receiving the news, and no matter how awful Camille felt telling the lie.

Chapter Nineteen

Vivian

2 March 1941.
Hôtel Ritz. Paris, France.

Vivian negotiated the long stretch of hallway that would bring her straight into a world of luxury and Germans and tried not to think about the gossip. Camille had done her job well, and now everyone suspected she was von Bauer's paramour, both in word and deed.

They were only half-right.

She spent her evenings with him, in the restaurant, the bar, at the opera house, private parties, and other events that required a woman on his arm. She'd shared kisses with him, allowed a little petting, only a little, but she hadn't been physically intimate with the man.

Tonight, that would change.

She'd toyed with von Bauer's affections too long, a miscalculation on her part. The teasing had made him more desirous of having her for his own. Only last night, his kisses had carried a hint of something deeper than liking, or even love. Obsession.

She felt it, the profound loneliness of her life. Every step that brought her closer to von Bauer brought a resounding echo of random things she remembered about her husband. The smell of his cologne. The sandpaper of his laugh when she said something clever. How she buried her head in his chest when they sat in a chair together. She'd made him work to win her, not so different from what she was doing with von Bauer. But where the Nazi wanted only to possess her, Rupert had demanded nothing but her heart.

Her feet completed the remaining steps to the restaurant. It was an odd world inside the Hôtel Ritz, one half-dedicated to the private indulgences of German soldiers, the other open to the public. There'd been a time when Vivian had been desperate to earn the favor of expats living inside these walls. She'd thought her money would buy her way into that select group of artists, writers, film stars, and fashion designers.

It had, but her beauty had foiled her, making her competition for the women and a prize to be captured by the men, as if she were a pretty piece of art. Something to be pulled out and admired, then set back in its case. She'd always despised being treated as an object. It had made her feel cheap and unlovable. Now, none of that mattered. Tonight, she would use the humiliation for a higher good.

At the restaurant's entrance, she met von Bauer's eyes across the room. A half smile played at his lips, and Vivian felt a sickening roll in her gut. The ghost of her greatest love crowded into the moment, offering comfort, strength, the nudge she needed to take the next step toward what she knew would surely be the end of her.

She shut her eyes for the briefest of moments, and when she opened them again, she was moving toward him. Her dress was silky and cool against her bare legs—no stockings for her, a small rebellion that kept her apart from the others who defied the ban on silk.

Vivian halted at the edge of the table. She could see von Bauer's face clearly, hard as stone and full of possessiveness. He stood, hand outstretched, palm up, waiting for her to answer his silent call. She felt the tension between them—a tether that drew her into his trap. She took his hand and watched, distantly, sickeningly, as *der Rab* pressed her knuckles to his lips.

The next few minutes were filled with their usual round of empty pleasantries. He complimented her dress, her face, her hair, all while he pulled out her chair, found his own, and snapped his fingers above his head. Vivian felt the intrusion of the waiter, and then, within seconds, she was holding a champagne coupe filled with the finest of French wines, and Hans-Dieter was making his customary toast. "To a memorable night."

She wanted to roll her eyes. Could he not come up with something new and original, a few words of substance? But that would make him more than what he was, perhaps even likable, a man with a bit of depth. That, she realized, would make matters so much worse. Better that he be predictable and possessive and chauvinistic.

As was his habit, he ordered for her. Mussels for the first course, a *plateau de fromage* next, sea bass for the main entrée, crème brûlée to finish. Vivian's stomach complained at the thought of all that rich food followed by a decadent dessert. But they were in Paris, and *der Rab* was a man prone to indulging himself. She still hadn't figured out his secret for staying so fit.

Over coffee, he took a long, languid puff from his cigarette and asked her about her day. It was a version of the same conversation they had following every meal they shared. But tonight. Oh, there were so many ways to answer, and yet really, only one.

"It was nothing special." A lie. She'd met with another Jewish family in need of papers, and Frank had insisted she try a different forger because he'd heard rumors her usual man was being followed by the Gestapo. "I had my hair done and bought a new dress. I read a magazine. How was your day?"

He brought the cigarette to his lips again and puffed, inhaling deeply this time, then releasing it with a long drawn-out breath. He appeared calm, but Vivian could tell he grew impatient. She watched the curl of smoke float toward her, feeling it curl around her and filtering through her nose, into her lungs, deep into her blood. Her head swam, but she held his gaze, watching him watch her, and she had the strangest conviction he knew exactly what was in her mind. And yet he didn't appear overly concerned that she didn't much like him. Her distain seemed to make him want her more.

She must do better, she told herself. Smiling, just a little, not too much, she took a sip of champagne. When it hit her mouth, the liquid burned on her tongue, flamed down her throat, and she had to fight the urge not to cough. She barely flinched. This was not her first night of deceit.

His eyes narrowed ever so slightly, but then cleared as he pushed back from the table. "We will finish this upstairs."

Vivian's nerves sang like a bow pulled across a violin string.

He noticed her hesitation. "One drink without eyes watching, judging. I do not like how others look at you, what they say about you. It does not reflect well on either of us."

She wanted to be flattered. She wanted to feel…something. But his face was very still as he spoke, almost unnaturally so, except for a vein beating at his temple, signaling more was happening under the surface. A kind of mute, frozen temper that wanted only a poke to find release. To appease him, she gave a slight shrug and took his offered hand. "What they say doesn't matter."

"It matters. I will not have your name bandied about like a common harlot's. You are much more than that, Vivian."

A smile, she told herself, *give him a smile to show your gratitude for his advocacy.*

"We will have that drink, and then…" He, too, smiled, the look of a snake charmer in his watchful eyes. "The rest of the evening will be up to you."

This was it. The inevitable moment when she crossed the

proverbial line. *Look behind you, Vivian. You already passed that marker when you pulled Camille into your scheme.*

Could she take the final step? Did she have a choice?

Vivian thought of the pretty French maid, and the other lost souls relying on her. She thought of the American government, and the nameless men deciding her fate with the swipe of a pen and the seizure of her money. They would not stop her. She would continue helping the innocent, but she would do it on her terms. Her way. That's what she told herself. What she almost believed. Almost, but not quite.

"As you wish, *der Rab.* We will have that drink in your suite, and then we shall see where the night leads." Though it pained her to do so, she gave him a flirty wink.

His rumble of laughter would have been appealing, if only she liked him more.

On legs that felt numb, she allowed him to escort her out of the restaurant. She was aware of the surreptitious looks, and the whispers that weren't really whispers.

Vivian tuned them out and wondered if he did the same, or if he was keeping a record of the people who dared to gossip about them. She watched him from the corner of her eye. He held silent, spine erect, eyes forward, face clear of expression, until they were well on their way to his suite—*her suite*—and he looked over at her with his blue eyes narrowed. "Does it bother you?" he asked. "The gossip?"

He'd rendered Vivian speechless, and she wondered if he truly cared about her feelings.

"It doesn't bother me." It was not a lie, not completely, not anymore. Even if she had not played her role in starting the rumors about their liaison, she would be immune.

"Good. This is good." He led her along. A deep breath on her part, squared shoulders on his, a hand to her back, a ride in the elevator. The next thing she knew, they were stepping into the marbled entryway of her former suite, and he was closing the door behind them with a soft click.

If he asked her if she wished to stay the night, she would tell him yes. Not yet. For now, she looked around what had once been her home. It was the same, but different. Not a single piece of clothing was strewn on the floor or in a chair, not a piece of furniture out of place.

In truth, there was no sign of von Bauer at all, which told Vivian three important pieces of information. One, he was as fastidious with his personal belongings as he was with his personal grooming. Two, the housekeeping staff were even more efficient under German occupation than they'd been before the enemy had confiscated the Place Vendôme side of the hotel. Finally, *der Rab* was so very German, down to the last exacting fiber of his being.

This was good information to have.

A strong grip on her shoulders from behind cut off the rest of her thoughts. He held her a little bit too hard as he turned her around to face him. His height was impressive. Even in her five-inch heels, she had to crane her neck to look into his pale blue eyes. What she saw made her wish she hadn't. That look, she'd seen in her father. *Der Rab* said the rest of the evening was up to her. He lied.

He would get what he wanted. *A fait accompli.* Her will, her choice, neither would matter to him. Ah, but they mattered to her. She was not without skills of her own. She would make him work for tonight. For her. Therein lay the control, the power.

His face leaned toward hers, close. Closer, closer.

Now. She told herself to move now. With a small, flirtatious smile, she slipped from his grasp and took a slow turn around the room, running her fingertip along a table, the edge of a chair, over to the ornate writing desk where she'd once kept her memories, personal letters, and forged documents for desperate refugees. Here, she noted ironically, were the first signs of the Nazi officer, in the pile of papers perfectly aligned next to a stack of ledgers. Pencils in a cup. Fountain pens, a letter opener.

All the accoutrements that belonged to a serious man assigned to conduct serious business. She'd thought him a soldier. Now she wondered. Just what did this man do for the Third Reich? She would make it her job to find out and pass on the information. He could have her body and use it for his own purposes, all while her mind worked against him, gathering what she could of his life as an SS officer.

"You are satisfied with your accommodations?" she asked, noticing that her voice was strained, and no, that would not do. "I apologize. It's none of my concern." She gave a jaunty toss of her head. "You mentioned a drink?"

"So I did." The low laugh rumbling from his throat could not hide the flaring blue fire of lust in his eyes. But he cooperated and poured amber liquid into two brandy snifters.

A tiny rueful smile flickered at the corner of his mouth as he handed her one of the glasses, keeping the other for himself.

They each took a sip, and Vivian knew, if she wanted to retain any self-respect, that she must control the inevitable. If only in the small way of being the first to initiate her ruin. She set down her glass, took his. The masculine hunger in his eyes grew deeper, more feral, as she slid her fingertips up his arms, along his shoulders. She traced the edge of his jawline, scratching the barely perceptible stubble, rough beneath her nails.

Lifting onto her toes, she closed the space between their mouths and asked in a husky whisper, "Am I standing too close?"

If she'd meant to unravel his self-control, she'd failed. He gripped her hair, tugged hard, pulling her face from his. "What game is this you play?"

Vivian made a helpless noise in her throat, one she hoped he misunderstood as willing submissiveness rather than fear. "I do not play games."

Truth, wrapped in a lie, coated with deception.

His fingers tangled in her hair and dug in deep, and this time, it was he who commanded the next move, she who followed. She knew what to expect, however, her mind recoiled from what was happening to her, taking her somewhere safe. She hid her true self in that place, shrouded behind a milky veil, a place wholly separate from reality and this man.

He could have her body. He could not have her mind, nor her soul, and especially not her heart. When he was through, when it was done, she stayed beneath the shrouded mist in her mind for another five minutes. Tears hung in her throat, razor-sharp, but she did not let them come.

She was not a young woman. She'd made bad decisions in her youth. *Der Rab* brought out the worst in her. Full circle, she thought, as she abandoned the ruse of sleep and padded across the room to the lavatory, or as the French called it, *le toilette*.

Alone, after the door clicked shut behind her, Vivian forced herself to look at her reflection in the mirror. Her eyes glinted with self-loathing, and she wiped the back of her hand across her mouth, again and again and again, but nothing could relieve her of the shame.

The pieces of her soul were too jagged to put back together. Pushing her fingertips against her forehead, she realized she had nothing to show for her sacrifice. She hadn't gotten a single piece of information out of *der Rab*. Nothing that could help the war effort. But the night wasn't over. All was not lost.

Exiting the lavatory, she found von Bauer had moved to the parlor. He was dressed in a robe, lounging in an ornate chair that Rupert had purchased for her in Milan. He appeared perfectly at home, as satisfied as a jungle cat the day after an important kill. Not quite meeting his eyes, she went to the wardrobe and grabbed one of his shirts, shrugged it over her head.

Most men considered the move a sign of intimacy shared. How easy they were fooled.

As if he could hear her thoughts, his cold blue eyes slid to the door, then back to her. "You are very good at this."

"You would prefer an innocent?"

He sat forward, resting his elbows on his knees. "I think you know the answer to that."

She did. He'd chosen her when others would have sufficed, a mature woman with life experience and, for all he knew, deep pockets.

"Come here," he ordered in the voice of a man with only half his hunger quenched.

She obeyed, wondering if he knew he'd just revealed something of himself, something underneath the Nazi. His desire for her was a weakness she could exploit. For months, he'd waged a war to get her into his bed. Now that he'd succeeded, Vivian would use his insatiable hunger for her to defeat him at his own game.

A battle with the outcome not yet decided.

Chapter Twenty

Rachel

April 1941.
Ezra Berman's Tailor Shop. Paris, France.

Winter brought heavy snow that lay thick on the streets and unseasonably low temperatures that strained the city's resources. Electricity failures and enforced blackouts were common, sending even the heartiest creatures scurrying for shelter. As January turned to February and February crept into March, the air remained frigid, and ice formed on the inside of the Bermans' apartment windows. The mood in Paris was as miserable as the weather. The occupiers were ruthless with their rules. The French police were worse.

Men in blue tunics positioned themselves alongside the gray-green-uniformed Germans. They were everywhere, questioning people in the streets, conducting random searches of people's homes. The curfew was tightened to 8:00 p.m. again, for all Parisians, not just Jews, and yet vandalism of Jewish businesses remained frequent and unchecked.

The Wozniaks' bakery had been only the first. Ezra Berman came home every night with tales of another business falling prey to vandals and ruffians looking to loot as much as spew their hate. Thus far, his tailor shop had been spared. How long would that continue?

The mood at the hotel had changed, at least toward Rachel, and in the worst possible way. Her hours had been cut to almost nothing, her wages so low they amounted to poverty level. She was forbidden to venture out of the laundry. She rarely saw Camille anymore, and when she did, it was only to collect whatever soiled linens she was there to deliver. Her friend was always quick with a kind word, but the war posed challenges for her as well. The girl was working too hard, working extra shifts Rachel would have taken had she been offered the opportunity.

Rachel was tired of being cold and afraid, always worrying. And the waiting, so much waiting, knowing the vandals were always looking to vent their disgust at a Jewish man earning a living that had catapulted him to the middle class. Even after all the violence, Ezra Berman believed obedience was their best route, their only route to survival. He displayed the sign that designated his shop as a Jewish-owned business. Rachel had begged him not to, she'd begged and begged. His response was always the same. "Our neighbors know we are Jewish. This is not something we can hide."

"Must you advertise to the vandals?"

"It is the law. We will obey this decree, as we have all the others."

"But, Papa. You might as well have put a target in the window."

Smiling fondly, he patted her on the head. "You worry too much, *córka*."

And he worried not enough.

A week later, Rachel's worst fears were realized. Vandals unleashed their anti-Semitism on her father's shop. They broke glass, sprayed ugly slurs on the walls, and ripped spools upon spools of valuable fabric into shreds.

Fortunately, no one was injured—that was what her father

said and her mother echoed. Rachel knew they were right, but that only seemed to add to the abuse. The cowards' destructive violence had happened overnight while the family slept in their beds two blocks away. Scheduled for a later shift at the hotel, Rachel would spend the morning washing the paint off the walls with Basia's help. Her brother was assigned to cleaning up the glass, while their parents inventoried what was lost. They tried desperately to salvage what could be saved or repaired, which Rachel feared was very little.

Circling her gaze over the destruction, she felt a rage so deep that she nearly howled from the pain. But it was her mother's face that brought true alarm. Her expression, as she sorted through the ruined bolts of cloth, was empty, as blank as a new piece of paper. Her eyes were open and seeing, but they contained nothing at all. Nothing.

Rachel's father showed similar signs of shock. His skin had gone gray and his lips slack. He sagged to the ground and kept plucking at the loose threads, plucking, plucking. Then, suddenly, his jaw clamped shut, his mind working frantically behind his dazed expression. He was probably thinking of their neighbors, the ones he'd sworn would protect them, or perhaps the French police, the government's decrees. Did any of it matter? Rachel looked around at the destruction. This was their reality now as Jews living in Paris.

No one would stand up for them. There would be no more talk of escape. The fight was over. Their very existence came down to one goal. Survival.

Basia, her face tight with anguish, brought a fresh bucket of water to where Rachel stood facing the wall of insults and slurs. "We should get started."

Rachel stared at the foul words slashed across the wall, her eyes landing on one of the slurs she often heard at work, barely whispered, constantly within earshot, spoken in French, not German. *Sale Juif.* Dirty Jew. Seeing the insult in plain sight, so bold and vicious, sent a queasy feeling through her stomach, and she broke out in a cold sweat. Terror and desperation were her constant companions. It was as if some huge curtain had been pulled back and she saw the situation in a new, more frightening light.

Sale Juif.

Another wave of nausea threatened. Struggling to bring the sensation under control, she placed her hand over mouth.

Slowly, the sickness retreated.

If only restoring the shreds of her dignity were so easy.

She didn't know what was worse. The shame or the fury. One brought humiliation, the other dark thoughts that made her question the nature of her character. The two emotions tangled, building into one hard knot of inevitability. Persecution was coming. And death.

Anger bled through her shame, the former all but wiping out the latter, and now Rachel knew which of the two emotions held dominance in her life. Rage, dark and red as the slashes of paint across the wall. The slurs weren't original. *Sale Juif.* But also, *Le Porc.* Swine. *Cafard.* Cockroach. *Rat.*

No, not original. But offensive. Reading the ugly words, knowing they were directed at her father, it was too much to bear. Her thoughts were as tangled as the gnarled roots of an ancient oak.

"Rachel."

Basia's soft voice, so devastated and hurt, but also worried. It was the worry that pushed Rachel into action. "I'm ready."

She wrung out the rag, flicked the last few drops into the bucket, and scrubbed. She scrubbed and scrubbed until her hands were chafed and her mind was as blank as her mother's face. As if hearing her thoughts, her mother came to stand beside her and wrapped an arm around her shoulders. They shared a tight smile. Then, together they faced the wall and stared at Rachel's handiwork. The words were gone, the bloodred now a smeared, sickly pink.

"You did a fine job."

It was a lie. Well-meaning, but still a lie. For her benefit or her mother's?

Rachel leaned her head on the older woman's shoulder. So thin, so bony, from worry as much as scarcity forced on them by the occupiers. Always the last in line for rationing coupons. The same was true at the baker's shop, the grocer, and often—too often—they were forced to go without. She pushed the thought away and reminded herself that she was alive and with her entire family. No one gone or disappeared or carted away. But as that thought arrived, it faded, and the wall became all she could see. They were being targeted because they were considered different, and for what? They'd done nothing wrong. "Why do they hate us so?"

"It's not personal, *maleńka*. It's their fear that makes them hate, and their lack of—"

"No, Mama, you're wrong. It is personal. All of it. This... *this*," she hissed, waving her hand in an arc that included the entire shop. "It's absolutely, undeniably personal. This attack, the destruction and slurs, it was directed at Papa and his shop because he followed the rules and put up the sign."

Her mother said nothing, her silence giving Rachel no comfort, only more confusion. More fear. The awful, weighty feeling stuck in her chest. Stepping back, until she was alone and isolated even from her mother, Rachel crossed her arms over her chest and hunched forward as if she could make herself smaller. She glared at the wall, the words unreadable now but there in the smeared paint, branded eternally on her mind.

Parisians had aligned themselves with the Nazis. They hated as strongly as their counterparts in Germany. They'd taken sides and had begun avoiding Jews on the streets. No eye contact, no use of given names, turning them into mere figures with faces. Not real people, but nameless creatures that breathed. Animal rather than human. Rachel couldn't see the end in her mind. But she knew nothing good was coming.

No, nothing good at all.

The Roundups

Chapter Twenty-One

Rachel

May 1941.
Paris, France.

The flat-eyed *l'agent de police* arrived on the Bermans' doorstep at twilight, when the sky leaned toward lavender, and the slow-moving breeze held the promising scent of summer. A beautiful night spoiled by the foul presence of the French police. He did not explain the reason for his sudden appearance, or why he held two small green postcards in his hand. He merely stared straight ahead, not speaking, not even looking at her, as if she was supposed to understand why he had come. Rachel knew this wasn't about the vandalism of her father's shop. That had been weeks ago.

Months and months of police indifference.

Still, he was here in an official capacity. Something in the air stirred around him, a menacing heat that sent her heartbeat thudding in the hollow of her throat. Whatever his purpose, it was not a piece of friendly business. He was taller than most policemen and seemed aggressively defiant with his broad shoulders thrown back and those savage eyes, a street thug who'd been given unchecked authority. Her chin tipped up. "May I help you?"

His hard face went harder still, his eyebrows slashing down in a scowl. When he spoke, his voice was measured, controlled. "Is this the Berman residence?"

Every line in Rachel's body tensed. This man, this sworn member of the French police, had come to perform an unpleasant task. "*Oui.*"

"Your name?"

"Rachel Berman."

"My business is not with you." He glared over her shoulder, where the rest of her family gathered. "I am here for Ezra Berman, and his eighteen-year-old son, Srulka."

Rachel's mind held only two words.

It begins.

She started to shut the door, unwilling to allow such a man inside her home, for whatever nasty business had brought him. But her father stepped in front of her. "I am Ezra Berman."

"These are for you and your son." He passed over two green postcards. "You will obey the summons or suffer the consequences." Having made his nasty little threat, he spun on his heel and left.

Silence fell in his wake, until Rachel's mother asked, "What do the cards say?"

Her father stared at her with a troubled look. "It is written in French."

This was his way of saying he didn't know the language well enough to decipher all the words. Rachel took one of the cards, a single slip of heavy green card stock, noting the other was identical to the first, but for the handwritten name. "It's from Police Headquarters in Paris, stamped with today's date."

She lifted her head, caught her father's scowl, then continued, "It says, 'Mr. Ezra Berman is invited to present himself in person, accompanied by one member of his family or by one friend, at 7:00 in the morning on 14 May 1941, for an examination of his situation. He is asked to provide identification. Those who do not present themselves on the set day and hour are liable for the most severe sanctions.'" Her hand began to shake so hard she nearly dropped the postcard. "It's signed in bold typeface, *Le Commissaire de Police.*"

Her mother gasped, and again, Rachel lifted her head. "Don't go, Papa."

"We must."

Rachel gripped his arm. "Please. I beg you. Don't go."

He gave her a sad smile, looking almost calm, but for the small twitch in his jaw. "This is nothing. An administrative formality."

It was more than that. Rachel knew it, and she suspected her father did, too. "Then let me go with you. It says you and Srulka are to report first thing tomorrow morning, with a family member. I'm assuming one of us would suffice for you both. Let it be me."

"I'll go, too," Basia offered.

"We will all go," her mother said, and Rachel was glad. It was right they stood together as a family, united and true.

The next morning dawned bright and warm. A slap in the face, Rachel thought. The sky should be weeping. Her father led the way down the street. The solemnity in his bearing, that sense of inevitability that seemed to shimmer off him, did nothing to calm her fears.

At the police station, he and her brother were immediately taken into custody with very little fanfare. It was all so orderly and coordinated, as if much planning had gone into the seizing of Jewish men eighteen and older who'd presented themselves as ordered. It was a shock, this punishment for their obedience. Before he was led away, her father looked over his shoulder and said to Rachel, "Take care of your mother."

"I... Yes, of course." She was talking to empty air. Her father and brother were already being manhandled and loaded onto an idling bus. With no chance to hug or say goodbye.

Everything had happened so fast, too fast. One moment, the Bermans were a family of five. The next, they were down to three, and as she watched her father and brother being led away, Rachel felt her skin prickle with a dark premonition. She had to steady herself with a hand on Basia's shoulder.

It was happening. The thing she'd most feared, her loved ones seized and taken away, and there'd been no time to react, no chance to speak in their defense. She looked to her mother, then to her sister. They, too, were frozen in shock, their eyes blinking, robbed of words.

"Why are you arresting them?" a woman shouted from the crowd of women left behind.

"What have they done?" another demanded.

Rachel echoed the same questions, her voice weak. Basia joined in as well. They were given a list of instructions as a response, with a one-hour deadline to supply the necessary items. Rachel returned to the police station alone, Basia choosing to stay behind with their mother.

As directed, she delivered two bags, each containing a blanket and sheet, a set of clothing, cutlery, a plate, a toiletry bag, a ration card, and enough food for twenty-four hours. She was not allowed to speak with her father or her brother, nor was she given the chance to deliver the bags to them herself. She noticed more buses, so many, rows of them at least five deep.

Against the odds, she caught a glimpse of her father in a window seat on the fourth bus in line. She rushed forward, shouting his name, and was severely rewarded with the smack of a police baton to the back of her thighs. She fell to her hands and knees. As she tried to stand, she was whacked again. The sting brought tears to her eyes.

"You will leave now." The voice was neither firm nor kind. "You do not belong here, mademoiselle." He did not attempt to help her stand but left her in a heap on the hard concrete.

"Where are you taking them?"

"To the train station and then on to a facility in Loiret."

His voice sounded nothing like before. It was no longer bland, but deep and ominous, almost creepy with unrestrained glee.

She had more questions, but he was already shoving aside another desperate woman, shouting at her, too. Frozen in her shock, with that angry French voice washing over her, Rachel watched the collection of dark suits and terrified eyes being loaded onto buses spitting smoke and reeking of diesel.

Jewish men—fathers and sons, brothers and uncles—herded like cattle, with but one purpose. To be taken to a facility in Loiret. No one explained why they were being taken. But Rachel knew. The monsters from her nightmares had come to life, wearing French uniforms, men corrupted by German propaganda. They'd joined in the false narrative of an elite race, one that didn't exist, would never exist. Once sworn enemies, now the French and Germans worked together, destroying their common foe, an entire race of innocent people.

Corrupted by the darkest part of their natures. The picture of true evil.

And Rachel could do nothing but watch from her spot on the ground. Watch and struggle to pull in gulps of air. Her breath refused to settle into a comfortable rhythm, instead ripping up her throat, shattering past her lips.

The last bit of her hope receded with unnatural quickness, like water draining through a sieve, and she slowly, awkwardly gained her feet. On legs gone numb, she made her way home, stumbling up and down the streets until she was in her own neighborhood. She found her sister and mother where she left them, at the small kitchen table, their heads bent close. Basia was whispering words of comfort. Her mother whispered back, in between low moans and soft sobs. Such a tender scene in a moment of quiet despair. But why whisper? Did they think if they raised their voices the situation would somehow grow worse?

It *was* worse, and Rachel had to tell her mother what she'd learned.

She opened her mouth, then shut it as something struck her.

Basia was sad, yes, but she was also remarkably calm, almost detached, which could mean only one thing. Her boyfriend had not received a green postcard. Jacob was safe from Nazi persecution. His father's connections and elevated status in French society protected him.

The sense of unfairness had her shutting the door with more force than intended. Two heads snapped up, and Rachel looked from one to the other, settling on her mother's face, seeking the woman from her childhood. She wasn't there. Her hair was unbound, and dark circles lay in crescents beneath her eyes. Rachel had the ugly task of relaying news that would only increase her pain.

"Tell us." Basia jumped to her feet. "Tell us what you know of Papa and Srulka."

Ignoring her sister, she hurried to her mother and took her hands. Brittle twigs under skin stretched too tight. So frail and thin. Rachel erased the images of that long row of buses and searched her mother's face, looking for the woman who'd raised her, fearing their roles were reversed now, perhaps permanently.

"Rachel!" Basia snapped out her name. "You are stalling."

It would be so easy to take out her frustration on her sister. But they needed to work together to keep their mother from breaking. After months of oppression at work, Rachel knew how to set her own feelings aside and do what must be done. She called on that skill now. "Papa and Srulka have been sent to a facility in Loiret."

Again, Basia made her demands. "Why? For how long? Can we see them, visit perhaps?"

"I don't know. I was told nothing, except to go away." She didn't add the part about the baton, though her skin still stung from the blow.

As reality was finally sinking in, Basia made no more demands. Her sudden silence was worse. Or so Rachel believed, until her mother began to sob. Big, choking sobs. "They will die. The Nazis will kill them."

Rachel's shoulders stiffened, but she kept her voice soothing. "We don't know that."

Her mother gave another wail of despair.

Rachel shared a look with her sister, who appeared equally powerless. She wanted to say the right thing, to do the right thing, but she also wanted the luxury of her childhood back. She wanted her mother to be the woman she'd always relied on, not this frail, devastated stranger.

If only she'd tried harder to keep her father from reporting to the police station. Had she argued more succinctly, with better words, perhaps he would have tossed the postcard into the trash. Perhaps he would still be here, he and Srulka, both safe and sound.

So many thoughts tangled in her mind, too many, and Rachel found her hands going to her hair and tugging at a curl, tugging and tugging, until she heard tearing. The pain was nearly welcome, a bare thread of feeling that wove past the shell she'd built around her heart.

Her mother watched her closely. Then she seemed to rally. She stood, took Rachel into her arms. And she had her mother back. She was here, in the tight embrace, and Rachel sagged into the warmth.

"You will see, *ketsl*. My sweet *córka*. This war will be over one day, and we will be reunited with your father and brother, if not sooner." Her mother pulled away, her gaze level. "With this hope in our hearts, we will take each day as it comes, one at a time."

Rachel wanted to feel her mother's confidence, but she couldn't forget what she'd seen in the eyes of those French policemen. The same look she'd witnessed in her coworkers at the hotel, and the Nazi soldiers on the streets. A fanaticism that transcended human goodness and touched on the ugliest of human nature.

It was all so hopeless. Suddenly, Rachel was a child again. That timid, frightened child pressed her face into her mother's shoulder and wept.

Chapter Twenty-Two

Vivian

11 March 1942.
Hôtel Ritz. Paris, France.

The worst part about becoming von Bauer's mistress wasn't the way he monopolized her social calendar, or the nightly rituals he insisted upon once they returned to his suite. No, the worst part was maintaining the lie in private. That she was getting better at it, the pretending she wanted to be with him, gave Vivian a quiet moment of despair.

She set the feeling aside and entered her room in the Rue Cambon building, something she rarely did now that she belonged, body and soul, to *der Rab*. She stopped at the mirror, squinted, sighed. She'd acquired new lines around her eyes and mouth, not many, and only if she looked hard. So, then, why her? There were younger, newer versions, all of them showing up on the arms of Nazis. Yet oddly, von Bauer preferred Vivian's maturity.

She should be flattered. She was not.

She thought of Hermann Göring's interest in her. No, not her. Her jewelry. With von Bauer acting as broker, the corpulent

Nazi had purchased nearly a dozen pieces from Vivian's collection. Though he was never fully satisfied. Her emerald necklace was the ultimate prize. The strange, greedy man had been waging a rather obvious war to have the treasure for his own.

Twice he'd approached her, through von Bauer, always with an offensive offer.

Twice she'd refused him. Tonight, she would allow the head of the *Luftwaffe* to achieve victory, for a ridiculous price, with *der Rab* once again acting as broker. He would think she relied on him. He would be right. Vivian needed the money to continue her clandestine work. More and more Jews required identity papers, exit visas, and a means of escape.

In that, at least, Vivian had not lost her way. She liked knowing that it was Hitler's second-in-command aiding her in the effort to save Jewish lives.

Course set, she went to the closet, lowered to her knees, and worked the slab of wood aside. Inside the box nested the necklace Göring coveted. She draped the jewels over her hand and let her eyes stray from one emerald to the next, each one more lovely than the last, a virtual fortune of perfectly formed gems. Strung together, they were worth millions in American dollars, ten times that in sentimentality. They'd been Rupert's gift to her on their wedding night.

Without him in her life, Vivian was a shell of her former self. She could admit that here, alone with the priceless necklace he'd given her resting coolly against her skin. She would honor her husband with the sacrifice of his gift, and pray the transaction saved many lives.

She searched her closet for the very dress to engage Göring's interest, this time with her in charge. She chose a silk gown in shimmering silver. The color and low neck would emphasize the emeralds. After fashioning her hair in a simple chignon, she gave her reflection one final glance, and knew she looked her best. She'd agreed to meet von Bauer for a predinner drink in the Little Bar.

At the entrance, she paused and surveyed the crowd. Some of the faces belonged to collaborators, others to resistance workers. And then there were those who played both sides. She moved deeper into the swirling cigarette smoke.

Frank greeted her with a nod.

She returned the gesture, then checked the room a second time. Von Bauer had not yet arrived. Excellent, she had time to pick her seat. She chose a small round table littered with overflowing ashtrays and half-empty glasses. There was only one chair. Again, excellent. The man needed to be reminded he didn't hold all the power in their relationship.

A quick repositioning of the chair and Vivian was facing the entrance, her back to the wall. The two women seated at the next table, each with at least three SS soldiers vying for their attention, eyed her with a look of contempt. Ironic. She'd supplied each of them with falsified papers that gave them very American names, Cook and Anderson, respectively, their Jewish heritage a thing of the past. All so they could stay in Paris and pretend there was no war. If those SS soldiers only knew who they were sniffing around.

Ah, but they didn't know.

Camille arrived at the table, her eyes briefly meeting Vivian's before she cleared away the carnage left by the previous guests. With the finesse of a carnival performer, she grabbed the last of the empty glasses while dropping a note into Vivian's lap. This had become their way of communicating now that von Bauer monopolized her time.

Using her own sleight of hand, Vivian hid the note in her purse and pulled out a tiny mirror. She checked her appearance, reapplied her lipstick, then replaced the tube. Before snapping the closure in place, she quickly scanned the note Camille had given her, penned in Frank's messy handwriting.

Ask him about the progress at Cité de la Muette.

Vivian frowned. She'd already passed along what she knew about the Nazis' plans for the abandoned apartment complex in Drancy. Originally, the German army had requisitioned the facility to house prisoners of war. However, the SS had become involved recently. Von Bauer oversaw logistics, and though she didn't have confirmation—yet—Vivian had overheard him speaking to a colleague on the telephone about the future of the site. The Nazis had big plans for the facility due its proximity to the railway.

She would find out more when she could. It was not always easy to gather information from *der Rab*. A small commotion at the bar's entrance drew her attention, and there he was. Her enemy, her lover. He'd yet to see her, and she was glad for the moment to cool her nerves. The shame that was always with her was strong tonight.

He will destroy me.

And perhaps she would return the favor. The thought became a silent vow in her head. But then their eyes met through the cloud of smoke, and something quicksilver passed between them. Something dark and inevitable. The feeling swelled and rose, filling her chest, warming her cheeks, rushing into her brain, and her shame took on an instant note of fear.

As if sensing her need for an ally, Camille reappeared. "Madame Miller, are you unwell?"

It wasn't the words but the look of concern on the girl's face that cut through her panic. "I'm fine." Camille didn't look convinced, so Vivian added, "Truly, I'm fine."

Or rather, she would be. When the war was over, and the enemy was vanquished. Von Bauer went on the move at the same time Camille shifted away, and Vivian placed a smile on her lips. Coy and mildly evasive.

He answered her silent call with a smile of his own, plus a knowing glint in his eyes. She knew that look. Saw it every night in his suite when they were alone. The man's appetite for her was strong, a raging fire that required little fuel on her part. What would happen to her when the flames of his desire became smoldering embers? He would discard her like yesterday's trash, though he would not let her go gently.

The man carried himself with the haughtiness of royalty, the pinnacle of Nazi entitlement, and as he paused at her table, Vivian saw the bitter truth in his face. He wanted to possess her completely, not just her body and soul, but her mind as well, and in that wanting was nothing pure or noble. She'd known this about him and had naively thought the knowledge gave her an advantage.

"We were to meet upstairs." He spoke calmly, but Vivian sensed the impatience boiling beneath the surface. He did not like playing games.

Neither did she. Yet they so often did. "I thought we were to meet here. Please—" she waved a hand over the table "—join me."

There was no seat for him take, which seemed to amuse him. One sidelong glance at the table of SS soldiers on his right and, as if he'd somehow communicated telepathically exactly what he wanted, an empty chair appeared. Von Bauer was soon settled across from her. No worries that his back faced the entrance. No concern that an enemy could walk up behind him. Such surety, such arrogance. Did nothing rattle *der Rab*?

"What are we drinking tonight, Vivian?"

"Champagne."

His hand lifted, and three heartbeats later, an open bottle of France's best champagne appeared at the table with two empty coupes. He filled a glass with the golden bubbles, handed it to her, then lifted his own in the air.

Vivian did the same. "What are we celebrating?"

"Us."

Indeed. She caught Camille watching her, the look of concern still swimming in her eyes. The girl's presence eased the anxiety gnawing inside her, and Vivian was able to touch the edge of her glass to his and return the toast. "To us."

There was silence after that, broken only by the jovial voices from SS officers and their female prey. No different than the man sitting across from her, his hawklike gaze set upon the jewels wrapped around her throat. "I see you wore the necklace tonight."

She shrugged. "One last hurrah."

His eyebrows lifted. "You are ready to part with the emeralds?"

This was a test, this blunt, tasteless conversation. "I am."

He held her stare, looking at her with the certainty of a man wielding great power. He reached out, his eyes still locked with hers, and rubbed his thumb along the back of her hand. "Would you like me to broker the deal?"

Hopelessness filled her, but she refused to let it show. "Please."

"Consider it done."

They made their way to the restaurant and, after an exquisite meal of scallops and baked sea bass, retired to his suite, where more champagne and strawberries awaited them. The decadence was criminal in a city where ration coupons were required to purchase the most basic food items and too many in Paris went without. This was not the place where Vivian's mind should go, not when *der Rab* was looking at her with a hunger she knew would take hours to quench.

"Get undressed," he barked.

She turned toward the bedroom.

"Here. Do it here. Do it now." He delivered the order in a bored tone. Never a good sign. When von Bauer spoke without inflection, or obvious intent, his behavior became unpredictable, and often turned cruel. Vivian had no idea what she'd done to put him in this mood, or if she was even the cause. What did it matter? She would bear the consequences, regardless.

"Vivian."

She jerked at the sound of her name, spoken in that low, terrible tone. She exhaled a long breath. Then, slowly, with great control, did as she was told, her eyes watering from the knowledge that *der Rab* had stolen everything from her, this suite, her antique furniture, the emeralds around her neck. But most of all, her dignity.

He approached her. She braced herself, toes curled into the carpet. She would not turn away. She would not show signs of weakness.

She would endure.

The bravado came hard, but it came. And she was grateful for that small piece of control in a game where women like her held so little power. As was her habit after the especially long nights, she left the bed soundlessly, donned her robe, and stepped out onto the balcony. The air was crisp. She hardly noticed. The tears she held back were born of fatigue. That's what she told herself.

Blinking hard, so hard her head swam, she wrapped her hands around the railing and stared down into the dark abyss below. In the afternoon light, she would be able to see the details of the manicured courtyard and watch the women taking tea at *La Terrasse*.

Tonight, she was alone.

Until a crow landed on the railing not two feet from her hand. It stared at her. Vivian stared right back, contemplating those small black eyes, so vacant and yet weirdly piercing. "Have you come to threaten or to warn?"

The bird cocked its head, shifted its weight, and then, with a squawk, flew away. Scared off by the sound of footsteps. Again, she braced herself for the moment his arms would rope around her. Or his hands would take her arms and spin her around to face him. One meant tenderness, the other pain. It was draining, always needing to keep track of his different moods.

The arms that came around her waist held on with a light, almost gentle hold. Tonight, it seemed, the placated, satiated man joined her on the balcony. "Come back inside," he whispered. "I have something to tell you."

She let him take her hand and lead her into the suite. She

assumed he would keep drawing her forward, back to the bedroom, but he let her go and indicated she sit with him on the brocade settee. If he appreciated her silence, it certainly didn't show. There was still the faintest tinge of hunger in him, humming just beneath the surface of his outward calm, and Vivian worried what it meant for the rest of the night.

But no, this impatience was different. Bigger, more pronounced.

"I have been awarded a promotion." The fire in his eyes glowed bright with self-importance. "The position will put me among the most trusted men among the *Führer's* inner circle. And I have you to thank."

"Me?"

"*Reichsmarschall* Göring has put in a good word on my behalf. It seems our transactions have pleased him."

He meant the sale of her jewelry.

That pleased look in his eyes made sense now. *Der Rab* was a driven man, viciously so. Did this promotion mean he would be transferred to Berlin? Vivian could not contain her smile. "Congratulations," she said in a husky whisper. "You are most deserving of this honor."

He liked it when she stroked his ego. But tonight, he merely shrugged. His gaze remained locked on hers, neutral and watchful, as if gauging her reaction. She gave him a bland smile.

"Does this mean you are leaving Paris?" She sounded a little too pleased. And that would not do. She must appear sad, or at least regretful that their time was up. So many emotions inside her, all of them lies, all of them true. Which one to present to him now?

"I will not be leaving Paris, no, only the Ritz. I have been ordered to move closer to my work in Drancy." He looked around the suite then. Perhaps calculating which pieces of *her* furniture were worthy enough to bring with him. No one would stop the theft. No one would even try.

"You will be moving to another hotel?"

"I have found a house that will better suit my elevated status."

Vivian knew what he meant. He'd seized a house—*a home*—from a Jewish family.

His nonchalance, his lack of affectation as he spoke, his complete disregard for the people he'd thrown out of their own home, these were the things that made him a monster. Suddenly, Vivian wanted to do violence to this man, even knowing he was bigger and stronger and could crush her with a single blow. She clenched her fists and breathed through the desire. It was so hard to push it down. Eventually, though, she was able to respond. "Tell me about the house."

It was the right thing to say, because he sat up straighter, a peacock preening over his newfound success. "It's three stories, each one decorated with tasteful furnishings and an art collection that would bring tears to the eyes of the greatest enthusiasts in Europe."

No amount of deep breathing calmed the renewed fury screaming in Vivian's veins. *Thief. Liar. Murderer.* How could he speak so calmly, with such confidence? "It sounds lovely."

"I admit, it's too much house for me, but it is the best in all of Drancy and, I believe, my due for the work I am to accomplish for the *Führer.*"

Here was her chance to discover what the Nazis planned for the former apartment complex. She said it quickly, before he could decipher her motive. "It must be important work."

He reached for her hand, their eyes locked, and he smiled. She smiled back, though it required great effort on her part. "I am to coordinate transportation of our detainees to concentration camps in Germany."

Detainees, meaning Jews. Vivian knew about the roundups. Everyone in Paris knew, though no one spoke of them, not in public. Not even in private. If no one talked about the horror taking place under their noses, it couldn't possibly be happening. A hideous, unconscionable rationalization that made Vivian sick at heart. But here, now, the silence of the French people worked in her favor. "Are there so many criminals in Paris that you need a separate facility?"

He eyed her with lips pressed together, a sure sign she'd trodden into dangerous waters. "Criminals, yes, in a manner of speaking. Once construction is complete, the facility will become a temporary detention center for Jews arrested in both Paris and the rest of France."

Vivian's mind stuck on one word. The worst of words. *Temporary*. The facility in Drancy was no longer a POW camp, or even a detention center for French Jews. No, it was to be nothing more than a way station for French Jews before they were sent to concentration camps inside Germany. The level of planning, the construction project itself, even von Bauer's own claim that his promotion put him in the upper echelon of Nazis, spoke of a large-scale operation. Thousands of souls would be seized and sent away, possibly killed.

This was another test, a way for *der Rab* to see if Vivian's ideology aligned with his. There were words she needed to say to secure his trust. Ugly, awful words. "A worthy project."

"It pleases me that you understand."

She looked away, mostly to hide her horror, and her own disgust at the words coming out of her mouth. She found her gaze wandering over the perfectly ordered room. Neat, clean, void of dirt and clutter. It came to her then, a way to gather more information than the bits and pieces she'd previously gleaned. It would mean going deeper into this man's world. But it would also mean no longer helping only few at a time, but hundreds. A lofty goal for one woman to undertake. But redemption just might be at the other end.

Could Vivian go into the viper's nest alone? Did she dare?

She had so few allies. None, that was, save one. It would mean more money for the girl, which would prove valuable if it became necessary to send her sister into hiding. It would also mean added danger. The choice would have to be up to Camille. But first, Vivian must insert herself into von Bauer's home. "This house you mentioned, the three-story mansion in Drancy, you will live there by yourself, or will your family be joining you?"

He stayed on the settee, reclining back, looking relaxed, completely at home, but his mouth tilted slightly up at one corner. "You are asking about my wife and children."

She nodded, knowing he'd mistaken the appalled tone in her voice for jealousy.

"The four of them will remain in Berlin."

Four. Vivian did the math in her head. One wife, three children. "I see."

Something came into his eyes, something dark and glittering and maybe a little cruel. "I can only imagine what you're feeling."

She wasn't feeling anything. That was the strange thing. She wanted to feel something—outrage, betrayal, grief for another woman. There was only a black emptiness where her soul should be, and an awareness that this man was exactly what she'd known him to be, a liar, a cheat. Married. The swine.

With the liquid grace of a dancer, Vivian reached for the silver case on the end table. She pulled out a cigarette, her eyes never leaving his face. Somewhere in the hotel, a door opened and closed with a bang, the sound moving through the air like a gunshot. Vivian didn't flinch. She lit a cigarette, took a long pull, pushed the smoke out in a slow, steady rhythm. This German was the worst of men. "You break your wedding vows very easily."

He tipped his head back, not an ounce of remorse. Yet another reason to despise him. "You worry about my wife, a woman you have never met?"

"I only wish to know what it is you want from me and if I am willing to give it."

Her response brought out his smile, the one she knew meant he was ready to play. "You wish this to be a negotiation." He gave a quick, satisfied nod. "This is good. Put your worries aside. Greta and I have not been intimate for years."

She saw it in him then, the rest of the lies that lived in his heart, the ability to think only of his own pleasure. Not even his own family came before his desires. He was the consummate Nazi, and a man of great ambition. Vivian could use both. In the time it took her to stroll to the balcony, pivot, and stand with the Paris night at her back, she had the makings of a plan in place.

Outside, a night creature cried, low and mournful. This was her last chance to be smart and end this farce. All it would take was a little outrage, a small jealous rant, and she would set fire to everything she'd built to this point.

She drew more smoke into her lungs. "The way I see it, you have been given an enviable position among your peers, and a large, elegant house, already furnished." She couldn't think about why that was. "Wielded properly, your career may go even further."

"What are you proposing, Vivian?"

She had his interest. Satisfaction filled her, but she only allowed her own grand ambitions to show on her face. "You will host exclusive dinner parties. The guest list will include only the most sought-after men and women in Paris. Everyone will seek an invitation into *your* inner circle. Many will be disappointed."

She saw the exact moment his aspirations took over his sense of caution. "And, of course, I will need a hostess for these exclusive gatherings."

"She should be a woman who understands how to make a man appear at his best."

"Tell me, Vivian." He moved quickly and took the cigarette from her hand, drew a long pull of smoke into his lungs, let it out in a rush. "Are you applying for the job?"

"You will not find a more experienced hostess."

He took his time responding. "This," he said at last, "I do not doubt."

"You will also want a housekeeper to keep your home in meticulous order."

"You have someone in mind." It was not a question.

"I do. A chambermaid here at the hotel. A young French-woman. Very pretty. Blonde, blue-eyed. I trust her completely."

The intent to deny her was in his eyes, in the way his head angled slightly off-center. Vivian had pushed too hard. She felt her anger flare, at him, at herself. She was tired of the manipulation, the games. She'd given von Bauer what he wanted, in a million different ways. He would now do the same for her. But it had to be his idea. "You will want to meet her, of course."

There was hesitation in him, still, but he also appeared intrigued. "She is blonde?"

"A very proper Aryan." How ugly that word sounded in her mouth.

"Tomorrow. You will bring the girl to me tomorrow, here, in this suite, at 5:00 p.m."

Vivian let him see only the smallest hint of triumph. "You will not regret this decision."

"I have made no decision."

Actually, he had. He just didn't know it yet. She moved in closer, until their bodies were touching, and their breaths had joined. "Tell me, *der Rab*. Tell me you want me by your side, warming your bed, planning your parties, and putting your name on every Parisian's lips."

His answer all but sealed their deal. "I look forward to meeting the chambermaid."

The Paris Housekeeper

Chapter Twenty-Three

Camille

12 March 1942.
Hôtel Ritz. Paris, France.

Camille answered the summons to Vivian's room with no small amount of trepidation. Life in the Ritz was fraught with danger. The most innocent of conversations could be interpreted a hundred different ways. Every collection of words exchanged could have hidden meaning. Alliances were made and broken. Friendships were questioned, especially between a chambermaid and a wealthy American widow.

Thus, they didn't speak in public, and kept eye contact brief. However, sometimes, Vivian called Camille to her room in the Rue Cambon building. She always prefaced their conversations by asking after Jacqueline. Camille never quite knew how to take the widow's interest in her sister. Did she truly care about the girl's progress?

There was another possibility, a more sinister one. Vivian could be gathering information for her Nazi lover. Then again, Camille knew the widow continued her work with Frank, often conducted via tiny handwritten notes, with Camille acting as courier.

Still, Vivian could be playing both sides. Hence Camille's unease. Even on this side of the hotel, where the regular guests stayed, she felt eyes on her. She looked up and down the corridor, over her shoulder, and sighed at her own paranoia. When, she wondered, would the need for subterfuge come to an end? Another six months, a year, five times that long?

The Americans were in the war now, something many French citizens had feared would never happen, but matters seemed worse, not better. The Germans were so strong, so angry, so determined to make the entire world their own.

Camille hesitated outside Vivian's door. Reluctance moved through her. The widow knew too much about her, and Camille knew too little about her in return. Her relationship with von Bauer was a favorite topic among the staff. Even Rachel, who never had a bad thing to say about anyone, not even the chambermaids who called her names, considered the widow the vilest of creatures. If only Camille could tell her friend the truth.

But no. She'd made a promise and, in truth, couldn't be sure Vivian wasn't every vile thing the gossips claimed. Had Camille put her trust in the wrong person? Unlikely. She knew some of Vivian's secrets. That bonded them.

Head lifted, mind clear, she knocked, quick and brusque. Vivian opened the door, and Camille recognized something in the woman's gaze that resided in her own tortured soul—a need for redemption. Two sides of the same coin.

"Come in, Camille."

She crossed the threshold. Once inside the room, she noted a strange sort of stillness on the air, silent but for the click of Vivian's heels on the entryway floor. Camille thought she heard something else, a breath of sound, but as she strained to make it out, the noise seemed to be only in her head. Vivian stopped at the window overlooking Rue Cambon but didn't turn to look out.

Her face was calm, her hands folded at her waist, and when she spoke, it was to ask, "How is your sister?"

An image of Jacqueline when she'd last visited flashed in Camille's mind. She'd been bent over a puzzle, a peaceful look on her face. Her entire bearing had been breathtakingly serene, and she repeated Dr. Garnier's assurance: "There is cause for hope."

Vivian smiled. "She's better, then?"

How best to answer? Nightmares still plagued the girl, and while she had many good days, she also had bad ones. Too many of them. "She's no worse."

Arms outstretched, Vivian came to her, took her hands in a gesture of solidarity. Not friend to friend, no. Something like mother to daughter, but not. "Then we focus on that."

Camille saw the sincerity in her eyes, heard it in her voice, felt it in her gentle grip, and she found herself admitting, "Her progress comes with a price."

"Most things do." The response came with a hint of bitterness.

Camille's sentiments exactly. She was tired, so very tired of her own helplessness, of never quite succeeding in bringing hope to others. Not only for Jacqueline, but for her mother and sisters. And then there was Rachel. Camille wasn't so consumed with her own worries that she didn't see the agony her friend suffered. The constant humiliations at work, the arrest of her father and brother.

"I have a proposition for you."

So lost in her own thoughts, it took Camille a moment to organize Vivian's words into meaning, and to realize the other woman had released her hands and was hovering over her like a benevolent being from a childhood fairy tale. "A...proposition?"

Vivian reached down and touched Camille's cheek. "It would

mean leaving your position here at the hotel, and the bar, but it will pay three times the salary you make now."

Camille blinked in astonishment. What, exactly, was Vivian suggesting? Was she offering her something illicit, something to do with her Nazi, or another one like him?

"What sort of position would pay so much to a woman like me?" Her voice cracked over the question, graceless and full of guilt. But also, hope. That horrible, awful, tempting emotion slithered through her, tempting her, coloring her perspective. In that moment, in every moment before, Camille knew—she knew—whatever opportunity Vivian was offering, she would consider seriously. For Jacqueline and her family, even for Rachel and hers. Yes, she would do anything to save the people she loved.

Anything.

"Von Bauer is setting up his own household outside the hotel. He needs a housekeeper, and I suggested you."

The man needed a housekeeper. Camille sank onto the arm of a nearby chair. "What would this job entail, exactly?"

"The usual. Cooking, cleaning, laundry." Vivian shook her head, the insult easy to read on her face. "What did you think I was suggesting?"

Camille cleared her throat. "I thought—"

"I *know* what you thought." Sighing, she went to an end table and picked up a silver cigarette case, rolled it around in her palm. She looked thoughtful and maybe a little tortured. "I suppose I should have expected this, even from you. I have played my role well, have I not?"

"We have all made hard choices in this war."

"True enough." She laughed, a hard, bitter sound, as she lit a cigarette and took a long, audible puff. Then several more. "Tell me, Camille, how far would you have gone, had I asked it of you?"

"For my sisters, my mother, there are no limits to what I would do."

They locked eyes, and Vivian's sharp gaze softened. "Even if that means living and working in the home of a Nazi? Can you do this, Camille? Can you cross this line?"

For her family? "Yes."

"I would, of course, be there as well. I would never allow you to do this alone. You know this, right? I will not let him harm you."

The promise was unexpected, and greatly appreciated. "Thank you."

"I must, however, warn you." Vivian ground out her cigarette in a ceramic dish. "Von Bauer is a hard, meticulous, demanding man. He will expect perfection."

"He is no different from any of the Germans living in the hotel."

"Think of them and multiply by ten. He misses nothing. There can be no mistakes, Camille. Not even small ones. Von Bauer has no forgiveness in him. I cannot stress this enough."

And Vivian had brought such a man into her life. Camille thought of him, and what she knew. Like the other Nazis in the hotel, he treated the staff with little respect. No smiles, no kind words. Only commands snarled out in his thick German accent. She found his behavior reprehensible, to be sure. But she only had to tolerate the callousness. For Rachel, it was a more complicated matter. Even squirreled away in the laundry, she wasn't fully safe.

Leaving the hotel would mean abandoning her friend. Camille nearly said no, but her family... Jacqueline. They were her priority. But perhaps there was a way to guarantee Rachel's security in her absence. "If I agree to this," she began, choosing her words carefully, "I will require something from you in return."

"Ah. You wish to bargain. I didn't expect that." Vivian straightened, and her entire demeanor took on a cool air. "All right, then, Camille. Make your request, and we will see what comes next."

Keep it vague, she told herself. *Provide no names.* "I would ask that you keep watch over my friend, as you've done for me."

A long moment passed, without a single change in Vivian's expression. "You ask much."

She asked not enough. Had done not enough. Small, insignificant things, a few kind words, standing up to the bullies. So very little when held up against the persecution Rachel suffered daily. The slurs were only the start. There was the banishment to the laundry. The heavy workload that seemed to grow heavier. Then there was the arrest of her father and brother. No, Camille had not done enough for her friend. "Please, Vivian. If I take this job, she will have no one to protect her."

Vivian's gaze flicked away. "I have explained why I cannot show the girl favor."

Because Rachel was Jewish. And Vivian openly cavorted with a Nazi. She had her reasons, yes, but now she was asking Camille to be a party to her schemes. A bold move that called for an equally daring response. "I ask only that you check on her, occasionally, and see she isn't harmed or put in unnecessary danger."

Another long pause, and then, as if knowing she was in the wrong, a slow, reluctant nod. "I will do this for you. But only if you secure the position with von Bauer."

"I thought the job was mine."

"Not yet. My word is not enough. He requires meeting you himself before making his final decision."

"He wishes to interview me?" Her voice was flat as she posed the rhetorical question, appalled even, and she wondered why she was so surprised. Had she thought she would never have to come face-to-face with the man? Had she assumed she would run his household without ever having to interact with him?

That's exactly what she'd thought. What she'd hoped. "When is the interview?"

"This afternoon at five. In his suite. Do not be late."

His suite. Camille would be alone with an exacting Nazi.

Her horror must have shown, because Vivian rushed on to say, "I will be in the room."

Camille forced herself to speak, bringing the words out in a rush before she lost her nerve. "Thank you, Vivian. If there's nothing else…" She waited, then continued when Vivian said nothing more. "I'll get back to my duties now."

"Five o'clock, Camille."

She arrived at von Bauer's suite at the agreed-upon time. Vivian answered the door with a brief nod and led Camille deeper into the room. "*Der Rab*, the chambermaid has arrived for your inspection."

Von Bauer looked up from his position in an overstuffed chair, a newspaper in his lap. He wore his SS uniform, nothing out of place. Even the iron cross was still pinned at the center of his collar, perfectly aligned with the middle of his chin.

Meticulous, indeed. Also, rude. He did not stand. He did not address Camille directly, but rather ran his gaze over her face, her hair, along her body, down to her toes. His inspection slowed to a crawl on the way back up to her face, a look of satisfaction in those cold, fathomless eyes the color of winter ice. Camille felt violated, as if his hands had performed the task rather than his gaze.

Vivian cleared her throat.

His eyes remained locked on Camille as he began the interview. In German. Camille pretended ignorance as he asked his questions. Two only. When she didn't respond, and he grew angry, she replied that she didn't speak German. He switched to French and posed his questions again. This time, she quickly, succinctly, gave her name and place of birth.

"You have the look of a good German girl." He said this with such approval that Camille thought she might be sick.

The interrogation began in earnest then. "What is in *coq au vin*?"

"Chicken and red wine."

"How many Cornish hens would you need to cook for a table of twenty?"

A trick question. The man was testing her. "One per guest, so twenty."

Some fifteen minutes later, he gave a single nod. "You have the job. I wish for you to begin two weeks from tomorrow."

Fifteen days. She had fifteen days to upend her life. "Thank you."

He flicked his hand in the air and, ignoring her now, said to Vivian, almost as an afterthought, "I trust you to make the arrangements for her relocation to my home."

Without waiting for a response, he went back to his newspaper. Vivian slipped her arm through Camille's and led her back to the foyer. At the door, she whispered, "You did well."

Later that night, alone at her kitchen table, staring at the hands that would clean a Nazi's house, Camille suffered more than a few doubts. She would be working directly for a high-ranking SS officer, living under his roof, seeing to his every need. Except, of course, the one Vivian met. It was all so sordid. And ugly.

But…Jacqueline. Camille's mother and sisters. Rachel and her family.

When she ran it over in her head, again and again, the choice was not so hard. Not when she considered the people she loved.

Chapter Twenty-Four

Rachel

March 1942.
The Berman Apartment. Paris, France.

Rachel pulled herself out of bed, dressed, and looked in the cracked mirror. Her cheeks were raw and red, no doubt from the heat and chemicals she encountered in the hotel laundry. The ravages didn't stop there. Her eyes were sunken in their sockets, and her stomach was so empty she barely had the energy to trudge into the next room, much less face another grueling day of washing bed linens and tablecloths and napkins. All while suffering the slurs and small persecutions that never failed to cut deep.

You, there. The Jewish girl. The label was more slur than description. The term echoed through her head at work, and now, at home. It beat in time with her footsteps as she half walked, half shuffled into the main living area.

The Jewish girl. The words floated through the fog in her brain, made worse by the lack of air in the apartment. The windows had been shut because of the rain. Three days of the watery assault. Hours upon hours of a bleak gray sky. Even inside the apartment, the light was dim and also gray. The electricity had been turned off by the French authorities, another persecution.

The Jewish girl. The entire staff called her that now, except Camille. Her only friend. The others treated Rachel with the barest hint of tolerance. Sometimes not even that. They would not break her. Every day she had a job was a victory over their bigotry and racism.

A glance outside told Rachel that dawn had surrendered fully to the morning, but the rain continued falling. She longed to be free of the soggy weather and her own dark mood. She wanted relief from the sorrow that grew each day there was no news from her father or brother. There'd been letters at first, filled with the assurances that they would be home soon.

Her mother had clung to those promises and found solace in her knitting. She made scarves for her husband and son at a frantic pace. And when the letters stopped, she simply made more, often unraveling previous creations or dipping into the skeins of yarn she'd collected before the Germans arrived. Whenever Rachel asked her why she kept at the task, the older woman would get a distant look in her eyes and say, "What else am I to do?"

What, indeed.

Rachel wanted to believe her father and brother were alive. She wanted never to hear the clacking of knitting needles in place of their laughter. She wanted desperately to eat something other than rotten cabbage.

Hurried footsteps sounded in the hallway. A dog barked. The door swung open, and Basia appeared on the threshold, looking pale, her eyes wide. The air seemed to shift under the force of her dismay. Something had rattled her, and Rachel ran to her, prepared for more bad news. Always, she thought, sorrow and grief showed up on their doorstep.

"Basia." Rachel tugged her sister into the sitting area, shutting the door behind them. "What's wrong? Why are you not at work?"

"It's happened." Tears wiggled to the edges of her lashes. "I have been dismissed."

Rachel wanted to comfort her sister, but Basia was shaking so hard, and now so was Rachel, and then the outrage came. "But you're the best seamstress in the fashion house. Mademoiselle Ballard has said so again and again."

"A girl arrived from Reims. Claudette. No, Paulette." Basia's voice was drenched with…something. Shock, confusion, bitterness? "She was young—your age, Rachel—and she was dressed quite elegantly."

"She was a client, then?"

Basia shook her head. "She came with a suitcase. And though her clothing was impeccable, it was clear something terrible had happened to her. I could see that right away, and all I thought to do was feel sorry for the girl."

Naturally, that would be Basia's first instinct. Good, kind, beautiful Basia. Rachel felt it again, that painful lurch of concern. Her sister was older, but in many ways more innocent than Rachel, with a heart that could not see evil in others because there was none in her. "Do you know what happened? Why she showed up on Mademoiselle Ballard's doorstep?"

Basia shook her head. The movement left a stray hair hanging low over her forehead, and she pushed the offending curl away with an impatient swipe. "I don't know, something to do with an arrest. Mademoiselle Ballard had been expecting her, I think."

There were so many thoughts in Rachel's head, but then she heard a sound and glanced over her shoulder, hoping to see her mother. And there she stood, looking so very frail and beaten. Ilka Berman had changed since the arrests. The loss of her husband and son, the absence of information, the sudden lack of letters, all of it had carved deep lines in her face and neck.

"This girl," Basia continued. "This Paulette, she came for a job with Mademoiselle, though she's never sewn a single stitch with her hand or a machine. Her only recommendation was a sketch pad of her drawings. I saw a few. Pretty dresses, the kind meant for parties, and absolutely, completely inappropriate for wartime. And yet..." Basia swallowed hard. "Mademoiselle gave her *my job*."

"It's an outrage," said Rachel with less force than she felt. "What are we going to do?"

How were they to survive on her pitiful wages alone?

Her mother drew her in close, and with what was a sterling effort, managed to sound nearly normal. "We will find a way."

How? They were living under German occupation, where nothing was guaranteed. The roundups kept coming. Thus far, Jewish women and children had been spared. But Rachel knew that would change one day.

A knock at the door cut through her thoughts. She slipped out from under her mother's arm and opened the door to Basia's boyfriend. He stood in the hallway, hat in hand, a nervous tick playing at the corner of his mouth. "Jacob? Were we expecting you?"

Had Basia called him to tell him her news? How? When? The Nazis had taken their telephone, along with the family's radio. How could he know his devastated girlfriend needed him?

Rachel was about to ask when Basia appeared beside her, and suddenly, his nerves were gone, replaced by a smile that suggested a brand of happiness that hadn't lived in this apartment since German soldiers marched on Paris.

"Mademoiselle Ballard told me you'd gone home—but what is this?" He took Basia's shoulders and studied her face. "You're crying."

"I lost my job this morning. I am no longer in Mademoiselle Ballard's employ."

"She didn't tell me this." His surprise at this news seemed genuine, but he didn't appear concerned. "I'm sorry. I know you enjoyed your job."

"I did. Oh, Jacob, I really did love my work." She paused, as if something suddenly occurred to her. "But why did you come to the fashion house, and now here?"

"I had to find you. I…" He looked at the others in the room, seeming to be momentarily unsure whether to continue, but not for long. "I have the most wonderful news. My father has given us his blessing to marry."

Basia's face transformed. But then she was frowning again, and shaking her head. "Oh, Jacob. This is not the right time."

"How can it not be right? I love you. I have loved you since you stood on the front stoop of my parents' home, come to fit the dress my mother had ordered from Mademoiselle Ballard."

She laughed a little, the sound a rusty version of the real thing. "I remember thinking you were the most handsome man I had ever met."

"Then marry me. Let us have something to celebrate in these dark times." He pulled her hands to his face and kissed each of palm. "Say yes and make me the happiest man in France."

"I can't marry you without my father here."

Ilka Berman entered the conversation, her voice surprisingly strong. "Your father would want you happy. More, he would want you settled. This is right."

"It doesn't feel right, Mama. Saying wedding vows without Papa and Srulka there to witness."

"We will tell them all about it when they are home once again."

Basia seemed to consider this. She slowly smiled at her mother, then at Jacob. "Yes, I'll marry you as soon as possible."

Jacob whooped. Basia laughed. Rachel's mother cried. As for Rachel, she swallowed down a surge of dread. *This is a mistake.* The thought skittered through her mind, instantly followed by another. *This union will end in tragedy.*

The wedding was scheduled for the end of the week. Mere hours after Rachel's final shift at the hotel, though none of them knew that at the time. She'd predicted she'd be let go, though not for the offense of stealing a towel that had mysteriously shown up in her locker.

For several endless seconds, Rachel had stood mortified, staring at the small peach washcloth with the hotel logo. "There's been a mistake."

"No mistake." Her supervisor grabbed her wrist, harder than necessary. "I found it in your locker. Explain yourself."

"I can't." She tried to keep her voice steady, tried to pull away from the menacing grip, but Madame Bergeron held on, her fingers digging into Rachel's flesh.

Camille, being Camille, immediately came to her defense. "Rachel didn't steal the towel. It's not in her nature."

"She is a Jew. All Jews lie and steal. *That* is their *nature*." Madame Bergeron spat the last like a swear word, her vehemence sending little flecks of spittle into the air. Then, suddenly, she released Rachel. "Clean out your locker."

The words hit like a slap in the face, and the humiliation rose up inside her, churning too quickly to be set aside, only endured.

"I said, *sortir de mon hôtel.*"

Leave my hotel. It was over. Done. No chance to defend herself, no mention of the wages owed her. The one thing that beat inside Rachel's head was *run. Before she has you arrested.*

She abandoned any thought of retrieving her personal belongings for fear of being accused of stealing again. She stayed only long enough to change her clothes. She was soon outside, standing on Rue Cambon, wondering how she would tell her mother. She would not cry. She would go home and face her family. Her feet took her the first few steps. Each one no easier than the last.

"Rachel, wait. Please." Camille ran to her, touched her arm, dropped her hand just as quickly. "I'll speak with the manager. I'll say the towel was mine."

"Then you will be let go, too."

"It doesn't matter. It's only a week before I—"

"Stop, Camille. Please stop. I know you mean well." And for that Rachel was grateful. "But there is nothing you can do."

"It's not right."

"No, it isn't." She tried to keep her voice steady, but it came out colder and sharper than she meant. "We both know this was inevitable. In truth, I'm relieved it's over and done."

Camille drew back, and then she sighed, slowly, and bit her chapped lips. "Is there anything I can do? Anything you need?"

So much. She needed so, so much. A job. A world not in chaos. Her father and brother home. She looked down and found her hands were shaking. Suddenly, she wanted her mother. "I only wish to go home."

Camille looked so sad, perhaps even grimly shattered, as if she understood Rachel's desire all too well. Her calm slipped a moment, and something came into her eyes, a kind of sorrow that spoke of apology, perhaps even guilt. "There's something I need to tell you."

"All right."

She looked mildly uncertain. "I have... That is, I will be... No, never mind. Now is not the time." Her jaw firmed, and she reached out a hand. "Will you be all right to walk home alone? I can ask—"

"I'll be fine on my own."

"Rachel—"

"I said, I'll be fine."

Undeterred by her sharp tone, Camille persisted. But Rachel held firm, and she finally relented. Rachel watched her retreat inside the hotel, feeling oddly bereft, as if their friendship had changed, though she couldn't think how. Her unhappy mood went unnoticed when she returned home. And she realized why. Basia was marrying the man of her dreams later that afternoon. Rachel decided to keep the news of her dismissal to herself until after the nuptials.

The exchange of vows lasted ten minutes and was, on the surface, no different from any other civil ceremony. Rachel didn't remember the words spoken, nor the promises the two made to one another. What she would remember was the way Basia looked at Jacob and he at her. The love in their eyes. The unquestionable devotion. The way Jacob held her sister's hand reverently in his. Yes, these were the things she would remember and would tell their children when they asked about their parents' wedding.

"I pronounce you man and wife."

A cheer went up among the small assemblage of family members. Hugs and happy tears ensued, and then Jacob whisked his new bride away for a brief honeymoon at one of the hotels where his father knew the owners and had thus pulled a few strings. Rachel tried not to be bitter that he could do so much for his new daughter-in-law and so little for her family.

What Rachel didn't know, what she didn't discover until she and her mother arrived home from the courthouse, was that Jacob and his father had more than a one-night honeymoon planned for his bride.

Dearest Sister,

By the time you read this, Jacob and I will be bound for Spain, then on to America. My new father-in-law, lovely man that he is, has made the arrangements himself. He secured the documents in my married name and has promised to do the same for you and Mama. And again, for Papa and Srulka once they return from wherever they have been staying.

Oh, dear sister. I happily await our reunion. Tell Mama I am safe and well and anxious to see her again very soon.

Love and kisses,

Mrs. Basia ~~*Berman*~~ *Lindon*

Rachel held the letter in her hand, realizing she'd been right. Basia and Jacob's union had ended in tragedy. Not for the married couple, but for the family her sister had left behind.

Chapter Twenty-Five

Camille

March 1942.
Hôtel Ritz. Paris, France.

Camille left for home with shame weighing her down. She'd failed Rachel. And now, the girl no longer worked at the hotel. Clearly, Madame Bergeron had been looking for a reason to dismiss her. The sour woman had probably planted the evidence herself. A gross injustice. Unfortunately, no amount of arguing could sway the woman to reconsider. Camille had tried. Upon returning to the locker room, she'd argued that a mistake had occurred.

The supervisor had remained unmoved.

Vivian had been her next step. She'd explained, in rather blunt terms, that it was one thing to look out for the girl, but quite another to intervene directly on her behalf. Then she'd switched topics and had gone on to explain Camille's duties in von Bauer's home and the logistics of moving her into the house itself.

That had brought on more regret. Camille should have told Rachel about her job. She hadn't wanted to upset the girl further, but really, she hadn't wanted her friend to think less of her. What a selfish, cowardly decision.

Upset with herself, Camille opted to walk to her apartment. She would make this trip only a few more times before moving into von Bauer's home. So caught up in her own thoughts, she'd failed to pay attention to her surroundings and found she'd wandered off course. She was in the second arrondissement now.

What had possessed her to take such a circuitous route home? She understood as soon as she rounded the corner and the Palais Berlitz loomed. Back in September of last year, the theater had shown *Le Juif et la France*, a film to educate Parisians on how to recognize the "racial" characteristics of Jews living among them.

Hoping to uncover the source of so much unreasonable hate, Camille had attended one of the showings. It had been a mistake. She'd sat through five minutes, perhaps less, wide-eyed and stunned at the irrationality of the Nazis' supposed science.

So impossible. So senseless.

Surely, she'd thought, she wasn't alone in her shock. She'd taken a quick glance to her right, back to her left, over the audience in general, and received a bigger shock. Her fellow moviegoers, most of them French, were nodding and laughing at the ridiculous images. And then, they were *agreeing* with the premise that Jews were substandard humans. Some were even taking notes, as if cataloging the physical traits that supposedly set a Jewish man or woman apart from the rest of them. Such bigotry.

Camille had been appalled, and rushed out of the building, trembling with revulsion and shame. What had she done to stop the madness from spreading through Paris? Pass a few notes in the Little Bar? Even Vivian Miller, a woman sleeping with the enemy, accomplished much with her forgery network. While

Camille thought only of her family, of Jacqueline, and little else. She'd befriended Rachel, but very few others.

Now, as she gazed up to where the giant movie poster had once hung with that hideous caricature of a male Jew, she was disgusted and sickened all over again, with her fellow Parisians— and herself. She plunged her hands deep in her pockets, down to their seams. Aware suddenly of a draft, crisp against her damp cheeks. She turned her head and caught sight of her reflection in a store window. Staring back was the truth Rachel must see as well.

Camille was one of *them.*

Non! She was not an Aryan. She only looked like one. It was the reason von Bauer had hired her to work in his home. He saw what was on the outside and decided she must surely be like him on the inside. And therein—possibly, maybe—lay Camille's means of redemption. As von Bauer's housekeeper, she would have access to his private life, his personal papers, perhaps even his work papers.

Was this her way to fight the enemy?

It would be dangerous. But she wouldn't be alone. Vivian would be there. Vivian, with her own secrets and clandestine work. Like the American, Camille would find a way to help more than just her family. She would help people unfairly persecuted, mostly Jewish men and women. If not all of them, then some. A few. Rachel and her family, at least.

Her mind full of possibilities, and only a little of the danger, she entered her building and made the climb to the third floor. The sight of the concierge shutting the door to her apartment sent a jolt of alarm through her. Camille knew the woman collected information about her tenants—who was doing what, where, and with whom. She'd seen the evidence of the woman's snooping. A misplaced book. A candle moved. A drawer left open.

"Bonjour," she said coolly. "You are looking for me?"

The woman spun around, her eyes blinking, clearly surprised

to be caught so completely. "Mademoiselle Lacroix, I didn't expect you home so soon."

Her response told Camille the concierge did indeed take note of her comings and goings. She was suddenly exhausted with this woman, and so many like her, neighbors monitoring neighbors, friends ratting out friends. This was what came from a bully regime that ruled with fear and very little else. "Was there something you needed?"

She stood tall. "You received a letter from Rennes."

The woman wanted to say more—Camille could read that much in her cagey expression—but to do so would reveal she knew the letter's contents. Though Camille wasn't surprised, she was annoyed. And prepared. She and Dr. Garnier had worked out a code to keep the censures, and nosy neighbors, unaware of Jacqueline's condition. Camille shot out her hand. "The letter?"

"I left it on your nightstand."

Camille said nothing.

"It seemed important, and I didn't want you to miss it."

Oh, yes, the concierge had read the letter. Every bit of it. But she'd gleaned little, and that brought some satisfaction.

Suddenly, Camille wanted to get to the letter.

She longed to read every vague, carefully worded sentence, knowing Garnier's kindness would emanate off the page and connect Camille to Jacqueline, and to him. Not wanting the concierge to see her eagerness, she engaged in a banal dissertation about the weather. The conversation lasted five minutes, an eternity. Then they said goodbye.

Inside the apartment, Camille found the letter exactly where Madame Thibodeaux claimed she would. She ran her fingertip over her name, penned in Garnier's signature loops and bold slashes. She could practically feel the warmth of his hand as it had crossed over the page. Would he have good news to share? Or bad? Taking a deep breath, she lifted the envelope's flap and pulled out the single slip of paper. The plain letterhead gave away nothing of the letter's origins. The message itself was short, and to the point, also exactly as they'd agreed.

Mademoiselle Lacroix.

No salutation, nothing but her name, written in his bold, masculine handwriting, and yet she felt his kindness wash over her.

I have only good news to report. The new fertilizer has proven most effective, and your favorite flower is blooming. A visit would be most welcome. I always appreciate your input when it comes to this particular variety. I still have much to learn.

Camille smiled—it felt good to smile. The gardening references had been Garnier's idea and were easy enough to decipher. New fertilizer meant a new treatment. Her favorite flower meant Jacqueline. He didn't sign the letter. That, too, had been agreed upon to protect Jacqueline. Camille reread Garnier's words, hearing his voice as if she were listening to his rich baritone giving her the report in person.

She let herself cry. Really cry. That felt good, too, as she sat on her bed and buried her face in her hands and sobbed. All her worries for Jacqueline, and her failure to help Rachel, found release in her tears. When the sobs turned to hiccups, she felt drained, but also fully committed to her new position as von Bauer's housekeeper and the possibility of doing more than merely clean his house.

What would Garnier think of her decision?

He would have to know. She'd grown to trust him. He would keep Jacqueline safe. She still worried about the Nazis turning their attention to mental patients in France. But with the Americans now in the war, and Hitler's obsession to be rid of all Jews in Europe, the threat to Jacqueline didn't seem as large as before. Camille could monitor the Nazis' position more closely while in von Bauer's home, another reason to take the position.

All that was left was telling Garnier.

She made the trip to Rennes two days later. As with her previous visits, she smiled at the guard and waited to be let in. He knew her by name. The rest of staff greeted her similarly.

After visiting with her sister, Camille found herself in Garnier's office, feeling a bittersweet sensation. It would be a very long time before she saw Jacqueline again, or her dedicated doctor who'd become a friend and confidant.

He sat across from her, the giant metal desk between them, his expression soft. "Camille, it's good to see you."

"You as well, Dr. Garnier."

"Pierre, please. I believe we are past such formalities."

"Pierre, then." She liked the sound of his name rolling past her lips. She liked his face, too. And his smile, the strength of his character. She liked it all. She liked him. The thought brought something warm spreading through her, something profound and inconvenient, and then she remembered why she'd come to Rennes. She frowned.

"You have something to tell me," he said.

Her frown deepened. How could he know her so well? She'd shared something of herself in their visits, this was true, and he'd done the same. She knew where he came from—Bordeaux— his schooling, and his decision to go into psychiatry after his own father's struggles following the war. That shared experience had brought them closer. But were they so connected that he could read her moods?

"You may speak freely, Camille. You have nothing to fear from me."

His amber eyes met hers then, and she could not for the life of her produce a single syllable. Would he judge her for her decision? Did she care what he thought of her?

Yes, she did. She cared very much.

She said it quickly. "I am leaving the Hôtel Ritz and have taken a new position as a housekeeper in a private home at three times my current wages."

For a moment, he said nothing, merely looked at her, searching her expression while nothing showed in his. Finally, he gave a short nod. "This decision was difficult. One you do not regret, but it brings you concern nonetheless."

This man was very good at his job. "The job is in the home of...of...a Nazi."

His countenance paled. For an instant, she saw a flash of sorrow in his eyes as he stood and came to sit in the empty chair beside her. He reached for her hand, held it gently. "You took this position for your sister. To pay for her care."

His understanding, it made her mind go blank. She looked at their joined hands. Why did the contact feel so natural? As if their palms were meant to touch like this, two magnets finding home. "Yes, I do this for Jacqueline. She is always my first concern. But also, my mother and other sisters. The bakery is struggling. They are struggling. I can't let them down."

"There is no other way?"

His scent wafted over her. He smelled of soap and new beginnings. Of promises not yet made. At the fanciful thought, she shook her head, very slowly. Lifting her chin, she said, "I have little education, few skills. No." She shook her head again. "There is no other way."

The grip on her hand grew tighter. "Don't return to Paris, Camille. Stay here. With me. You can be *my* housekeeper. You—"

"—have too many people relying on me." She pulled her hand free. "Don't try to change my mind. We both know you can't pay me what von Bauer will."

"No, I don't have that kind of money, but there are ways I can protect you and your family."

The temptation was strong. "Why? Why are you offering this to me, a total stranger?"

"We aren't strangers."

No, they weren't. And she very much wanted what he offered. Perhaps he could keep her safe, and Jacqueline, too. But her mother and sisters? And what of Rachel? What right did Camille have to hide away in this man's promise of safety, when her friend faced a far graver future? Since the day she'd left Jacqueline alone with their father, Camille had failed the people who relied on her most. She would not run from her duty now.

"I should go." She stood.

Pierre scrambled to his feet a moment too late. She was halfway to the door, her hand reaching for the handle.

"Camille, wait." He strode around her in three long strides, his stance nonthreatening, but barring her exit all the same. "Don't do this. Don't take this terrible job. It's too dangerous."

"Please, Pierre, you're standing too close. I can't think with you so near."

He moved not an inch.

"People rely on me. You must let me fulfill my duty, or I won't be able to live with myself. I can't run from this." Not this time. "I wish I could, but no. This is my destiny."

He took a breath. She could feel the shudder pass through him, the one that matched her own. "You ask too much, Camille. It isn't in me to let someone I care about walk into danger."

"As long as the Nazis occupy France, and spread their hate, we are all in danger."

To his credit, he didn't argue. "If he hurts you..."

"I'll be smart. Please. Don't make this any harder than it already is."

"All right. But before you go, I want you to remember this address." Finally, he stepped back, then rattled off a number and the name of a street.

She nodded.

He said the address again, then insisted she repeat it.

"Why? What is the significance?"

"It's where I live. My private residence. If anything changes, if you sense you're in danger, come to me. Promise me, Camille. Promise you will come to me."

Her answer was to repeat the address two more times, ending with, "Take care of my sister."

"Always." He placed a tender kiss to her forehead, so soft she thought she imagined it. Then it was his turn to make a quiet demand. "*Va avec Dieu*, Camille."

Go with God. She tucked the words in her heart and, with one final glance over her shoulder, left Rennes, praying that when next she returned to him, the war would be over, and France had been swept clean of every German snake from her soil.

Chapter Twenty-Six

Rachel

25 March 1942.
The Berman Apartment. Paris, France.

Every day, when dawn broke over the city, and Rachel woke to the realities of her life—her father and brother gone, her lost job, Basia's abandonment—all she wanted to do was burrow beneath the covers and never come out. She didn't, no matter how powerful the pull. Her mother needed her.

This morning, though, after five days of unemployment, when she heard the clack of knitting needles, the desire to indulge in her own self-pity grabbed her by the throat. But no. She tossed a shawl over her shoulders and let her nose guide her to where her mother sat near the stove, their pitiful breakfast simmering in a foul, sickly stench.

How long, Rachel wondered, would they have gas flowing through the burners? Their very survival hung in the balance. Why, why had Basia left without ensuring they were cared for and fed? Had she not thought, even a little, about them? She claimed she would send for them. Yet they heard nothing.

Bitterness took root, and Rachel watched her mother set aside her knitting in favor of standing at the stove, staring vacantly into the pot. Ilka Berman seemed especially frail this morning. She'd always been a small woman. Now she appeared impossibly petite and fragile, as if she were shrinking inside herself.

The thought had barely settled when her mother looked up. The grief on her face, naked and bare, sent a slice of pain straight through Rachel's heart. The woman she'd always known was missing. In her place was this broken creature. Alive, yes, but broken. Rachel wanted her mother back, but their roles had reversed. She was the adult now, Ilka Berman the child.

A knock at the door startled them both, and Rachel spun around to stare at the slab of wood, fearing what stood on the other side. *Is this it? Have they come to arrest us?*

The knock came again, but there were no shouts to open up, or demands to let them in. Not the police, then. Someone else.

Her mother must have come to the same conclusion because she shuffled toward her bedroom without another word. Rachel pulled the folds of her shawl tighter around her shoulders and answered the door. Camille stood in the hallway, an unreadable expression on her face. Rachel blinked in surprise. She hadn't seen her friend since she'd been dismissed from the hotel. She'd missed their walks home together when their schedules had aligned. So why did she resent the girl's appearance on her doorstep this morning? Had it come too soon? Too late?

What did it matter? Her friend was here now, and Rachel was being rude. Camille had been nothing but kind to her. Then why did she wish her gone? Why this need for solitude when she'd always hated being alone?

"Camille," she said, in what she hoped was a pleasant tone. "Come in."

As she stepped into the apartment, the shadows from the hallway rolled away, and Rachel got a good look at Camille's face. Her eyes held such utter bereavement that Rachel's first thought was of death. "Has something happened to your family?" She thought a moment, remembered her friend's burdens. "Is it your mother? Your sisters? Has one of them fallen ill?"

"No, no. They are well. Or rather—" she pressed her lips together, sighed "—as well as can be expected, considering."

"But something *is* wrong. I can see it clearly on your face."

Sighing again, she glanced away, glanced back. "I have come to tell you something important, but I don't think you're going to like it."

Her nervousness was contagious, and Rachel set a tentative hand on her shoulder. "Here," she said, pointing to the sofa. "Sit down. And tell me what you've come to say."

"I can't stay long. I have to—" She cut herself off, abruptly, and her gaze fell to the bag looped around her forearm. "Oh, I almost forgot. I brought you this."

Rachel took the bag, looked inside, and saw food. So much food. Pastries and salted meats and cheeses and bread that smelled freshly baked. Her mouth watered. Her stomach growled. She didn't know what to say, except the first thing that came to her mind. "How?"

"I confiscated what I could from the hotel kitchens."

Again… "How?"

"Yesterday, before I left, I saw that Chef was about to toss these leftovers in the waste bin. I offered to do it on my way home. He seemed happy to be free of the task," she said, pulling the opening wider. Together, they peered inside the bag. "Or maybe he knew I had other plans for the food and decided not to stop me."

Rachel stared dumbfounded at her friend.

Basically, Camille had risked her job to steal food for her. She could have been arrested or stopped by a German soldier. Her friend had gone to great risk to supply Rachel with much-needed food. Her generosity was too much. Darkness and silence filled the moment. And Rachel's shame swelled. But also, her hunger, and the impossibility of refusing this gift.

The words *thank you* were tangled up inside her pride. She

couldn't seem to push those two simple words of gratitude past her lips. *I must.*

"Tha—" She clutched the bag of delicacies to her chest, the scent of yeast and butter powerful in her nose. "Thank you, Camille. I'm grateful."

And she was. So very, very grateful. And yet, also resentful. So very, very resentful.

"I'm sorry it took me this long to come. I have been embroiled in my own…" She trailed off, and silence fell between them again.

Rachel could tell this transaction was as uncomfortable for her friend as it was for her, but she didn't have it in her to ease the woman's distress. Camille, with her blond hair and blue eyes and perfect Aryan features, could not know what it was like to be Rachel. She could not know the prejudices and persecutions she endured. She could not know what it meant to be Jewish in German-occupied France.

Everything Rachel had been, had dreamed of being, everything she'd planned for herself and her future—it was all cast in a bruised, purplish shade of gray. She felt helpless. Her father and brother were missing, arrested for no reason. She didn't know what had become of them. All Rachel and her mother could do was wait for news. They waited and waited and waited. For days, weeks, then months. It was as if Papa and Srulka had vanished into a spool of smoke rolling off the Seine.

"It's dreadful, what Madame Bergeron did to you," Camille was saying. "She shouldn't have let you go over something she had to know you didn't do."

Yes, dreadful. How easy it had been for the housekeeping supervisor to dismiss her. She hadn't even bothered to look remorseful. Rachel had been furious at first. But reality had set in, and then lumps of horrid, charred fear had followed. No other hotel would hire her. She'd tried. She'd looked for work in all sorts of places. Restaurants, boardinghouses, even a few seedy bars.

Now Rachel and her mother were reduced to accepting charity. She started to tremble with anger and humiliation, and Camille was still talking about the Ritz. "...I have quit my job at the hotel."

But why? "Was it..." *For me?* she nearly asked. Had Camille quit out of solidarity for their friendship? That couldn't be right. She needed the job. Rachel searched her friend's face for an answer and saw uncertainty. That couldn't be right, either. Camille was French-born with the looks of a perfect German. Any number of establishments would hire her.

"I have taken a job as a private housekeeper in Drancy."

"Drancy? Is it closer to your home?"

"It's about the same distance."

"I still don't understand," Rachel said.

"I know. I'm not making myself clear. This is hard to say. I have taken the position of housekeeper with *Herr Sturmbannführer* von Bauer."

Rachel's shock came out in a low, horrified growl. Camille was going to work for a Nazi? "What? *Why?*"

"It's complicated."

"Then explain it to me. Explain, Camille, why you choose to work in the home of a Nazi, when you claim to be my friend."

"I *am* your friend."

"And yet you align yourself with the enemy."

"It's not like that." Camille hopped to her feet and went to stand by the window. She made a show of scrutinizing its wooden frame, scratching at a mark on the glass, turning back around. "He's paying me three times what I make at the Ritz. My family needs the money, Rachel. And really, when you consider the actual work I'll be doing, it's no different than working as a chambermaid at the hotel."

Rachel recognized the shame in her friend's eyes, but it wasn't enough to erase her actions. "It's one thing, Camille, to clean the rooms occupied by Germans staying at the Ritz. But to move into the home of a Nazi, live under the same roof?

This is a foul choice. He could do anything he pleases with you. To you. He could—"

"He won't. Vivian is moving into the house as well."

"As his mistress."

Camille frowned. "Don't judge her so harshly. She is an ally, not the enemy."

"You're telling me that Vivian Miller, that horizontal collaborator, has orchestrated this new position for you in her lover's house?" The taste of betrayal was back in Rachel's throat, right there, then on the edge of her tongue. Oh, how she wanted to lash out. Why did Camille trust the American widow so completely?

"I will find a way to continue bringing you food."

Rachel nearly slapped her friend's face, so offended was she by her words. It took every ounce of self-control to keep her hand from moving. "You should leave now."

The seconds that followed were among the longest Rachel had ever endured. Nothing but sound filled the moment, noises from the outside world, where people were living and surviving by any means possible. No different than the two of them.

The thought should have softened Rachel toward her friend.

It did not.

She stood frozen in a tableau of pain and rage. Whatever trust and affection had been between her and Camille was gone. They were both in this war, just as before, but now each was in her own private battle for her family.

It was another terrible loss. Another abandonment. Rachel felt her temples pulse, her vision blur. Eventually, as the sound of a motorcar passed on the street below, she gave up her stillness, as did Camille. They moved in tandem toward the entryway, neither speaking.

The motor grew faint in the distance. An apartment door from somewhere down the hallway creaked open. A baby's distressing wail came thin and reedy from the floor below. "Rachel, please, I don't want to leave with you angry at me. I want you to know this wasn't an easy decision. I have to think about my family. I know you understand that. I—"

"Go." She yanked open the door. "Go now."

"If that's what you want."

"It is."

Camille stepped into the hallway, gave her a sad smile, and was gone a second later. Only once her footsteps faded completely did Rachel let out a slow, quiet cry of regret.

What had she done?

Exactly what she needed to retain what small shred of dignity she had left. *Dignity will not fill your belly.* But it did feed her soul. She chastised herself for thinking she'd done something wrong by sending Camille away. She gave one short, final sigh then returned to her apartment and the sound of her mother's knitting.

She'd never felt more alone.

Chapter Twenty-Seven

Camille

27 March 1942.
Von Bauer's Home. Seine-Saint-Denis Department.
Paris, France.

Two days after her disastrous visit with Rachel, Camille prepared to move into von Bauer's home. She greeted the morning with mixed emotions. She'd forsaken the people she cared about for the very reason that she cared. The only ally she had left was Vivian, a woman who, quite literally, slept with the enemy for reasons she claimed were for the greater good.

Camille wanted to believe her. She did believe her, mostly.

The sky was utterly cloudless as she followed the directions Vivian gave her. The hard, bold light was an affront to the gravity of her new life. She thought of Pierre Garnier. Though she'd burned his letters, and had vowed no more visits to Rennes, she'd buried his entreaty in her heart. *Va avec Dieu.* Go with God.

But did God go with her?

She didn't feel His presence, not that she'd turned to Him for guidance. At least, not in prayer. And not for a very long time. Her father's funeral had been the last time she'd stepped inside a church. So now, as she stood outside a different church composed of a slate roof and red brick, she prayed for God's protection. Maybe she should take Pierre up on his offer. How much easier it would be to rely on such a man, and together figure out how to keep Jacqueline safe and feed her family. But what about Rachel? And her mother?

Rachel had sent Camille away, looking insulted and betrayed, and in hindsight, Camille couldn't blame her. She'd entered her friend's home like some guardian angel from on high, offering food she hadn't even prepared herself, then admitting she would be working for a Nazi. She'd been thoughtless, and now Camille vowed, as she stood on holy ground, her face turned to heaven, that she would find a way to ease her friend's suffering.

Turning onto a cobblestoned street, she took in the ornate mansions with their manicured front lawns, well-tended gardens, massive windows, and rows upon rows of wrought-iron balconies on the second and, in most cases, third stories.

At the third house on her right, she checked the address, frowning. Of course von Bauer would claim the largest house on the block. The gate was unlocked, so she pushed through and maneuvered up the long, curving drive, toward the three-story house. The white facade was eye-blinkingly bright. Gleaming windows dotted the structure at precise, regular intervals.

The brass knocker on the front door was fashioned in the shape of a lion's head. It had vacant, staring eyes and a fat metal ring held between his teeth. Ignoring the pointy fangs, she slammed the knocker several times against the wood beneath those mean, snarling teeth.

She heard the click of a lock, and then von Bauer stood in the doorway, outfitted in his uniform. He hit her with the full force of that intense gaze. Then, as he'd done during her interview, he gave her a slow, cold inspection. "You're late."

"I apologize." She gave no defense or explanation. He had to know that only Germans were allowed to ride in cars, and thus she'd been forced to take the crowded Métro. A dicey prospect at the best of times, worse now that an on-time arrival was rarely guaranteed.

After yet another head-to-toe inspection that left her feeling exposed, he opened the door wider and, with a hitch of his chin, indicated she should enter the house. She slipped inside, giving him a wide berth, and looked around. There was a lot of marble, black lacquered furniture, and shiny gold fixtures.

Von Bauer maneuvered around her. The strike of his heels echoed in the cavernous foyer. "This is the total of your luggage?"

"It... Yes."

"Follow me."

Before she could respond, he was leading her down a dark corridor, to an impossibly tiny room. She peered inside and counted a bed, a chest of drawers, a rug, a washbasin, and nothing else. "This is where you will live. Leave your suitcase and come with me."

She did as commanded, wondering where Vivian was. She nearly asked, but he was handing her a ring of keys connected to a long chain. "You will wear these, always."

"Understood." She clipped the antique chatelaine at her waist. There were other ways she could carry the keys, but this requirement told Camille much about von Bauer. Madame Bergeron had worn a similar key ring at her waist. When he presented her uniform, a perfect replica of the one she'd worn as a chambermaid, she knew her suspicions were correct. This was a man who cared about appearances.

He explained her duties in short, rapid sentences that made his French sound as guttural as his German. He gave her no restrictions on roaming the house, only that she must keep every room spotless, even the ones he never used. He finished his pompous speech by handing her a slip of paper. "This is the menu for tonight. You will change nothing."

Giving her no time to ask questions, he exited the back door with a promise that he would return at seven o'clock sharp and expected dinner precisely thirty minutes later.

Once he was gone, Camille studied the menu and gasped. She was to create a five-course, elegant dinner for two. She was to serve champagne with the appetizer, a dry red with the main course, and a rare cognac after the dessert course. She was doomed to failure. In agony, she read to the bottom of the page and gave a sigh of relief. Von Bauer had included a name and telephone number to contact for the ingredients and another for the wine. She made the phone calls and, after explaining the situation, was guaranteed delivery by noon.

That done, Camille went about investigating the house. She started in the kitchen, taking note of the stove, the oven, the industrial-size sink. At the pantry, she discovered someone had completed most of the shopping for the next two weeks. No rationing, it would seem, for SS officers and their mistresses. And certainly, no quotas adhered to, as evidenced by the massive sacks of flour, butter, sugar, and coffee. Also, cheese, pasta, bread. Fresh vegetables. Camille fumed over the extravagance. If nothing else, she would find a use for the leftovers.

For now, she set her mind on exploring the rest of the house. The ticking of a grandfather clock guided her back to the foyer. Its long shadow spread across the marble floor, the tip pointing directly to a winding staircase that led to the top two floors. Deep breath. She placed her hand on the banister, took another deep breath, and made the climb to the top. A dusty attic with nothing but an empty crate. She moved down to the second level.

There she found the master bedroom. Signs of von Bauer's demand for order were in the straight edges and precise positioning of the furniture. Expected, of course. But also, there were pieces of Vivian here, too. A fashion magazine on an end table, stray red hairs on the decorative pillows, a bottle of red nail varnish in the bathroom, the dent in the pillow where she'd slept beside von Bauer. It gave Camille a jolt to see the physical proof of how far the American was willing to go to save innocent lives.

Taking a final spin, she cataloged the art on the wall, most done by the masters, the exquisite furnishings, the bulk of them antiques. In the closet, she found von Bauer's clothes arranged by color, mostly uniforms and several tailored suits. Vivian's dresses hung in another closet along with her smart skirts and matching jackets. Her jewelry and furs, the ones Camille had once helped her hide, were back in her possession, resting in their cases.

Surely, von Bauer would have had questions when she'd retrieved the items from their hiding places. Or had he been the one to discover them? Had he returned them to Vivian only after he'd taken her as his mistress?

Either scenario was possible, the result ultimately the same. Both of them getting what they wanted.

Oh, Vivian, how real is this charade of yours?

Camille was shaking by the time she walked out of the closet, both worried for her friend and suspicious of her loyalties. Her skin felt too tight on her face, and she wondered what else she would find if she dared look deep enough.

She dared.

A more thorough search revealed signs of the previous owners. A monogrammed handkerchief at the back of a drawer. A child's paper doll crushed under the sofa's cushions. Something shiny from beneath the armoire had her crouching down and pulling free a small book of some kind. With it caught between her splayed fingers, the heaviness indicated a precious metal had been forged for the cover, silver perhaps. She flipped open the lid and, after a bit of spinning and turning, realized she'd originally had the book upside down. Or was it backward? Flipping from left to right, no, right to left, she studied the foreign script, mostly letters and slashes in a language she didn't know. Except that she did know. Or suspected. She was holding a small, decorative Hebrew Bible.

She washed out her lungs with long, deep breaths of air, but nothing could erase her outrage, or her personal guilt. She was to live and work in this house, and be well paid for her efforts, while others suffered.

Clutching the book to her heart, Camille bit down on her bottom lip, and prayed for the family who'd toiled to make this beautiful house their home. *Please, Lord, keep them safe.* Her next prayer was more personal. *Forgive me.*

She'd allowed herself to believe her reasons for taking this job were morally right. So long as her loved ones were safe, she would be absolved. But in this room, with this beautiful, embellished book resting against her beating heart, the truth could not be ignored: von Bauer had confiscated this home from a Jewish family. And Camille was complicit.

Forgive me, Lord.

Did Vivian know? Had she even tried to steer von Bauer to another house?

Camille looked for answers in the rest of the rooms upstairs. She found little to explain this travesty, and nearly gave up hope, until she entered von Bauer's private study on the first floor. Here, she prayed, would be the answers she sought. Shelves filled with books wrapped around three of the four walls. A row of windows covered the remaining one. Camille walked over to take in the view, and there was her outrage again, clogging in her throat.

A gazebo built in an octagonal shape sat at the very edge of the lawn. The ivy had been left to grow wild, winding up each of the eight columns. A short path threaded between flower beds. There was a look of neglect, telling Camille that the previous occupants had been gone for some time. She returned her attention to the study itself.

Von Bauer adhered to his ruthless order in his private domain, and that, she decided, was to her advantage. She went straight to his desk and got down to work, sorting through the various files, all in German. Camille was glad she'd kept her knowledge of the language to herself. Von Bauer hadn't bothered to put his important work under lock and key. Did he think her inability to speak his language rendered her impotent?

The more she read, the more Camille learned about the Drancy facility. She discovered the number of buildings completed to date, the ones still under construction, the direct connection to the railway. She even found a list of the SS soldiers directly under von Bauer's command, and their specific job duties. With every piece of information gleaned, Camille thanked her mother for insisting she learn the language her father mumbled in his sleep.

Her eyes landed on the word *Durchgangslager*. It took her a moment to piece together the root word with the rest, and when she finally put it all together, her palm slammed against her mouth. The Germans had no plans to keep prisoners of war at the Drancy facility. They'd turned the failed housing project into a *Durchgangslager*. A transit camp for the Jews rounded up in Paris, as well as the rest of France. They were held at the facility only temporarily before being sent to concentration camps in Germany, but mostly Poland.

Camille blinked, shocked. Stunned. Her mind went immediately to Rachel. Was this the fate of her friend's father and brother? She had to know. If what she suspected was true, it would not give Rachel peace. But it would give her friend answers.

Flipping through the file in her hand, then another, and another, Camille eventually found a list of names, their accompanying ages, the dates of their arrests, and their assigned destination. Nazis were quite the meticulous record keepers. Camille ran her fingertip down the list of names, checking dates, moving quickly, her eyes following the same path on each page.

Then: she paused. Gasped. Felt the burn of tears. Everything in her went waxy and hard. There, beneath her finger. Ezra Berman, age fifty-six, arrested on 14 May 1941, sent to Pithiviers in Loiret, transferred to Drancy nine months later, then sent on to a concentration camp in Poland. Auschwitz. A sob slipped past her rigid lips as she read the next line. Srulka Berman, age eighteen, arrested on 14 May 1941, sent to Pithiviers in Loiret, then to Drancy, then also to Auschwitz.

Another sob rose in Camille's throat. This time, she buried her grief and anger. She had to tell Rachel. Would her friend even open the door? After her last visit, Camille wasn't sure. But she had to try.

Tomorrow. She would go tomorrow.

Another thought came, one that brought such urgency that Camille collapsed into the chair, the hinges barely creaking under her slight weight. More arrests were happening every day. Most of the detainees to date had been Jewish men, immigrants first, then French-born. Would women and children be next? Camille continued her search through the files and ledgers, biting her tongue to keep her howls of outrage silent. She found nothing concrete, nothing but an uneasy feeling in the pit of her stomach. Von Bauer had documentation of what had already occurred.

Nothing of what was to come.

That didn't mean Rachel and her mother were safe. Resolve pushed Camille to her feet. Panic for her friend sent her flipping through every file again. Such a cold, hard collection of data. Men who would keep these sorts of records would think nothing of killing every Jew in France, including women and children.

Camille must find a way to get Rachel and her mother out of Paris. The women would need new identity cards, travel visas, transportation, a route of escape. Camille knew of only one person who could gain all four. The person who kept putting her off. But now matters were worse. Dire, even. Oh, yes, she would approach Vivian. And this time, she would not be ignored.

Chapter Twenty-Eight

Vivian

March 1942.
Von Bauer's Home. Seine-Saint-Denis Department.
Paris, France.

Vivian entered von Bauer's house, mentally choosing her wardrobe for dinner while also reviewing her meeting with Frank Meier. Her forger had been arrested, or so she assumed now that he'd missed two of their scheduled meetings. This had left her with a significant time constraint for her current project. She'd turned to the Ritz's bartender to find her another. He'd introduced her to a Turkish fellow with a long résumé of successfully forged documents and a quick hand. She'd hired him on the spot for a set of identity papers she owed a couple looking to escape Europe with their daughter who'd been born with a clubfoot.

She'd met the girl today, a sweet child of thirteen. Her curly red hair and green eyes were a reminder of Vivian's younger self, and in that moment, she'd vowed to the child's parents that she would get them out of France. It was a promise she meant to keep. They'd been appreciative, impossibly so, and their gratitude had been a balm to her soul.

The sensation had faded almost instantly. How many lives would Vivian need to save to erase the nights she spent in von Bauer's bed?

Frowning, she stepped into the foyer and paused. The air felt different. She'd barely taken three steps when she heard someone call out. "Hello? Is someone there?"

Vivian recognized the voice at once and remembered Camille had been slated to move in today.

The sound of footsteps heralded the girl's appearance, her eyes wild and unfocused. And Vivian knew the cause. "He's given you the menu for tonight's meal."

It was to be Camille's first test. Vivian had recognized *der Rab*'s intentions and had stocked the pantry herself, in an effort to assist the girl. The cooking. The presentation. The serving. The acquiring of special ingredients. That would all be up to her.

She was still thinking about the impossible task von Bauer had set before Camille when she realized the girl hadn't said a word. She stood in the foyer, her face covered in shadows, and Vivian was instantly on the move, hurrying toward her, desperate to understand the source of her agitation. She took her painfully thin shoulders, felt the trembling in her own bones, and one thought filled her mind. Von Bauer had assaulted her. She should not have brought the girl into this house. Wrong, so wrong of her. She'd been selfish, attempting to provide herself with an ally. Instead, she'd brought devastation into Camille's young life.

"What's happened?" she asked. "Did he hurt you?"

She shook her head.

Her relief was short-lived. "Your sister? Has she taken a turn for the worse?"

Camille whimpered softly, as if she couldn't hold back her

emotions, and Vivian knew that whatever had occurred, it was bad. Very bad.

"Tell me, Camille, tell me what's happened."

Finally, the girl seemed to get ahold of herself and produced some semblance of control, at least in the way she held her body, her spine now straight as an iron rod. "It's the round-ups," she began. Then came the soft whimper again. "They... It... But... Vivian! It's ghastly. Just *awful*. I need to do something, but what?"

Vivian's legs were suddenly weak, and she wanted to sit, but she didn't give in to the sensation. "Your sister." She swallowed back the bile rising from her stomach. "They took her."

"No. Praise God, Jacqueline is safe in the care of her doctor." For a brief second, something sweet and lovely passed in the girl's eyes. Then instantly vanished. "It's Rachel's father. Her brother, and others like them." Her eyes filled with a fevered expression, something between terror and panic, but also fury. "They have been sent to a camp in Poland. To a...a death camp."

"You are sure of this? They were sent to a death camp, not an internment camp?"

"The numbers don't add up." She put her head in her hands and spoke through her splayed fingers. "Too many are being sent to the same facility. No one camp could house so many."

Such specific information did not come from innocent sources. "You know this, how?" Vivian took the girl by the arm, practically dragging her to a chair before forcing her to sit. "Tell me, Camille, how did you come by this information?"

The girl shook her head, her eyes not quite meeting Vivian's. "It doesn't matter."

Oh, but it did. Vivian couldn't bear to think what *der Rab* would do if he caught the girl rummaging through his personal correspondence. Even Vivian didn't dare it. "Camille." Fear coated her voice, and the girl winced in response. Good.

She should be as afraid. "You cannot take such risks. *Mon Dieu*, you cannot search his private office."

Vivian thought, at first, that maybe the girl understood the danger she'd put herself in. She nodded, after all, but she did so absently, and then words were rolling out of her mouth in a rush. "I fear the arrests will include women and children next."

"But you said your sister was safe."

"The Nazis don't seem concerned with the mentally ill in France. It is the Jews they target here." Camille stared at the floor. When she looked up, her face appeared gaunt and shadowed, as if resistant to light. "What of Rachel, and her mother? We must help them."

At last, the source of the girl's anxiety became clear. "You're worried about your Jewish friend, the chambermaid from the Ritz you asked me to watch over."

It was the wrong thing to say. The floodgates opened, and Camille's concern for her friend drenched the room. "A single decision, a sweep of a pen, that's all it would take, and the next round of arrests would include all Jews, not just male immigrants."

Vivian's gut told her Camille had cause to worry. Only yesterday, she'd witnessed the arrest of a wealthy French Jew who'd thought himself safe because of his money and connections in the foreign office. The Gestapo and the French police came in the afternoon, in broad daylight, working in tandem. Vivian had been taking tea with Coco Chanel, doing her best to ferret out the designer's loyalties, at Frank Meier's request.

The scene had played out quickly. A man seized, his female companion as well, the latter screaming, the former earning a fist to his face for resisting. Vivian shuddered at the memory. She would not wish such a fate for Camille's friends. She would not wish that for Camille, either. "You must not look through von Bauer's files ever again."

The girl made a choking sound in her throat. "Can you help

Rachel and her mother? You are the only person I know who can get them out of France."

There was such trust in Camille's eyes. Vivian didn't want to be the cause of all that unbridled hope staring back at her. She was not that powerful or connected, and, more importantly, not at all certain she would be able to acquire the necessary documents, much less the rest. A viable escape route, an escort through the mountains, transportation once they were in Spain. Money. Her network had grown, true, but one false move and the links were broken. "This is not a small thing you ask."

Camille's face suddenly went fierce, eyebrows drawn low. "How many more roundups will it take before good people stop looking the other way and start standing against evil? How many fractured families must watch their loved ones stolen from them?"

Vivian didn't have answers to the girl's questions. She didn't have solutions.

"Please, I beg you. Help my friends."

She would have to call in favors, the few she had left. But if Vivian refused to help Camille and her friends were arrested... No, it didn't bear thinking. "I will consider this, on one condition."

"Anything," Camille vowed.

"You must never snoop among von Bauer's private papers again. No, don't interrupt me." She lifted a hand when Camille opened her mouth. "This is not negotiable. If I am to help your friend—"

"—and her mother."

Vivian nodded. "If I am to help these women, you will not put yourself in danger ever again. Say it, Camille. Say you will never snoop among von Bauer's things again."

"Never again."

"It will take time."

The girl looked into Vivian's eyes, her gaze steady. "You'll do it?"

"I'll do it." As if to mark the occasion, the clock struck the hour. Two chimes, echoing in Vivian's mind, over and over, long past the final strike, long past Camille's departure to the kitchen. Alone, she closed her eyes and, still hearing the clock in her head, thought: *Two chimes for two lives.* As with the Jewish family she'd met this morning, Vivian made a silent vow to Rachel and her mother. *I will not fail you.*

She would make it her life's mission to help them escape France. She would do it for Camille. For Rupert's legacy. But, most of all, for all the people she couldn't save. That was her vow. That was her promise.

Chapter Twenty-Nine

Rachel

1 April 1942.
The Berman Apartment. Paris, France.

Rachel tried not think about her disastrous visit with Camille. But the words they'd exchanged, and the ones they hadn't spoken, weren't easy to dismiss. A week had come and gone, and with each day that passed, she wondered why she didn't regret her own behavior more. She'd always been able to see both sides of an argument. But life had turned hard, with the sorrows too great and the joys too few. And somewhere along the way, Rachel had lost a piece of herself. The part that embraced the notion of fairness.

Camille had meant well—she understood that—and the food she'd confiscated from the hotel had restored some of her mother's strength. Rachel's as well, giving her the energy to stand in long lines for whatever rationed food was available.

Which wasn't much. Food was scarce everywhere, but nearly nonexistent for Jews, who were forced to stand at the back of every line. She should have shown more gratitude for Camille's gift. Rachel blamed her rudeness on her constant worry for her

father and brother, for her absent sister who still hadn't con-
tacted them.

She wanted to howl in frustration, if only she could find the
desire. The emptiness inside, this awful absence of feeling, it
was as if the darkness in her life had dug a deep pit in her very
core. Every free moment, she poured all her feelings out onto
the pages of her journal, but nothing could erase the silence
that crept into her soul every night as she laid her head on her
lumpy pillow. Despair ate at her. She tried to wait out the sensation, to go blank, or simply disappear into nothingness, but
always, something pulled her back from the abyss.

The sound of the door creaking on its hinges did so now,
and then a soft, familiar voice said, "Rachel? Madame Berman? Are you home?"

Rachel swiveled in her chair, craning her neck to glimpse
the friend she'd banished from the apartment. Camille Lacroix
was proving to be a stubborn woman.

"Hello?" came the tentative greeting again, the hinges creaking louder, a stark reminder that the locks had been taken along
with the telephone and wireless. They'd even shut off the water.
"Rachel?"

"Camille." Her heart thrummed at the sight of her friend,
now standing inside the apartment, another bag slung over her
shoulder. More charity, so very needed yet so very unwelcome.
In that moment, Rachel forgot her remorse over their last meeting, and the childhood lessons on politeness her parents had in-
stilled in her, and asked, bluntly, irritably, "Why are you here?"

"Please don't turn me away." Camille moved deeper into the
room, a contrite look on her face, but all Rachel could see was
the satchel she carried. Her very survival, her mother's as well,
was collected inside that nondescript canvas bag.

"I come with news."

Not good news, Rachel sensed.

"It's about your father and brother."

No, not good news. But information she desperately wanted.

To her shame, her mind wasn't on her father, or her brother, but on her empty stomach. She couldn't take her eyes off the bag slung over Camille's shoulder. And what it meant. Survival.

A sick feeling filled Rachel, guilt that her desire for food outweighed her need for answers. She didn't want to be this selfish, but there was no room for noble pursuits on an empty belly. Rachel had to think about her mother. And the promise she'd given her father in the police station on the day of his arrest. She sighed, knowing she would accept Camille's charity, and this time, she would show more gratitude.

"Come in." She stepped forward and was suddenly aware of the stench coming off her own unwashed body, and how the wavy locks of her hair that had once been her shining glory hung in greasy clumps. The way her clothes hung on her emaciated frame and gave her the look of an underfed child.

Camille touched her arm as she moved past, the connection brief, and yet that small kindness brought a burning sensation to the back of Rachel's throat. At least one person in Paris didn't view her as vile. One person who, even in Rachel's current state, saw her as human.

One person. A friend.

Again, Rachel regretted her earlier resentment. Or rather, she wanted to feel regret, but she couldn't seem to swallow it down completely.

Camille set the bag on the table without a single hint of pity in her movements, and for that, at least, Rachel was grateful. For that, she could muster up the courage to say two simple words. "Thank you."

"I wish it was more."

The tears clogging in her throat moved into her eyes, and Rachel had to swallow several times to hold them back. When she was finally able to speak again, the words came out in a rush. "You said you have news?"

"Can we sit?"

No, she wanted to shout. *No, no, no!* She didn't want to sit.

She didn't want to hear what Camille had learned. She wanted to continue believing her father and brother would come home. Any day, they would walk through the door. But the sadness in Camille's eyes, the hunch of her shoulders, told a different story, and Rachel knew they were gone for good. At least her mother was still abed and wouldn't have to hear the truth from anyone but Rachel.

"All right, let's sit." She pulled out a chair at the kitchen table. Camille did the same, then reached across the divide and took Rachel's hand. Her touch was nearly as gentle as before, and Rachel's resentment ignited all over again.

Camille looked so strong, so healthy, so safe in the knowledge she was not a target of Nazi hate. She was also loyal and did not have to come bearing food and important news, and Rachel wanted this meeting to be easier. "Tell me what you know."

"My employer works at the facility in Drancy, the one the German army originally slotted as a camp for prisoners of war."

"Originally?" Rachel's mind hooked on that one word, dreading what it meant, but needing to know the truth. "But not anymore?"

"No." Her friend gave a sad shake of her head. "The SS took command and turned the compound into a transit camp."

"A transit camp?" Rachel asked, unable to comprehend what this information meant for her father and brother. Except that maybe, sadly, she did.

"It's a facility where the Nazis hold detainees before trans-porting them to…to…other, uh—" she swallowed "—detainee centers in Germany and, as I recently discovered, Poland."

Rachel lost her breath a moment. "Detainee centers." She squeezed out the words past her suddenly parched lips. "You mean concentration camps."

"*Oui*, yes. Concentration camps." Camille looked stricken, the color leaking from her face, as surely as Rachel felt the heat leaving her own.

There it was again, that tingle of recognition that her father and brother were lost. She felt the fatigue of the past year pull on her heart, and her next words were full of grief. "Tell me the rest, Camille. All of it."

"My employer is a scrupulous record keeper. He has ledgers that list the names of Jewish males arrested in the French and German roundups, where the detainees were initially sent and for how long they were there. There are other lists that have the date of their transfer to Drancy, and then..." She swallowed again, then looked up to the ceiling, as if searching for her next words in the cracked plaster. "The date they were transported out of France to a concentration camp in Poland. It's called Auschwitz."

Rachel felt her fingers tightening into fists. Her teeth gnashed together. And the taste in her mouth grew foul and bitter. "You found my father and brother in these ledgers."

Grief filled her friend's gaze. "They were sent to Auschwitz."

Rachel heard the words, and knew them to be terrible, but she also had hope. Her father and brother were alive. They were in Poland, at a concentration camp. Not dead. Alive, and... and... The moment of relief was squashed instantly by the sight of tears in her friend's eyes. "What aren't you telling me?"

"They were sent to Auschwitz with thousands of other men. The trains leave daily. Daily, Rachel, and always to the same destination, to a single concentration camp."

Camille was openly crying now. So was Rachel, big, fat tears she didn't bother wiping away, because the numbers told a harrowing tale that could not be dismissed. Auschwitz was a death camp. Rachel's father and brother had been sent to a death camp. She couldn't breathe.

When will this nightmare be over?

Never. It would never be over until the Germans were defeated. Not even then. Too many innocent souls had already been lost. Her father. Her brother. Both surely gone. No. No! Her mind would not accept this awful news.

Camille was talking again, but Rachel didn't want to hear

any more. She wanted to hit something, someone. Camille. How satisfying it would be to take out her anger on her friend.

"It's your only chance, Rachel. You and your mother must leave Paris."

She'd said nearly the same words to her father two years ago. And now, it was Rachel denying the idea. "How? Our identity cards mark us as Jews."

"I have a plan to secure new documents for you and your mother, including travel visas."

It was exactly what Basia had promised. Would Camille have greater success? Or would she disappear as her own sister had done?

"Say you come through with these new documents." Her fears, her hopes and dreams, the instinctual need to survive, all of it was buried in the shaky tenor of her voice. "What then?"

"We are working on a plan to get you out of the city, then out of France entirely."

"Who is we?"

Camille broke eye contact. "It's better you don't know."

Rachel's mind calculated wildly. This chance of escape would mean leaving France and giving up hope her father and brother would somehow return, but it would also mean saving her mother. "How long will it take to coordinate our escape?"

"A few weeks, maybe longer, maybe less. It depends on the forger. Do I have your permission to continue this escape plan?"

She thought of her mother, which made her decision for her. "I'd like to know the details. Barring that, yes."

They spoke only a few minutes longer, with Rachel also agreeing to let her friend continue bringing her food in the interim, and Camille promising not to fail her.

When Rachel closed the door behind her, her mind was reeling from all that she'd learned. Could grief and hope exist at the same time? How did she mourn her father and brother while feeling unconscionable relief that she could possibly save her mother?

The older woman emerged from her room, looking frantically around. "I heard the door. Is it… Are they…?"

"It was only my friend, Camille." Rachel picked up the satchel her friend had conspicuously left and set it on the kitchen table. "She brought us more food."

"Oh." Her mother rummaged through the contents of the canvas bag, her movements listless and somewhat indifferent.

Rachel watched her, her love a physical ache in her chest. Ilka Berman was all the family she had left, and she'd promised her father she would keep her safe. Escaping France was the only way she could do that. It would not be easy convincing her mother to leave. Did Rachel tell this fragile shell of a woman that they could escape France, but only if they gave up waiting for the men in their family to return?

There were so many unknowns, and too many details that hadn't been put into place. No, Rachel decided, she would not tell her mother what she'd learned from Camille. For now, she would carry this burden alone.

Chapter Thirty

Camille

June 1942.
Von Bauer's Home. Seine-Saint-Denis Department.
Paris, France.

Two months later, and after several successful deliveries of food to Rachel and her mother, Camille still waited for Vivian to pull together the Bermans' escape plan. Each time she visited Rachel, she had few details to share. She saw the grief in her friend and knew it would be hard to leave Paris, but it was the best way to start a new life where the Nazis couldn't hurt her.

That place would not be in Europe. Wireless broadcasts reported German victories daily. America's entry in the war had not slowed them down. But Hitler was so caught up in winning the war on the continent, while pushing toward Russia, that he had not put troops on American soil.

In that, Camille found hope for Rachel and her mother. They would be safe on the other side of the Atlantic. Vivian claimed she was working on the details, but her assertions that "these things take time" and "many details must fall into place" brought Camille great concern.

She entered the kitchen still pondering the delays that kept cropping up and set her mind on tonight's task. Von Bauer was hosting an intimate dinner party for four. Vivian would be the only woman at the table. He'd given Camille precise instructions, as was his habit, before exiting the house this morning.

The menu was to include vichyssoise as the first course, a fruit salad with strawberries and bananas, followed by sea bass and asparagus for the main dish. She was to end the night with individual chocolate soufflés that must rival any Michelin three-star restaurant in Paris. He also expected fine wines and a minimum of three centerpieces of fresh-cut flowers arranged in crystal vases. Camille had searched the house for the elusive vases. Vivian suggested she try the basement, which brought no small amount of dread. Camille had avoided that area of the house, for personal reasons, and it had never been a problem. Until today.

Having put off the task long enough, she opened the door and stood perfectly still as memories from another time, in another basement, assaulted her. Even now, seven years after that horrible day, she could hear Jacqueline's screams in her head. The smells were in her nose as well. The scent of gunpowder, her father's blood, mixed with death. No, she couldn't go down into the basement.

She had to do it.

Von Bauer would know she'd avoided this trip into the dark recesses of the house. There was no choice. She took her first tentative step, bracing for the images she kept hidden in her mind. They came quickly and followed her to the bottom of the stairs. The smell was nearly unbearable, a nausea-inducing mix of mold and wet wool and something that came from a dead animal. Some sort of rodent, she guessed. A rat.

Would she never be free of the monstrous little creatures?

Camille found a lone light bulb hanging by a single wire and pulled on the string. The scurrying of claws over concrete, the flash of black fur, a pink tail, and then she was blissfully alone with only the terrible stench.

Dust bunnies scattered under her foot, warning she was the first in a long time to venture this deep into the bowels of the house. That should have comforted her. But spiders stared at her from their sticky webs suspended in the corners. She looked away and focused on the racks full of forgotten canned goods. Sacks of flour and sugar, butter and coffee filled another. Nearly every item was neatly aligned side by side and in bulk.

Had that been von Bauer's doing? Vivian's? Or perhaps, the previous occupants had anticipated shortages and prepared accordingly. That would explain the layers of dust. Camille thought back and remembered that Vivian's suggestion to look for the vases in the basement had been a passing remark, not a definitive solution.

She found several vases on one of the shelves and breathed a sigh of relief as she clutched three of them to her. Deed done, she worked her way back to the stairwell, her pace fast and nimble. Then something cold snaking around her ankles made her scream. She nearly shot up the steps but took an instant to look down and saw it was only a draft. Coming from where?

A quick scan revealed the windows were shuttered from the inside.

Something nagged at her, a memory she couldn't quite catch. There, then gone. Head cocked, she moved closer to the shelves with the canned fruit and, aha, she felt the draft again, coming from beneath the rack itself. Perhaps there was a hole in the wall.

That would explain the rodents.

Setting the vases on the floor, she peeked beneath the rack. There was a thin gap running parallel to the floor. That vague memory nagged at her again, and she stood, the key ring slapping against her hip bone as she wiped her hands on the apron. The memory tugged harder, bringing images slowly, eventually, into focus.

Another room. A large piece of furniture.

Vivian's furs, hidden away. Of course. Of course. Camille moved the rack aside, which required a lot of pulling and pushing and moving from one side to the other. And yes. There it was. The outline of a small door. There was no handle, only a padlock. After several misfires, Camille found the key. The door swung inward, and a whoosh of stale air swept over her. Well, well. She'd found a secret tunnel. Where did it go?

She checked her watch. There were hours before von Bauer's return. She needed only a few minutes. Hurrying now, she retrieved a flashlight from the kitchen and, steeling herself against her awful, awful memories, she made the descent back into the basement.

A sound had her stopping midway down. She held her breath, waited. Listened. Nothing. Just an old house with old bones settling into itself. Blowing out a breath, she continued. At the edge of the tunnel, sweat broke out on her forehead, and her stomach tried to jump to her throat as she stared at the nothingness in front of her. She flicked on the light and, yes. It was indeed a tunnel, cut into soil and rocks.

Again, she tried to work out where it led, knowing there was only one way to find out.

She took a tentative step, swept the light left to right, up and down. Another step. Another sweep. She continued in this manner. Step, sweep. Step, sweep. The narrow passageway was supported by wooden joints and beams that required Camille to bend low or risk hitting her head.

An uneasy feeling grabbed her. A sense that this was not a place where happiness had lived. The previous owners of the house came to her. A family of Jews, targeted by Nazis.

She did not like the conclusions that filled her mind. She called out, "Hello?"

An echo was her only response.

Suddenly afraid of what she would find, she thought to turn back, but the smell of death was absent, and some inner need urged her forward, a sense that she must—*must*—find out what lay at the other end of this tunnel. Each step required courage she hadn't tapped into since coming upon her father in their basement. Time seemed to bend and shift, taking Camille back to that moment of dark discovery. She nearly turned back, but no.

You can do this.

The tunnel got smaller and then, suddenly, opened into a larger space, no longer made from dirt and rocks supported by wood beams but a room made of concrete. Not a room, a bunker, sturdy but hastily constructed, as evidenced by the cracks in the floor.

Camille passed the light through the space. The beam landed on a small cot with a blanket and pillow. A woman's hairbrush lay discarded on the milk crate beside it, along with a small stockpile of candles, matches. To her right stood another cot, and still another. The third one was half the size as the other two. For a child, no doubt, and that made Camille's heart twist in her chest. She found a tattered stuffed bear and a picture book for toddlers, the pages worn from constant use.

Something thin and shiny caught her eye from one of the cracks. Camille wiggled it free, and a long gilt chain unspooled in her hand. At the end hung a six-point star. The Star of David.

A Jewish family had lived here. Probably the owners of the house. They were gone now. And by all accounts, had left in a hurry. Or had they been dragged out? No, Camille would have seen evidence of a struggle. She would have also seen signs that von Bauer knew about this bunker.

This bunker had kept the family hidden—and alive. The thought brought Camille a level of peace, and she immediately thought of Rachel. If Vivian failed to come through with an escape plan, Rachel and her mother could hide in here, at least temporarily, right under von Bauer's nose. A desperate last resort, but it was a better plan than none at all.

Chapter Thirty-One

Rachel

June 1942.
The Berman Apartment. Paris, France.

The Vichy government passed another ordinance on the seventh day of June. Every Jew in Paris was required to wear a yellow star sewn on the outside of their clothing. The punishment for not doing so was arrest.

It was bad enough that they'd shown a film last year detailing the physical traits of a Jew so that Parisians could identify them properly. Now they were to mark themselves with this star, sufficiently setting them apart from other French citizens, labeling them as something to be avoided, ignored, or, in some cases, mistreated in public.

Humiliation to go with her empty stomach.

Rachel's salvation was her journal. She filled page after page with thoughts too intense to share with her mother. The book had become a chronicle of her lost hope and growing resentment. She held nothing back in her writings. She ranted. She railed. If only her father had trusted their neighbors less. If only they'd left Paris in the mass exodus. *If. Only.* Rachel flung her pencil across the room. It hit the floor, slid across the room, and landed with a thud against the baseboard. Her stomach twisted and growled.

Food. She and her mother needed food. It would mean standing at the back of more lines, wearing the hideous yellow star. She thought of Camille then, both wishing her friend would come bearing another satchel of food and dreading the moment she would be forced to take the charity so faithfully offered. Or maybe, Camille would come with the promised escape plan, and Rachel could flee Paris with her mother.

Would Ilka Berman leave the city, the country itself?

Not if she believed her husband and son would one day return. Rachel had yet to find the words to tell her mother what she knew of their fate. She'd tried on several occasions, but something always held her back. Right now, finding food was her priority. It would be good to get out of the apartment. The silence, the lack of male voices, was all too much.

Swallowing her pride, Rachel put on the dress with the yellow star. She would walk the streets today, bearing the mark of a Jew, but she would do it with her head high, her gaze steady. She would not show shame, as the Nazis and Vichy government wanted of her. The more restrictions they put on her, the more men they rounded up and sent away, the more pride Rachel found in who she was. A Jew.

"Rachel," her mother called from the kitchen. "Are you going somewhere?"

"*Oui*, to stand in line for bread."

"It's not safe to go out alone."

It was no more dangerous than staying at home. The French police, and their German counterparts in the Gestapo, knew where they lived. Any day, a member of either police force could show up at their door again. This time, to arrest the Berman women left behind.

Rachel's stomach rolled in on itself, reminding her of the empty hole that required filling.

"I don't know how long I'll be." It could take hours, half the day, perhaps right up until curfew. Sighing, she grabbed her handbag, the ration coupons tucked inside, and, rather optimistically, looped her arm through an empty basket in case she was lucky enough to find a shop willing to serve a Jewish woman wearing a yellow star.

Her mother met her at the door. "I'm coming with you."

Rachel hesitated only a moment. The stubborn set of her mouth and jaw was reminiscent of the woman from her childhood. She wanted to spend time with that woman, her mother. "I'd like that."

"We must stand together."

Emotion rolled up Rachel's throat. Her mother had been strong like this, once upon a time, vibrantly alive, and even if this was only a brief glimpse into the woman she remembered, it was enough. "I love you, Mama."

Her mother gave her a fierce hug in response.

"You can carry this." Rachel passed over the basket, and they took to the streets hand in hand. The noise was shocking, made louder after weeks of silence in the apartment.

Paris was the same, and yet different. What had once been Rachel's city, her home, was now foreign territory. French children ran past them and shouted at each other, horns honked, bicycles whooshed by. Along the thoroughfare, shops and restaurants were open for business but with signs barring Jews entry.

Her mother averted her gaze, and she now wore the look of quiet despair. "How are we to buy bread if we are not allowed in any of the usual shops?"

"I don't know. We must try, though." Bold words, but as they continued up one street and down another, apprehension crawled up Rachel's throat.

Wandering gazes locked onto the yellow star on her dress. Few of the eyes that met hers seemed shocked. Some people smiled at Rachel and her mother. Others gave a silent nod. A few offered covert winks. But most looked away or whispered behind their hands. Centuries of assimilation in French society, and this was what it meant to be a Jew in Paris.

Rachel would not be intimidated. She would show pride in who she was, embrace her identity. She'd been born a Jew, a whole and deserving woman, with thoughts and dreams and feelings that could be hurt. With flesh that could be destroyed. Her fingers tightened around her mother's hand, but she swallowed the bitter remarks on her tongue. For Ilka Berman's sake, Rachel would keep from antagonizing the people who so clearly thought to antagonize her.

"I have never felt more conspicuous," her mother whispered out of the side of her mouth.

Conspicuous, yes. But not alone. Other Jewish women had taken to the streets. She nodded to one, an older woman, her yellow star prominent on her perfectly pressed dress. Their eyes held for only a moment, but an entire world of meaning passed between them that could not be put into words.

Sufficiently bolstered, Rachel adjusted the bag she'd slung over her shoulder. It was heavier than it looked, due to the books and journals she stuffed inside, along with some of her mother's yarn. No locks meant anyone could walk into the apartment and take what they pleased.

They attempted a line at a bakery and were immediately shooed away. They tried another and another, always with the same response.

Finally, they found one that allowed them to join the back of the queue. They waited, arms linked, and quietly, boldly, endured the stares, the whispers, the slurs. Rachel had thought herself desensitized, but her time at the Ritz had not prepared her for the German soldier standing guard at the bakery's entrance. "Jews are not allowed in this shop."

All that time, wasted. There was no other place to go but home.

They arrived at the apartment defeated, empty-handed, bellies still so very empty. Another day without food. They could not last much longer. Escape was their only chance for survival.

Rachel slumped on the sofa and thought: *Please, Camille, come through for us.*

Chapter Thirty-Two

Camille

14 July 1942.
Von Bauer's Home. Seine-Saint-Denis Department.
Paris, France.

Camille's patience had all but vanished. Just this morning, she'd pressed Vivian again for news of Rachel and her mother's escape. The American had given her the same vague answer as always. "These things take time."

Time, Camille feared, was the one commodity the Bermans didn't have, and so she'd pressed harder. Vivian had admitted she was having trouble securing the identity cards. But assured Camille it was "nothing we can't overcome."

She'd then gone on to say that she'd met with the young woman who would escort Rachel and her mother out of Paris. The route would take them into the Free Zone, then over the Pyrenees mountains, and eventually into Spain. Once there, they would be free.

The explanation had eased Camille's mind, somewhat. But now, as she served the main course of sea bass and asparagus to von Bauer and his guests, she shook with frustration. A sense of foreboding ate at her. *Get ahold of yourself.* Von Bauer would notice if her hand shook.

He made impossible demands, often expecting Camille to be two people. Cook the meal. Serve the meal. She placed the first plate in front of von Bauer, as instructed, and moved counterclockwise around the table, finishing with Vivian. He watched her with those spooky, pale eyes, making her feel uncomfortable and somehow dirty.

There were only four people at the table tonight. Vivian, von Bauer, the commandant of the Drancy camp, and one other man who wore the blue tunic of the French police. His face had a lot of nose and very little chin, plus shockingly small black eyes set deep in hollow sockets. The German was not so completely unappealing as his French companion, but not as attractive as von Bauer, either.

All but attempting to melt into the woodwork, Camille stared at Vivian, and realized she was on edge, too, even though she looked quite at home among all these terrible men. Her eyes flicked to von Bauer, just once. Whatever she saw in his face made her flinch.

Camille wanted to sympathize with the American. But there she was, dripping in colorful jewels and dressed in a fashionable gown. She was the picture of a queen happily holding court. Laughing, smiling, drinking expensive champagne. Camille had a sudden, almost violent urge to grab her friend and shake some sense into her. What was Vivian thinking, enjoying the masculine attention instead of securing the necessary documents for the Bermans' escape?

She promised to come through for them, at great risk to herself.

It was the simple, complicated truth, and so Camille swallowed her irritation and removed the empty plates before serving the next course. She made her sweep around the table once again, placing the final dish in front of Vivian. She turned to go. Von Bauer stopped her retreat. "We will take our coffee in the blue parlor."

"I'll help with the tray," Vivian suggested, waiting until they were alone to explain. "I wanted to speak with you while he's occupied with his *friends*."

Not sure what she heard in the other woman's voice, Camille set down the dirty dishes and began preparing a tray with coffee she'd brewed earlier, sugar, cream, and plated the individual soufflés.

"I have unfortunate news." Looking over her shoulder, Vivian leaned in close and said, "There's been an unexpected development in our little project."

Camille stiffened. "What kind of development?"

"My forger was arrested," she said, her voice barely audible.

Camille tried to speak. To no avail. The devastation she felt for Rachel, but also her concern for the forger, left her unable to think clearly. "Have they…" *Hurt him? Killed him? Sent him to a concentration camp?* How did she ask such questions? "Is he…?"

"I don't know his fate."

"I'm sorry." The words beat in her ears, heartfelt, yet also unhelpful.

Vivian looked at Camille in that way she sometimes had, as if she knew what she was thinking. "There is another who will supply the papers." She touched her arm. "I will succeed in our quest, Camille. Your friends will soon be free of this nightmare country."

Another promise made, in a time when there were no guarantees. Camille thought of her sister then, and Pierre Garnier's promise, spoken with the same ferocity, and she felt a little less anxious. But also, overwhelmed. The utter uselessness of so few brave souls up against men like the ones sitting in the parlor, drinking coffee with real sugar and cream, while making their sinister plans to rid the world of good, innocent people.

Frustration lodged lump-like in her throat. "You will tell me when the plans are complete?"

"You will be the first to know."

Mind working through other alternatives if Vivian failed,

Camille picked up the tray and left the kitchen ahead of her friend. The light was brighter in the sitting room, alarmingly so. She squinted. The Frenchman was talking in German—as if that alone would prevent her from eavesdropping—which, as far as he knew, it did. His hands moved rapidly, a sense of glee apparent in every rotation of those bony wrists. "Once we have the bulk of them in the Vél d'Hiv, we will begin busing them to your facility for immediate departure to…?" He lifted a brow.

"We'll decide that on our end." This from von Bauer, his voice filled with finality.

"Sehr gut." The Frenchman spoke in the tone of a seasoned businessman discussing a shipment of goods rather than people.

Needing details, wanting them for Rachel's sake, Camille moved closer. Only at the last minute did she remember to force a vacant look in her eyes as she served the coffee. Behind that expression, her mind worked quickly, straining to catch every word.

As the conversation continued, she realized Drancy was officially under the control of the French police. That made sense. They orchestrated most of the roundups. The SS oversaw the housing of the detainees and their eventual transportation to German-run concentration camps. A team effort that proved France's official collaboration with their occupiers. Camille found herself engulfed in a rage so strong that she had to look away for fear of revealing her thoughts.

"How many do you anticipate in this mass arrest?" asked von Bauer.

"Somewhere between twenty and thirty thousand Parisian Jews."

This outrageous number seemed to confuse the two Nazis, Camille as well. Von Bauer spoke the question they were all thinking. "There can't be that many Jewish males left in Paris."

"There aren't." The Frenchman puffed out his chest. A peacock showing off his plume. "This roundup will include women and children."

Von Bauer was not impressed, as evidenced by his look of disbelief. "I wasn't aware the French police had that sort of manpower."

"We have enough. After all, we are talking about Jewish women and children. They are like cows, stupid and weak. They will go willingly."

Camille bit the inside of her bottom lip to keep from shouting at the ugly little man. The tinny taste of blood rolled across her tongue. The French police could not be so cruel, so vicious. They couldn't, they wouldn't, arrest women and children. But of course, they could. And they would. She saw the truth in the beady black eyes flashing with sick satisfaction.

Fragments of feeling wanted to bleed through her horror. Rachel. Her mother. She had to warn them. No, she had to get them out of Paris, tonight. She looked at Vivian and saw no help there. Her vague, bored expression seemed far too real. Besides, only minutes ago, she'd told Camille the forged documents weren't ready. There had to be another way. Another option, another— The bunker. Of course!

The bunker.

Von Bauer would never think to look for Jews hiding beneath his house. It would be dangerous. But with the proper amount of subterfuge, Camille could hide Rachel and her mother for a few days, maybe longer. Her hands clasped together at her waist. The feel of the ridiculous chatelaine imprinted against her wrist gave her an idea. There was only this one set of keys. She could lock the doors after von Bauer left for work and unlock them before he arrived home, he none the wiser. If he made to return unexpectedly, he would have to knock to get inside.

It could work. Camille would make it work. Time was her greatest enemy. She carefully, slowly moved toward the exit, then realized she was still required to wait on these foul, awful men with their foul, awful plans. She forced herself to remain calm and show nothing of her knowledge on her face.

Von Bauer called for a refill. Camille poured more coffee

into his cup, moving as if her body belonged to someone else, a woman who didn't comprehend the German language. She scanned the occupants of the room from beneath her lashes, understanding as she hadn't before why this small group of men had come here tonight. Players in another roundup that would be the worst one yet. Finally, she served the last of the coffee, took a deep breath, and slipped out of the room, her pace slow and steady so she didn't call attention to herself.

Hovering in the hallway, empty tray in hand, she strained to hear the rest of their evil plans. She knew the roundups were to take place, she knew where the women and children would be taken, at least initially, but she didn't know the ultimate destination for all those innocent souls. Or the dates. She heard the rustle of papers being handed off from one man to another. Every detail would be written on those pages. She would have to wait until the household was asleep and, slim though the possibility was, pray the documents didn't walk out the door with von Bauer's superior officer.

Stitching her lips tightly together, Camille returned to the kitchen and made herself clean the remains of the dinner party as quickly as possible. Her eyes lit on the half-eaten food on three of the four plates. Such waste.

A noise sounded behind her, and she froze, hands submerged in soapy water. Vivian came to stand beside her. Her face was pale, and her green eyes swam with unspoken grief. "I didn't know you spoke German."

Vivian sighed. "Until I saw your face just now, I didn't know you did, either." She shook her head in defeat. "I'll do my best to expedite the process we've already put into motion. I don't know how long we have before the roundup. That horrid little Frenchman didn't reveal the date aloud. He merely handed von Bauer the paperwork."

So, the information *was* in writing. Camille simply needed to get a look at the documents to know how to proceed. This was her opportunity to tell Vivian about the bunker. Something held her back. She trusted the American only to a point. And so, instead of confessing her plan for the Bermans, she said simply, "I pray there's enough time before the arrests begin."

"As do I." Vivian turned to go then, paused at the door. "This world we live in. It is very—" she sighed "—ugly."

"It is."

Camille waited until the house went dark and the sounds from von Bauer's room had gone quiet to make her inquiry. There was still a chance she'd misunderstood about the roundup. But that would mean Vivian had misunderstood as well.

That seemed highly unlikely, and so she entered von Bauer's study, careful not to make a sound. The room was coated in darkness, made darker by the cloud cover outside. A steady rain had begun falling from the sky. Camille tiptoed to von Bauer's desk. *Please, please, let him be in possession of the documents.*

He was.

Please. Please. Let me be wrong about the roundups.

She was not.

The plan was for tens of thousands of Jews to be rounded up in a single day and contained in the Vél d'Hiv, a stadium used mostly for indoor bicycle races. Camille searched for the date of the roundup, gasped at what she found. Vivian's efforts would not be enough to save Rachel and her mother. The arrests were to begin two days from now, at sunrise.

Camille had failed so many people in her life. Her father. Her sister. Even, on some level, her mother. She would not fail the Bermans. Mouth set, she replaced the documents exactly where she'd found them. At the door, she gave the room a quick scan to ensure she'd left no signs of herself behind. Satisfied, she left the way she'd come.

A great crash of thunder sounded in the distance outside the kitchen. She flinched so hard her teeth rattled. The rain began to fall in earnest, scratching at the glass, like someone trying to get in, or to warn her to get out. Hurry, hurry. So little time. She should wait until tomorrow night when the weather was better. But… Wouldn't it be easier to avoid notice in the rain? The sentries would be less diligent performing their duties.

Decision made, Camille pounded over the distance from the kitchen to the back door. Her whole body was trembling by the time she exited the house. She had to get to Rachel. Tonight. She had to convince her friend to hide in the home of a German SS officer. A Nazi. No small task.

She made the trip on foot, thankful for the rain that kept the soldiers on patrol huddled deep within their coats, their attention on staying dry rather than catching young Frenchwomen on a mission to save her friends.

When Camille finally stood outside the Bermans' apartment, the irony was not lost on her. Much like the day the Germans invaded Paris, this time it was Camille standing in the hallway of a run-down building, urgently standing before a closed door, hoping—praying—she wasn't too late.

Chapter Thirty-Three

Rachel

15 July 1942.
Paris, France.

Rachel didn't know what woke her. Sometime before midnight, she'd fallen into a fitful sleep, her dreams plagued with Nazi flags in the hands of French policemen. She sat up, blinking hard, the stale air filling her lungs. After a long pause, she heard it again. Two sounds. The rumble of thunder in the distance and the sound of the front door squeaking open. Her first thought was: *Gestapo.* They'd come for her and her mother. But then she heard her name whispered.

She knew the owner of that voice.

Camille.

With a sense of urgency, Rachel threw off the covers and hurried out of the room, her footsteps silent in the gloom. She knew which of the floorboards creaked, which ones held her weight without making a sound. Rain clouds covered the moon outside, turning the dark room darker still. She stumbled, righted herself on the edge of a ladder-back chair.

The lack of light told her it was still the middle of the night, or perhaps early morning. Hard to know with the rain coming down in hard sheets. The sound of footsteps came from the entryway, and for a minute Rachel thought of the French police again.

"Rachel?"

Hearing something akin to panic, Rachel froze. The clouds shifted, and a thin trickle of moonlight illuminated her friend, standing inside the apartment. Her clothes were wet, her hair all but plastered to her head. "Camille, why are you—"

"Hurry." Her eyes were wide and glistened like hard glass. "You must come with me. Now. You and your mother. There isn't much time. They're coming for you."

"The Gestapo?"

She shook her head, her eyes heavy with insistence and something else. Panic. "The French police. They've scheduled another roundup."

Her earlier confusion slid into bone-chilling fear. "When?"

"Soon. And this time—" Camille's voice hitched "—they will arrest women and children."

Rachel felt her cheeks go hot. "How do you know this?"

"It doesn't matter. Wake your mother. We must go."

Go? Where? Where could a Jewish woman and her mother hide in a city swarming with enemies?

Before she could ask the question, her mother appeared, her eyes full of weary acceptance. "We will go with you now, Camille. It's time."

It wasn't until she and her mother were dressed, each carrying a small bag of their most important possessions, that Rachel realized, like her mother, she trusted Camille.

A snap of lightning brightened the night, a pitchfork in the sky, and she found herself asking, "Where are you taking us?"

"To Drancy."

Her blood turned to ice, and her earlier confidence vanished. Panic became a living, breathing thing writhing in her empty belly. She tried to ignore the sensation, to hold it back, squeeze it down. But she couldn't stifle a squeak of alarm.

Camille was quick to reach to her. "I do not take you to the detainment center. I am taking you home with me."

Rachel felt relief rush through her, hot and unexpected. Then came the fear. Cold and furious. "You mean, to the Nazi's home?" she hissed.

"Yes, and no." The rain streamed over her, turning the long golden locks into thick, unruly clumps. "There is a hidden bunker beneath the house. The entrance is in the basement. And before you protest, von Bauer doesn't know about the secret room."

"Does his mistress?"

"The fewer people who know of its existence, the safer it is for you."

That wasn't an answer.

"We should get moving." Camille touched her arm. "It's a long walk, and we must keep to the shadows to avoid detection. Even in the rain, there are patrols."

Rachel knew her friend was right, but for her mother's sake, she couldn't let her question go unanswered. "Is Vivian Miller aware of the bunker?"

"I am the only one who knows. It's not ideal, I know. But, Rachel, they're coming for you and your mother. What choice do you have but to trust me?"

She saw the dark honesty in her friend's gaze, the desire to protect her, friend to friend, sister to sister. It was there on the tip of her tongue, every feeling, every nuanced emotion. She imagined it all spilling out. The gratitude she felt. But also, the anger. White-hot fury that she had to rely on someone outside her family for her survival.

At least you have someone watching out for you. Others didn't. *Be grateful.*

Rachel gave the briefest of nods and, after taking her mother's arm, followed Camille through the shadows, over the wet streets, back into the shadows. After what felt like hours, with her mother leaning heavily against her now, she finally chanced a whispered, "Are we close?"

"Nearly there. Just over the next rise."

The rain slowed to a spitting drizzle. Rachel glanced down at her mother, as she'd done throughout the journey, and saw her fatigue. For a moment, there was a roaring in her ears, as if she were forging through gallons of water rather than raindrops.

Camille stopped at a wrought-iron gate that led into a court-yard. Rachel took in the massive three-story house looming above them. The walls were made of white stone, something grand, possibly marble. The windows were dark, like hollow eyes cut into a pale, unforgiving face. Vines crawled up the columns of a gazebo off to her left, reminding Rachel of snakes, lizards, and vipers. The stuff of nightmares.

Reaching for a ring of keys at her waist, Camille unlocked the gate and stepped through. Rachel and her mother followed her. "We'll enter through the back. Hurry now. The sun will be rising soon."

She was right. The night sky had taken on a purplish tint. Soon the world would go pink and orange, and the French police would begin coordinating last-minute details for their roundups. Rachel and her mother could not be caught outside. They could not be caught inside, either.

Again she glanced at her mother before taking the next step. Ilka Berman looked exhausted, which was expected after their trek across half of Paris on empty stomachs, but she also appeared resolved. That evident will to live gave Rachel permission to continue trusting her friend. Camille led them around the house and let them in through an unassuming door. They were in some sort of mudroom now, which spilled into a kitchen on the left and housed yet another door on their right.

Gaze locked with Rachel's, Camille pushed open that second door and stepped aside.

A row of stairs descended into a tomb-like darkness that

reeked of mold and something equally pungent. There was a railing. Just as Rachel put her hand on the wood, she heard a soft click, and then a faint light came on. She took a step, but Camille stopped her. "Me first."

Happy to let her friend lead, she watched as Camille disappeared down the steps. Another soft click—barely a hint of sound—and then more dim light shone at the foot of the stairs. That, Rachel knew, was her cue to guide her mother into the basement.

At the bottom of the stairs, she discovered the space was mostly a storage area. Brooms and mops in one corner, racks of metal shelves filled with canned goods in another. So much food. Enough to feed a small regiment of German soldiers, and that brought back her anger. She stubbed her toe on something hard and had to slap her hand over her mouth to keep silent.

Camille set her hands on one of the racks. "Help me move this."

Rachel went to the other side, placed her hands on the cold metal, and pushed. Camille pulled. And then, there was yet another door, this one cut right into the wall.

"Follow me." Camille reached for a flashlight sitting on a small shelf above the door and, using its narrow beam, entered what seemed to be a long, narrow tunnel.

Even knowing Camille was showing her trustworthiness, always taking the first step into the unknown, Rachel couldn't seem to make her feet move. "We have trusted her this far," her mother reminded her. "What are a few more steps? Go, *ketsl*, my *córka*. I am right behind you."

The first step into the cool, velvety cave proved the hardest. But she took it. As she continued along the narrow passageway, some unnamed fear stabbed in her throat. The dark seemed to close in around her, like a hard, ruthless fist. She stood still in the deep, black nothingness, her breath shallow, cold prickling over her skin.

"Keep going," her mother whispered.

Rachel took another step and again froze. She could feel the dark earth swallowing her whole. Then, suddenly, she was done being scared and was moving faster. The tunnel eventually emptied into a rather large room. A sprawling concrete monster, no windows, no ventilation, no light beyond the small torch in Camille's hand. The space was more like a prison cell than a bunker, and Rachel realized someone else had lived here once, at least temporarily.

Where were they now?

She would probably never know.

"I need to go. The rest of the household will want their breakfast soon. I'll come back in a few hours, and we'll discuss our next steps." Camille stepped around Rachel, pausing to say, "In the meantime, I left some bread, cheese and water on the table between the two largest cots."

She disappeared into the tunnel with a final promise to return soon. The door shut next. The heavy scrape of metal followed. Then Camille was gone, and Rachel and her mother were alone in a concrete bunker, beneath a Nazi's home.

She felt a sudden twist of fury, and a lot of fear. How had her life come to this? How could so many presumably good people look the other way? It was all too much to bear, and Rachel wanted to cry. So, she cried.

Her mother came to her with a piece of torn cloth in her hand. Without saying a word, she reached up and wiped away Rachel's tears. "We will get through this, *schatzeleh*. For the memory of your father and brother, yes? We will survive for them."

"You…you know what happened to Papa and Srulka?" She had to say their names, had to honor them in that small way.

"I overheard your conversation with your friend."

"Oh, Mama. I'm so sorry."

"As am I. Now, chin up. For our *mishpokhe*, we will be strong. We will live for those who have died."

Rachel hadn't known her mother could summon such inner strength when her body was so fragile, and she promised herself she would find the same fortitude inside herself. She would do it for her mother and, as Ilka Berman said, for the ones they'd lost.

Chapter Thirty-Four

Camille

15 July 1942.
Von Bauer's Home. Seine-Saint-Denis Department.
Paris, France.

Camille couldn't make the journey down into the basement in the few hours she'd promised. Vivian, usually quick to leave the house, often at the same time as von Bauer, lingered over her coffee. Camille wanted to yell at her to go away. But there she sat. At the little round table by the window, her legs crossed. She took unhurried, dainty sips from her cup while Camille cleaned the breakfast dishes. She said nothing, simply drank and watched. Watched and drank. Until Camille was sick with frustration and worry for the women she'd left in the bunker.

It was possible, even probable, that Rachel and her mother thought she'd abandoned them. Camille set aside the plate she'd been drying, turned, and held Vivian's stare. Some sixth sense made her pulse ripple beneath her skin. She went hot all over, and she knew, just knew, that Vivian was aware of their uninvited guests.

Slowly, Vivian placed her cup on the saucer. "We need to discuss what happened last night."

Camille's mind went instantly blank. She could not have responded had Vivian put a gun to her head.

"I'm afraid the news is not good."

She knows. To come so close, only to fail Rachel and her mother. Always the same. Her efforts never enough. She felt a few self-pitying drops trail down her cheeks. But then she took a deep breath and scrubbed them away. Crying would gain nothing. "What do you know?"

"I was able to wheedle the actual dates for the roundups out of von Bauer." She didn't say how she'd come by the information, and quite frankly, Camille had no desire to ask. "The arrests will begin early tomorrow morning and continue into the next day, however long it takes the French police to gather up the remaining Jews living in Paris."

Camille tried not to show her surprise or relief. Vivian didn't know about Rachel and her mother. She thought she was supplying Camille with new information. "Tomorrow?" she croaked, reminded anew of the terrible crime the French police would commit. "So soon?"

"I'm sorry, Camille. Time has run out for your friends. I wish I had been quicker finding a proper forger. I wish I could have coordinated their escape sooner. I wish—" she lifted her gaze, and in her eyes Camille saw the look of a stricken woman "—many, many things."

Camille could ease Vivian's mind. She could tell her about the bunker. But the stakes were high. And two lives were solely in her hands. The possibility of Vivian betraying them was slim, but it *was* possible. "What if I told you that they have a place to hide temporarily? Would you continue arranging their escape?"

"What do you mean, hide?" Vivian's gaze sharpened. "Where would they hide? Who would hide them?"

Two questions, with but one answer too dangerous to utter. "Perhaps there is at least one brave soul left in Paris."

"Brave? No, not brave. Reckless. Foolhardy. An open invitation for the Gestapo to come knocking on their door."

Camille's heart ached with something like regret. She'd thought Vivian courageous. But her words spoke of self-preservation. "If I am able to guarantee they will not be arrested in the roundup, will you continue setting up their escape?"

"What have you done, Camille?" Vivian's voice was sharp as the edge of a blade.

"It's better you don't know."

"Tell me, where are they hiding?"

Camille ignored the question. "Will you continue working on their behalf?"

Not quite meeting her eyes, Vivian swiveled her head and stared out the window overlooking the backyard where the gazebo stood. Her agitation was palpable.

"Were they just words, Vivian? Or did you mean what you said? Do you *wish* to help my friend and her mother?"

Slowly, Vivian settled back in her seat. Slowly, she looked at Camille. Slowly, she said, "I will continue as if there are to be no roundups."

"Thank you."

There was no need for further discussion. That didn't keep Vivian from having the last word. "Be careful who you trust, Camille. Enemies come in the most unlikely of packages."

Hearing more than the obvious warning, a premonition even, Camille found herself unable to take a decent pull of air. The sensation was like a noose around her neck, not yet tight, but already making it hard to breathe.

"Did you hear me, Camille?"

"I heard you."

"Good." Saying nothing more, Vivian exited the kitchen and then, moments later, the house itself. Camille locked the door behind her and waited an additional half hour before making the journey down the basement stairs. The sound of her heels on the wooden steps dragged her back to that other time, to that other basement. She bit her lip, looked back over her shoulder, forced herself to continue.

At the bottom, she scanned the immediate area, saw that nothing was out of place, and only then allowed herself to breathe easy. Flexing her cold fingers, she gripped the metal rack and pushed it aside. The lock gave way with only a small battle, and Camille stepped into the dark tunnel. A miniscule pinprick of light escaped from the bunker on the other end of the corridor. Camille groped her way forward, the tiny beacon her guide.

There was the sound of breathing, hers, and then she heard the soft murmurs. She cleared her throat. "Rachel? Madame Berman? It's me, Camille."

She finally entered the bunker itself and found Rachel and her mother exactly as she'd left them. Sitting side by side on a single cot, their arms tightly linked.

Rachel's gaze met Camille's. Her lips were somehow a little twisted, as if there were thoughts in her head she struggled to keep from blurting out all at once. In stark contrast, her mother was completely closed off. Her gaze empty and unfocused, she hummed something beneath her breath, a song Camille had never heard. "I'm sorry I was gone so long. But I'm— Oh." She glanced at the untouched plate of food. "You didn't eat."

"We had other things on our mind," Rachel said, her face tightly disapproving, though her voice was a whisper of its usual self. "Food was low on the list."

"Again, I'm sorry." The words rang insincere and hollow in this moldy, dank bunker. "I never intended to be gone so long."

More excuse-making. Why couldn't Camille get this right?

Rachel readjusted herself on the cot, her gaze moving to the chatelaine hooked at Camille's waist. "Did you have to bolt the door behind you?"

The question told Camille much. Rachel had explored the bunker and the tunnel beyond, where she'd then checked the door leading into the basement.

"I didn't secure the lock to keep you in," she said, simply and from the heart. "I did it to keep *him* out."

The expression on Rachel's face could not be described as transformed, but her frown wasn't so deep. And her lips weren't so tight. "I see. Yes, of course."

The courage it took to come to that moment of acceptance humbled Camille. Shamed her, even. She'd been so blindly focused on getting Rachel and her mother safely hidden that she hadn't thought what it must be like for them to face an uncertain future, indefinitely holed up in this soulless bunker, with no talk of escape.

Surely, they had questions. How could they not?

The solution came to Camille suddenly, like a swift nudge to her shoulder. Knowing it was the right course of action, she reached out one hand to Rachel, the other to her mother. "Come upstairs with me now. We'll get you some breakfast, and after you're feeling stronger, we'll discuss plans for your escape and—"

"Upstairs? You want us to come upstairs with you? Now?"

"Yes, now. So I can explain."

"We can't go upstairs." Rachel jumped to her feet and shoved herself back. Back, back, back until she was flush against the concrete wall. "It's not safe. Von Bauer—"

"Won't be home for hours. Nor will Vivian. Rachel." Camille inched toward her friend, slowly, her hand still outstretched. "I promise you, it's safe. I've locked all the doors from the inside, and I am in sole possession of the keys. No one can get in without me letting them in."

Rachel's eyes went wide and a little wild, and Camille could tell by the way she scrubbed at them with her sleeve that she was trying not to cry. "I don't know what to do. I want to trust you, but I...I'm scared. I don't want to be, but I am. All the time. I hate feeling like this."

She closed her eyes, and Camille realized she'd rescued her friend from one life in a cage, only to throw her into another.

"This bunker is only temporary. One day soon you will be free of this awful house, and safely on your way to Spain. It will happen. I ask only that you trust me a little while longer."

Rachel drew a long breath. "*Trés bien*. I—" She glanced briefly at her mother, who gave a very small nod. "That is, *we* will trust you a little longer."

Chapter Thirty-Five

Rachel

August 1942.
Von Bauer's Home. Seine-Saint-Denis Department.
Paris, France.

Two weeks later, Rachel lay flat on her back, her forearm flung over her eyes. She couldn't sleep. Too many thoughts floating in her head. Her father and brother. Her sister. Too much silence from her mother on the next cot. And too little variation in their daily routine.

The web of monotony was a strange sort of torture. Every morning started the same, with the sound of metal scraping across concrete. Next, a key rattling in a lock. Hushed footsteps. Then Camille's soft voice telling Rachel and her mother, "You can come upstairs now."

Sighing, Rachel turned from her back onto her front, blinked into the vast nothingness of the darkened room, and remembered that first morning upstairs. The sunshine had been a shock, blinding her, and then the smells had rolled in. Sweet, creamy scents mixed with another equally pleasant, almost forgotten aroma. Camille had poured the coffee into two mugs and had presented a basket of croissants with butter and jam—*real* butter and sugary jam—and Rachel had been too overwhelmed with guilt to partake in any of it. Not when she thought of other French Jews, mostly women and children, who were at the mercy of the French police.

Camille had insisted she eat.

Rachel had resisted.

Even when her friend had gently reminded her that she would need her strength for the journey across France, Rachel had not been able to indulge. Only when she realized her mother was taking her lead, and refusing to eat as well, did she pick up one of the pastries. Halfway through her second croissant, Rachel had looked around and realized the house must be enormous with a kitchen so large. "You are tasked with cleaning this entire house on your own, or are there others who come to assist during the day?"

"No others. Only me. I also cook and see to the laundry."

Rachel had blinked in astonishment. "But that's impossible."

Camille shrugged. "I am paid well, and when exhaustion nearly overtakes me, I think of my family. And now, I will also think of you and your mother."

There was nothing of the martyr in her voice, only conviction, and Rachel had felt a lump in her throat. How quick she'd been to judge her friend for taking this job. "Let me help you with some of your household duties."

"And I will cook," her mother had added.

They were the first words she'd spoken since their arrival in the kitchen, and Rachel reached out to squeeze the older woman's hand. "Yes, you will cook, and I will clean, and your job, Camille, will not be quite so hard."

The protests came at once. "Absolutely not. After last night, rest is what you need. Now, finish up your breakfast, and I will take you back downstairs."

Back downstairs. A fluttering panic rose in Rachel's chest. Back. Downstairs. Into the dark and the mold and the suffocating silence that seemed to come alive once the lock clicked into place. "Please, Camille. Work is just what we need. Give us something to do. We'll polish the silver, sweep the floors, scrub the laundry." Anything to forestall going back into that wretched room. "It will help us feel a little bit normal."

Camille's protests had eventually subsided and, after that first morning, they'd quickly found a rhythm. There was a risk, always a risk, that the Nazi would come home unexpectedly, and because of that, it was agreed that Rachel and her mother would spend only a few hours out of the bunker. A few blessed hours when honest work held their fears and paranoia at bay.

Now Rachel lay awake, and when she shivered, it was not entirely at the thought of the man who lived upstairs. It was from knowing the stillness in the bunker would dissolve without warning, and her mother would dip into the dream that plagued her every night without fail.

Suddenly, Rachel could not bear the wait. She lit a candle, then reached out, thinking to shake the older woman awake. But she'd moved too late. Her mother was already beginning to thrash about in the dim light. Her legs kicked out in protest of the images in her head. She muttered in a confused mix of Yiddish and French and Polish, none of it making any sense. All of it breaking Rachel's heart.

She rolled off her cot and knelt on the floor beside her mother. "Mama. Shh. It's a dream. Only a dream. Wake up." She smoothed a hand over the sweating brow. "You need to wake up now. It's a dream, only a dream."

More thrashing of arms and legs. And now her head joined the riotous dance.

"*Mama!* Wake up!"

Suddenly, Ilka went still, deathly still. Then her eyes popped open, and she was instantly, fully awake. It was not reassuring, staring into her mother's tortured expression swollen with tears and heartbreak. "We should not have left our home, *ketsl*. They will come back."

"They aren't coming back." It was never easy, saying those terrible words.

"My Ezra, *meyn harts*, he will find a way home. We will be gone. And then he will think we gave up hope."

She was wrong. They could not give up something that was already lost. "Papa and Srulka are gone."

Rachel saw the denial in her mother's eyes, and then the awful moment of acceptance for what could not be changed. Sleep would not come for either of them now. She stood, bent over her mother's small form. "Here, let me help you sit up, and then I will read out loud while you knit."

The smallest spark of life came into her mother's eyes, and for that alone, Rachel would have endured the clacking of needles. But as they sat together under the candlelight, and her mother began to knit in earnest, Rachel realized something rather shocking. The sound that had once brought such loath-some dread now supplied an endless source of comfort. Such that she found herself asking, "Will you teach me?"

"I'd like nothing more."

For the next several hours, Ilka Berman patiently guided Rachel through the process of knitting scarves for men who would never wear them.

Chapter Thirty-Six

Vivian

September 1942.
Von Bauer's Home. Seine-Saint-Denis Department.
Paris, France.

Now that he was tasked with transporting French Jews to Poland, von Bauer left for the transit camp early in the mornings and arrived home later and later in the evenings. This schedule suited Vivian. She spent the bulk of her days at the Hôtel Ritz, continuing her charade as a wealthy American. Between luncheons with her so-called friends and, on rare occasions, taking tea with Coco Chanel or other notorious collaborators, she pushed Frank to acquire the forged documents for Camille's friends.

There always seemed to be a new delay. What should have taken weeks was taking months. She would push harder this afternoon. This morning, however, she hesitated outside the breakfast room, gathering her strength before confronting the man she'd grown to loathe even more than her own wicked choices.

Von Bauer had left her alone last night, which had been a

great comfort, but also a great concern. His passion was waning. He would soon discard her. She wasn't concerned who her replacement would be, until she took her place at the table and watched the wicked man leer at Camille as she set down a plate of pastries.

In her blackest dreams, Vivian had not thought he would turn his eye toward the girl. She'd wondered. But he'd been so dismissive of Camille's country manners she'd let the thought go. However, now, she realized her mistake. The girl was beautiful, and von Bauer's animal instincts were strong, barbaric even. All those envious female eyes that followed Vivian whenever she was on his arm, they had no idea how fortunate they were he'd chosen her over them.

Looking at him now, taking him in as she would a casual stranger, she saw nothing of the monster, only the handsome soldier in the crisp uniform. The iron cross at his neck was perfectly aligned with his Adam's apple, not a centimeter off-center. Ah, but when it came to his personal pleasure, he was not a man so concerned with outward control.

He was a selfish brute with a preference for causing pain.

Vivian approached the table at a steady, sweeping pace. Again, von Bauer's gaze followed Camille out of the room. She knew that look, what it meant, and she would not be a party to the loss of the girl's innocence. No, no.

A sharp, determined sound moved through her throat.

At last, von Bauer swung his gaze in her direction. "I told you to sleep in."

"I have much to do for tonight's party."

"That's why I hired a housekeeper." Displeasure threaded through his voice.

Vivian shrugged. "I prefer to take care of the centerpieces myself. The girl doesn't have an eye for such things."

"Nevertheless. I require for you to attend parties as my hostess. Smile, entertain, and make me look good. The rest, you will leave to the French girl."

As if on cue, Camille reappeared and began gathering the dirty dishes off the table. The swine watched her every move. Vivian knew that sly tilt of his head, the touch of awareness in his gaze, the stillness that belonged to a predator poised to strike.

She felt an odd sinking in her stomach as her mind flashed on the memory of his initial pursuit of her. She'd known he would get what he wanted. Her only decision had been whether to cooperate or use the situation to her advantage. The outcome would have been the same, but by controlling a portion of the process, she'd kept a small piece of her dignity intact.

It would not be the same for Camille.

Vivian had made a gross error in judgment. She'd brought the girl into this home, only to become von Bauer's prey. At least he hadn't touched her yet, but he would—if Vivian didn't intervene.

Von Bauer rose suddenly, and Vivian did the same. He kissed her on the mouth, a cold, unenthusiastic peck, and she knew, without a doubt, that he was done with her.

"I will be home in time for the party," he said, taking her by the shoulders with a grip that told her he expected complete obedience. "Wear the blue dress and matching sapphire necklace."

There was a distance in his eyes as he issued the command, but he kissed her again. And in the space of that second kiss, she let herself be the woman he thought her to be—needy, a little desperate, reliant solely on him. She even managed a shaky sigh, added a bit of unease to the sound, going for uncertain, fragile.

Her performance did the trick. He drew back, looking pleased. Good. Let him think he'd subdued her rebellious nature.

Putting a hint of nerves in her demeanor, she walked with him to the back door, a direct route through the kitchen. She didn't trust him alone with Camille. He moved around the girl, but only just barely. His sleeve brushed her arm.

She did not react, not a shudder, not a flinch. Not a smile. Clever girl.

Camille locked the door behind him and went to the sink, where she began washing the breakfast dishes. Vivian took in the young woman's appearance. Not a crease out of place, or wrinkle to mar the cut of the fabric on her thin frame.

A beautiful girl, who followed her employer's instructions to the letter, but when Vivian looked closer, she also saw the exhaustion in her blue eyes. And the worry. Did she understand what von Bauer wanted? "Take care, Camille. Do not find yourself alone with him. He is not to be trusted."

"No, he is not."

Vivian had underestimated the girl. Still. "Lock your bedroom door at night."

"Always."

"Good. Excellent. You understand." A faint noise from somewhere in the house caused the girl to jump. Nothing more than the house settling, but Camille gazed frantically over her shoulder, toward the mudroom. The worry had returned in her gaze, and something else. A sort of paranoid watchfulness. Thinking she knew the cause, Vivian touched Camille's arm, squeezed gently. "Have you received news about your sister?"

She shook her head.

"This is a good thing, yes?"

She nodded. "I will only hear if the news is—" She stopped abruptly, and cleared her throat, looked to the door. The window. The walls themselves.

"Dire?"

This time, a sigh leaked from her lips, pulled from somewhere deep inside her. *"Oui."*

"If not your sister, what keeps you from sleeping?"

A scared expression replaced the worry. "You heard me moving around last night?"

Something there, in her gaze. Guilt, secrets, they hung in the air, the implications of a lie swirling. "You're exhausted. I assume you lose sleep over your sister."

Camille visibly relaxed. "Thoughts of her keep me up, but

also, I worry about all those people in the roundup, and the terrible days they spent in that arena without food and water. Mothers, daughters, sisters, aunts. What did they do but live their lives and work hard to provide for their families?"

"You are thinking about your friend," Vivian said. "You're worried she will be taken."

Camille dipped her head, but not before she glanced to a spot just over Vivian's shoulder. "She won't be taken."

Vivian's eyebrows lifted. "You seem certain of this."

Camille's eyes shifted again, and she bunched her lips, considering. "I am, very."

The pointed look, the tapping of her foot, the inability to gaze directly at Vivian, meant the young woman was hiding something. But what?

"Do you want me to continue with our plans?"

"Yes. Please. Rachel and her mother cannot stay in France indefinitely."

"The details of their journey are nearly complete. I will pick up the documents in a few days. In the meantime, come, let's review their escape route one more time."

They studied the map together, with Vivian pointing out the first rendezvous point and the second if there was trouble early on. Camille listened without comment, repeating everything only after Vivian was through. "Okay," Vivian said, pushing away from the table. "I meet with the forger later today."

"Be careful, Vivian."

She took each of Camille's hands in hers. "I won't let you down."

"I know it, and I thank you, for myself and for them."

There was nothing else to say. Determined to do this one thing for Camille, and her Jewish friends, Vivian went to the mirror in the foyer and checked her appearance. Camille stood behind her, sharing her reflection as she pinned her hat at a jaunty angle. "I'll be back shortly, and your friend's terrible nightmare will nearly be over."

Vivian would make it be so. Then she would w̶
ting Camille free from von Bauer. She would sell he
and the tapestries, whatever it took to provide for th̶
woman's future. As for herself, her fate had been sea̶
moment she'd become von Bauer's mistress.

The Betrayal

Chapter Thirty-Seven

Rachel

16 September 1942.
Von Bauer's Home. Seine-Saint-Denis Department.
Paris, France.

Two months had passed since Rachel and her mother became willing captives in the concrete bunker beneath a Nazi's home. Two months since they'd discovered the house had originally belonged to another Jewish family. The blink of an eye in the span of a lifetime. An eternity for two women anticipating rescue, when all they received were excuses.

Waiting, always waiting, for the sound of metal scraping against concrete. For the whoosh of air to swirl through the tunnel. For Camille to call out so Rachel and her mother could spend a few precious hours aboveground.

This was a mistake, she thought for the thousandth time. A stupid, shortsighted mistake. As if trapped in her mother's nightmares, she wondered how her father and brother would find them, should they survive. Or Basia. How would she know where to look? A sob trailed up her throat. Rachel stifled the sound in her blanket. When she looked up, her mother's eyes were on her, searching her face. "I'm all right," she whispered.

The older woman kept her gaze locked on Rachel's face, saying nothing. She'd stopped speaking in full sentences weeks ago, with barely a word uttered in recent days. The silence was another casualty in this room. A concrete cage shared with bugs and rats and the ghosts of a family that had come before them. Rachel reached for the stuffed bear, hugged it close as if she were a child.

In many ways, she was a child. But also, a very old woman. Older even than her mother. Her dreams and desires had drilled down to a single, impossible wish for her family to be restored. She wanted to be the young, hopeful girl before France had declared war on Germany. She wanted to argue with her brother. To share clothes with her sister. Rachel didn't want riches. She didn't want pretty things. Her family together, each of them safe and alive, that's all she craved.

Before her mother had gone silent, her last words were, "You're a good girl. Strong and courageous like our ancestors."

But Rachel didn't feel strong and courageous. She felt the gnawing, unrelenting shame of being reduced to an animal. Her humiliation never relented. Hiding in a tiny concrete room, waiting for Camille to open the door for a small taste of freedom, only to be shut back in before the dreaded Nazi arrived home for his evening meal and parties.

You are alive. Your mother is safe.

The sound of metal scraping across concrete heralded temporary relief from the bunker. Rachel scrambled to her feet and reached for her mother, who rose significantly slower.

"It's good to get out of this room," Rachel said, unsure which of them she was trying to convince.

The door swung open, and she caught the tiny glimmer of light on the other side of the tunnel. Everything inside her knotted. For two months, she'd seen that beacon and taken this route with her mother every morning, their arms linked, their feet shuffling over wood and concrete and then dirt, back to concrete. Each time, the dark frightened her just a little bit more. It seemed to grow more sinister with each trip.

Camille stood before them, her smile one of apology. But there was something else in her, too, a nervousness that told Rachel she was on edge about something. "What's happened?"

"He was late leaving the house. He—" she looked at the ground "—he's gone now."

"And Vivian?"

"Gone, too."

Camille was hiding something from Rachel. It was in the way she kept dropping her chin. But Rachel didn't ask. There were some things that occurred upstairs she simply didn't want to know.

"I've made breakfast. Come and eat."

Rachel took the stairs after Camille and entered the mudroom a step behind her. In the kitchen, her eyes locked on the food. The smells were amazing, and her stomach rumbled. She ignored it. She must work first, then rest. "What needs doing first?"

"Nothing until after you and your mother have eaten."

Camille set a basket of croissants and honey on the table and all but pushed Rachel in a chair. She poured two mugs of hot coffee—added cream and sugar—and then placed several more *viennoiseries* on the table, each with a thick slab of butter. Real butter.

In the past two months, Rachel and her mother had eaten better than they had in the past two years. She'd watched the older woman gain weight, even as she grew more and more silent. She was glad her mother was growing stronger, but her silence made Rachel feel so alone.

She put it out of her mind, as much as she could, and dug into the delicacies Camille provided. They discussed their route to freedom, as they did every morning. They would need to be physically strong to make the journey. With that in mind, she took a hefty bite of a croissant and thought about the next few hours. There was always plenty of work to do in a house this size.

She remembered that first day, when her friend had refused help. No more now that her employer hosted his Nazi friends in his Nazi house nearly every night. Their days had taken on something of a routine, and Rachel was glad for the work. She cleaned, polished the silver, set the table, changed bed linens. Her mother helped mostly with the cooking. Rachel took her final bite and asked, "How many at the party tonight?"

Camille made a face. "Twenty. It's to be some sort of celebration. He wants fresh flowers placed throughout the house." She made another face, this one full of frustration. "Would you dust the rooms on the first floor, while I gather the blooms?"

"Whatever you need."

Camille reached to her but didn't make contact. Her hand dropped slowly. "I wish—"

"I know." Rachel cut her friend off before she could voice her sorrow over the situation. "I wish it, too. But really, I don't mind the work."

It was better than sitting on her cot in the bunker, trapped inside with only a sliver of candlelight, not knowing whether it was day or night or when she would be able to venture out.

"If you're sure…"

She nodded. "I am."

"*Très bien.*" Camille picked up an empty basket and pulled out a tool that looked like scissors with thicker blades that curved into two deadly points. Garden shears, Rachel surmised, though she'd never actually cut a fresh flower before.

A burning desire to follow her friend outside had Rachel standing. She navigated the short distance without thinking about what she was doing. She wanted to walk in the sunshine. Just for a minute. She reached for the door handle, and just as quickly dropped her hand. It was so hard to stay inside the house. She wanted to smell the fresh air, to have the sticky sweet scent of flowers in her nose, and to feel real dirt beneath her fingers.

Too dangerous. Rebellion moved through her. Bitterness. She swallowed it all down, as she'd done for months, hating the surge of ingratitude spiraling through her. She should not resent her confinement, and so she wouldn't.

Rag in hand, she left her mother mixing dough and moved

into the main portion of the house. She removed dust from every piece of antique furniture that had once belonged to a wealthy Jewish family. And just like that, the resentment was back in her heart.

This time, Rachel let the feeling come. She let it fuel her movements through the first room, into the next, and the one after that. She'd nearly worn herself out by the time unfamiliar scents drew her back into the kitchen. Her mother stood at the stove, stirring some sort of soup in an enormous pot.

Rachel had seen this picture of her mother a hundred times, a thousand. Time seemed to shift and bend. Her vision narrowed, blurred, and Rachel was transported back to her childhood.

Love so profound rocked her into motion.

She closed the distance in two strides. "Mama," she whispered, wrapping her arms around the soft waist. *I cannot lose you.* In many ways, she already had. She'd lost her mother to the silence. But in the most important way, Ilka Berman was still her mother, her anchor in this terrible storm.

"What is the meaning of this?"

The furious voice had Rachel spinning around and locking gazes with a pair of stunned green eyes. "Madame Miller," she sputtered, "I thought Camille locked the front door. I thought—"

"I have a key. I have always had a key. What I want to know is how *you* got into this house? More to the point, where is Camille? Camille!" She shouted the girl's name, her gaze shooting swiftly around the kitchen. "Camille! Where are you?"

During the woman's torrent, Rachel moved in front of her mother, effectively shielding her from the outraged American. She stood her ground, heart pounding, knees threatening to give out, and chose to answer the least complicated of the questions. "Camille is outside, cutting flowers for tonight's party."

Silence met her words. Long, endless silence.

Get out. The words echoed in her mind. *Take your mother by the arm and get out of this house.* As if sensing her desire to flee,

Vivian stepped directly in her path, her face devoid of emotion. "Do not think to escape until I have my answers."

Air tightened in her lungs. *It's over.*

The trek in the middle of the night. The months of confinement. None of it had been enough to keep her mother safe. *Get out.* The command permeated every thought swirling in her head. *Get out.*

She couldn't. She mustn't.

She must.

If Vivian Miller held them here until her lover returned—

The back door swung open, and Camille appeared, her gaze running over the scene as frantically as Rachel's blood rushed in her veins.

"Vivian," she managed to say, her voice hitching over each syllable. "You're—" she cut a quick glance to Rachel "—you weren't supposed to be back until later."

The American jabbed a finger in the air in Camille's general direction. "You are keeping them here?" Her voice hit yet another octave. "In *this* house?"

"It made sense. There is a—"

"It *made sense*? Not even a little does this make sense. You said they were in a safe place. This house is not a safe place. I can only assume you've gone mad." Camille flinched as if the other woman had slapped her, but Vivian continued without seeming to notice. "Do you know what he'll do to you, to all of you—" she swept her hand in a wide arc "—if he finds them in this house?"

"Technically, they aren't living in the house."

"Then where? If I am to keep this secret, I must know the truth." The American's fear was clear. Also clear, Rachel saw, was her concern. Concern for Camille, and for herself, but what about Rachel? Her mother?

Was she at all worried about them?

"There is a bunker beneath the house," Camille was saying, "with only one access point through the basement. I found it by accident. I'm certain he doesn't know it exists."

"You're certain, are you?"

"Yes."

Vivian took a deep breath, but it was clear she was still upset. "Explain this to me, Camille, and start at the beginning. But first, lock the back door. And you, stay away from the windows." This last part was for Rachel.

"We know," Rachel said with no small amount of resentment.

"Good. This is good. Now, while Camille locks the door, introduce me to this woman, whom I assume is your mother."

Trying not to shake, Rachel stepped to her mother and pulled her flush against her, so close she could smell the earthy scent of her sweat. "Mama, this is Madame—"

"Vivian. My name is Vivian."

"Vivian," Rachel corrected herself, eyeing the American with open suspicion. She wore a dress that looked custom-made to fit her curvy figure beneath a fur stole thrown around her shoulders. Fur, in September. Such extravagance. It was as if the war hadn't touched her life. Of course it hadn't. She was the mistress to a powerful SS officer, as much an enemy to Rachel as her Nazi lover who'd stolen this house from a Jewish family. "This is my mother, Ilka Berman."

"Come, Ilka. I can call you Ilka, yes?"

Rachel's mother nodded.

"Excellent. All right, Ilka, come and sit here." With a gentleness Rachel hadn't known the woman capable of, Vivian shut off the stove and guided her mother to a chair at the table then sat beside her. "You, too, Rachel. Sit. Over there, across from us."

Rachel took the chair Vivian indicated. When Camille returned, Vivian's calm was fully restored. Camille's was not.

"Now, enlighten me about this secret hiding place beneath the house that no one seems to know about but the three of you."

Camille did as Vivian directed, explaining how she'd found the secret door in the basement while looking for crystal vases. She detailed the first time she'd ventured down the tunnel that led to the bunker, and the subsequent night she'd con-

vinced Rachel and her mother to hide there. "That was two
months ago."

The widow had questions. Most of them for Camille, but
there were a few only Rachel could answer. *Is it only you and
your mother?* Yes, only the two of us. *What do you do for enter-
tainment?* I read and write in my journal. *Do you have a plan for
escape if von Bauer becomes suspicious?*

Rachel and Camille answered simultaneously. "No."

"Then we will make one soon." Vivian returned her attention to Camille and spoke only to her, as if Rachel and her
mother were not in the room. "One thing is certain. You cannot continue hiding them in this house for long. It's too dangerous. We will move up our plan for their escape."

Our plan? Just how involved was Vivian and, more to the
point, why? Why was she helping Rachel and her mother? What
could she possibly gain? Question after question rolled through
her mind, all pertaining to Vivian Miller's motives.

Her eyes locked on the American's face, and the other woman
seemed to know instantly what was in her thoughts. "Why I
have chosen to help you is complicated. Just know that you can
trust me, Rachel. You and your mother."

She wanted to believe her. How could she? This woman
had shown herself an opportunist in her choice of lovers. The
clothes she wore. The comfortable life she led. No, Vivian asked
too much of them.

"I will have your new identity cards later tonight," she said,
gaining her feet. "All that is left is the final preparations for your
escape through the south of France, which will require a few
tweaks now that we're moving the date up by several weeks. I
will meet with the *passeur* while I'm in town."

"Can it be done in time?" Camille asked. "This rearrang-
ing of the timeline?"

Vivian's response was a slow, cynical shake of her head. "Anything can be done in the Occupied Zone, for a price."

Chapter Thirty-Eight

Vivian

16 September 1942.
Von Bauer's Home. Seine-Saint-Denis Department.
Paris, France.

Vivian sat at her dressing table and confronted her weary reflection. The woman looking back at her was the same as always, but somehow different tonight. New lines showed around her eyes, and the muscles in her lower back were like steel cords, perpetually braced for an attack. Her vibrancy was gone, as was the flirtatious twinkle in her eyes.

No longer her husband's Vivi, but Vivian, a woman who'd made morally questionable choices. The toll of those choices showed in her reflection. The cheekbones were not quite so prominent, the skin around her jawline not quite so firm. She was glad her husband wasn't here to witness what she'd become. *Oh, Rupert. How I miss you. How I miss the woman I was with you.*

She briefly shut her eyes, and with very little effort could see him smiling at her, his hand outstretched, drawing her to him. It would be so easy to answer his call. Not yet. A young woman and her mother were counting on her to do the right thing. There was also Camille, who needed her protection from a black-hearted Nazi bent on stealing her innocence.

Sighing, Vivian reached up her hand and dragged her fingertip over the frown line forming across her forehead. She would not survive this war. She felt the truth of it in her bones. She would not escape her fate, but Rachel and her mother could.

The pieces were in place. Vivian had seen to the details herself and then passed them on to Camille only an hour ago. Two nights from now, the Bermans would be met by an escort in the woods a mile down the road. They would journey through central France, then over the Pyrenees and into Spain. Their specific route was known only to their guide.

Two more nights before they were away, two more parties to endure, and then Vivian would deal with von Bauer. She had plans for him. But those would have to wait. For now, she paid attention to the finishing touches of her makeup, rouging her cheeks, powdering her face, and then the final step. The application of the contraband lipstick. Elizabeth Arden's Victory Red.

Satisfied, she nodded at her reflection and returned the tube to its hiding place next to the identity cards. A dark foreboding slid down her spine as she moved to the open window. Just as quickly, she stepped back in alarm. A raven perched on the ledge, devouring the remains of his dinner, what looked to be a dead rodent of some kind. He paused, glanced in her direction, and gave an irritated squawk before settling back in.

Shivering, she turned away and stepped into her dress. Did she have the courage to go through with this act of rebellion? She'd chosen not the blue, as ordered, but a figure-hugging gown made of deep red silk. She draped a strand of rubies around her neck, their bloodred fire as much a statement as the dress. A last-minute change of plans left her hair hanging loose. She wore no gloves, no rings on her fingers. No jewels on her wrists.

Von Bauer would demand payment for her defiance, once they were alone.

Her heart took an extra hard beat, the only reaction she allowed herself, and left the room. Most of the guests had already arrived. The bulk were SS officers, but there were also members of the French police. All of them wore their mistresses on their arms. Too much laughter rang from those women, coupled with too many clever smiles, a cruel mockery to the innocent Jews in the basement, and the French housekeeper in her room down the hall.

One of the policemen approached her, an oily smile on his lips. "Madame Miller."

"Monsieur Colbert." She smiled at one of Paris's highest-ranking policemen. "How lovely to see you again."

She sounded almost, nearly, sincere.

He bent over the hand she offered at the end of her limp wrist. *"Enchanté."*

Vivian continued smiling, though it took great effort. Colbert was a big man who'd lost considerable weight recently. A ploy to fit in with his fellow Frenchmen who suffered from the perils of rationing. Skinny now, but waiting to become big again, once the war was over. And he was still talking—simpering, actually. "It would be my honor to escort you in to dinner."

"I would welcome your company."

A grown man blushing. It was not a pretty sight, especially on the jowly face that hadn't quite caught up with the rest of the slim frame.

He continued making banal conversation. It didn't take long to ferret out that he required only a few nods and a serene smile. Vivian caught von Bauer watching them, his gaze narrowed. His disapproval wrapped around her, even as Colbert's nasally voice filled her ears. So much condemnation in one man, so much adoration in the other.

Eventually, von Bauer's patience wore out, and with a hitch of his chin, he made his intentions known. She excused herself as gracefully as she could. As she answered the summons, their eyes locked, and held.

"Good evening, *der Rab*." The use of his nickname was intentional, meant to show deference.

He was not fooled. He seized her arm at the elbow and squeezed harder than was necessary, a silent warning to speak nothing but happy words in front of his guests. His gaze roamed her face, then lowered over her gown. There was an air of censure in his appraisal, but also ownership, as if she were his possession. And why wouldn't he look at her that way? She *was* his possession. "You're wearing red." Barely concealed rage filled his voice, but the smile on his face was for the others in the room, as were his next words: "I requested blue."

She swallowed back the catch in her throat and forged ahead with their unpleasant charade. "I thought you said red."

"Perhaps I did."

Oh, yes. There would be retribution on his part and the endurance of pain on hers.

The party dragged on and on. Vivian was exhausted long before the last guest departed.

Unfortunately, her evening wasn't over.

As predicted, von Bauer proved true to his nature. She endured his cruelty. When he was finished with her, she looked at his sleeping form.

How could such a pleasing face mask the evilest of hearts? *Der Rab.* Harbinger of death. The Ice Queen was no match, after all. Vivian was finished pretending she had a chance of survival in their contest of wills. She would get Rachel and her mother away tonight. Then she would end this farce between them.

She went to her own room down the hall. Her eyes caught on a thin strip of moonlight splashing over the remains the crow had left on the window's ledge. Bile rose in her throat, but she set it aside and went to the telephone. She dialed the number two nights earlier than planned and said into the telephone, "We go tonight."

There was no conversation, no questions, just two words, *"Très bien."*

It would take at least an hour for the *passeur* to arrive at the designated meeting place. Plenty of time to get the Bermans to the rendezvous point. Vivian would take them there herself. When they were safely gone, she would return to the house and deal with von Bauer.

One of them would not meet the morning alive, that much she vowed. *Der Rab* would pay the cost for all the men who'd hurt Vivian. But first, Rachel and her mother. Vivian grabbed her purse, dug down to the false bottom, reached underneath, and…

No!

It couldn't be. It wasn't possible. She'd been so careful.

Overturning the bag, she dumped out the contents on her bed and, heart stuck in her throat, rummaged through the scattered items. Everything was in order, except. The identity cards were gone. And the tube of red lipstick. That, too, was missing.

He knows.

How? How had he found her out? Or had he known about her clandestine work all along? No, he'd been enamored with her, driven to possess her. Not even *der Rab* could fake that level of obsession. So then, how?

She searched the purse again.

The hidden compartment was still empty. The identity papers were gone. She struggled to breathe through her panic and tried to remember when she'd last checked the hidden compartment. This evening, before the party. He must have slipped away during the after-dinner drinks. At least he didn't know Rachel and her mother were in the house.

They were safe.

It was Vivian who was in trouble.

There was a sudden explosion of fear inside her, pumping fast and hard through her veins, giving her the strength to dress in the clothing she'd picked out months ago in anticipation of this confrontation. Plain brown slacks, stark white blouse, sensible shoes, face free of makeup. The true Vivian would meet her fate tonight, free of any mask.

Bracing herself, she went in search of the predator who'd taken everything from her.

She would slap the swine awake.

He wasn't in his bed. She checked his study next. Not there, either. She moved to the foyer and shut her eyes, thinking, listening. Camille's room? No. No! She headed for the hallway, her feet at a run, but then she heard a faint sound, ice clinking against crystal. Relief had her stumbling to a halt. She quickly righted herself and, balance restored, pushed through the door leading into the formal dining room.

He sat in his usual spot at the head of the table, an open bottle of French cognac beside him, a half-empty glass in his hand. In the dim moonlight, he was more shadow than man. She drew closer and saw the darkness of his gaze, the clothing he wore. Black pants, black shirt and, she knew without looking down, black jackboots. Everything about him radiated danger. She should put as much distance between them as possible.

But no.

There was a burning rage inside her now, something volatile and focused on this one man, who, by default, represented all the others in her past. All but Rupert. Her father, her first boyfriend, a lecherous doctor in the Italian hospital. All of them had used her, hurt her, beaten her. Von Bauer was their equal in every way.

Oh, yes, Vivian thought, this noxious, twisted thing between them ended tonight.

"Darling," she said, placing a soft note in her voice that hinted at seduction. "What are you doing up so late?"

"I could ask the same of you."

They both sounded so reasonable. The expression that crossed his face—a twist of rage—that was not so reasonable. Nor was the pounding of her heart against her ribs. For a moment, she thought he would jump to his feet and pounce on her. That was the level of unchecked violence she saw in his eyes.

He remained perfectly still, though, his hand perversely steady as he poured more of the amber liquid. He lifted the now full glass and took a deep swallow. "You think me a fool."

"No. I think you're a monster."

Something feral came from his mouth, a terrible slur against her womanhood. Then, with a flick of his wrist, the crystal tumbler went flying by her head, missing her ear by inches.

The sound of glass shattering against the wall caused her to jump.

She tried to remember her husband. Rupert. Sweet, calming, good-hearted Rupert. He'd shown her how to connect to the goodness inside her.

This man sitting before her, he brought out only the dark and ugly in her, a woman capable of hate and worse. He rose, and a hollow of dread opened in her mind. He moved closer, his eyes locked on her face, and she felt the heat of his anger as he raised his hand.

Not to hit her, but to show her what he held in his fist. The identity cards.

"What do you plan to do with these, Vivian?" His voice was a challenge, a provocation. "The workmanship is quite good."

"I don't know what you mean."

"Give me the name of your forger."

"I know of no such person."

"A name, Vivian."

She backed away, even as he stepped closer, until she came up against the door and felt it give under her weight.

"He's a true master at his craft." He continued advancing on her. His breathing was heavy now, his eyes shining with contempt and too much alcohol in his system.

Her whole body shook, but she wouldn't run from this confrontation. She was through tamping down her emotions, swallowing then back. *Think, Vivian. Distract him from Rachel and her mother.* "I've done nothing wrong."

"You hid official documents in a secret compartment in your purse. Documents that do not belong to you. This is the action of a woman with much to hide."

"I can explain."

"I've been good to you," he growled, and in his eyes she saw something else besides evil, a sort of hurt she hadn't expected, as if she'd wounded him with her duplicity. "I made you my mistress. I gave you jewelry. I threw parties in your honor and moved you into my house."

She laughed at that. The rage boiling inside her had reached a new level, and this man, like all the others before him, thought he held all the power. "You are *nothing*," she said, her voice low and feral. "I despise the very sight of you."

The words felt like fire in her throat, but von Bauer didn't appear to hear her. Or maybe he simply didn't care what she thought of him. "I have given you every luxury a woman could want, and this is how you repay me." He threw the leather booklets at her. "With forged documents for foul Jews. You are a common liar, a thief, and a leech." His hand went to her throat, the fingers curling ruthlessly into her flesh. "What else are you hiding from me?"

He shifted his weight, and she made her move, wheeling backward through the door. Too fast, too fast. She crashed to the floor. Struggled to her feet. A kind of strangled howl followed her, more like a roar, and he was on her, a hand closing over her shoulder, moving down to her biceps, fingers digging hard. She tried to wrench herself free.

He was too strong.

All she could do was cry out as he pulled her toward the sweeping stairwell, up, up, up, to the second floor, down the hallway, into her bedroom. Still holding her arm, he began tossing the room, upending drawers, throwing open cabinets. "You will find nothing here."

Ten minutes later he stopped. Pivoted. Looked around the room. Then he went to the telephone and picked up the receiver.

"Who…who are you calling?"

The smile he gave her distorted his face into a gruesome mask of contempt. "The director of the Gestapo in Drancy."

Vivian blanched. She could not let him make that call. She grabbed the cord and yanked, hard. The receiver flew out of his hand and landed on the carpet with a thud. She scrambled to grab it and, seizing the entire piece of equipment, crawled to the window on her hands and knees, dragging the phone with her.

Out it went, breaking into a million pieces on the ground below.

He roared his fury. "There are other telephones in the house."

He dragged her out into the hallway.

Think, Vivian. Think.

She'd made so many terrible choices, some for the right reasons, but not all. She'd endured humiliation and pain. But she'd never been forced to fight for her life, not like this. She'd thought herself good and moral, deep down, where it counted. She'd thought herself ready for death. She'd been wrong. About all of it. She had one final card to play, presented as a bluff. Could it work?

Could she fool him into thinking she was simply tossing out words and making things up to save her own neck?

The risk to the others in the house was great. But so was her will to survive. Her mind grappled with right and wrong, good and evil, even as he dragged her down the stairs to the first floor. They entered his study, and when he reached for the telephone there on his desk, she knew she had one chance. One final chance to save herself. Vivian was not strong, after all. She was weak. And selfish. *Forgive me.*

The words were in her head, whispered like a prayer, but spoken to whom? Rachel? Camille? Herself? *Forgive me forgive me forgive me forgive me.* She knew what she was going to do, even as she knew it was completely, utterly wrong.

One chance. Throw out a bluff that wasn't really a bluff.

Von Bauer had the phone in his hand now, and she made her threat. "You turn me over to the Gestapo," she warned, "and, so help me, I'll…I'll…" *Say it, Vivian. Say it.* "I'll tell them about the Jews living in your house. You will attempt to deny knowledge of this, but I will be very good with my arguments. I will manufacture proof. You will be tried for treason, *der Rab*, and I will happily watch you hang by your neck until you are dead."

He froze. The phone dangling between his fingers. "What is this lie you tell? It is—"

"No lie." She nearly laughed at his shocked expression. Apparently, she wasn't the only one in this house concerned with their own survival. "They are right under your nose and have been for months."

She immediately realized what she'd done. She'd betrayed three innocent people to save herself. Her father had been right. She was a worthless human being. But maybe she could fix this mess. "You think yourself superior, clever? You are nothing but a man who has been living with Jews in his house. The Gestapo will come see for themselves. And when they find evidence that I will plant, they will never believe you didn't know."

"You will not tell this lie."

His panic was real, but so was hers.

What have I done? "Yes, I will tell this lie. This great, bold lie. And I will tell it to the Gestapo, over and over, until they are forced to believe me. They will question you, *der Rab*. They will wonder. You will carry this stain. Then your career will be over."

He searched her face. "Why do you tell this lie? Who are you protecting?"

"I protect only myself."

"That is your greatest lie yet." Releasing her, he changed direction, a new determination in his strides. "Let's ask the house-keeper about the lies you tell. Or perhaps—" he gave Vivian a thoughtful look "—she is the Jew you protect."

"Leave Camille alone. She's done nothing wrong."

"We shall see, won't we?"

He marched toward the back of the house, with Vivian hard on his heels, clawing at his arm, begging him to stop and listen.

"The time for listening is over."

Chapter Thirty-Nine

Camille

16 September 1942.
Von Bauer's Home. Seine-Saint-Denis Department.
Paris, France.

Caught in that uncertain moment between sleep and wakefulness, Camille felt the air shift. Something was coming toward her. Not a nightmare. It felt too real. She ripped herself awake and sat up abruptly, blinking into the inky darkness.

She heard it then. The shouting. The angry tones. She caught only a few words, a mix of German and French—*lie, housekeeper, Jews.* Her breath wheezed out, jamming in her throat on the way back in. She shoved out another hiss of air. With the same brute force, she came to her feet, just as she heard wood cracking, hinges releasing. She'd barely understood what was happening when her door flew open, giving her no time to find her robe and slippers.

Von Bauer appeared on the threshold, cloaked in shadows. His hand reached out, switching on the light, blinding her momentarily. Her arm was suddenly gripped in one of his hands, a large clump of her hair in the other. "Are there Jews in this house? Tell me, Camille. Are there?"

She glanced over at Vivian and knew, in that instant, that her friend had revealed their secret. The sting of betrayal burned in her throat as she kept her eyes locked on her friend's watery eyes. Vivian looked sickly and shaken. And guilty. So guilty. Camille didn't want to see that dull, stricken expression. She didn't want to know why the river of tears tracked down her cheeks. Because that would mean she'd trusted the wrong person.

Vivian lifted her hands in a helpless gesture, pressed them to her face, while von Bauer kept shouting at Camille, demanding to know. "Are you harboring Jews in my house?"

Camille dragged in another breath. "There are no Jews in this house."

"You lie."

It wasn't a lie. The bunker was technically under the gazebo. "There are no Jews in this house."

He yanked her hair harder. Her scalp was on fire now, the air trapped in her lungs. She would have screamed out in pain, had she the breath. Von Bauer's hand came up and connected with her face. Pain exploded in her cheek, even as her eyes connected with Vivian's again. She willed her friend to explain herself, to step into the fray, to do something. Anything. There was only emptiness in the eyes staring back.

Camille felt her fury rising. *How could you?* she wanted to shout. But to do so would be to confirm whatever tale Vivian had told von Bauer. She set her fury aside. Her mind needed to be clear to fight the beast yanking her across the room, out the door, and into the hallway. She couldn't think, couldn't breathe. The pain. It stole all reason. Any minute, her hair would rip right off her head. Then she would be free. Free to protect Rachel and her mother.

How? How could she keep them safe?

By remaining silent. By refusing to confirm von Bauer's suspicions.

Vivian was saying something that Camille couldn't make out over the roaring in her head. Outside the dining room, von Bauer released her. The sudden move sent her stumbling into the wall, falling awkwardly to the ground. Vivian moved in close and pushed her hair off her forehead.

With her expression, that abyss of guilt in her eyes, the unspoken apology, Camille nearly reached to her in return. But then von Bauer was retrieving something on the floor, two somethings, waving them near her face. "What do you know about these?"

Clarity of mind eluded her, along with her vision. She couldn't focus, not on his words or the small leather books he held in his hands. The identity cards. She closed her eyes, just for a minute.

A mistake.

Von Bauer was grabbing her again, the identity cards falling to the ground. Rachel's and her mother's freedom was right there, at her feet, and Camille couldn't reach for them because he was dragging her out into the hallway, up the stairs, to the second floor and its host of shut doors.

From room to room, he shoved her inside, Vivian following in their wake, saying nothing—yet another betrayal—as he barked the same question, over and over: "Is this where you keep the Jews?"

Her answer was always the same. "There are no Jews in this house."

Camille's head started to clear, the situation coming into focus. Vivian had betrayed Rachel and her mother, but why? To save herself. Nothing else made sense. Except, if Vivian wanted to save herself, why was she still here, in this house, clawing at von Bauer's arm and finally, *finally*, using her voice to enter the fray? "Leave the girl alone!"

Why wasn't she running to safety, if she truly cared only for herself? Camille wanted to reach to her, to beg her to explain why she'd betrayed them, but her answer would not solve the problem of von Bauer's wrath.

He was bearing down on her again. "Where are the Jews?"

Another glance in Vivian's direction told Camille her friend had revealed some things, but not everything. "There are no Jews in this house."

"Did you help them escape?"

Truth. She would give him truth. "No." *Not yet.* The words echoed in her mind. The plan to get Rachel and her mother away had taken too long to execute, and now they would be discovered.

Von Bauer's hands came up again. This time, he went for her throat. She writhed under his hold, kicked at his shins. "I give you a position of trust," he ground through his bared teeth. "And you defile my goodwill by bringing Jews into my home."

This man, his eyes black with fury, he was going to kill her. Camille didn't want to die. She tore at his hands, swiped at his face, felt her limbs go limp from the effort to keep awake. To stay alive. A kaleidoscope of images played in her head. Her sister. Sweet, tortured Jacqueline. How would she survive without the money Camille sent? She'd failed again.

But maybe not.

The doctor. Pierre Garnier. He would care for Jacqueline in her stead. Images of Camille's mother came next, her sisters. They were there in her mind, so clear, but then blurry. Slipping away from her, along with her will to fight. She kept her eyes closed, tight and secure in the darkness swelling over her.

"Let her go!"

Camille opened her eyes. Vivian was in her line of vision, something large in her hands. A porcelain vase. Camille heard a crack, then she was falling to the floor, and von Bauer was falling with her. He spoke in slurred, unintelligible German. She couldn't make out what he was sputtering, only the fury behind the words.

Her gaze scanned the room, looking for a way out, an escape. There. The door. Still open. She didn't remember climbing to her feet, or looking at the prone man, fighting to keep his eyes open. He failed. Vivian joined Camille on the floor. Breathing hard, she pressed her fingertips to a spot on his neck.

"Is he dead?" Camille whispered, crab walking away.

Vivian placed her ear close to his nose. "He's alive."

Camille didn't know what to do with the information. Around her, the room started to go gray, her vision grayer, as if she was looking through a wall of smoke. Vivian scrambled to her feet. A moment of staring down at von Bauer, and then she was reaching for Camille.

Instinct had her shrinking back. Vivian's hand fell to her side. Camille tried to remember the woman she'd trusted so completely, who'd listened to her story about her father, and sympathized with her sister's plight, who'd set her up in this job at three times the wages she'd been making at the hotel.

That woman was a deception. The Vivian Miller standing before her was a stranger, an opportunist only out for herself. No different from the man lying unconscious on the floor.

"We must get them out tonight," the stranger said. "Now, Camille, before he wakes up."

She was right. But it was impossible. "Nothing is in place."

"It will be. I made the call an hour ago."

Camille felt a flash of anger. The possibility of an early escape had always been there. It had taken Vivian's betrayal to expedite the process. Camille glanced down at von Bauer, so still and silent on the floor, pieces of the shattered vase in his hair.

Maybe he *was* dead.

The edges of the room felt fuzzy and gray again, closing in around her.

Vivian reached to her, an apology in her eyes, and Camille wanted to believe this was a woman she could trust. It hurt to admit that there was still a connection between them, flawed and based on lies as much as truth, but so very real. She couldn't find it in her to hate this woman. She couldn't find it in her to forgive Vivian, either. "How could you—"

"We have much to do to see them safely away."

"Yes." The word came out reedy and weak. "Yes, we must hurry." There were two precious lives depending on Camille setting aside her own sense of disillusionment and calling on every bit of her internal strength.

"Retrieve the identity cards, then change your clothes and meet me in the basement."

"What about him?"

They both looked at von Bauer's prone form. "Leave him to me."

There was something terrible in Vivian's voice, a finality that Camille didn't want to understand, for fear of learning one more ugly thing about a woman she'd considered a friend and mentor. Rachel and her mother were her only concern now.

Vivian had failed them. Camille would not.

Chapter Forty

Rachel

17 September 1942.
Von Bauer's Home. Seine-Saint-Denis Department.
Paris, France.

Rachel had gotten her days and nights confused. With no windows, it was always dark in her world. Darkness layered on top of darkness, cut only by the pitiful candlelight in the bunker. Nothing to do but write in her journal. She looked down at the words she'd written only moments before, their meaning lost to her now. Compelled, she drew her fingernail over the loops and swirls. Her resentment seemed to be fading, perhaps because she knew what lay ahead two days from now. Or was it only one now?

What time was it? Her watch said twelve o'clock. Was that twelve noon or twelve midnight? She couldn't remember, and that just made her more frustrated.

With a snap, she shut the journal and stowed it away in her satchel, then checked the contents of the bag she would carry on her journey to freedom. It would be a grueling journey, both physically and mentally. A dangerous one, too, with the threat of capture and betrayal, possibly even an ambush.

Frowning at the direction of her thoughts, she rustled through the clothing. Counted the three shirts, touched the extra sweater, the two pairs of thick socks. Her journal, her favorite two novels by Dumas. Finally, her hand found the garden shears she'd pilfered the day Vivian Miller had found them out.

All was in order. All was ready. Except for the identity cards Vivian promised she would secure today—yesterday? Rachel really disliked losing her sense of time.

She disliked everything about her enforced captivity. *Better than a concentration camp.*

Her mother lay asleep on the cot farthest from the tunnel, snoring softly. She was fully dressed, like Rachel, ready to leave in an instant. Her face looked peaceful, the color of pale pink roses back in her cheeks. Ilka's health was almost fully restored because of the food Camille fed them and the work that pulled them out of the bunker for a few hours every day. Despite her obvious recovery, would the older woman be able to make the demanding journey to freedom? Camille had been very clear that escape would require fortitude, resolve, and physical strength.

If her mother faltered, Rachel would shore her up. If she fell behind, Rachel would pull her along. On her own back, if that's what it took to guide the beloved woman to safety.

A sound from the other side of the tunnel had her surging quickly to her feet. She checked her watch again, read the time—again—but couldn't make her mind accept that it was probably a quarter past midnight. Even if it was a quarter past noon, it was too soon for their escape. Something must have gone wrong.

Rachel hurried to the edge of the bunker. From her vantage point, the tunnel was a molten abyss of nothingness, the gaping mouth of a monster, open and ready to swallow her whole.

The familiar scrape of metal on cement sounded from the other end. The noise moved through her like a jolting stream of electricity. More noise from the basement, footfalls, something dropping, the squeak of female voices. Camille and Vivian. She couldn't make out what they were saying. Slowly, she crept through the tunnel. Camille was there and, yes, Vivian. But they weren't talking. They were shouting, arguing.

Rachel stood in the shadows in a kind of mute, frozen state. Who would greet her from the other side? Camille, always Camille. But also, tonight, Vivian. There had never been talk of the American involving herself in the actual escape.

The door slid open, letting in a thread of light, enough to reveal her friend standing in the basement, and Vivian behind her. Both looked shattered. Both were trembling.

"It's time," Camille said, pressing two small leather books into Rachel's hand, while Vivian added, "Go get your mother, Rachel. And be quick about it."

Panic iced Rachel's limbs, holding her in a perpetual pause. "Why now?"

"No time to explain," the two said simultaneously.

She felt as much as heard their impatience. Something had gone wrong. She made a split-second decision and rushed back into the shadows. She would trust Camille. She must. Vivian, too, though instinct told her the American was the cause for moving up their departure.

"Mama," she shouted in the darkness, her eyes flicking over the corridor.

Her feet took her the final steps, and she was back in the concrete tomb. Despite the months of preparation, Rachel was caught in a moment of desperate confusion. What was she supposed to do next? She'd forgotten. Her gaze circled the bunker, then landed on her mother, already awake, fully dressed, her travel bag slung crossways over her shoulder. "Come. We go now, *córka.*"

Rachel blinked at the longest string of words out of her mother's mouth in weeks. The exact motivation she needed to gather her own bag. She took her mother's hand, but halfway between the bunker and basement, more noises sounded from upstairs, heavy footfalls. The kind that belonged to a man. There was the sound of something dropping. A hard thud. Another voice, female, shouting in accented French, then German. Something clanging.

More clanging. Another thud, followed by a brief cry of pain. Footfalls. Shouts. Then, furious muttering close by, too close to be coming from anywhere but the basement itself.

The sound of metal scraping against metal came next, a crash, the rush of air, followed by a voice, a man's voice, slightly slurred, as if he were drunk. Or—

"Come out, you filthy Jews. I know you're in there."

Camille's voice came next, muted, but clear, and surprisingly steady. "I told you, *Herr Sturmbannführer*, there are no Jews in this house."

The use of his formal rank was the signal for Rachel and her mother to stay hidden in the bunker. But what if the Nazi entered the tunnel and continued further still? Every plan they'd discussed had been contingent on Camille and Vivian outmaneuvering von Bauer.

But he was here, mere feet away, and Rachel needed to know just how bad things had become.

Signaling her mother to wait where she was, she took a few steps and peered into the shadows. Her heart gave a little pop. The Nazi held Camille against him, a pistol pressed to her temple. His eyes were glassy and muddied with rage. Where was Vivian? Rachel scanned the basement, caught sight of a lump on the floor beside an overturned rack. The shouting, the clanging, the crash, the thud, they all made a sick sort of sense now.

"Come out," von Bauer shouted. "Or I'll shoot your friend."

Rachel slipped back to where her mother waited just inside the bunker. She had an impossible decision to make, with no good outcome. She couldn't leave Camille imprisoned in a Nazi's viselike embrace, with the mouth of a gun pressed to her head. But Rachel couldn't put her mother in danger, either. The situation was hopeless. And one thing was certain:

the Nazi would eventually come through the tunnel, either now, or after he killed Camille.

"Hide," she whispered in her mother's ear. "Under your cot."

"You will hide with me." Her mother began pulling her back toward the bunker.

The grip on her arm was surprisingly strong. But Rachel's resolve was stronger. She was done hiding in this hole like a captured animal. She would fight her way out. Or die trying. The garden shears. She opened her bag and began searching. Her efforts were cut short by the Nazi's final threat.

"This is your last chance. Come out now, or your friend won't live to see the dawn." The click of the weapon's hammer pulling back punctuated his words. "You have five seconds."

He started counting. One, two, three...

Rachel stepped into the light, into her greatest fears realized, unarmed, shoulders squared, chin lifted. "Here I am."

Chapter Forty-One

Vivian

17 September 1942.
Von Bauer's Home. Seine-Saint-Denis Department.
Paris, France.

Pain seeped through every breath, crushing Vivian's ribs. Heat crept over her. Her eyes refused to open. A voice in her head tempted her to let go. Give up the fight. Her betrayal left a black, gaping hole, swallowing light and time and the final piece of her soul that had once been good. This wasn't how her life was supposed to end. She wasn't supposed to die before achieving redemption.

The need to do the right thing was a storm in her belly, drawing her toward light and goodness, away from the evil she'd done to the people who'd trusted her with their lives. All three women were in this house because of her. All three were in jeopardy because of her.

Only in sacrifice could she make amends.

That was her prayer now, her reason to push past the self-pity that wanted to overwhelm her sense of right and wrong. *It's not over.* Not while she still had breath in her lungs. *You can still make things right.*

She flinched at the wail of pain screaming through her head. No, not *her* pain. The cry came from another. Camille. Vivian cracked open an eye, slammed it shut, pulling away from the yellow rectangle of light. She tried again, surveying the scene. Von Bauer was hurting the young woman.

He would not win this fight.

Gritting her teeth, she rolled to her stomach, climbed to her hands and knees, set one foot on the cement, then the other. A tear dripped onto her hand. Not just one, but many. They seemed to spring from her eyes on their own, a sign of her rage. Vivian only ever cried when she was very, very angry.

Her head pounded. Her insides shook. On the outside, she was calm as death itself. She stood, faced the tunnel, and what was this? Rachel was there, looking glorious, an avenging angel ready to face a legion of demons.

Von Bauer's lips lifted in an ugly grin. His eyes were as black as a raven's wing as he lowered the gun from Camille's head and pointed the weapon at Rachel.

No!

"Der Rab!" Vivian's voice bounced off the wall, harsh and bitter, and the pistol veered in her direction. The tip angling straight for her heart. "You're a coward," she ground out. "Like all bullies."

His eyes went wild with indignation, shock. "You're supposed to be dead. I hit you hard enough to kill you."

"And yet I stand before you now."

He pounced. No hesitation. No warning. She was ready. With a hard swipe of her hand, she knocked the pistol to the ground. A bullet discharged on its way down, hitting the cement feet away from Vivian. Muttering curses in German, sprinkled with French, he reached for the weapon. At the same moment, she kicked him in the groin. The blow drove him to his knees.

She slid a frantic glance toward Camille. *Go,* she shouted in her head. *Now.* "Run!"

Vivian didn't wait to see if the girl obeyed. Her eyes were locked on von Bauer. His face was twisted in pain. Breathing hard, he scrambled to his feet. She let him. They would finish this eye to eye.

"You made a gross error in judgment, *der Rab*." Her voice was calm, baiting, the Ice Queen dripping in every syllable. "You threw parties for your Nazi friends and crowed about your work. You told tales about the thousands of Jews you sent to their death. All while you had two of them living right under your feet."

He grabbed her, yanked her close, so close their noses pressed together. Her stomach churned in disgust. But her fear was gone, vanished with her dignity. She didn't see a man leaning into her. She saw only the hard edges of a face gone mad with rage, his purpose clear. He would kill her. He would use his fists, or the pistol at his feet, or whatever weapon he could find.

He started with his fists. The blows came hard, painful, unrelenting.

Vivian fought back, but she was no match for his superior strength.

Even in her strange and suspended state, she felt the air leave her lungs, felt the breathy half sob crawl up her throat. Out of the corner of her eye, she saw Camille and the other two finish their climb up the stairs. Only once they disappeared did Vivian breathe a sigh of relief.

Her momentary distraction foiled her. Von Bauer struck a hard blow to her chin. Her eyes rolled back in her head. Then: the sharp bite of the cement floor met her broken body. She kicked out and brought von Bauer down with her. The crack of his skull filled the air.

Relief refused to come. Monsters like him weren't so easily defeated.

Vivian could smell the scent of whiskey and cigars wafting off him. Then he came to life, crawling over her, cloaking her with his hate. His hands snaked around her neck.

"You will take your last breath with me watching your life drip away."

"You will join me in death," she vowed. Her voice came out muffled, barely clear enough to hear, but von Bauer's eyes narrowed. He'd understood her. Blood ran alongside his face, and the skin around his mouth had gone gray. The color of death.

She clawed at his wrists, moved her hands to his face, felt the satisfaction of connection, then the moment of freedom when his grip loosened and slipped away completely. His hand snaked out, reaching for the gun. Her hand was moving, too, of its own volition. Her fingers closed over the barrel. So did his.

They grappled for control. A shot rang out. A screech of agony lodged in her own belly. Pain lanced through her, slithered up to her chest, merging with her ragged breaths until she couldn't tell where the agony began and where it ended. Her lungs constricted. The air was leaving her body. No air. No air. She couldn't breathe. The pressure was too great.

She could feel her will to fight draining from her. Not yet. Not. Yet.

Von Bauer's grip slipped, just enough, and Vivian had the pistol. She squeezed off another bullet. A third one.

He collapsed on top of her. She shoved him, hard, and he rolled onto his back. Eyes wide and unblinking, face blank.

It was done.

Blackness edged her vision. She shut her eyes, expecting to find Rupert waiting for her there. She saw nothing but the poisonous condition of her soul. Vivian dissolved to the ground and prayed she'd done enough to gain absolution.

Chapter Forty-Two

Rachel

17 September 1942.
Von Bauer's Home. Seine-Saint-Denis Department.
Paris, France.

Rachel would never know where her mother found the strength to control her fear. One minute, she was staring—gaping, actually—at the battle between Vivian and the Nazi. The next, her hand was on Rachel's arm, pulling her in a stumbling run across the basement floor, up the stairs, through the back door, and out into the moonlit night. Camille's footsteps pounded behind them. Her friend's voice was a nonsensical buzz in Rachel's ears. She heard words, but they were disjointed and tinny. Camille seemed to be giving them instructions, something about the *passeur* waiting for them a mile down the road, just on the edge of the forest.

Rachel already knew where they were supposed to go. Camille had given her the route in very specific terms. She'd shown Rachel a map and had drilled her relentlessly until she could see every twist and turn in her mind. She even knew the street names, though without the benefit of light, that information was useless.

Now she recalled every detail. Right at the first corner, go two blocks, another right, continue four more blocks, a left. Another left, right, right, left. Her bag slammed into her hip, and her breath came in snatches. Rachel focused only on the route.

Another left.

The residual heat of the day turned the air into a wet, sticky stew smelling of something quite foul. How close were they to the detention center? Too close, she decided, and was happy for the lack of light.

A hard right.

Rachel kept her mother close, nearly fused to her right hip. Camille moved in on the other side, sufficiently flanking the older woman. They shared a look over her head, and in Camille's eyes, Rachel saw the apology Vivian hadn't given. She also recognized a deep sense of kinship. Rachel would miss this woman, her friend, she would miss her very much.

But this wasn't the time for sentiment. She should be thinking only of the next step in the difficult journey ahead. They took the final corner, and Rachel looked to Camille again. A hundred unspoken thoughts passed between them. Rachel didn't want tears. They came anyway.

Now it was her turn to feel sorrow and regret. Not only for this friend she would never see again, but also, irrationally, for Vivian Miller. In the final moment, when it mattered most, she'd sacrificed herself. That's what Rachel would remember. No matter how many times she relived the moment when von Bauer had pointed the gun at her, she would remember the American distracting him before he could shoot her.

She's also the reason you're on the run. With identity cards and American passports she'd provided.

Betrayal and sacrifice. Opposite sides of a very complicated coin.

"We're here," Camille said, her voice barely a whisper on

the light breeze. They entered through the dense tree line. The night was thicker in the woods, the air stagnant, as if holding its breath. The unseasonable heat had Rachel's hair sticking to her forehead. Frustrated, she shoved it aside, and sensed her mother watching her.

"We will survive this," she said. "For the ones we've lost."

Rachel didn't think twice. She grabbed her mother in a tight, clumsy hug. "Yes. We will survive. For Papa and Srulka."

A dull light flashed in the distance, just a shimmer. Then a girl came into view, wearing men's clothing far too big for her small frame and a floppy hat that covered half her face. She was young, younger even than Rachel, and agonizingly thin. "I am Paulette." She spoke French with the accent of privilege. "I will be your *passeur*, your escort."

There was something tragic about the girl, something that transcended class and rank, and Rachel felt an instant connection.

Camille shifted into the thin beam of light, drawing Paulette's attention. "This is Rachel and her mother, Ilka."

The girl frowned. "I was told to expect only two, a mother and daughter."

"That's right." Camille nodded. "I'm not making the journey."

"Why not?" Rachel reached to her friend, the scene in the basement fresh in her mind. "You can't go back to that house."

"I can't leave Vivian."

"Yes, you can. She is the woman who…" *Betrayed us.* Rachel didn't say the words, but they hung in the air between them. "What if she didn't survive? What if he did? Don't go back, Camille. Please."

"I won't abandon her. I can't. And there is my family to consider. They need me." She held Rachel's stare. "No, I can't leave France."

In that moment, Rachel understood Camille in ways she hadn't before. She felt a moment of shame. For all her doubts concerning this woman. A woman who'd offered her charity and a place to hide. And that slippery, elusive gift of all: hope. "Thank you, *mon ami*. I won't forget what you've done for my mother and me."

"I would do it all again."

"I know."

They reached for each other and held on tight. So tightly that Rachel could feel the thud of Camille's heartbeat. They said not a word. They made no promises to meet again after the war. This was the end for them. Their friendship would not be rekindled once the weapons were laid down. *"Merci,"* she said again.

"De rien."

They pulled apart, and Camille was turning one way, Paulette another. Rachel realized she had one last gift to give her friend. "Camille, wait." She reached inside her bag and pulled out the garden shears. "For protection."

There was nothing left to say. Rachel took her mother's hand, and together, they followed their escort deeper into the woods. To Spain, or to capture. Around the fire, or through it. Either way, they would soon be free.

Chapter Forty-Three

Camille

September 1942.
Von Bauer's Home. Seine-Saint-Denis Department.
Paris, France.

Camille ran all the way back to the house, keeping away from the streetlights. She moved quickly, ignoring the sting in her lungs. The back door stood ajar, just as she'd left it.

Vivian and von Bauer were still inside. Camille feared what she would find in the basement. She knew it would not be pleasant. She lingered a moment, her heartbeat heavy in her ears. A surge of dread shook through her.

She suddenly felt numb all over. She couldn't feel her fingers, or her toes. She searched for some hint of deeper feeling, but nothing came. Maybe a twinge of something, a faint wish for things to have gone differently tonight. That the plan she and Vivian had developed so carefully would have gone off without a hitch.

The garden shears weighed heavy in her grip. A deadly weapon, if used properly. Camille entered the house. The mudroom was absent of sound. Still, she paused and listened for some sign of what she would find in the basement. The door stood open. There was no use for it. She would have to go down. Clutching the shears tight, she pushed forward and took the stairs one at a time. An unpleasant odor met her halfway down, metallic and sharp.

Blood. She'd smelled it before, in another basement. Images flooded her vision, urging her to turn around and play the coward. Was this moment real, or another nightmare?

A muffled groan brought the answer, the sound exceptionally female.

This was no dream. And Vivian needed Camille's courage, as her sister had once needed it. Down, she went down the steps, into cement and dust and…death. Those were the scents she smelled, blood and death. Her grip slipped, and the garden shears clattered to the floor.

Two bodies lay on the basement floor, side by side, blood pooling around them.

Everything went dark in Camille's mind. The room took a slow, sickly spin, and what little light was cast from the single bulb faded to gray. She shook her head, viciously, forcing her vision to clear. She moved in closer. Von Bauer lay on his back, his eyes blank, a hole in his head, one more in his chest.

Camille took a wide circle, stopping next to the other body, careful to avoid the thick red liquid spreading across the cement. A dark stain of blood spooled at Vivian's waist. *Don't be dead. Don't be dead.*

"Vivian." *Don't be dead.* Camille reached down and shook her friend's shoulder. "Wake up. Please, please wake up."

No response. Nothing.

"Vivian," she said again, her voice softer, calmer.

A small movement, slight and nearly nonexistent, then the lifting of a perfectly manicured hand, the nails lacquered the same color as the liquid spreading across the cement.

"Camille?" The sound of her name seemed to come from a great distance. "Are they safely away?"

"They are safely away."

Vivian tried to lift her head. A centimeter, perhaps less, that was all she could manage before collapsing back against the cement with a thud. "Von Bauer?"

Camille didn't need to look twice. "Dead."

"Good," she whispered.

Camille knelt beside her friend, and took her cold hand, so cold, too cold. "Don't move," she said. "I'm going to get you help."

But...where? Who? Who could she trust?

"Too late," Vivian wheezed.

The need to argue came fast, but Vivian's eyes opened again, and something passed between them, a silent knowledge that her injuries were too great to survive, and even if she overcame the bullet wound in her stomach, she would not defeat a Nazi's inquisition. Vivian would be executed for shooting an SS officer.

"Run." The word gurgled from Vivian's throat. "Run, Camille."

"I can't leave you." *I can't let you die alone.* Without thinking about the blood, Camille cradled Vivian's head in her lap. "I'll stay with you until—" she shut her eyes "—the end."

Vivian shifted. The movement instigated a coughing fit so hard Camille feared it would bring the end sooner. "Shh," Camille soothed. "Don't talk."

"I'm sorry. I...I...thought to blackmail him. I—" she pulled in a shaky breath "—I miscalculated. He...von Bauer. Bad man. Evil in his heart." She reached up, touched Camille's cheek where he'd hit her. "I thought it was the only way to save us all."

To save yourself. No matter how Camille turned Vivian's actions in her mind, she always came back to that. The woman had acted out of self-preservation first, then honor.

"Not for me. I did it for you. For Rachel and her mother."

Her French had an American accent now, the words barely distinguishable. "One day, you'll see that."

There had been other ways to protect their secret.

"Miscalculated," she wheezed. "Forgive me."

Camille wanted to offer Vivian redemption. She couldn't say the words.

"Leave me, Camille. It's too late. Save yourself. They can't find you here."

They. The Gestapo.

Run. The word was in her head now. Urgent. Echoing. Vivian gripped her arm with a show of strength that seemed to surprise them both. "Run!"

Camille watched the color drain from Vivian's face and her body go limp. And then, she was gone. *Run.* She took only enough time to change into clean clothes and sort out her route. She knew where she would go, had always known from their first meeting that he would be a haven. For her sister, and for her.

There was only one thing left to do. She ran.

Unable to stop herself, she looked over her shoulder, not once, but again and again. The house loomed large at first, sinister, the windows like cavernous eyes full of judgment and condemnation. She hadn't abandoned Vivian, but the relief of leaving her behind was similar to how Camille had felt when she'd first arrived in Paris.

Much had changed since then. Her sister was better, her own guilt far less heavy to bear. She glanced at the house a few more times. The structure eventually receded in the distance, smaller, less menacing. When it was but a dot on the horizon, Camille faced forward, knowing she wouldn't look back ever again. She felt a hard tug of sorrow for the woman lying in the basement beside her lover. A woman who'd betrayed Camille and Rachel, and then had atoned for her duplicity in a single act of sacrifice.

Camille would forgive Vivian. One day.

The sky turned purple overhead, and the first signs of dawn colored the horizon. Camille moved deeper into the woods, staying undercover while the sun shone. When night fell, she ventured closer to the road. By day two, the rain blew in from the west, soaking her to the bone. With the rain came mud and treacherous divots in the slippery dirt. Camille had been wise to don her boots, but she'd dressed for the heat. Not the cold, wet rain.

I did it for you, Vivian had said. *One day, you'll see that.*

Now there were divots in her heart as well as underfoot. But her eyes remained dry. The sky cried for her, for the rest of the afternoon and deep into the night.

For days, Camille wove in and out of the wooded areas that ran parallel to the road. Countless hours of fearing that every unknown noise meant she'd been discovered by a German patrol. She slept, but rarely. Sometime in the middle of the third, fourth, possibly fifth night, she arrived at the address in Rennes that Pierre had made her memorize. She'd studied a map of the city months ago and, as she'd insisted with Rachel and her mother, had gone over every twist and turn until she knew the route by heart.

Light shone from within the little house, making it look cozy and warm. Tired and thirsty, her energy spent, Camille stumbled up the walk, and somehow found the strength to scratch at the door.

Twenty seconds, that's all it took, and Pierre Garnier opened the door. He stood with the light at his back, the soft glow caressing his dark hair. He was fully dressed, as if he'd been waiting for her arrival for some time. His smile was as inviting as his home. "Camille." He peered around her. "You are alone?"

She managed a nod, more a lifting and lowering of her chin. She blinked away the need to cry and then, suddenly, she was inside the house, the door shut behind her. A heartbeat later, his arms wrapped her in a long, desperate hug. She clung, shamelessly, but so did he, and as he held her just as fiercely as she held him, every terrible fear she'd harbored during her journey washed away.

Eventually, Pierre shifted. He held her a little bit away, his gaze running over her face, then from her head to her toes. "You're hurt. Come, let me check your injuries."

The request was from a man of medicine, but his voice was filled with a personal intimacy that superseded his profession. "It's not my blood."

He visibly relaxed. Then his spine stiffened again. "The SS officer?"

"*Dead*. He… Oh, Pierre, he's dead. I didn't kill him," she rushed on to say. "But they…the Gestapo, they will think I had a hand in his death. So, I ran. I came here."

"On foot?"

"It took me five days, I think. Maybe it was a week. I have lost track of time, and I—"

He gave her no chance to say more. She was back in his arms, surrounded by his heat, relishing his strength. The tears fell at last, big, bone-rattling sobs.

"It's okay," he assured her, rubbing her back in slow, easy strokes. "You're safe, Camille. You're safe now." He repeated the words until they were as real to Camille as the air in her lungs.

Her sobbing eventually turned to hiccups, and slowly, she put space between them. She looked into the eyes that had always drawn her in. Now they promised everything she'd forgotten how to want and things she'd never known could be hers.

"When was the last time you ate?"

The doctor was back, and she found herself smiling. "Three days ago, possibly longer."

"Food first. And then you will rest."

She would remember the next hour as the warmest, safest of her life. Pierre wrapped her in a blanket, started a fire, then served her a cup of hot, watered-down tea. No sugar, no lemon, yet it was the sweetest brew she'd ever tasted. Because he'd made it for her. He served her a piece of bread and some soft cheese, a meal fit for a queen. That's how it went down. How she would remember the taste.

"Thank you for coming to me," he said, sitting across from her, his eyes full of questions she could tell he wanted to ask, but he was too polite to push the conversation on her after her ordeal.

Why was he so kind? She didn't know what to do with all that kindness. "I didn't kill him," she blubbered through another onslaught of tears.

"I believe you." He took her hand, held it nestled between his larger ones. "Can you tell me what happened?"

She did. Every bit of it.

He put his hand to her cheek. She could feel his heartbeat in his palm, like a balm to the bruise von Bauer had inflicted, no doubt an ugly greenish color by now. "I'm sorry for your loss," he said. "But I'm glad you listened to your American friend. She was right. They will think you are to blame and are probably searching for you as we speak."

"I know."

He dropped his hand and moved to sit beside her. "I won't let them find you." He kissed her forehead, her cheek, and ended with the lightest touch to her lips. "Am I scaring you?"

"You're really not." In his slow, soft smile she saw the quiet integrity that had always drawn her to him, so different from the man intent on killing her.

She swallowed away the sudden sensation of hands wrapped around her neck, but it was as if Pierre could read her mind. His fingertips touched the tender spot on her throat. "I will protect you, Camille. No matter how long this war lasts, I will hide you in this house, and keep you safe. You and your sister, you are both safe in my care."

Lost for words in the face of such integrity, more sincere than any wedding vows, Camille couldn't speak. But she could smile. Oh, how she smiled.

He smiled back.

The last of her apprehension wore away. Something new took its place, something wholesome and good. Everything she'd done—all her mistakes, the years of guilt—they were being washed away with each new breath. Camille felt swept clean by this man, her story rewritten. A different, hopeful tale that didn't include tragedy and failure.

They spoke a little longer, but now that her stomach was full, a languid flowering of warmth seeped through her, and she couldn't keep up her end of the conversation.

"That's it. Bed for you." He scooped her up and set her down on a soft mattress, then pulled the covers up to her chin. "Sleep now, *ma charmante fille*." He kissed her forehead. "We'll talk more in the morning."

"I'd like that."

He smiled that beautiful, pure smile of his, and she was flooded with a sense of peace. There would be no nightmares tonight, not with Pierre watching over her, and as she looked deep into his eyes, eyes that held hers with unwavering faithfulness, Camille knew she would spend the rest of her life with this man.

Epilogue

Camille

June 1976.
Site of the Drancy Internment Camp.
Seine-Saint-Denis Department. Paris, France.

Despite her family's insistence she stay in the taxi until they reached their destination, Camille asked the driver to pull over. When she climbed out onto the sidewalk, her husband made to join her. She waved him off. "I want to walk the final blocks alone."

"Camille—"

"Please, Pierre."

He didn't look happy, but as was so often the case in their thirty-three years of marriage, he didn't attempt to push his will onto hers, either. He wasn't always so accommodating. While Camille could be bone-stubborn at times, so, too, could he. Especially when it came to her. He'd kept his vow to keep her safe since that fateful night she stumbled up his front stoop.

She'd loved him desperately every day since.

And he still didn't look happy. "If you're sure—"

"I am, very."

He nodded, then said the words that had given her strength at a time when she'd needed it most. "*Va avec Dieu*, Camille."

Go with God. "Always." As she stared into his concerned eyes, she thought of their life together, and the two beautiful daughters they'd created, each of them celebrated pastry chefs like their mother, both with the look of their father in their eyes and their mother's blond hair. And, of course, there was Jacqueline. Restored fully, thriving, and working alongside Pierre as a psychiatrist in the hospital where she'd found her own healing. She had stayed behind so that Pierre could make the trip.

Camille was so very blessed to have such a lovely, happy family. She whispered a prayer of thanks for God's grace and mercy on her life. "I'll be along shortly," she told her husband, closing the door with a soft click. "I promise. I won't linger."

She watched the taxi drive off, noting how three pairs of eyes turned in her direction. Smiling, she lifted a hand to reassure them she was fine. And she was. After stretching her legs, she began covering ground at a steady pace, looking not toward the house that carried so many memories of pain and death, but ahead—toward the buildings that had once served as a detainment center for 100,000 Jewish citizens. No less a study in torture.

The individual structures had remained intact, but the double rows of barbed wire were long gone, as were the guards who had been a strange mix of German SS soldiers, Gestapo, and, much to France's shame, the *gendarmerie*. The French military police.

Camille took a breath and held it for a long time. Her heart went hard as the truth hit her. All those living souls passing through this detention center and unceremoniously shoved into cattle cars. Most had not survived the ordeal, but some had, including Shelomo Selinger, the sculptor of the *Le Monument de la Déportation*.

The dedication of the memorial had been the reason Camille agreed to make this journey to Drancy, not the other ceremony planned an hour later. She really didn't want to attend that one and had tried every avenue to squelch it. The French government would not be swayed.

Attendance for the first ceremony was impressive. Already hundreds of people filled the chairs set in neat rows before the monument. The mood was appropriately somber. No band played. No happy greetings or laughter rang out.

Camille was handed a program, and she took a moment to view the sculpture that was to be dedicated in honor of the all the lives lost. It was a fittingly dreary day for the ceremony, the sun long hidden behind gray clouds. A clap of thunder gave Camille chills, as if God himself was making his opinion known about the horrors that had occurred on this very ground.

She exhaled a shaky breath, drew in another, and circled the piece of art.

Inside her program was an explanation, though she could have figured out most of it on her own. The main sculpture depicted interlacing figures in wrenching poses of prayer, agony, and death. In the center of the piece, the block represented ten men, the number needed to recite the kaddish. At the bottom, the wavelike pattern evoked the fire in which so many Jews died.

The images were heartrending and terrible and Camille couldn't seem to catch her breath. She shouldn't have sent her family away. She wanted them with her now, especially Pierre. As if knowing she needed him, her husband appeared at her elbow. Seeing her grief reflected in his gaze, she was glad he'd found her.

"Come, Camille." His voice was gentle, his hold even more so. "Our daughters are waiting for you at our seats."

"I'm not finished viewing the monument."

"Take your look, then. But I go with you."

Arm in arm with her husband, Camille read the verse from the Book of Lamentations. *Behold and see, if there is any pain like my pain.*

Her thoughts went to Rachel, and the pain she'd suffered from the loss of her father and brother. A pain she'd had to live with for over thirty-five years. Camille was glad she'd found her friend again. It had taken two decades, and though they hadn't been able to accomplish a face-to-face reunion yet, they'd kept in touch via letters and telephone calls.

Like Camille, Rachel had lived a happy, productive life after the war. She'd married a man she'd met during her escape. They'd produced seven healthy children, four girls and three boys. There were twenty grandchildren in total, and several on the way. While raising her family in New York, with her mother's moral support before she died two years later, Rachel had started her own cosmetic company. Her husband was the main chemist, and her sister, Basia, acted as the creative director.

"Please, everyone, take your seats."

Pierre guided Camille to where their daughters waited near the back. The ceremony was appropriately solemn. Several people gave speeches, but it was the artist's words that brought home the reality of what had occurred on this property. "I designed *Le Monument de la Déportation* to transmit to future generations the emotions felt by us, the survivors of Nazi camps, the horrors of what we endured, and the guilt we share over the ones we lost."

He finished with a request for a moment of silence for the souls who did not survive.

From across the rows of bowed heads, Camille's gaze connected with Rachel's. She knew her friend at once. She still had the look of her younger self. The only change was that her once dark hair was now styled in a sleek gray bob that highlighted her cheekbones.

The ceremony concluded after Selinger finished his speech.

Minutes after the ribbon cutting, Camille was hugging Rachel just as fiercely as she had in the forest barely a mile from where they now stood.

"It's so good to see you," they said simultaneously, then pulled away to smile into each other's eyes. Introductions were made, which took considerable time since most of Rachel's brood and several of her extended family had made the trip from America to France.

An hour after the first ceremony, the second one began.

"I really don't want to go through with this," Camille told her husband.

Pierre patted her hand. "Now, now, my dear. You aren't getting out of this that easily."

At least the crowd was considerably smaller, fewer than a hundred people, which included Rachel's family, Camille's husband and daughters, and some French dignitaries, even the president himself, Valéry Giscard d'Estaing.

Giscard d'Estaing's speech was blessedly brief. "We are here today to present the highest recognition for service to France, to a most worthy recipient, Madame Camille Lacroix Garnier." He called her to the podium, and when she stopped before him, he draped a medal around her neck. "France thanks you for your service."

The applause was loud and long, and Camille's cheeks grew hot with embarrassment as she returned to her seat. She didn't deserve this recognition and had tried on several occasions to convince the government to reconsider giving her the Legion of Honor. There were many others more worthy, she'd argued, thinking of Vivian and her vast network that had coordinated Rachel and her mother's escape. Camille's part had been small, hardly worth mentioning.

The bureaucrats had disagreed.

"Without Madame Garnier's act of bravery," the president was saying, "the woman I now have the honor of introducing would not be here to tell her story. Please, welcome to the podium one of France's greatest success stories, Madame Rachel Berman Horowitz."

The applause for Rachel was even louder and longer than for Camille, and that, she thought, was exactly the way it should be.

Rachel thanked the French president, greeted the guests with her beautiful smile, then launched into a speech Camille hadn't known she would be giving. "I'm here not to tell you my story, but the one I share with this woman." She smiled at Camille. "My friend, Camille Lacroix, now Camille Garnier, a humble Paris housekeeper who was with me during the darkest time in France's history."

As Rachel told their combined story, Camille relived the memories with the rest of the audience. She felt the fear all over again, the hot rage and unspeakable grief. The despair. But also, the guilt and shame over the French people's collective indifference to the plight of their Jewish neighbors. "Camille, please join me up here for this next part."

Once again, Camille walked to the podium. This time, there were tears in her eyes.

"For two months, this woman hid my mother and me in the home where she worked. She kept us safe and alive and did it right under the nose of a Nazi. I have no doubt she would have taken a bullet to save us. In fact, she nearly did."

Rachel paused and looked briefly at Camille. In that moment of silent connection, they honored the woman who *had* taken a bullet to save them. Vivian Miller would never be venerated for her sacrifice. She'd been judged a traitor and a collaborator by the French government, a murderess by the Germans, while the Americans had used her money to fund their own war effort. She'd died in disgrace and would only be lauded for her sacrifice in Camille's and Rachel's shared memories of that harrowing night.

"If you think one person can't make a difference in the fight against tyranny," Rachel continued, "I'm here to tell you you're wrong. This woman is a testament to what happens when a single brave soul does the right thing. Camille didn't just save my life. She made many of yours possible. And so, I ask, would my family please rise and stand in recognition of this woman, my friend?"

Nearly fifty people surged to their feet.

"Camille, the people who stand before you now, do so because I survived the war. This, my friend—" she swept her arm over her considerable family "—is your legacy as much as mine."

The applause that broke out was the loudest and longest yet.

* * * * *

Author's Note

As with all my books, this one began in the library. I didn't have much of a story. I knew I wanted to go back to France. I also knew I wanted three heroines who would be underestimated, possibly untested, but were also interconnected in some way. Each would require a strong reason to sacrifice for the people she loved. That's all I knew as I explored some amazing acts of heroism by seemingly ordinary women in WWII Europe. Each story was more inspiring than the last, but I didn't find this book's inspiration until I discovered Irena Gut's heroic deeds.

Irena was the housekeeper for a Nazi officer in Poland. She managed to hide twelve Jews in her employer's basement for two years. All of them survived, but not without some very close calls and a personal sacrifice by Irena. Her story is remarkable. I highly recommend you read about her life and the tragedies that led to her incredible feats in her autobiography, *In My Hands: Memories of a Holocaust Rescuer*.

While Irena was the initial inspiration for Camille, the character morphed and changed into something wholly different and very, very French. I needed Camille to have a good reason to stay in Paris during the war and ultimately work in a

Nazi's home. That was key. Again, I went back to the library and came across the Nazi medical program that was responsible for the murder of thousands of mentally and physically disabled patients. According to one source, by the summer of 1940, this horrible euthanasia program had become common knowledge among Germans and in other countries. For story purposes, I gave Camille access to this information and a sister with a malady that put her jeopardy.

Rachel's character also required significant thought. There were many ways I could have portrayed her. But when I discovered the assimilation of so many French Jews, she formed fully in my mind. Most of these men and women believed they were safe, mainly because they didn't openly practice the Jewish faith. History shows us they were mistaken. In fact, the French government passed their own anti-racial laws separate from their occupiers. Moreover, it was the French police who coordinated most of the mass arrests, including the July 1942 Vel d'Hiv roundup that targeted women and children.

By this point, victims of these arrests were sent directly to the Drancy internment camp, where they were unceremoniously loaded into train cars and deported to Auschwitz. While far too many innocent lives were lost, Shelomo Selinger was not among them. The celebrated sculptor survived nine German death camps, and two death marches. In memory of the innocent men and women who passed through Drancy, he created *Le Monument de la Déportation*. Again, for story purposes, I created a dedication ceremony, with Camille and Rachel in attendance. I also reworked the timeline concerning the United States Ambassador to France. William Bullitt Jr. was actually terminated from his position in July 1940. I took a little creative license and pushed that date to later in the year to fit within Vivian's story arc.

Many thanks to my amazing editor, Melissa Endlich, who guided me through the editorial process with patience and expertise. You always make my books better, Melissa. The extent of my gratitude cannot be put into mere words. You're the best! I also want to thank the art department and the sales and marketing team at Harlequin. You never fail to make my books shine.

Thank you to my readers for taking this journey with me through German-occupied Paris. I couldn't do what I love without your ongoing support. For fans of *The Widows of Champagne*, I left you an Easter Egg. It comes with my deepest gratitude for your loyalty. Cheers!

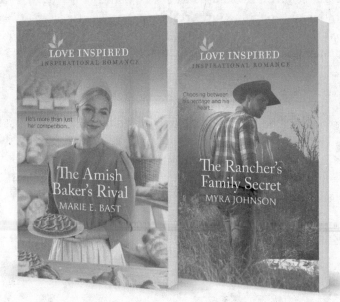